I0639205

Tales from the

Italian and Spanish

Three complete novels, one Italian and two Spanish

Manzoni's "Betrothed Lovers"
Cervantes' "Don Quixote" and
Valdés' "Marta y Maria"

Four other famous stories:

Valera's "Pepita Jiménez"
Aleman's "Guzman of Alfarache"
Mendoza's "Lazarillo of Tormes"
and Quevedo's "Paul of Segovia"

159 Short Stories
118 Italian
41 Spanish Tales of To-day
49 Translated for the first time for this set
26 Stories of Love and Revenge
34 Stories of Heroism and Romance
58 Stories of Humor and Adventure

Originals of famous literary works: "Patient Grisel-da," "Romeo and Juliet," and "Merry Wives of Windsor" (Shake-speare), the stories of "Gil Blas," and some of the comedies of Moliére, and of the grand opera, "Cavalleria Rusticana."

32 Illustrations, chiefly from famous paintings

Full explanatory introductions to each volume, with descriptive historical notes to many of the stories.

Stories of Humor   Stories of Revenge
Stories of Adventure   Stories of Romance
Stories of Love   Stories of Local Color

Authors Represented

Italian

Manzoni, Boccaccio, Machiavelli, Masuccio, Fogazzaro, D'Annunzio, Verga, ·Deledda, De Roberto, Da Porto, De Marchi, Firenzuola, Capuana, Bandello, Neera, Manni, Fiorentino, Boito, Giacosa, ˙Sabbadino, Ojetti, Pirandello, Rovetta, Palmarini, Gozzi, Da Ceno, Bottari, Doni, Sacchetti, Sanvitale, Parabosco, Cinthio, Soave, Sozzini, Lando, Grazzini, Colombo, Fucini, Malespini, Serao, Brevio, Straparola, Da Lodi, De Amicis, Erizzo, Granucci, Fortini, Martini, Sansovino, Castelnuovo, Bisaccioni, Illicini.

Spanish

Cervantes Velera, Valdés, Galdos, Calderon, Aleman, Mendoza, Quevedo, Ibañez, Picón, De Truba, Pardo-Bazan, Caballero, De Alarçón, Selgas, Nieto, Antor, Blasco, Solano, De Anellano, Calson, Ruiz, Becquer, Hartzenbusch.

Mexico:
López-Portillo y Rojas
De Zayas

Chile:
Gana y Gana
Varas

Cuba:
Castellanos

Venezuela:
Blanco-Fombona

Costa Rica:
Guardia

Peru:
Palma

Colombia:
Isaacs

Argentine:
Ugarte

Philippines:
Rizal

"THE TOWNSPEOPLE SPREAD THE FAME OF HER VIRTUES AND
CROWNED HER WITH A HALO OF RESPECT AND SANCTITY"

(The original a drawing by John Lewis)

TALES
FROM THE
ITALIAN
AND
SPANISH

A NEW SORT OF FICTION

REALISM AND ROMANCE,
ADVENTURE AND HUMOR,
REVEALING THE SOUL
OF THE LATIN LANDS

IN EIGHT VOLUMES
ILLUSTRATED

WILDSIDE PRESS

Copyright 1920
By THE REVIEW OF REVIEWS CO.

TALES FROM THE SPANISH

PEPITA JIMÉNEZ

BY

JUAN VALERA

AND

MARTA AND MARIA

BY

ARMANDO PALACIO VALDÉS

With Four Illustrations

Contents

PEPITA JIMÉNEZ AND MARTA Y MARIA

	PAGE
INTRODUCTION TO PEPITA JIMÉNEZ	xi
"NESCIT LABI VIRTUS"	1
PARALIPOMENA	44
INTRODUCTION TO MARTA Y MARIA	93
CHAPTER I	95
In the street.	
CHAPTER II	102
The Soiree at the Elorza Mansion.	
CHAPTER III	127
The Nine Days' Festival of the Sacred Heart of Jesus.	
CHAPTER IV	145
How the Marquis of Penalta became the Duke of Thuringen.	
CHAPTER V	165
The road to perfection.	
CHAPTER VI	183
In search of a canary.	
CHAPTER VII	201
Husband or soul.	
CHAPTER VIII	216
As you like it.	
CHAPTER IX	230
Excursion to El Moral and the Island.	
CHAPTER X	243
The excursion continued.	
CHAPTER XI	262
A strange circumstance.	
CHAPTER XII	272
Gathered threads.	

PEPITA JIMÉNEZ AND MARTA Y MARIA

                                                                    PAGE

CHAPTER XIII   293
    In which are told the labors of a Christian virgin

CHAPTER XIV   314
    Pallida Mors.

CHAPTER XV   332
    Let us rejoice, beloved!

CHAPTER XVI   350
    The Marquis of Penalta's dream.

Illustrations

PEPITA JIMÉNEZ AND MARTA AND MARIA

PAGE

"The townspeople spread the fame of her virtues
and crowned her with a halo of respect and sanctity" .   .   .   .   .   . *Frontispiece*

"Two lovely girls . . . dressed like peasants, but with
the greatest neatness and even elegance" .   .   17

"Don Pedro danced with Pepita as also with the most
attractive among her maids"   .   .   .   89

Don Serapio never tired of ogling the ladies   .   .   115

v

THE publishers desire to express their grateful acknowledgment for permission to use in this volume portions of Pepita Jiménez, by Juan Valera, copyrighted by William Heinemann, London, and an abridgement of Marta y Maria, by Armando Palacio Valdés, translated by Nathan Haskell Dole, copyrighted by Thomas Y. Crowell, New York.

TALES FROM THE SPANISH

———

PEPITA JIMÉNEZ

BY

JUAN VALERA

INTRODUCTION

IF a chorus of praise can make a book great, *Pepita Jiménez* is one of the greatest books of the nineteenth century. When, in 1874, it issued from the press at Madrid, the distinguished English critic, Mr. Edmund Gosse assures us, " it enjoyed a success which had not been paralleled, and has not since been surpassed, in the history of modern Spanish literature. This book still remains, after a quarter of a century and after the large development of fiction in Spain, the principal, the typical Spanish novel of our days."

When we remember that the most interesting development of Spanish literature in the nineteenth century is the novel and that *Pepita Jiménez* is indeed a landmark because it first attracted international attention to Spanish fiction, we see how high is Gosse's praise. A brilliant English writer goes further: Coventry Patmore declares *Pepita Jiménez* is a specimen of that "complete synthesis of gravity of matter and gayety of manner which is the glittering crown of art, and which outside of Spanish literature is to be found only in Shakspere, and even in him in a far less obvious degree." Even the most authoritative student of Spanish literature, Mr. James Fitzmaurice-Kelley, avers with scholarly solemnity that Juan Valera is intrinsically Spanish, " a great creative artist and the embodiment of a people's genius," and adds that he will be read as long as Spanish literature endures.

But the book does not need this chorus of praise to make it great. It was written by one who knew mankind widely and thoroughly. The son of wealthy parents, he secured an education in college and law school without gaining the reputation of a bookworm. Instead, says one of his biographers, he was conspicuous wherever he went for his success with the ladies, his wild freaks at the gaming table, his crazy escapades, his feats of horsemanship, his prowess as a *toreador*. Possibly this sowing of wild oats helped fit him for the diplomatic career which his father had selected for him. He started out modestly as *attaché* to the Spanish embassy at Naples, but his suave manners of the politely incredulous man of the world secured frequent promotions until at the age of thirty he was secretary of legation at St. Petersburg. Returning to his native country, he at once entered politics and soon held a position in the cabinet. After a term as minister at Frankfort, he again became a prominent figure in the intellectual and social life of Madrid. His most important diplomatic position was from 1884 to 1886 as ambassador to the United States.

To the urbanity of the diplomat he joins the authoritative insight of the student and the philosopher. In his fiftieth year he spent much time in reading the Spanish mystics of the seventeenth century. The ecstasies of these fathers of the church over divine joys suggested to this man of the world, who had come to look on life with serene amusement as a brilliant and diverting comedy, the plan of confronting this fervent mysticism with the brighter ardor of natural instinct. As a result he portrayed with rare dramatic sympathy the unavailing struggles of a young theological student against the innocence and beauty of Pepita.

Such a struggle, depicted by a master hand, reveals the quintessence of Spanish life. As Gosse says, the book is " singularly in sympathy with Spanish character. In a country where the shades of feeling are violent, this one story reflects them all, yet with a discretion so perfect, a good-humor so absolute, that no one is offended. *Pepita Jiménez* is Spain itself, in microcosm—Spain with its fervor, its sensual piety, its rhetoric and hyperbole, its superficial passion, its mysticism, its graceful extravagance. . . . It is, what is not a common thing, a genuine novel of manners. Its landscape, of a sumptuous Andalusian fertility, has we know not what of primitive and simple, broad and glowing. Against it move six or seven figures, clearly de-fined and distinguished, perfectly new and perfectly vivid types. The treatment of these types is often very subtle, especially that of the father Don Pedro, who is perhaps the most wholly delightful personage in the story."

It is this subtlety and delicacy of treatment, in addition to the " fresh and joyous sympathy with human nature in an absolutely novel phase," which William Dean Howells points out, that explains the perpetual charm of the story. In its present form, where certain passages chiefly of a theological nature are omitted, that charm is pervasive. The equally absorbing drama, in which spiritual fervor gains the better of earthly love, is presented in the other novel of this volume, that masterly narrative of *Marta and Maria*.

Pepita Jiménez

" Nescit labi virtus "

THE reverend Dean of the Cathedral of ——, deceased
a few years since, left among his papers a bundle of
manuscript, tied together, which, passing from hand to
hand, finally fell into mine, without, by some strange
chance, having lost a single one of the documents contained
in it. Inscribed on this manuscript were the Latin words
I use above as a motto, but without the addition of the
woman's name I now prefix to it as its title; and this inscription has probably contributed to the preservation of
the papers, since, thinking them, no doubt, to be sermons,
or other theological matter, no one before me had made
any attempt to untie the string of the package, or to read
a single page of it.

The manuscript, being all in the same handwriting, it may
be inferred is that of the reverend dean; and, as taken
together, it forms something like a novel, I at first thought
that perhaps the reverend dean wished to exercise his
genius in composing one in his leisure hours; but, looking
at the matter more closely, and observing the natural simplicity of the style, I am inclined to think now that it
is no novel at all, but that the letters are copies of genuine
epistles which the reverend dean tore up, burned, or returned to their owners, and that the narrative part only,
designated by the pedantic title of *Paralipomena*, is the
work of the reverend dean, added for the purpose of completing the story with incidents not related in the letters.

However this may be, I confess that I did not find the
reading of these papers tiresome; I found them, indeed,

rather interesting than otherwise; and as nowadays everything is published, I have decided to publish them too, without further investigation, changing only the proper names, so that if those who bear them be still living they may not find themselves figuring in a book without desiring or consenting to it.

The letters contained in the first part seem to have been written by a very young man, with some theoretical but no practical knowledge of the world, whose life was passed in the house of the reverend dean, his uncle, and in the seminary, and who was imbued with an exalted religious fervor and an earnest desire to be a priest.

We shall call this young man Don Luis de Vargas.

The aforesaid manuscript, faithfully transferred to print, is as follows.

I

LETTERS FROM MY NEPHEW

March 22d.

DEAR UNCLE AND VENERABLE MASTER:
Four days ago I arrived in safety at this my native village, where I found my father, the reverend vicar, our friends and relations, all in good health. The happiness of seeing them and conversing with them has so completely occupied my time and thoughts, that I have not been able to write to you until now.

You will pardon me for this.

Having left this place a mere child, and coming back a man, the impression produced upon me by all those objects that I had treasured up in my memory is a singular one. Everything appears to me more diminutive, much more diminutive, but also more pleasing to the eye, than my recollection of it. My father's house, which in my imagination was immense, is, indeed, the large house of a rich husbandman, but still much smaller than the seminary. What I now understand and appreciate better than formerly is the country around here. The orchards, above all, are delightful. What charming paths there are through them! On one side, and sometimes on both, crystal waters flow with a pleasant murmur. The banks of these streams are covered with odorous herbs and flowers of a thousand different hues. In a few minutes one may gather a large bunch of violets. The paths are shaded by majestic trees, chiefly walnut and fig trees; and the hedges are formed of blackberry-bushes, roses, pomegranates, and honeysuckle.

The multitude of birds that enliven grove and field is marvelous.

I am enchanted with the orchards, and I spend a couple of hours walking in them every afternoon.

My father wishes to take me to see his olive plantations, his vineyards, his farmhouses; but of all this we have as yet seen nothing. I have not been outside of the village and the charming orchards that surround it.

It is true, indeed, that the numerous visits I receive do not leave me a moment to myself.

Five different women have come to see me, all of whom were my nurses, and have embraced and kissed me.

Everyone calls me Luisito, or Don Pedro's boy, although I have passed my twenty-second birthday; and everyone inquires of my father for *the boy*, when I am not present.

I imagine I shall make but little use of the books I have brought with me to read, as I am not left alone for a single instant.

The dignity of squire, which I supposed to be a matter for jest, is, on the contrary, a serious matter. My father is the squire of the village.

There is hardly anyone here who can understand what they call my caprice of entering the priesthood, and these good people tell me, with rustic candor, that I ought to throw aside the clerical garb; that to be a priest is very well for a poor young man; but that I, who am to be a rich man's heir, should marry, and console the old age of my father by giving him half a dozen handsome and robust grandchildren.

In order to flatter my father and myself, both men and women declare that I am a splendid fellow, that I am of an angelic disposition, that I have a very roguish pair of eyes, and other stupid things of a like kind, that annoy, disgust, and humiliate me although I am not very modest, and am too well acquainted with the meanness and folly of the world to be shocked or frightened at anything.

The only defect they find in me is that I am too thin through over-study. In order to have me grow fat they propose not to allow me either to study or even to look at a book while I remain here; and, besides this, to make me eat of as many choice dishes of meats and confectionery as they know how to concoct in the village.

It is quite clear—I am to be stall-fed. There is not a single family of our acquaintance that has not sent me some token of regard. Now it is a sponge-cake, now a meat-salad, now a pyramid of sweetmeats, now a jug of sirup.

And these presents, which they send to the house, are not the only attentions they show me. I have also been invited to dinner by three or four of the principal persons of the village.

Tomorrow I am to dine at the house of the famous Pepita Jiménez, of whom you have doubtless heard. No one here is ignorant of the fact that my father is paying her his addresses.

My father, notwithstanding his fifty-five years, is so well preserved that the finest young men of the village might feel envious of him. He possesses, besides, the powerful attraction, irresistible to some women, of his past conquests, of his celebrity, of having been a sort of Don Juan Tenorio.

I have not yet made the acquaintance of Pepita Jiménez. Everyone says she is very beautiful. I suspect she will turn out to be a village beauty, and somewhat rustic. From what I have heard of her I cannot quite decide whether, ethically speaking, she is good or bad; but I am quite certain that she is possessed of great natural intelligence. Pepita is about twenty years old, and a widow; her married life lasted only three years. She was the daughter of Doña Francisca Galvez, the widow, as you know, of a retired captain,

" Who left her at his death,
As sole inheritance, his honorable sword."

as the poet says. Until her sixteenth year Pepita lived with her mother in very straitened circumstances—bordering, indeed, upon absolute want.

She had an uncle called Don Gumersindo, the possessor of a small entailed estate, one of those petty estates that, in olden times, owed their foundation to a foolish vanity. Any ordinary person, with the income derived from this estate, would have lived in continual difficulties, burdened by debts, and altogether cut off from the display and ceremony proper to his rank. But Don Gumersindo was an extraordinary person—the very genius of economy. It could not be said of him that he created wealth himself, but he was endowed with a wonderful faculty of absorption with respect to the wealth of others; and in regard to dispensing, it would be difficult to find anyone on the face of the globe with whose maintenance, preservation, and comfort, Mother Nature and human industry ever had less reason to trouble themselves. No one knows how he lived; but the fact is that he reached the age of eighty years, saving his entire income, and adding to his capital by lending money on unquestionable security. No one here speaks of him as a usurer; on the contrary, he is considered to have been of a charitable disposition, because, being moderate in all things, he was so even in usury, and would ask only ten per cent. a year, while throughout the district they ask twenty and even thirty per cent., and still think it little.

In the practice of this species of industry and economy, and with thoughts dwelling constantly on increasing instead of diminishing his capital, indulging neither in the luxury

5

of matrimony and of having a family, nor even of smoking, Don Gumersindo arrived at the age I have mentioned, the possessor of a fortune considerable anywhere, and here regarded as enormous, thanks to the poverty of these villagers, and to the habit of exaggeration natural to the Andalusians.

Don Gumersindo, always extremely neat and clean in his person, was an old man who did not inspire repugnance.

The articles of his modest wardrobe were somewhat worn, but carefully brushed and without a stain; although from time immemorial he had always been seen with the same cloak, the same jacket, and the same trousers and waistcoat. People sometimes asked each other in vain if anyone had ever seen him wear a new garment.

With all these defects, which here and elsewhere many regard as virtues, though virtues in excess, Don Gumersindo possessed excellent qualities; he was affable, obliging, compassionate; and did his utmost to please and to be of service to everybody, no matter what trouble, anxiety, or fatigue it might cost him, provided only it did not cost him money. Of a cheerful disposition, and fond of fun and joking, he was to be found at every feast and merrymaking around that was not got up at his expense, which he enlivened by the amenity of his manners, and by his discreet although not very Attic conversation. He had never had any tender inclination for any one woman in particular, but, innocently and without malice, he loved them all; and was the most given to complimenting the girls, and making them laugh, of any old man for ten leagues around.

I have already said that he was the uncle of Pepita. When he was nearing his eightieth year she was about to complete her sixteenth. He was rich; she, poor and friendless.

Her mother was a vulgar woman of limited intelligence and coarse instincts. She worshipped her daughter, yet lamented continually and with bitterness the sacrifices she made for her, the privations she suffered, and the disconsolate old age and melancholy end that awaited her in the midst of her poverty. She had, besides, a son, older than Pepita, who had a well-deserved reputation in the village as a gambler and a quarrelsome fellow, and for whom, after many difficulties, she had succeeded in obtaining an insignificant employment in Havana; thus finding herself rid of him, and with the sea between them. After he had been a few years in Havana, however, he lost his situation on account of his bad conduct, and thereupon began to shower letters upon his mother, containing demands for money. The latter, who had scarcely enough for herself and for Pepita, grew desperate at this, broke out into abuse, cursed herself and her destiny with a perseverance but little resembling the theological virtue, and ended by fixing all her hopes upon settling her daughter well, as the only way of getting out of her difficulties.

In this distressing situation Don Gumersindo began to frequent the house of Pepita and her mother, and to pay attentions to the former with more ardor and persistence than he had shown in his attentions to other girls. Nevertheless, to suppose that a man who had passed his eightieth year without wishing to marry, should think of committing such a folly, with one foot already in the grave, was so wild and improbable a notion, that Pepita's mother, still less Pepita herself, never for a moment suspected the audacious intentions of Don Gumersindo. Thus it was that both were struck one day with amazement when, after a good many compliments, between jest and earnest, Don Gumersindo, with the greatest seriousness and without the least hesitation, proposed the following categorical question:

" Pepita, will you marry me? "

Although the question came at the end of a great deal of joking, and might itself be taken for a joke, Pepita, who, inexperienced though she was in worldly matters, yet knew by a certain instinct of divination that is in all women, and especially in young girls, no matter how innocent they may be, that this was said in earnest, grew as red as a cherry and said nothing. Her mother answered in her stead:

7

"Child, don't be ill-bred; answer your uncle as you should: 'With much pleasure, uncle—whenever you wish.'"

This "with much pleasure, uncle—whenever you wish," came then, it is said, and many times afterward, almost mechanically from the trembling lips of Pepita, in obedience to the admonitions, the sermons, the complaints, and even the imperious mandates of her mother.

I see, however, that I am enlarging too much on this matter of Pepita Jiménez and her history; but she interests me, as I suppose she should interest you too, since, if what they affirm here be true, she is to be your sister-in-law and my stepmother. I shall endeavor, notwithstanding, to avoid dwelling on details, and to relate briefly what perhaps you already know, though you have been away from here so long.

Pepita Jiménez was married to Don Gumersindo. The tongue of slander was let loose against her, both in the days preceding the wedding and for some months afterward.

In fact, from the point of view of morals, this marriage was a matter that will admit of discussion; but, so far as the girl herself is concerned, if we remember her mother's prayers, her complaints, and even her commands—if we take into consideration the fact that Pepita thought by this means to procure for her mother a comfortable old age, and to save her brother from dishonor and infamy, constituting herself his guardian angel and his earthly providence, we must confess that our condemnation will admit of some abatement. Besides, who shall penetrate into the recesses of the heart, into the hidden secrets of the immature mind of a young girl, brought up, probably, in the most absolute seclusion and ignorance of the world, in order to know what idea she might have formed to herself of marriage! Perhaps she thought that to marry this old man meant to devote her life to his service, to be his nurse, to soothe his old age, to save him from a solitude and abandonment embittered by his infirmities, and in which only mercenary hands should minister to him; in a word, to

8

cheer and illumine his declining years with the glowing beams of her beauty and her youth, like an angel who has taken human form. If something of this, or all of this, was what the girl thought, and if she failed to perceive the full significance of her act, then its morality is placed beyond question.

However this may be, leaving aside psychological investigations that I have no authority for making, since I am not acquainted with Pepita Jiménez, it is quite certain that she lived in edifying harmony with the old man during three years, that she nursed him and waited upon him with admirable devotion, and that in his last painful and fatal sickness she ministered to him and watched over him with tender and unwearying affection, until he expired in her arms, leaving her heiress to a large fortune.

Although more than two years have passed since she lost her mother, and more than a year and a half since she was left a widow, Pepita still wears the deepest mourning. Her sedateness, her retired manner of living, and her melancholy, are such that one might suppose she lamented the death of her husband as much as though he had been a handsome young man. Perhaps there are some who imagine or suspect that Pepita's pride, and the certain knowledge she now has of the not very poetical means by which she has become rich, trouble her awakened and more than scrupulous conscience; and that, humiliated in her own eyes and in those of the world, she seeks, in austerity and retirement, consolation for the vexations of her mind, and balm for her wounded heart.

People here, as everywhere, have a great love of money. Perhaps I am wrong in saying *as everywhere;* in populous cities, in the great centres of civilization, there are other distinctions which are prized as much as, or even more than money, because they smooth the way to fortune, and give credit and consideration in the eyes of the world; but in smaller places, where neither literary nor scientific fame, nor, as a rule, distinction of manners, nor elegance, nor discretion and amenity in intercourse, are not to be either valued or understood, there is no other way by which to adjust the social hierarchy than the possession of more or less money, or of something worth money. Pepita, then, in the possession of money, and beauty besides, and making a good use, as everyone says, of her riches, is today respected and esteemed in an extraordinary degree. From this and the surrounding villages the most eligible suitors, the wealthiest young men, have crowded to pay their court to her. But, so far as can be seen, she rejects them all, though with the utmost sweetness, for she wishes to make no one her enemy; and it is commonly supposed that her soul is filled with the most ardent devotion, and that it is her fixed intention to dedicate her life to practices of charity and religious piety.

My father, according to the general opinion, has not succeeded better than her other suitors; but Pepita, to fulfil the adage that "courtesy and candor are consistent with each other," takes the greatest pains to give him proofs of a frank, affectionate, and disinterested friendship. She is unremitting in her attentions to him, and when he tries to speak to her of love she brings him to a stop with a sermon delivered with the most winning sweetness, recalling to his memory his past faults, and endeavoring to undeceive him in regard to the world and its vain pomps.

I confess that I begin to have some curiosity to know this woman, so much do I hear her spoken of; nor do I think my curiosity is without foundation, or that there is anything in it either vain or sinful. I myself feel the truth of what Pepita says; I myself desire that my father, in his advanced years, should enter upon a better life; should forget, and not seek to renew, the agitations and passions of his youth; and should attain to the enjoyment of a tranquil, happy, and honorable old age. I differ from Pepita's way of thinking in one thing only: I believe my father would succeed in this rather by marrying a good and worthy woman who loved him, than by remaining single. For this very reason I desire to become acquainted with Pepita, in order to know if she be this woman; for I am to a certain extent troubled

—and perhaps there is in this feeling something of family pride, which, if it be wrong, I desire to cast out—by the disdain, however honeyed and gracious, of the young widow.

If my situation were other than it is, I should prefer my father to remain unmarried. Then, being the only child, I should inherit all his wealth, and, as one might say, nothing less than the position of squire of the village. But you already know how firm is the resolution I have taken. Humble and unworthy though I be, I feel myself called to the priesthood, and the possessions of this world have but little power over my mind. If there is anything in me of the ardor of youth, and the vehemence of the passions proper to that age, it shall all be employed in nourishing an active and fecund charity. Even the many books you have given me to read, and my knowledge of the history of the ancient civilizations of the peoples of Asia, contribute to unite within me scientific curiosity with the desire of propagating the faith, and invite and animate me to go forth as a missionary to the Far East. As soon as I leave this village, where you, my dear uncle, have sent me to pass some time with my father, and am raised to the dignity of the priesthood, and, ignorant and sinner as I am, feel myself invested by free and supernatural gift, through the sovereign goodness of the Most High, with the power to absolve from sin, and with the mission to teach the peoples —as soon as I receive the perpetual and miraculous grace of handling with impure hands the very God-made man, it is my purpose to leave Spain, and go forth to distant lands to preach the Gospel.

I am not actuated in this by vanity. I do not desire to believe myself superior to other men. The power of my faith, the constancy of which I feel myself capable, everything after the favor and grace of God, I owe to the judicious education, to the holy teaching, and to the good example I have received from you, my dear uncle. . . .

Farewell, uncle. In future I will write to you often, and as much at length as you recommend me, if not quite so much so as today, lest I should appear prolix.

II

TALES FROM THE SPANISH

March 28th.

The dinner at the house of Pepita Jiménez, which I mentioned to you, took place three days ago. As she leads so retired a life, I had not met her before; she seemed to me, in truth, as beautiful as she is said to be, and I noticed that her amiability with my father was such as to give him reason to hope, at least judging superficially, that she will yield to his wishes in the end, and accept his hand.

As there is a possibility of her becoming my stepmother, I have observed her with attention; she seems to me to be a remarkable woman, whose moral qualities I am not able to determine with exactitude. There is about her an air of calmness and serenity that may come either from coldness of heart and spirit, with great self-control and power of calculating effects, accompanied by little or no sensibility; or that may, on the other hand, proceed from the tranquillity of her conscience and the purity of her aspirations, united to the purpose of fulfilling in this life the duties imposed upon her by society, while her hopes are fixed, meantime, upon loftier things, as their proper goal. What is certain is that, either because with this woman everything is the result of calculation, without any effort to elevate her mind to a higher sphere, or, it may be, because she blends in perfect harmony the prose of daily life with the poetry of her illusions, there is nothing discernible in her out of tone with her surroundings, although she possesses a natural distinction of manner that elevates her above and separates her from them all. She does not affect the dress of a provincial, nor does she, on the other hand, follow blindly the fashions of the city; she unites both these styles in her mode of dress in such a manner as to appear like a lady, but still a lady country-born and country-bred. She disguises to a great extent, as I think, the care she takes of her person. There is nothing about her to betray the use of cosmetics or the arts of the toilet. But the whiteness of her hands, the color and polish of her nails, and the grace and neatness of her attire denote a greater

12

regard for such matters than might be looked for in one who lives in a village, and who is said, besides, to despise the vanities of this world and to think only of heavenly things.

Her house is exquisitely clean, and everything in it reveals the most perfect order. The furniture is neither artistic nor elegant, nor is it, on the other hand, either pretentious or in bad taste. To give a poetic air to her surroundings, she keeps in the rooms and passages, as well as in the garden, a multitude of plants and flowers. There is not, indeed, among them any rare plant or exotic, but her plants and flowers, of the commonest species here, are tended with extraordinary care.

Canaries in gilded cages enliven the whole house with their songs. Its mistress, it is obvious, has need of living creatures on which to bestow some of her affection; and besides several maid-servants, that one would suppose she had selected with care, since it cannot be by mere chance that they are all pretty, she has, after the fashion of old maids, various animals to keep her company—a parrot, a little dog, whose coat is of the whitest, and two or three cats, so tame and sociable that they jump up on one in the most friendly manner.

At one end of the principal saloon is a species of oratory, whose chief ornament is an *Infant Jesus,* carved in wood, with red and white cheeks and blue eyes, and altogether quite handsome. The dress is of white satin, with a blue cloak full of little golden stars; and the image is completely covered with jewels and trinkets. The little altar on which the figure is placed is adorned with flowers, and around it are set pots of broom and bay; and on the altar itself, which is furnished with steps, a great many wax tapers are kept burning. When I behold all this I know not what to think, but for the most part I am inclined to believe that the widow loves herself above all things, and that it is for her recreation, and for the purpose of furnishing her with occasions for the effusion of this love, that she keeps the cats, the canaries, the flowers, and even the *Infant Jesus* itself, which, in her secret soul, perhaps does not occupy a place very much higher than the canaries and the cats.

It cannot be denied that Pepita Jiménez is possessed of discretion. No silly jest, no impertinent question in regard to my vocation, and, above all, in regard to my approaching ordination, has crossed her lips. She conversed with me on matters relating to the village, about agriculture, the last crop of grapes and olives, and the means of improving the methods of making wine, expressing herself always with modesty and naturalness and without manifesting any desire of appearing to know more than others.

My father was at his best; he seemed to have grown younger, and his pressing attentions to the lady of his thoughts were received, if not with love, at least with gratitude.

There were present at dinner, the doctor, the notary, and the reverend vicar, who is a great friend of the house and the spiritual father of Pepita.

The reverend vicar must have a very high opinion of her, for on several occasions he spoke to me apart of her charity, of the many alms she bestows, of her compassion and goodness to everyone. In a word, he declared her to be a saint.

In view of what the vicar has told me, and relying on his judgment, I can do no less than wish that my father may marry Pepita. As my father is not fitted for a life of penance, in this way only could he hope to change his mode of life, that up to the present has been so dissipated, and settle down to a well-ordered and quiet, if not exemplary, old age.

When we reached our house, after leaving that of Pepita Jiménez, my father spoke to me seriously of his projects. He told me that in his time he had been very wild, that he had led a very bad life, and that he saw no way of reforming, notwithstanding his years, unless Pepita were to fall in love with and marry him.

Taking for granted, of course, that she would do so, my father then spoke to me of business. He told me that he was very rich, and would leave me amply provided for in his will, even though he should have other children. I answered him that for my plans and purposes in life I needed very little money, and that my greatest satisfaction would always consist in knowing him to be happy with wife and children, his former evil ways forgotten. My father then spoke to me of his tender hopes with a candor and eagerness that might make one suppose me to be the father and the old man, and he a youth of my age, or younger. In order to enhance the merit of his mistress and the difficulties of his conquest, he recounted to me the accomplishments and the excellences of the fifteen or twenty suitors who had already presented themselves to Pepita, and who had all been rejected. As for himself, as he explained to me, the same lot, to a certain extent, had been his also; but he flattered himself that this want of success was not final, since Pepita showed him so many kindnesses, and an affection so great that, if it were not love, it might easily, with time and the persistent homage he dedicated to her, be converted into love.

There was, besides, in my father's opinion, a something fantastic and fallacious in the cause of Pepita's coldness, that must in the end wear away. Pepita did not wish to retire to a convent, nor did she incline to a penitential life. Notwithstanding her seclusion and her piety, it was easy to see that she took delight in pleasing. Her neatness and the exquisite care she took of her person had in them little of the cenobite. The cause of her coldness, then, my father declared to be, without a doubt, her pride—a pride to a certain extent well founded. She is naturally elegant and distinguished in appearance; both by her force of character and by her intelligence she is superior to those who surround her, no matter how she may seek, through modesty, to disguise it. How, then, should she bestow her hand upon any of the rustics who up to the present time have been her suitors? She imagines that her soul is filled with a mystic love of God, and that God only can satisfy it, because thus far no mortal has crossed her path intelligent enough and agreeable enough to make her forget even her image of the *Infant Jesus*. "Although it may seem conceited on my part," added my father, "I flatter myself that I am the happy man." . . .

April 8th.

The amusements of the country, in which, very much against my will, I am compelled to take part, still go on.

My father has taken me to see almost all his plantations, and he and his friends are astonished to find me not altogether ignorant in matters pertaining to the country. It would seem as if, in their eyes, the study of theology, to which I have dedicated myself, were incompatible with a familiarity with Nature. How much have they not wondered at my knowledge, on seeing me discriminate, among the vines that have only just begun to sprout, the common from the choice varieties! How much have they not wondered, too, at my being able to distinguish, among the young plants in the fields, the shoots of the barley from those of the bean; at my being familiar with many fruit and shade trees; at my knowing the names of many plants, even, that grow spontaneously in the woods, as well as something of their properties and virtues!

Pepita Jiménez, who has heard through my father of the delight I take in the gardens here, has invited me to visit one that she owns at a short distance from the village, and eat the early strawberries that grow there. This caprice of Pepita's to show so many little attentions to my father, while, at the same time she declines his addresses, seems to me at times to partake somewhat of coquetry, and to be worthy of reprobation. But when next I see her, and find her so natural, so frank and so simple, this bad opinion is dispelled, and I cannot believe her to have any other end in view than to maintain the friendly relations that exist between her and our family.

Be this as it may, yesterday afternoon we went to Pepita's garden. It is charmingly situated, and as delightful and picturesque a place as one can imagine. The river, that by means of innumerable drains waters almost all these

'TWO LOVELY GIRLS . . . DRESSED LIKE PEASANTS, BUT WITH THE
GREATEST NEATNESS AND EVEN ELEGANCE"

(From a sketch by John Lewis)

gardens, falls into a deep ravine, bordered on both sides by white and black poplars, osiers, flowering oleanders, and other leafy trees. The waterfall, clear and transparent, precipitates itself into this ravine, sending up a cloud of spray, and then follows its tortuous course by a channel formed for it by Nature herself, enameling its banks with a thousand plants and flowers, and just now covering them with a multitude of violets. The declivity at the end of the garden is full of walnut, hazel, fig, and other fruit trees; and in the level portion are beds planted with strawberries and vegetables, tomatoes, potatoes, beans, and peppers.

There is also a little flower-garden, with a great abundance of flowers, of the kinds most commonly cultivated here. Roses especially abound, and of these there are innumerable varieties. The gardener's house is prettier and cleaner than the houses of its class that one is accustomed to see in this part of the country; and near it there is another smaller building, dedicated to the use of the mistress of the place, where Pepita regaled us with a sumptuous collation. The pretext for this collation was the strawberries, to eat which was the chief purpose of our visit. The quantity of strawberries, considering the earliness of the season, was astonishing. They were served with the milk of goats, belonging also to Pepita.

There were present at this banquet the doctor, the notary, my aunt Casilda, my father, and myself, and of course the indispensable vicar, spiritual father, and, more than spiritual father, admirer and perpetual eulogist of Pepita.

By a sort of sybaritic refinement, it was not by the gardener, nor his wife, nor the son of the gardener, nor by any other rustic, that we were served at this banquet, but by two lovely girls, confidential servants, in a manner, of Pepita's, dressed like peasants, but with the greatest neatness and even elegance. They wore gowns of gay-colored cotton, short and confined at the waist, and around their shoulders silk handkerchiefs. Their lustrous and abundant black hair, without covering, was braided and arranged in a knot behind; and in front they wore curls confined to the head by large hairpins, here called *caracols*. Above the knot, or *chignon*, they each displayed a bunch of fresh roses.

Pepita's attire, except that it was black and of rich material, was equally unpretending. Her merino gown, made in the same style as those of her maids, without being short, was yet not long enough to catch the dust of the ground. A modest handkerchief of black silk covered also, according to the usage of the country, her shoulders and bosom; and on her head she wore no other ornament, either flower or jewel, than that of her own blond tresses.

The only particular, with respect to Pepita, in which I observed a certain fastidiousness, and in which she departed from the customs of the country people, was in wearing gloves. It is evident that she takes great care of her hands, and is, perhaps, to a certain extent, vain of their beauty and whiteness, as well as of her rose-colored and polished nails; but if this be so, it is to be pardoned to the weakness of the flesh; and indeed, if I remember aright, I think that St. Teresa, in her youth, had this same species of vanity, which did not prevent her, however, from becoming a great saint.

In truth, I can understand, even though I do not excuse, this little piece of vanity. It is so distinguished, so aristocratic, to possess a beautiful hand! I even think, at times, that there is something symbolic in it. The hand is the instrument by which we execute our works, the sign of our nobility, the means by which the intellect gives form and shape to its artistic conceptions, by which it gives reality to the mandates of its will, by which it exercises the dominion that God conceded to man over all other creatures. The rough, strong, sinewy, horny hand—it may be, of a laborer, a workman—testifies nobly to this dominion, but on its rudest and least intellectual side. The hands of Pepita, on the contrary, transparent almost, like alabaster, but rosy-hued, and in which one can almost see the pure and subtle blood circulate that gives to the veins their faint bluish tinge—these hands, I say, with their tapering fingers and unrivaled purity of outline, seem the symbol of the magic power, the mysterious dominion, that the human spirit holds and exercises, without the intervention of material force, over all those visible things that are the creation of God by a direct act of His will, and which man, as the instrument of God, improves and completes. It would be impossible to suppose that anyone with hands like Pepita's should have an impure thought, a gross desire, an unworthy purpose at variance with the purity of the hands that would be called upon to put them into effect.

It is unnecessary to say that my father appeared as much charmed with Pepita, and she as attentive and affectionate toward him, as always; though her affection seemed, perhaps, of a character more filial than he could have wished. The fact is, that my father, notwithstanding the reputation he has of being in general but little respectful or reverent toward women, treats this one woman with such respect and consideration that not even Amadis, in the most devoted period of his wooing, showed greater toward Oriana. Not a single word that might shock the ear, no indelicate or inopportune compliment, no coarse jest, of the kind the Andalusians permit themselves so frequently to employ, does he ever indulge in. Hardly does he dare say to Pepita, " What beautiful eyes you have ! " and, indeed, should he say so, he would only speak the truth, for Pepita's eyes are large, green as those of Circe, expressive, and well-shaped.

And what enhances their beauty is that she seems unaware of all this, for there is not to be detected in her the slightest wish to please or attract anyone by the sweetness of her glances. One would say she thought eyes were only made to see with, and for no other purpose; the contrary of what I suppose to be the opinion, according to what I have heard, of the greater number of young and pretty women, who use their eyes as a weapon of offense, or as a sort of electric battery, by means of which to subdue hearts and captivate them. Not like those, indeed, are Pepita's eyes, wherein dwell a peace and a serenity as of heaven. And yet it cannot be said that there is anything of coldness in their glances. Her eyes are full of charity and sweetness. They rest with tenderness on a ray of light, on a flower, on the commonest object in Nature; but with greater tenderness still, with signs of a softer feeling, more human and benign, do they rest on her fellow-man, without his daring to imagine in that tranquil and serene glance, however young or handsome or conceited he may be, anything more than charity and love toward a fellow-man, or, at most, a friendly preference. . . .

Our garden-party was decorously merry. We talked of flowers, of fruit, of grafts, of planting, and of innumerable other things relating to husbandry, Pepita displaying her knowledge of agriculture in rivalry with my father, with myself, and with the reverend vicar, who listens with open mouth to every word she utters, and declares that in the seventy-odd years of his life, and during his many wanderings, in the course of which he has traversed almost the whole of Andalusia, he has never known a woman more discreet or more judicious in all she thinks and says.

On returning home from any of these excursions, I renew my entreaties to my father to allow me to go back to you, in order that the wished-for moment may at last arrive in which I shall see myself elevated to the priesthood. But my father is so pleased to have me with him, he is so happy here in the village, taking care of his plantations, exercising the judicial and executive authority of squire, paying homage to Pepita, and consulting her in everything as his Egeria, that he always finds, and will find perhaps for months to come, some plausible pretext to keep me here. Now he has to clarify the wine of I know not how many casks; now he has to bottle more wine still; now it is necessary to hoe around the vines; now to plough the olive-groves and dig around the roots of the olives; in short, he keeps me here against my wishes—though I should not say " against my wishes," for it gives me great pleasure to be with my father, who is so good to me. . . .

PEPITA JIMÉNEZ

May 4th.

It is strange that in so many days I should not have had time to write to you, but such is the fact. My father does not let me rest a moment, and I am besieged by visitors.

In large cities it is easy to avoid seeing visitors, to isolate one's self, to create for one's self a solitude, a Thebaid in the widst of the tumult; in an Andalusian village, and, above all, when one has the honor of being the son of the squire, it is necessary to live in public. Not only now to my study, but even to my bedroom, do the reverend vicar, the notary, my cousin Curritò, the son of Doña Casildo, and a hundred others, penetrate without anyone daring to oppose them, waken me if I am asleep, and carry me off with them wherever they wish.

The clubhouse here is not a place of amusement for the evening only, but for all the hours of the day. From eleven o'clock in the morning it is full of people, who chat, glance over a paper to learn the news, and play at *hombre*. There are persons here who spend ten or twelve hours a day at this game. In short, there is as much enjoyment here as one could well desire. In order that this enjoyment may be uninterrupted there are a great many amusements. Besides *hombre,* there are many other games at cards. Checkers, chess, and dominoes are not neglected. And, finally, there is a decided passion for cock-fighting. . . .

In the past few days I have had occasion to practice patience in an extreme degree, and to mortify my self-love in the most cruel manner. My father, wishing to return Pepita's compliment of the garden-party, invited her to visit his villa at the Pozo de la Solana. The excursion took place on the 22d of April. I shall not soon forget the date.

The Pozo de la Solana is about two leagues distant from the village, and the only road to it is a bridle-path. We all had to go on horseback. As I never learned to ride, I had on former occasions accompanied my father mounted on a pacing mule, gentle, and, according to the expression of Dientes the muleteer, as good as gold, and easier of motion than a carriage. On the journey to the Pozo de la Solana I went in the same manner.

My father, the notary, the apothecary, and my cousin Currito were mounted on good horses. My aunt, Doña Casilda, who weighs more than two hundred and fifty pounds, rode on a large and powerful donkey, seated in a commodious side-saddle. The reverend vicar rode a gentle and easy mule like mine.

As for Pepita Jiménez, who, I supposed, would go also mounted on a donkey, in the same sort of easy saddle as my aunt—for I was ignorant that she knew how to ride—she surprised me by making her appearance on a black and white horse full of fire and spirit. She wore a riding-habit, and managed her horse with admirable grace and skill.

I was pleased to see Pepita look so charming on horse-back, but I soon began to foresee and to be mortified by the sorry part I would play, jogging on in the rear beside my corpulent aunt Casilda and the vicar, all three as quiet and tranquil as if we were seated in a carriage, while the gay cavalcade in front would caracole, gallop, trot, and make a thousand other displays of their horsemanship.

I fancied on the instant that there was something of compassion in Pepita's glance as she noted the pitiable appearance I no doubt presented, seated on my mule. My cousin Currito looked at me with a mocking smile, and immediately began to make fun of me and to tease me.

Confess that I deserve credit for my resignation and courage. I submitted to everything with a good grace, and Currito's jests soon ceased when he saw that I was invulnerable to them. But what did I not suffer in secret! The others, now trotting, now galloping, rode in advance of us, both in going and returning. The vicar and I, with Doña Casilda between us, rode on, tranquil as the mules we were seated upon, without hastening or retarding our pace.

I had not even the consolation of chatting with the vicar, in whose conversation I find so much pleasure, nor of wrapping myself up in my own thoughts and giving the rein to my fancy, nor of silently admiring the beauty of the scenery around us. Doña Casilda is gifted with an abominable loquacity, and we were obliged to listen to her. She told us all there is to be told of the gossip of the village; she recounted to us all her accomplishments; she told us how to make sausages, brain-puddings, pastry, and innumerable other dishes and delicacies. There is no one, according to herself, who can rival her in matters pertaining to the kitchen, or to the dressing of hogs, but Antoñona, Pepita's nurse, and now her housekeeper and general manager. I am already acquainted with this Antoñona, for she goes back and forth between her mistress's house and ours with messages, and is in truth extremely handy—as loquacious as Aunt Casilda, but a great deal more discreet.

The scenery on the road to the Pozo de la Solana is charming, but my mind was so disturbed during our journey that I could not enjoy it. When we arrived at the villa and dismounted, I was relieved of a great load, as if it had been I who carried the mule, and not the mule who carried me.

We then proceeded on foot, through the estate, which is magnificent, of varied character and extensive. There are vines, old and newly planted, all on the same property, producing more than five hundred bushels of grapes; olive-trees that yield to the same amount; and, finally, a grove of the most majestic oaks that are to be found in all Andalusia. The water of the Pozo de la Solana forms a clear and deep brook, at which all the birds of the neighborhood come to drink, and on whose borders they are caught by hundreds, by means of reeds smeared with bird-lime, or of nets, in the center of which are fastened a cord and a decoy. All this carried my thoughts back to the sports of my childhood, and to the many times that I too had gone to catch birds in the same manner.

Following the course of the brook, and especially in the ravines, are many poplars and other tall trees, which, together with the bushes and the shrubs, form a dark and labyrinthine wood. A thousand fragrant wild flowers grow there spontaneously, and it would, in truth, be difficult to imagine anything more secluded and sylvan, more solitary, peaceful, and silent than this spot. Even in the fervor of noonday when the sun pours down his light in torrents from a heaven without a cloud, the mind experiences the same mysterious terror as visits it at times in the silent hours of the night. One can understand here the manner of life of the patriarchs of old, and of the primitive shepherds and heroes; and the visions and apparitions that appeared to them of nymphs, of gods, and of angels, in the midst of the noonday brightness.

As we walked through this thicket, there arrived a moment in which, I know not how, Pepita and I found ourselves alone together. The others had remained behind.

I felt a sudden thrill pass through me. For the first time, and in a place so solitary, I found myself alone with this woman; while my thoughts were still dwelling on the noontide apparitions, now sinister, now gracious, but always supernatural, vouchsafed to the men of remote ages.

Pepita had left the long skirt of her riding habit in the house and now wore a short dress, that did not interfere with the graceful ease of her movements. She had on her head a little Andalusian hat, which became her extremely. She carried in her hand her riding-whip, which I fancied to myself to be a magic wand by means of which this enchantress might cast her spells over me.

I am not afraid to transcribe here these eulogies of her beauty. In this sylvan scene she appeared to me more beautiful than ever. The precaution recommended in similar cases by ascetics, to think of her beauty defaced by sickness and old age, to picture her to myself dead, the prey of corruption and of the worm, presented itself, against my will, to my imagination; and I say *against my will*, for I do not concur in the necessity for such a precaution. No thought of the material, no suggestion of the evil spirit, troubled my reason or infected my will or my senses.

What did occur to me was an argument—at least to my

mind—in disproof of the efficacy of this precaution. Beauty, the creation of a Sovereign and Divine Power, may indeed be frail and ephemeral, may vanish in an instant; but the idea of beauty is eternal, and, once perceived by the mind, it lives there an immortal life. The beauty of this woman, such as it manifests itself today, will disappear in a few short years; the graceful form, those charming contours, the noble head that raises itself so proudly above her shoulders; all will be food for loathsome worms; but—though the material must of necessity be transformed—its idea, the creative thought—abstract beauty, in a word—what shall destroy this? Does it not exist in the Divine Mind? Once perceived and known by me, must it not continue to live in my soul, triumphing over age and even over death?

I was meditating thus, striving to tranquilize my spirit and to dissipate the doubts which you have succeeded in infusing into my mind, when Pepita and I encountered each other. I was pleased and at the same time troubled to find myself alone with her—hoping and yet fearing that the others would join us.

The silvery voice of Pepita broke the silence, and drew me from my meditations, saying:

"How silent you are, Don Luis, and how sad! I am pained to think that it is perhaps through my fault, or partly so at least, that your father has caused you to spend a disagreeable day in these solitudes, taking you away from a solitude more congenial, where there would be nothing to distract your attention from your prayers and pious books."

I know not what answer I made to this. It must have been something nonsensical, for my mind was troubled. I did not wish to flatter Pepita by paying her profane compliments, nor, on the other hand, did I wish to answer her rudely.

She continued:

"You must forgive me if I am wrong, but I fancy that, in addition to the annoyance of seeing yourself deprived today of your favorite occupation, there is something else that powerfully contributes to your ill-humor."

"And what is this something else?" I said; "since you have discovered it, or fancy you have done so."

"This something else," responded Pepita, "is a feeling not altogether becoming to one who is going to be a priest so soon, but very natural in a young man of twenty-two."

On hearing this I felt the blood mount to my face, and my face burn. I imagined a thousand absurdities; I thought myself beset by evil spirits; I fancied myself tempted by Pepita, who was doubtless about to let me understand that she knew I loved her. Then my timidity gave place to haughtiness, and I looked her steadily in the face. There must have been something laughable in my look, but either Pepita did not observe it, or, if she did, she concealed the fact with amiable discretion; for she exclaimed in the most natural manner:

"Do not be offended because I find you are not without fault. This that I have observed seems to me a slight one. You are hurt by the jests of Currito, and by being compelled to play—speaking profanely—a not very dignified *rôle*, mounted, like the reverend vicar with his eighty years, on a placid mule, and not, as a youth of your age and condition should be, on a spirited horse. The fault is the reverend dean's, to whom it did not occur that you should learn to ride. To know how to manage a horse is not opposed to the career you intend to follow, and I think, now that you are here, that your father might in a few days give you the necessary instruction to enable you to do so. If you should go to Persia, or to China, where there are no railroads yet, you will make but a sorry figure in those countries as a bad horseman. It is possible even that, by this oversight, the missionary himself may come to lose prestige in the eyes of those barbarians, which will make it all the more difficult for him to reap the fruits of his labors."

This and other arguments Pepita adduced in order to persuade me to learn to ride on horseback; and I was so convinced of the necessity of a missionary's being a good horseman, that I promised her to learn at once, taking my father as a teacher.

"On the very next expedition we make," I said, "I shall ride the most spirited horse my father has, instead of the mule I am riding today."

"I shall be very glad of it," responded Pepita, with a smile of indescribable sweetness.

At this moment we were joined by the rest of the party, at which I was secretly rejoiced, though for no other reason than the fear of not being able to sustain the conversation, and of saying a great many foolish things, on account of the little experience I have had in conversing with women.

After our walk my father's servants spread before us on the fresh grass, in the most charming spot beside the brook, a rural and abundant collation.

The conversation was very animated, and Pepita sustained her part in it with much discretion and intelligence. My cousin Currito returned to his jests about my manner of riding and the meekness of my mule. He called me a theologian, and said that, seated on muleback, I looked as if I were dispensing blessings. This time, however, being now firmly resolved to learn to ride, I answered his jests with sarcastic indifference. I was silent, nevertheless, with respect to the promise I had just made Pepita. The latter, doubtless thinking as I did—although we had come to no understanding in the matter—that silence for the present was necessary to insure the complete success of the surprise that I would create afterward by my knowledge of horsemanship, said nothing of our conversation. Thus it happened naturally and in the simplest manner, that a secret existed between us; and it produced in my mind a singular effect.

Nothing else worth telling occurred during the day.

In the afternoon we returned to the village in the same manner in which we had left it. Yet, seated on my easygoing mule and at the side of my aunt Casilda, I did not experience the same fatigue or sadness as before.

During the whole journey I listened without weariness

to my aunt's stories, amusing myself at times in conjuring up idle fancies. Nothing of what passes in my soul shall be concealed from you. I confess, then, that the figure of Pepita was, as it were, the center, or rather the nucleus and focus, of these idle fancies.

The noonday vision in which she had appeared to me, in the shadiest and most sequestered part of the grove, brought to my memory all the visions, holy and unholy, of wondrous beings, of a condition superior to ours, that I had read of in sacred authors and in the profane classics. Pepita appeared to the eyes and on the stage of my fancy in the leafy seclusion of the grove, not as she rode before us on horseback, but in an ideal and ethereal fashion—as Venus to Æneas, as Minerva to Callimachus, as the sylph who afterward became the mother of Libusa to the Bohemian Kroco, as Diana to the son of Aristæus, as the angels in the valley of Mamre to the Patriarch, as the hippocentaur to St. Anthony in the solitude of the wilderness.

That the vision of Pepita should assume in my mind something of a supernatural character, seems to me no more to be wondered at than any of these. For an instant, seeing the consistency of the illusion, I thought myself tempted by evil spirits; but I reflected that in the few moments during which I had been alone with Pepita near the brook of the Solana, nothing had occurred that was not natural and commonplace; that it was afterward, as I rode along quietly on my mule, that some demon, hovering invisible around me, had suggested these extravagant fancies.

That night I told my father of my desire to learn to ride. I did not wish to conceal from him that it was Pepita who had suggested this desire. My father was greatly rejoiced; he embraced me, he kissed me, he said that now not you only would be my teacher, but that he also would have the pleasure of teaching me something. He ended by assuring me that in two or three weeks he would make me the best horseman of all Andalusia; able to go to Gibraltar for contraband goods, and come back laden with tobacco and cotton, after eluding the vigilance of the custom-house officers; fit, in a word, to astonish the riders who show off their horsemanship in the fairs of Seville and Mairena, and worthy to press the flanks of Babieca, Bucephphalus, or even of the horses of the sun themselves, if they should by chance descend to earth, and I could catch them by the bridle.

I don't know what you will think of this notion of my learning to ride, but I take it for granted you will see nothing wrong in it.

If you could but see how happy my father is, and how he delights in teaching me. Since the day after the excursion I told you of, I take two lessons daily. There are days on which the lesson is continuous, for we spend from morning till night on horseback. During the first week the lessons took place in the courtyard of the house, which is unpaved, and which served us as a riding-school.

We now ride out into the country, but manage so that no one shall see us. My father does not want me to show myself on horseback in public until I am able to astonish everyone by my fine appearance in the saddle, as he says. If the vanity natural to a father does not deceive him, this, it seems, will be very soon, for I have a wonderful aptitude for riding.

"It is easy to see that you are my son!" my father exclaims with joy, as he watches my progress.

My father is so good that I hope you will pardon him the profane language and irreverent jests in which he indulges at times. I grieve for this at the bottom of my soul, but I endure it with patience. These constant and long-continued lessons have reduced me to a pitiable condition with blisters. My father enjoins me to write to you that they are caused by mortification of the flesh.

As he declares that within a few weeks I shall be an accomplished horseman, and he does not desire to be superannuated as a master, he proposes to teach me other accomplishments of a somewhat irregular character, and sufficiently unsuited to a future priest. At times he proposes to train me in throwing the bull, in order that he may take me afterwards to Seville, where, with lance in hand, on the plains of Tablada, I shall make the braggarts and the bullies stare. Then he recalls his own youthful days, when he belonged to the body-guard, and declares that he will look up his foils, gloves, and masks, and teach me to fence. And, finally, as my father flatters himself that he can wield the Sevillian knife better than anyone else, he has offered to teach me even this accomplishment also. . . .

Yesterday was the Feast of the Cross, and the village presented a very animated appearance. In each street were six or seven May-crosses covered with flowers, but none of them was so beautiful as that placed by Pepita at the door of her house. It was adorned by a perfect cascade of flowers.

In the evening we went to an entertainment at the house of Pepita. The cross which had stood at the door was now placed in a large saloon on the ground-floor, in which there is a piano, and Pepita presented us with a simple and poetic spectacle—one that I had seen when a child, but had since forgotten.

From the upper part of the cross hung down seven bands or broad ribbons, two white, two green, and three red, the symbolic colors of the theological virtues. Eight children, of five or six years old, representing the seven sacraments, and holding the seven ribbons that hung from the cross, performed with great skill a species of contra-dance. The sacrament of baptism was represented by a child wearing the white robe of a catechumen; ordination, by another child as a priest; confirmation, by a little bishop; extreme unction, by a pilgrim with staff and scrip, the latter filled with shells; marriage, by a bride and bridegroom; and penance, by a Nazarene with cross and crown of thorns.

The dance was a series of reverences, steps, evolutions, and genuflections, rather than a dance, performed to the sound of very tolerable music, something like a march, which the organist played not without skill, on the piano.

The little dancers, children of the servants or retainers

of Pepita, after playing their parts, went away to bed loaded with gifts and caresses.

The entertainment, in the course of which we were served with refreshments, continued till twelve; the refreshments were sirup served in little cups, and afterwards chocolate with sponge-cake, and meringues and water.

Since the return of spring Pepita's seclusion and retirement are being gradually abandoned, at which my father is greatly rejoiced. In future Pepita will receive every night, and my father desires that I shall be one of the guests.

Pepita has left off mourning, and now appears, more lovely and attractive than ever, in the lighter fabrics appropriate to the season, which is almost summer. She still dresses, however, with extreme simplicity.

I cherish the hope that my father will not now detain me here beyond the end of this month at farthest. In June we shall both join you in the city, and you shall then see how, far from Pepita, to whom I am indifferent, and who will remember me neither kindly nor unkindly, I shall have the pleasure of embracing you, and attaining at last to the happiness of being ordained.

May 7th.

Pepita, as I mentioned to you before, receives every evening from nine to twelve.

Four or five married ladies of the village, and as many more unmarried ones, including Aunt Casilda, are frequent visitors; as well as six or seven young men, who play at forfeits with the girls. Three or four engagements are the natural result.

The sedate portion of the company are the same as usual. These are, as one may say, the high functionaries of the village—my father, who is the squire, the apothecary, the doctor, and the reverend vicar.

Pepita plays *hombre* with my father and the vicar and a fourth player.

I am at a loss to know in which division to place myself. If I join the young people, my gravity proves a hindrance

31

to their games and flirtations; if I stay with the elders, I must play the *rôle* of a looker-on in things I have no knowledge of. The only games of cards I know are the *burro ciego*, the *burro con vista*, and a little *tute* or *brisca crusada*.

The best course for me to pursue would be to absent myself from the house altogether, but my father will not hear of this. By doing so, according to him, I should make myself ridiculous.

My father shows many signs of wonder when he sees my ignorance in certain things. That I should not know how to play even *hombre* fills him with astonishment.

"Your uncle has brought you up quite out of the world," he says to me, "cramming you with theology, and leaving you in the dark about everything else you ought to know. For the very reason that you are to be a priest, and can neither dance nor make love in society it is necessary that you should know how to play *hombre*. Otherwise, how are you going to spend your time, unhappy boy?"

To these and other arguments of a like kind I have been obliged to yield, and my father is teaching me at home to play *hombre*, so that, as soon as I have learned it, I may play it at Pepita's. He wanted, also, as I already told you, to teach me to fence, and afterwards to smoke and shoot and throw the bar; but I have consented to nothing of all this.

"What a difference," my father exclaims, "between your youth and mine!"

And then he adds, laughing:

"In substance it is the same thing. I, too, had my canonical hours in the quarters of the Life-Guard: a cigar was the censer; a pack of cards, the hymn-book; and there were never wanting other devotions and exercises of a more or less spiritual character."

Although you had warned me of my father's levity of disposition, on account of which I have lived with you for twelve years of my life—from the age of ten to that of twenty-two—yet his sayings, altogether too free at times, perturb and mortify me. But what is to be done? Although I cannot reprove him for making use of them, I do not, on the other hand, applaud or laugh at them. The strangest part of it is, that my father is altogether another person when he is in the house of Pepita. Never, even by chance, does he utter a single phrase, a single jest of the kind he is so prodigal of at other times. At Pepita's my father is propriety itself. He seems, too, to become every day more attached to her, and to cherish greater hopes of success.

My father continues greatly pleased with me as his pupil in horsemanship. He declares that in four or five days I shall have mastered the art, and that I shall then mount Lucero, a black horse bred from an Arab horse and a mare of the race of Guadalcazar, full of fire and spirit, and trained to all manner of curvetings.

" Whoever succeeds in getting on the back of Lucero," my father says to me, " may venture to compete in horsemanship with the centaurs themselves; and that you shall do very soon."

Although I spend the whole day out-of-doors on horseback, in the clubhouse, or at Pepita's, I yet steal a few hours from slumber, sometimes voluntarily, sometimes because I cannot sleep, to meditate on my situation and to examine my conscience. The image of · Pepita is always present to my mind. " Can this be love?" I ask myself. . . .

Every other consideration, every other object, is of no avail to destroy her image. It rises up between the crucifix and me; between the most sacred image of the Virgin and me; I see it on the page of the religious book I am reading.

Yet I do not believe that my soul is invaded by what in the world is called love. And even if this were so, I would do battle against this love, and conquer in the end.

The daily sight of Pepita, the hearing her praises sounded continually, even by the reverend vicar, preoccupy me; they turn my spirit toward profane things, and withdraw it from its proper meditations. But no—I do not yet love Pepita; I will go away from hence and forget her.

While I remain here I will battle valiantly. I will wrestle with the Lord in order to prevail with Him by love and submission. My cries shall reach Him like burning arrows, and shall break down the buckler wherewith He defends and hides Himself from the eyes of my soul. I will fight like Israel in the silence of the night and the Lord shall wound me in the thigh, and shall humble me in the conflict, in order that, being vanquished, I may become the victor.

May 12th.

Before I had any intention of doing so, my dear uncle, my father persuaded me to ride Lucero. Yesterday, at six in the morning, I mounted the beautiful wild beast, as my father calls Lucero, and we set out for the country. My father rode a spirited chestnut.

I rode so well, I kept so firm a seat, and looked to such advantage on the superb animal, that my father could not resist the temptation of showing off his pupil; and about eleven in the morning, after resting at a farm he owns half a league distant from here, he insisted on our returning to the village and entering by the most frequented street, which we did, our horses' hoofs clattering loudly on the paving-stones. It is needless to say that we rode by Pepita's house, who for some time past is to be seen occasionally at her window, and who was then seated at the grating of a lower window, behind the green shutter.

Hardly had Pepita heard the noise we made than, lifting up her eyes and seeing us, she rose, laid down the sewing she had in her hands, and set herself to observe us. Lucero, who has the habit, as I learned afterwards, of prancing and curveting when he passes the house of Pepita, began to show off, and to rear and plunge. I tried to quiet him, but as there was something unfamiliar to him in the ways of his present rider, as well as in the rider himself, whom perhaps he regarded with contempt, he grew more and more unmanageable, and began to neigh and prance, and even to kick. But I remained firm and serene, showing him that I was his master, chastising him with the spur, touching his breast with the whip, and holding him in by the bridle. Lucero, who had almost stood up on his hind legs, now humbled himself so far as to bend his knees gently and make a reverence.

The crowd of idlers who had gathered around us broke into boisterous applause. My father called out to them:

" A good lesson that for our braggarts and blusterers ! "

And observing afterwards that Currito—who has no other occupation than to amuse himself—was among the crowd, he addressed him in these words:

" Look at that, you rascal ! Look at the theologian now, and see if you don't stare with wonder, instead of laughing at him ! "

And, in fact, there Currito stood open-mouthed, stock-still with amazement, and unable to utter a word.

My triumph was great and assured, although unsuited to my character. The unfitness of the triumph covered me with confusion. Shame brought the blood to my cheeks. I must have turned as red as scarlet, or redder, when I saw that Pepita was applauding and saluting me graciously, while she smiled and clapped her beautiful hands.

In short I have been adjudged a man of nerve, and a horseman of the first rank.

My father could not be prouder or happier than he is. He declares that he is completing my education; that in me you have sent him a book full of wisdom, but uncorrected and unbound, and that he is now making a fair copy, and putting it between covers.

On two occasions I played *hombre* with Pepita. Learning *hombre,* if that be a part of the binding and the correcting, is also done with.

The night after my equestrian feat Pepita received me with enthusiasm, and—what she had never ventured, nor perhaps desired, to do before—she gave me her hand.

Do not suppose that I did not call to mind what so many moralists and ascetics recommend in like cases, but in my inmost thoughts I believed they exaggerated the danger.

Those words of the Holy Spirit, that it is as dangerous to touch a woman as a scorpion, seem to me to have been said in another sense. In pious books, no doubt, many phrases and sentences of the Scriptures are, with the best intentions, interpreted harshly. How are we to understand otherwise the saying that the beauty of woman, this perfect work of God, is always the cause of. perdition? Or how are we to understand, in a universal and invariable sense, that woman is more bitter than death? How are we to understand that he who touches a woman, on whatever occasion or with whatsoever thought, shall not escape without stain?

However, I made answer rapidly within my own mind to these and other similar counsels; I took the hand that Pepita kindly extended to me, and pressed it in mine. Its softness made me comprehend all the better the delicacy and beauty of the hand that until now I had known only by sight.

According to the usages of the world, the hand, once given, should always be given on entering a room and on taking leave. I hope that in this ceremony, in this evidence of friendship, in this manifestation of kindness, given and accepted in purity of heart, and without any mixture of levity, you will see nothing either evil or dangerous.

As my father is often obliged of an evening to see the overseer and others of the country people, and is seldom free until half-past ten or eleven, I take his place with Pepita at the *hombre* table. The reverend vicar and the notary are generally the other partners. We each stake a penny a point, so that not more than a dollar or two changes hands in the game.

As the game thus possesses but little serious interest, we interrupt it constantly with pleasant conversation, and even with discussion on matters foreign to the game itself, in all which Pepita displays such clearness of understanding, such liveliness of imagination, and such extraordinary grace of expression as to astonish me.

I find no sufficient motive to change my opinion with

respect to what I have already said in answer to your suspicions that Pepita perhaps feels a certain liking for me. She manifests toward me the affection she would naturally entertain for the son of her suitor, Don Pedro de Vargas, and the timidity and shyness that would be inspired by a man in my position, who, though not yet a priest, is soon to become one.

Nevertheless, as I always speak to you in my letters as if I were kneeling before you in confessional, I desire, as is my duty, to communicate to you a passing impression I have received on two or three occasions. This impression may be but an hallucination or a delusion, but I have none the less felt it.

I have already told you in my former letters that the eyes of Pepita, green as those of Circe, are frank and tranquil in their gaze; she does not seem to be conscious of their power, or to know that they serve for any other purpose than to see with. When she looks at one, the soft light of her glance is so clear, so candid, and so untroubled that, instead of giving rise to any evil thoughts, it seems to give birth to pure thoughts, and leaves innocent and chaste souls in untroubled repose, while it destroys every incitement to evil in souls that are not chaste. There is no trace of ardent passion, no fire to be discovered in Pepita's eyes. Their light is like the mild ray of the moon.

Well, then, notwithstanding all this, I fancied I detected, on two or three occasions, a sudden brightness, a gleam as of lightning, a swift, devouring flame in her eyes as they rested on me. Can this be the result of a ridiculous vanity, inspired by the arch-fiend himself?

I think so. I believe it is, and I wish to believe it.

The swiftness, the fugitive nature of the impression make me conjecture that it had no external reality, that it was only an illusion.

The serenity of heaven, the coldness of indifference, tempered, indeed, with sweetness and charity—this is what I always discern in Pepita's eyes.

TALES FROM THE SPANISH

Nevertheless, this illusion, this vision of a strange and ardent glance, torments me.

My father affirms that in affairs of the heart it is the woman, not the man, who takes the first step; but that she takes it without thereby incurring any responsibility, and with the power to disavow or retract it whenever she desires to do so. According to my father, it is the woman who first declares her passion through the medium of furtive glances, which she afterwards disavows to her own conscience if necessary, and of which he to whom they are directed divines, rather than reads, the significance. In this manner, by a species of electric shock, by means of a subtle and inexplicable intuition, he who is loved perceives that he is loved; and when at last he makes up his mind to declare himself, he can do so confidently, and in the full security that his passion is returned.

Perhaps it is these theories of my father, to which I have listened because I could not help it, that have heated my fancy and made me imagine what has no existence in reality. . . .

May 19th.

It was not a dream; it was not madness; it was the truth: she lets her eyes rest upon me at times with the ardent glance of which I have told you. There is in her glance an inexplicable magnetic attraction. It draws me on, it seduces me, and I cannot withdraw my gaze from her. On such occasions my eyes must burn, like hers, with a fatal flame, as did those of Ammon when he turned them upon Tamar; as did those of the prince of Shechem when they were fixed upon Dinah.

When our glances thus meet, I forget even God. Her image rises up within my soul, the conqueror of everything. Her beauty outshines all other beauty; the joys of heaven seem to me less desirable than her affection. An eternity of suffering would be little in exchange for a moment of the infinite bliss with which one of those glances which pass like lightning inundates my soul.

PEPITA JIMÉNEZ

When I return home, when I am alone in my room, in the silence of the night, I realize all the horror of my position, and I form good resolutions, only to break them again.

I resolve to feign sickness, to make use of any pretext so as not to go to Pepita's on the following night, and yet I go.

My father, confiding to the last degree, says to me when the hour arrives, without any suspicion of what is passing in my soul:

"Go you to Pepita's; I will go later, when I have finished with the overseer."

No excuse occurs to me; I can find no pretext for not going, and instead of answering "I cannot go," I take my hat and depart.

On entering the room I shake hands with Pepita, and as our hands touch she casts a spell over me; my whole being is changed; a devouring fire penetrates my heart, and I think only of her. Moved by an irresistible impulse, I gaze at her with insane ardor, and at every instant I think I discover in her new perfections. Now it is the dimples in her cheeks when she smiles, now the roseate whiteness of her skin, now the straight outline of her nose, now the smallness of her ear, now the softness of contour and the admirable modeling of her throat.

I enter her house against my will, as though summoned there by a conjurer, and no sooner am I there than I fall under the spell of her enchantment. I see clearly that I am in the power of an enchantress whose fascination is irresistible.

Not only is she pleasing to my sight, but her words sound in my ears like the music of the spheres, revealing to my soul the harmony of the universe; and I even fancy that a subtle fragrance emanates from her, sweeter than the perfume of the mint that grows by the brookside, or the wood-like odor of the thyme that is found among the hills.

I know not how, in this state of exaltation, I am able

39

to play *hombre,* or to converse rationally, or even to speak, so completely am I absorbed in her.

When our eyes meet, our souls rush forth in them and seem to join and interpenetrate each other. In that meeting a thousand feelings are communicated that in no other way could be made known; poems are recited that could be uttered by no human tongue, and songs are sung that no human voice could sing, and no guitar accompany.

Since the day I met Pepita by the Pozo de la Solana I have not seen her alone. Not a word has passed between us, yet we have told each other everything.

When I withdraw myself from this fascination, when I am again alone at night in my chamber, I set myself to examine coolly the situation in which I am placed; I see the abyss that is about to engulf me yawning before me; I feel my feet slip from under me, and that I am sinking into it. . . .

No resource is left me but flight. If, before the end of the month, my father does not go with me, or consent to my going alone, I shall steal away like a thief, without a word to anyone.

June 6th.

Pepita's nurse—now her housekeeper—is, as my father says, a good bag of wrinkles; she is talkative, gay, and skilful, as few are. She married the son of Master Cencias, and has inherited from the father what the son did not inherit—a wonderful facility for the mechanical arts, with this difference: that while Master Cencias could set the screw of a wine-press, or repair the wheels of a wagon, or make a plow, this daughter-in-law of his knows how to make sweetmeats, conserves of honey, and other dainties. The father-in-law practiced the useful arts; the daughter-in-law those that have for their object pleasure, though only innocent, or at least lawful pleasure.

Antoñona—for such is her name—is permitted, or assumes, the greatest familiarity with all the gentry here. She goes in and out of every house as if it were her own. She says *thou* to all the young people of Pepita's age, or four or five years older; she calls them *niño* and *niña,* and treats them as if she had nursed them at her breast.

She behaves toward me with the same familiarity; she comes to visit me, enters my room unannounced, has asked me several times already why I no longer go to see her mistress, and has told me that I am wrong in not going.

My father, who has no suspicion of the truth, accuses me of eccentricity; he calls me an owl, and he, too, is determined that I shall resume my visits to Pepita. Last night I could no longer resist his repeated importunities, and I went to her house very early, as my father was about to settle his accounts with the overseer.

Would to God I had not gone!

Pepita was alone. When our glances met, when we saluted each other, we both turned red. We shook hands with timidity and in silence.

I did not press her hand, nor did she press mine, but for a moment we held them clasped together.

In Pepita's glance, as she looked at me, there was nothing of love; there was only friendship, sympathy, and a profound sadness.

She had divined the whole of my inward struggle; she was persuaded that Divine love had triumphed in my soul— that my resolution not to love her was firm and invincible.

She did not venture to complain of me; she had no reason to complain of me; she knew that right was on my side. A sigh, scarcely perceptible, that escaped from her dewy, parted lips, revealed to me the depth of her sorrow.

Her hand still lay in mine; we were both silent. How was I to tell her that she was not destined for me, nor I for her; that we must part forever?

But though my lips refused to tell her this in words, I told it to her with my eyes; my severe glance confirmed her fears; it convinced her of the irrevocableness of my decision.

All at once her gaze was troubled; her lovely countenance, pale with a translucent pallor, was full of a touching expression of melancholy. She looked like Our Lady of

Sorrows. Two tears rose slowly to her eyes, and began to steal down her cheeks.

I know not what passed within me—and how to describe it, even if I knew?

I bent toward her to kiss away the tears, and our lips met in a kiss.

A rapture unspeakable, a faintness full of peril, invaded our whole being. She would have fallen, but that I supported her in my arms.

Heaven willed that we should at this moment hear the step and the cough of the reverend vicar, who was approaching, and we instantly drew apart.

Recovering myself, and summoning all the strength of my will, I brought to an end this terrible scene, that had been enacted in silence, with these words, which I pronounced in low and intense accents:

" The first and the last! "

I made allusion to our profane kiss; but, as if my words had been an invocation, there rose before me the vision of the Apocalypse in all its terrible majesty. I beheld Him who is indeed the First and the Last, and with the two-edged sword that proceeded from His mouth He pierced my soul, full of evil, of wickedness, and of sin.

All that evening I passed in a species of frenzy, an inward delirium, that I know not how I was able to conceal.

I withdrew from Pepita's house very early.

The anguish of my soul was yet more poignant in solitude.

When I recalled that kiss and those words of farewell, I compared myself with the traitor Judas, who made use of a kiss to betray; and with the sanguinary and treacherous assassin Joab, who plunged the sharp steel into the bowels of Amasa while in the act of kissing him.

I had committed a double treason; I had been guilty of a double perfidy; I had sinned against God and against her.

I am an execrable wretch. . . .

June 18th.

This is the last letter I shall write to you. On the 25th I shall leave this place without fail.

I shall soon have the happiness of embracing you. Near you I shall be stronger. You will infuse courage into me, and lend me the energy in which I am wanting.

A tempest of conflicting emotions is raging now in my soul. The disorder of my ideas may be known by the disorder of what I write.

Twice I returned to the house of Pepita. I was cold and stern. I was as I ought to have been, but how much did it not cost me!

My father told me yesterday that Pepita was indisposed, and would not receive.

The thought at once assailed me that the cause of her indisposition might be ill-requited love.

Why did I return her glances of fire? Why did I basely deceive her? Why did I make her believe I loved her? Why did my vile lips seek hers with ardor, and communicate the ardor of an unholy love to hers?

But no; my sin shall not be followed, as its unavoidable consequence, by another sin!

What has been, has been, and cannot be undone; but a repetition of it may be avoided—shall be avoided in future.

On the 25th, I repeat, I shall depart from here without fail.

The impudent Antoñona has just come to see me. I hid this letter from her, as if it were a crime to write to you.

Antoñona remained here only for a moment.

I arose, and remained standing while I spoke to her, that the visit might be a short one.

During this short visit she gave utterance to a thousand mad speeches, which disturbed me greatly. Finally, as she was going away, she exclaimed, in her half-gypsy jargon:

"Get away—you deceiver! you villain! My curse upon you! You have made the child sick, and now you are killing her by your desertion. May witches fly away with you, body and bones!"

Having said this, the fiendish woman gave me, in a coarse, vulgar fashion, six or seven ferocious pinches below the shoulders, as if she would like to tear the skin from my back in strips, and then went away, looking daggers at me.

I do not complain. I deserve this brutal jest, granting it to be a jest. I deserve that fiends should tear my flesh with red-hot pincers.

Grant, my God, that Pepita may forget me! Let her, if it be necessary, love another, and be happy with him! Can I ask more than this, of Thee, O my God!

My father knows nothing, suspects nothing. It is better thus.

Farewell for a few days, till we see and embrace each other again!

How changed will you find me! How full of bitterness my heart! How lost my innocence! How bruised and wounded my soul!

II

PARALIPOMENA

HERE end the letters of Don Luis de Vargas. We should therefore be left in ignorance of the subsequent fortunes of these lovers, and the simple and ardent love-story would have remained without an ending, if one familiar with all the circumstances had not left us the following narrative:—

No one in the village found anything strange in the fact of Pepita's being indisposed, or thought, still less, of attributing her indisposition to a cause of which only we, Pepita herself, Don Luis, the reverend dean, and the discreet Antoñona, are thus far cognizant.

They might rather have wondered at the life of gayety that Pepita had been leading for some time past, at the daily gatherings at her house, and the excursions into the country in which she had joined. That Pepita should return to her habitual seclusion was quite natural.

Her secret and deeply rooted love for Don Luis was hidden from the searching glances of Doña Casilda, of Currito, and of all the other personages of the village of whom mention is made in the letters of Don Luis. Still less could the public know of it. It never entered into the head of anyone, no one imagined for a moment, that the theologian, the *saint*, as they called Don Luis, could become the rival of his father, or could have succeeded where the redoubtable and powerful Don Pedro de Vargas had failed—in winning the heart of the lovely, graceful, coy, and reserved young widow.

Notwithstanding the familiarity of the ladies of the village with their servants, Pepita had allowed none of hers to suspect anything. Only the lynx-eyed Antoñona, whom nothing could escape, and more especially nothing that concerned her young mistress, had penetrated the mystery.

Antoñona did not conceal her discovery from Pepita, nor could Pepita deny the truth to the woman who had nursed her, who idolized her, and who, if she delighted in finding out and gossiping about all that took place in the village, being, as she was, a model scandalmonger, was yet, in all that related to her mistress, reticent and loyal as but few are.

In this manner Antoñona made herself the confidante of Pepita; and Pepita found great consolation in unburdening her heart to one who, though she might be coarse and vulgar in the frankness with which she expressed her sentiments, was not so either in the sentiments or the ideas that she expressed.

In this may be found the explanation of Antoñona's visits to Don Luis, as well as of her words, and even of the ferocious and disrespectful pinches, given in so ill-chosen a spot, with which she bruised his flesh and wounded his dignity on the occasion of her last visit to him.

Not only had Pepita not desired Antoñona to carry

45

messages to Don Luis, but she did not even know that she had gone to see him. Antoñona had taken the initiative, and had interfered in the matter simply because she herself had wanted to do so.

As has already been said, she had with wonderful perspicacity discovered the state of affairs between her mistress and Don Luis.

While Pepita herself was still scarcely conscious of the fact that she loved Don Luis, Antoñona already knew it. Scarcely had Pepita begun to cast on him those furtive glances, ardent and involuntary, which had wrought such havoc—glances which had been intercepted by none of those present when they were given—when Antoñona, who was not present, had already spoken of them to Pepita. And no sooner had those glances been returned in kind, than Antoñona knew that also.

There was but little left, then, for the mistress to confide to a servant of so much penetration, and so skilled in divining what passed in the inmost recesses of her breast.

Five days after the date of Don Luis's last letter our narrative begins.

It was eleven o'clock in the morning. . . . Pepita had risen as the reverend vicar was about to take his leave. After closing the door she stood for a moment immovable in the middle of the room—her gaze fixed on space, her eyes tearless. A poet or an artist, seeing her thus, would have been reminded of Ariadne, as Catullus describes her, after Theseus has abandoned her on the island of Naxos. All at once, as if she had but just succeeded in untying the knot of a cord that was strangling her, Pepita broke into heartrending sobs, let loose a torrent of tears, and threw herself down on the tiled floor of her apartment. There, her face buried in her hands, her hair unbound, her dress disordered, she continued to sigh and moan.

She might have remained thus for an indefinite time if Antoñona had not come to her. Antoñona had heard her sobs from without, and hurried to her apartment. When she saw her mistress extended on the floor, Antoñona gave way to a thousand extravagant expressions of fury.

"Here's a pretty sight!" she cried; "that sneak, that blackguard, that old fool, what a way he has to console his friends! I shouldn't wonder if he has committed some piece of barbarity—given a couple of kicks to this poor child, perhaps; and now I suppose he has gone back to the church to get everything ready to sing the funeral chant, and sprinkle her with hyssop, and bury her out of sight without more ado."

Antoñona was about forty, and a hard worker—energetic, and stronger than many a laborer. She often lifted up, with scarcely more than the strength of her hand, a skin of oil or of wine weighing nearly ninety pounds, and placed it on the back of a mule, or carried a bag of wheat up to the garret where the grain was kept. Although Pepita was not a feather, Antoñona now lifted her up in her arms from the floor as if she had been one, and placed her carefully on the sofa, as though she were some delicate and precious piece of porcelain that she feared to break.

"What is the meaning of all this?" asked Antoñona. "I wager anything that drone of a vicar has been preaching you a sermon as bitter as aloes, and has left you now with your heart torn to pieces with grief."

Pepita continued to weep and sob without answering.

"Come, leave off crying, and tell me what is the matter. What has the vicar said to you?"

"He said nothing that could offend me," finally answered Pepita.

Then, seeing that Antoñona was waiting anxiously to hear her speak, and feeling the need of unburdening herself to someone who could sympathize more fully with her, and with more human feeling, Pepita spoke as follows:

"The reverend vicar has admonished me gently to repent of my sins; to allow Don Luis to go away; to rejoice at his departure; to forget him. I have said yes to everything; I have promised him to rejoice at Don Luis's departure; I have tried to forget him, and even to hate him. But,

47

look you, Antoñona, I cannot; it is an undertaking superior to my strength. While the vicar was here I thought I had strength for everything; but no sooner had he gone than, as if God had let go His hold of me, I lost my courage, and fell, crushed with sorrow, on the floor. I had dreamed of a happy life at the side of the man I love; I already saw myself elevated to him by the miraculous power of love—my poor mind in perfect communion with his sublime intellect, my will one with his, both thinking the same thought, our hearts beating in unison. And now God has taken him away from me, and I am left alone, without hope or consolation. Is not this frightful? The arguments of the reverend vicar are just and full of wisdom; for the time, they convinced me. But he has gone away, and all those arguments now seem to me worthless—a tissue of words, lies, entanglements, and sophistries.

"I love Don Luis, and this argument is more powerful than all other arguments put together. And if he loves me in return, why does he not leave everything and come to me, break the vows he has taken, and renounce the obligations he has contracted? I did not know what love was; now I know—there is nothing stronger on earth or in heaven. What would I not do for Don Luis? And he—he does nothing for me! Perhaps he does not love me. No; Don Luis does not love me. I have deceived myself; I was blinded by vanity. If Don Luis loved me, he would sacrifice his plans, his vows, his fame, his aspirations to be a saint and a light of the Church, he would sacrifice all to me. God forgive me, what I am about to say is horrible, but I feel it here in the depths of my heart, it burns here in my fevered brow: for him I would give even the salvation of my soul!"

"Holy Virgin!" exclaimed Antoñona.

"It is true; may our blessed Lady of Sorrows pardon me—I am mad—I know not what I say. I blaspheme!"

"Yes, child; you are talking indeed a little naughtily. Heaven help us! To think how this coxcomb of a theologian has turned your head! Well, if I were in your place, I would not take Heaven to task, which is in nowise to blame, but the jackanapes of a collegian, and I would have it out with him, or never again call myself Pepita Jiménez. I should like to go hunt him up, and bring him here to you by the ear, and make him beg your pardon and kiss your feet on his knees."

"No, Antoñona; I see that my madness is contagious, and that you are raving too. There is, in fact, nothing left for me to do but what the reverend vicar advises. And I will do it, even though it should cost me my life. If I die for him, he will then love me; he will cherish my image in his memory, my love in his heart; and God, who is so good, will permit me to see him again in Heaven with the eyes of the soul, and will let our spirits mingle together and love each other there."

Antoñona, although of a rugged nature, and not at all sentimental, on hearing these words felt the tears start to her eyes.

"Good gracious, child!" she said; "do you want to make me take out my handkerchief and begin to bellow like a calf? Calm yourself, and don't talk about dying, even in jest. I can see that your nerves are very much excited. Shan't I bring you a cup of fine-flower tea?"

"No, thanks; leave me—you see how calm I am now."

"I shall close the window, then, to see if you can sleep. How should you feel well when you have not slept for days? The devil take that same Don Luis, with his fancy for making himself a priest! A nice price you are paying for it!"

Pepita had closed her eyes; she was calm and silent, weary now of her colloquy with Antoñona.

The latter, either thinking she was asleep, or hoping her to be so, bent over Pepita, imprinted a kiss softly and slowly on her white forehead, smoothed out the folds of her dress, arranged the windows so as to leave the room in semi-obscurity, and went out on tiptoe, closing the door behind her, without making the slightest noise.

While these things were taking place at the house of Pepita, Don Luis de Vargas was neither happier nor more tranquil in his. . . . He was allowing himself to be tormented by opposing thoughts that made war on each other, when Currito, without asking leave or license, entered his room.

Currito, who had held his cousin in very slight esteem so long as he was only a student of theology, now regarded him with wonder and veneration, looking upon him, from the moment when he had seen him manage Lucero so skilfully, as something more than human.

To know theology and not know how to ride, had discredited Don Luis in the eyes of Currito; but when Currito saw that, in addition to his learning, and to all those other matters of which he himself knew nothing, although he supposed them to be difficult and perplexing, Don Luis could also keep his seat so admirably on the back of a fiery horse, his veneration and his affection for his cousin knew no bounds. Currito was an idler, a good-for-nothing, a very block of wood; but he had an affectionate and loyal heart.

To Don Luis, who was the idol of Currito, happened what happens with all superior natures when inferior persons take a liking to them. Don Luis permitted himself to be loved—that is to say, he was governed despotically by Currito in matters of little importance. And as for men like Don Luis there are hardly any matters of importance in common daily life, the result was that Don Luis was led about by Currito like a little dog.

"I have come for you," the latter said, "to take you with me to the clubhouse, which is full of people today, and unusually gay. What is the use of sitting here alone gazing into vacancy, as if you were waiting to catch flies?"

Don Luis, without offering any resistance, took his hat and cane, as though the words were a command, and saying, "Let us go wherever you wish," followed Currito, who led the way, very well pleased with the influence he exercised over his cousin.

The clubhouse was full of people, owing to the festivities of the morrow, which was St. John's Day. Besides the gentry of the village, many strangers were there who had come in from the neighboring villages to be present at the fair and the vigil in the evening.

The principal point of reunion was the courtyard, which was paved with marble. In its center played a fountain, which was adorned with flower-pots containing roses, pinks, sweet-basil, and other flowers. Around this courtyard ran a corridor or gallery supported by marble columns, in which, as well as in the various saloons that opened into it, were tables for *hombre,* others with newspapers lying on them, others where coffee and other refreshments were served, and finally, lounges, benches, and several easy-chairs. The walls were like snow, from frequent whitening; nor were pictures wanting for their adornment. There were French colored lithographs, a minute explanation of the subject of each being written, both in French and in Spanish, below. Some of them represented scenes in the life of Napoleon, from Toulon to St. Helena; others, the adventures of Matilda and Malek-Adel; others, incidents in love and war, in the lives of the Templar, Rebecca, Lady Rowena, and Ivanhoe; and others, the gallantries, the intrigues, the lapses, and the conversions of Louis XIV. and Mademoiselle de la Vallière.

Currito took Don Luis, and Don Luis allowed himself to be taken, to the saloon where were gathered the cream of the fashion, the dandies and *cocodés* of the village and of the surrounding district. Prominent among these was the Count of Genazahar, of the neighboring city of ——. The count was an illustrious and much admired personage. He had made visits of great length to Madrid and Seville, and, whether as a country dandy or as a young nobleman, was always attired by the most fashionable tailors.

The Count of Genazahar was a little past thirty. He was good-looking, and he knew it; and could boast of his prowess in peace and in war, in duels and in love-making. The count, however—and this notwithstanding the fact that he had been one of the most persistent suitors of Pepita—had received the sugar-coated pill of refusal that she was accustomed to bestow on those who paid their addresses to her and aspired to her hand.

The wound inflicted on his pride by this rejection had never quite healed. Love had turned into hatred, and the count lost no occasion of giving utterance to his feelings, holding Pepita up on such occasions to ridicule as a prude.

The count was engaged in this agreeable exercise when, by an evil chance, Don Luis and Currito approached and joined the crowd that was listening to the odd species of panegyric, which opened to receive them. Don Luis, as if the devil himself had had the arrangement of the matter, found himself face to face with the count, who was speaking as follows:

" She's a cunning one, this same Pepita Jiménez, with more fancies and whims than the Princess Micomicona. She wants to make us forget that she was born in poverty, and lived in poverty until she married that accursed usurer, Don Gumersindo, and took possession of his dollars. The only good action this same widow has performed in her life was to conspire with Satan to send the rogue quickly to hell, and free the earth from such a contamination and plague. Pepita now has a hobby for virtue and for chastity. All that may be very well; but how do we know that she has not a secret intrigue with some plowboy, and is not deceiving the world as if she were Queen Artemisia herself?"

People of quiet tastes, who seldom take part in reunions of men only, may perhaps be scandalized by this language. It may appear to them indecent and brutal even to the point of incredibility; but those who know the world will confess that language like this is very generally employed in it, and that the most amiable and agreeable women, the most honorable matrons, if they chance to have an enemy, or even if they have none, are often made the subjects of accusations no less infamous and vile than those made by the count against Pepita; for scandal, or, to speak more accurately, disrespect and insult, are often indulged in for the purpose of showing wit and effrontery.

Don Luis—who from a child had been acustomed to the consideration and respect of those around him, first, of the servants and dependants of his father, who gratified him in all his wishes, and then of everyone in the seminary, where, as well because he was a nephew of the dean, as on account of his own merits, he had never been contradicted in anything, but on the contrary, always pleased and flattered—stood, when he heard the insolent count thus drag in the dust the name of the woman he loved, as if a thunderbolt had fallen at his feet.

But how undertake her defense? He knew, indeed, that although he was neither husband, brother, nor other relative of Pepita's, he might yet come forward in her defense as a man of honor; but he saw well the scandal this would give rise to, since, far from saying a word in her favor, all the other persons present joined in applauding the wit of the count. He, already the minister almost, of a God of peace, could not be the one to give the lie to this ruffian, and thus expose himself to the risk of a quarrel.

Don Luis was on the point of departing in silence; but his heart would not consent to this, and striving to clothe himself with an authority which was justified neither by his years nor by his countenance, where the beard had scarcely begun to make its appearance, nor by his presence in that place, he began to speak with earnest eloquence in denunciation of all slanderers, and to reproach the count, with the freedom of a Christian and in severe accents, with the vileness of his conduct.

This was to preach in the desert, or worse. The count answered his homily with gibes and jests; the bystanders, among whom were many strangers, took the part of the jester, notwithstanding the fact that Don Luis was the son of the squire. Even Currito, who was of no account whatever, and who was, besides, a coward, although he did not laugh, yet made no effort to take the part of his friend, and the latter was obliged to withdraw, disturbed and humiliated by the ridicule he had drawn on himself. . . . In the seclusion of his own apartments, he gave himself up undisturbed to his thoughts.

He had been sunk in them for a long time, seated before his desk, with his elbows resting upon it, when he heard a noise close by. He raised his eyes and saw standing beside him the meddlesome Antoñona, who, although of such massive proportions, had entered like a shadow, and was now watching him attentively, with a mixture of pity and of anger.

Antoñona, taking advantage of the hour in which the servants dined and Don Pedro slept, had penetrated thus far without being observed, and had opened the door of the room and closed it behind her so gently that Don Luis, even if he had been less absorbed in meditation, would not have noticed it.

She had come resolved to hold a very serious conference with Don Luis, but she did not quite know what she was going to say to him. Nevertheless, she had asked heaven or hell, whichever of the two it may have been, to loosen her tongue and bestow upon her the gift of speech—not such grotesque and vulgar speech as she generally used, but correct, elegant, and adapted to the noble reflections and beautiful things she had in her mind and wanted to express.

When Don Luis saw Antoñona he frowned, and showed by his manner how much this visit displeased him, at the same time saying roughly:

"What do you want here? Go away!"

"I have come to call you to account about my young mistress," returned Antoñona, quietly, "and I shall not go away until you have answered me."

She then drew a chair toward the table and sat down in it, facing Don Luis with coolness and effrontery.

Don Luis, seeing there was no help for it, restrained

his anger, armed himself with patience, and, in accents less harsh than before, exclaimed:

"Say what you have to say!"

"I have to say," resumed Antoñona, "that what you are plotting against my mistress is a piece of wickedness. You are behaving like a villain. You have bewitched her; you have given her some malignant potion. The poor angel is going to die; she neither eats nor sleeps, nor has a moment's peace, on account of you. Today she has had two or three hysterical attacks at the bare thought of your going away. A good deed you have done before becoming a priest! Tell me, wretch, why did you not stay where you were, with your uncle, instead of coming here? She, who was so free, so completely mistress of her own will, enslaving that of others, and allowing her own to be taken captive by none, has fallen into your treacherous snares. Your hypocritical sanctity was doubtless the lure you employed. With your theologies and your pious humbugs you have acted like the wily and cruel sportsman, who whistles to attract the silly thrushes only to strangle them in the net."

"Antoñona," returned Don Luis, "leave me in peace. For God's sake, cease to torture me! I am a villain; I confess it. I ought not to have looked at your mistress; I ought not to have allowed her to believe that I loved her; but I loved her, and I love her still, with my whole heart; and I have given her no other potion or philter than the love I have for her. It is my duty, nevertheless, to cast away, to forget this love. God commands me to do so. Do you imagine that the sacrifice I make will not be—is not already—a tremendous one? Pepita ought to arm herself with fortitude and make a similar sacrifice."

"You do not give even that consolation to the unhappy girl," replied Antoñona. "You sacrifice voluntarily, on the altar, this woman who loves you, who is already yours—your victim. But she—how do you belong to her that she should offer you up as a sacrifice? What is the precious jewel she is going to renounce, what the beautiful

55

ornament she is going to cast into the flames, but an ill-requited love? How is she going to give to God what she does not possess? Is she going to try to cheat God, and say to Him: ' My God, since he does not love me, here he is; I offer him up to you; I will not love him either.' God never laughs—if He did, He would laugh at such a present as that!"

Don Luis, confounded, did not know what answer to return to these arguments of Antoñona, more atrocious than her former pinches. Besides, it was repugnant to him to discuss the metaphysics of love with a servant.

"Let us leave aside," he said, "these idle discussions. I cannot cure the malady of your mistress. What would you have me do?"

"What would I have you do?" replied Antoñona, more gently and with insinuating accents: "I will tell you what I would have you do. If you cannot cure the malady of my mistress, you should at least alleviate it a little. Are you not saintly? Well, the saints are compassionate, and courageous besides. Don't run away like an ill-mannered coward, without saying good-by. Come to see my mistress, who is sick. Do this work of mercy."

"And what would be gained by such a visit? It would aggravate her malady, instead of curing it!"

"It will not do so; you don't see the matter in its proper light. You shall go to see her, and, with your honeyed tongue and the gift of talk that Nature has bestowed upon you, you will put some resignation into her soul, and leave her consoled for your departure; and if you tell her, in addition to this, that you love her, and that it is only for the sake of God you are leaving her, her woman's vanity, at least, will not be wounded."

"What you propose to me is to tempt God; it is dangerous both for her and for me."

"And why should it be to tempt God? Since God can see the rectitude and the purity of your intentions, will He not grant you His favor and His grace that you may not yield to temptation during the visit to her, which it is

56

but justice you should make? Ought you not to fly to her
to deliver her from despair, and bring her back to the
right path? If she should die of grief at seeing herself
scorned; or if, in a frenzy, she should seize a rope and
hang herself to a beam, I tell you, your remorse would be
harder to bear than the flames of pitch and sulphur that
surround the caldrons of Lucifer."

"This is horrible! I would not have her grow desperate. I shall arm myself with courage—I will go to see
her."

"May Heaven bless you! But my heart told me you
would go. How good you are!"

"When do you wish me to go?"

"Tonight, at ten o'clock precisely. I will be at the
street door waiting for you, and will take you to her."

"Does she know you have come to see me?"

"She does not—it was all my own idea; but I will prepare her cautiously, so that the surprise, the unexpected
joy of your visit may not be too much for her. You
promise me to come?"

"I will go."

"Good-by. Don't fail to come. At ten o'clock precisely
I shall be at the door."

And Antoñona hurried away, descended the steps two
at a time, and so gained the street.

It cannot be denied that Antoñona displayed great
prudence on this occasion, and that her language was so
dignified and proper that some may think it apocryphal,
if there were not the very best authority for all that is
related here; and if we did not know, besides, the wonders
—the natural cleverness—a woman may work when she is
spurred on by interest or by some strong passion.

Great, indeed, was the affection Antoñona entertained
for her mistress, and, seeing her so much in love and in
such desperate case, she could do no less than seek a
remedy for her ills. The consent she had succeeded in
obtaining from Don Luis was an unexpected triumph; and

in order to derive the greatest possible advantage from this triumph, she was obliged to make the most of her time, and to use all her worldly wisdom in preparing for the occasion.

Antoñona had suggested ten as the hour of Don Luis's visit, because this was the hour in which Don Luis and Pepita had been accustomed to see each other in the now abolished or suspended gatherings at the house of the latter. She had suggested this hour also in order to avoid giving rise to scandal or slander; for she had once heard a preacher say that, according to the Gospel, there is nothing so wicked as scandal, and that the scandalmonger ought to be flung into the sea with a millstone hung round his neck.

Antoñona then returned to the house of her mistress, very well satisfied with herself, and with the firm determination so to arrange matters that the remedy she had sought should not prove useless, or aggravate instead of cure Pepita's, malady. She resolved to say nothing of the matter to Pepita herself until the last moment, when she would tell her that Don Luis had asked her of his own accord at what hour he might make a farewell visit, and that she had said ten.

In order to avoid giving rise to talk, she determined that Don Luis should not be seen to enter the house, and for this the hour and the internal arrangement of the house itself were propitious. At ten the street would be full of people, on account of the vigil, which would make it easier for Don Luis to reach the house without being observed. To enter the hall would be the work of a moment, and Antoñona, who would be waiting for him, could then take him to the library without anyone seeing him.

All, or at least the greater part, of the handsome country-houses of Andalusia are in construction double rather than single houses. Each of these double houses has its own door. The principal door leads to the courtyard, which is paved and surrounded by columns, to the parlors and the other apartments of the family; the other to the inner yards, the stable and coach-house, the kitchens, the mill, the wine-press, the granaries, the buildings where the oil, the must, the alcohol, the brandy, and the vinegar are kept in large jars; and the cask stores, or cellars, where the wine, new and old, is stored in pipes or barrels. This second house, or portion of a house, although it may be situated in the heart of a town of twenty or twenty-five thousand inhabitants, is called the *farm-house*. The overseer, the foreman, the muleteer, the principal workmen, and the domestics who have been longest in the service of the master are accustomed to gather here in the evenings, during the winter, around the enormous fireplace of a spacious kitchen, and in summer in the open air, or in some cool and well-ventilated apartment, and there chat or take their ease until the master's family are about to retire.

Antoñona was of opinion that the colloquy or explanation which she desired should take place between her mistress and Don Luis required tranquillity, and should be interrupted by no one; and she therefore determined that, as it was St. John's Eve, the maid-servants of Pepita should be tonight released from all their occupations, and should go to amuse themselves at the farm-house, where, in union with the rustic laborers, they might get up impromptu amusements, to consist of the recitation of pretty verses, playing the castanets, and dancing jigs and fandangoes.

In this manner the dwelling-house—without other occupants than Pepita and herself—would be silent and almost deserted, and suited to the solemnity and undisturbed quiet desirable in the interview she had planned, and on which perhaps—or rather to a certainty—depended the fate of two persons of such distinguished merit.

While Antoñona went about turning over and arranging in her mind all these things, Don Luis had no sooner been left alone than he repented of having proceeded with so much haste, and weakly consenting to the interview Antoñona had asked of him. As he reflected upon it, it seemed to him more full of peril than those of Œnone or

Celestina. He saw before him all the danger to which he voluntarily exposed himself, and he could see no advantage whatever in thus making in secret and by stealth a visit to the beautiful widow.

To go and see her in order to succumb to her attractions and fall into her snares, making a mockery of his vows, and placing not only the bishop, who indorsed his petition for a dispensation, but even the holy Pontiff, who had conceded it, in a false position, by relinquishing his purpose of becoming a priest, seemed to him very dishonorable. It was, besides, a treason against his father, who loved Pepita and desired to marry her; and to visit her in order to undeceive her in regard to his love for her, seemed to him a greater refinement of cruelty than to depart without saying anything.

Influenced by these considerations, the first thought of Don Luis was to fail, without excuse or warning, to keep his appointment, and leave Antoñona to wait in vain for him in the hall; but then, as Antoñona had, in all proba- bility, already announced his visit to her mistress, he would, by failing to go, unpardonably offend, not only Antoñona, but Pepita herself.

He then resolved on writing Pepita a very affectionate and discreet letter, excusing himself from going to see her, justifying his conduct, consoling her, manifesting his tender sentiments toward her, while letting her see that duty and Heaven were before everything, and endeavoring to inspire her with the courage to make the same sacrifice as he him- self was making.

He made four or five different attempts to write this letter. He blotted a great deal of paper which he after- wards tore up, and could not, in the end, succeed in getting the letter to his taste. Now it was dry, cold, pedantic, like a poor sermon or a schoolmaster's discourse; now its contents betrayed a childish apprehension, as if Pepita were a monster lying in wait to devour him; now it had other faults not less serious. In fine, after wasting many sheets of paper in the attempt, the letter remained unwritten. . . . He felt as if the room, though a large one, was too small to contain him. Starting to his feet, he paced with rapid strides up and down the floor, like some wild animal in his cage, impatient of confinement. At last, although—being summer—the window was open, he felt as if he could remain here no longer, lest he should suffocate for want of air; as if the roof pressed down upon his head; as if, to breathe, he needed the whole atmosphere; to walk, he required space without limits; to lift up his brow and exhale his sighs and elevate his thoughts, to have nothing less than the immeasurable vault of heaven above him.

Impelled by this necessity, he took his hat and cane and went out into the street. Thence, avoiding everyone he knew, he passed on into the country, plunging into the leafiest and most sequestered recesses of the gardens and walks that encompass the village and make for a radius of more than half a league a paradise of its surroundings.

We have said but little, thus far, concerning the personal appearance of Don Luis. Be it known, then, that he was in every sense of the word a handsome fellow—tall, well-formed, with black hair, and eyes also black and full of fire and sweetness. His complexion was dark, his teeth were white, his lips delicate and curling slightly, which gave to his countenance an appearance of disdain; his bearing was manly and bold, notwithstanding the reserve and meekness proper to his sacred character. The whole mien of Don Luis bore, in a word, that indescribable stamp of distinction and nobility that seems to be—though this is not always the case—the peculiar quality and exclusive privilege of aristocratic families.

On beholding Don Luis one could not but confess that Pepita Jiménez was æsthetic by instinct.

Don Luis hurried on with precipitate steps in the course he had taken, jumping across brooks and hardly glancing at surrounding objects, almost as a bull stung by a hornet might do. The countrymen he met, the market-gardeners who saw him pass, very possibly took him for a madman.

Tired at last of walking on aimlessly, he sat down at the foot of a stone cross near the ruins of an ancient convent of St. Francis de Paul, almost two miles from the village, and there plunged anew into meditation, but of so confused a character that he himself was scarcely conscious of what was passing in his mind.

The sound of the distant bells, calling the faithful to prayer, and reminding them of the salutation of the angel to the Most Holy Virgin, reached him in his solitude through the evening air, and at last drew Don Luis from his meditations, recalling him once more to the world of reality.

The sun had just sunk behind the gigantic peaks of the neighboring mountains, making their summits—in the shape of pyramids, needles, and broken obelisks—stand out in bold relief against a background of topaz and amethyst—for such was the appearance of the heavens, gilded by the beams of the setting sun. The shadows began to deepen over the plain, and on the mountains opposite to those behind which the sun was sinking the more elevated peaks shone like flaming gold or crystal.

The windows and the white walls of the distant sanctuary of the Virgin, patroness of the village, situated on the summit of a hill, and of another small temple or hermitage situated on a nearer hill called Calvary, still shone like two beacon lights touched by the oblique rays of the setting sun.

Nature exhaled a poetic melancholy, and all things seemed to intone a hymn to the Creator, with that silent music heard only by the spirit. The slow tolling of the bells, softened and almost lost in the distance, hardly disturbed the repose of the earth, and invited to prayer without distracting the senses by their noise. Don Luis uncovered his head, knelt down at the foot of the cross, the pedestal of which had served him as a seat, and repeated with profound devotion the *Angelus Domini*.

The shades of evening were gathering fast, but when Night unfolds her mantle, and spreads it over those favored regions, she delights to adorn it with the most luminous stars and with a still brighter moon. The vault of heaven did not exchange its cerulean hue for the blackness of night; it still retained it, though it had assumed a deeper shade. The atmosphere was so clear and pure that myriads of stars could be descried shining far into the limitless depths of space. The moon silvered the tops of the trees, and touched with its splendor the waters of the brooks that gleamed, luminous and transparent, with colors as changeful and evanescent as the opal. In the leafy groves the nightingales were singing. Herbs and flowers shed a rich perfume. Countless multitudes of glow-worms shone like diamonds or carbuncles among the grass and wild flowers along the banks of the brooks. In this region the firefly is not found, but the common glow-worm abounds, and sheds a most brilliant light. Fruit-trees still in blossom, acacias, and roses without number, perfumed the air with their rich fragrance.

Don Luis felt himself swayed, seduced, vanquished by this voluptuousness of Nature, and began to doubt himself. It was necessary, however, to fulfil his promise and keep his appointment.

Deviating often from the straight path, hesitating at times whether he should not rather push forward to the source of the river, where, at the foot of a mountain and in the midst of the most enchanting surroundings, the crystal torrent that waters the neighboring gardens and orchards bursts from the living rock, he turned back, with slow and lingering step, in the direction of the village.

In proportion as he approached it, the terror inspired by the thought of what he was about to do increased. He plunged into the thickest of the wood, hoping there to behold some sign, some wonder, some warning, that should draw him back. He thought often of the student Lisardo, and wished that, like him, he might behold his own burial. But heaven smiled with her thousand lights, and invited to love; the stars looked at each other with love; the nightingales sang of love; even the crickets amorously vibrated their

63

sonorous elytra, like troubadours thrumming a serenade. All the earth, on this tranquil and beautiful night, seemed given up to love.

There was no warning; there was no sign; there was no funeral pomp. All was life, peace, joy.

Where was now his guardian angel? Had he abandoned Don Luis as already lost; or, deeming that he ran no risk, did he make no effort to turn him from his purpose? Who can say? Perhaps from the danger that menaced him would in the end result a triumph? St. Edward and Queen Edith presented themselves to the imagination of Don Luis, and strengthened his resolution.

Engrossed in these meditations, he delayed his return, and was still some distance from the village when ten, the hour appointed for his interview with Pepita, struck from the parish clock. The ten strokes of the bell were ten blows that, falling on his heart, wounded it as with a physical pain —a pain in which dread and treacherous disquiet were blended with a ravishing sweetness.

Don Luis hastened his steps, that he might not be too late, and shortly found himself in the village.

The hamlet presented a most animated scene. Young girls flocked to wash their faces at the spring outside the village; those who had sweethearts, that their sweethearts might remain faithful to them; and those who had not, that they might obtain sweethearts. Here and there women and children were returning from the fields, with verbena, branches of rosemary, and other plants, which they had been gathering to burn as a charm. Guitars tinkled on every side, words of love were to be overheard, and everywhere happy and tender couples were to be seen walking together.

The vigil and the early morning of St. John's Day, although a Christian festival, still retain a certain savor of paganism and primitive naturalism. This may be because of the approximate concurrence of this festival and the summer solstice. In any case, the scene tonight was purely mundane and not religious. All was love and gallantry.

PEPITA JIMÉNEZ

In our old romances and legends the Moor always carries off the beautiful Christian princess, and the Christian knight receives the reward of his devotion to the Moorish princess on the eve or in the early morning of St. John's Day; and the traditionary custom of the old romances had been, to all appearances, preserved in the village.

The streets were full of people. The whole village was out of doors, in addition to the strangers from the surrounding country. Progress, thus rendered extremely difficult, was still further impeded by the multitude of little tables laden with *nougat,* honey-cakes, and biscuits, fruit-stalls, booths for the sale of dolls and toys, and cake-shops, where gypsies, young and old, by turns fried the dough, tainting the air with the ōdor of oil, weighed and served the cakes, responded with ready wit to the compliments of the gallants who passed by, and told fortunes.

Don Luis sought to avoid meeting any of his acquaintances, and, when he caught sight by chance of anyone he knew, he turned his steps in another direction. Thus, by degrees, he reached the entrance to Pepita's house without having been stopped or spoken to by anyone. His heart now began to beat with violence, and he paused a moment to recover his serenity. He looked at his watch; it was almost half-past ten.

" Good heavens ! " he exclaimed; " she has been waiting for me nearly half an hour."

He then hurried his pace and entered the hall. The lamp by which it was always lighted was burning dimly on this particular evening.

No sooner had Don Luis entered the hall than a hand, or rather a claw, seized him by the right arm. It belonged to Antoñona, who said to him under her breath:

" A pretty fellow you are, for a collegian ! Ingrate ! good-for-nothing ! vagabond ! I began to think you were not coming. Where have you been, imbecile ? How dare you delay, as if you had no interest in the matter, when the salt of the earth is melting for you, and the sun of beauty awaits you ? "

While Antoñona was giving utterance to these complaints, she did not stand still, but continued to go forward, dragging after her by the arm the now cowed and silent collegian. They passed the grated door, which Antoñona closed carefully and noiselessly behind them. They crossed the courtyard, ascended the stairs, passed through some corridors and two sitting-rooms, and arrived at last at the door of the library, which was closed.

Profound silence reigned throughout the house. The library was situated in its interior, and was thus unaccessible to the noises of the street. The only sounds that reached it, confused and vague, were the shaking of the castanets, the tinkle of the guitar, and the murmur of the voices of Pepita's servants, who were holding their impromptu dance in the farm-house.

Antoñona opened the door of the library and pushed Don Luis toward it, at the same time announcing him in these words:

"Here is Don Luis, who has come to take leave of you."

This announcement being made with due ceremony, the discreet Antoñona withdrew, leaving the visitor and her mistress at their ease, and closing the door behind her. . . .

The visit began in the most grave and ceremonious manner. The customary salutations were mechanically interchanged, and Don Luis, at the invitation of Pepita, seated himself in an easy-chair, without laying aside his hat or cane, and at a short distance from her. Pepita was seated on the sofa; beside her was a little table on which were some books, and a candle, the light from which illuminated her countenance. On the desk also burned a lamp. Notwithstanding these two lights, however, the apartment, which was large, remained for the greater part in obscurity. A large window, which looked out on an inner garden, was open on account of the heat; and although the grating of the window was covered with climbing roses and jasmine, the clear beams of the moon penetrated through the interlaced leaves and flowers, and struggled with the light of the lamp and candle. Through the open window came,

66

too, the distant and confused sounds of the dance at the farm-house, which was at the other extremity of the garden, the monotonous murmur of the fountain below, and the fragrance of the jasmine and roses that curtained the window, mingled with that of the mignonette, sweet-basil, and other plants that adorned the borders beneath.

There was a long pause—a silence as difficult to maintain as it was to break. Neither of the two interlocutors ventured to speak. The situation was, in truth, embarrassing. They found it as difficult to express themselves then, as we find it now to reproduce their words; but there is nothing else for it than to make the effort. Let us allow them to speak for themselves, transcribing their words with exactitude.

" So you have finally condescended to come and take leave of me before your departure," said Pepita; " I had already given up hope that you would do so."

The part Don Luis had to perform was a serious one; and, besides this, in this kind of dialogue, the man, not only if he be a novice, but even when he is old in the business and an expert, is apt to begin with some piece of folly. Let us not condemn Don Luis, therefore, because he also began unwisely.

"Your complaint is unjust," he said. " I came here with my father to take leave of you, and, as we had not the pleasure of being received by you, we left cards. We were told that your health was somewhat delicate, and we have sent every day since to inquire for you. We were greatly pleased to learn that you were improving. I hope you are now much better."

" I am almost tempted to say I am no better," answered Pepita, " but, as I see that you have come as the ambassador of your father, and I do not want to distress so excellent a friend, it is but right that I should tell you, that you may repeat it to him, that I am much better now. But it is strange that you have come alone. Don Pedro must be very much occupied indeed, not to accompany you."

"My father did not accompany me, madam, because he does not know that I have come to see you. I have chosen to come without him, because my farewell must be a serious, a solemn, perhaps a final one, and his will naturally be of a very different character. My father will return to the village in a few weeks; it is possible that I may never return to it, and, if I do, it will be in a very different character from my present one."

Pepita could not restrain herself. The happy future of which she had dreamed vanished into air. Her unalterable resolution to vanquish this man, at whatever cost, the only man she had loved in her life, the only one she felt herself capable of loving, seemed to have been made in vain. She felt herself condemned at twenty years of age, with all her beauty, to perpetual widowhood, to solitude, to an unrequited love—for any other love was impossible for her. The character of Pepita, in whom obstacles only strengthened and rekindled her desires, with whom a determination, once taken, carried everything before it until it was fulfilled, showed itself now in all its violence and without restraint. She must conquer, or die in the attempt. . . .

She continued: "I have had the audacity to ask of Heaven that you should allow yourself to be vanquished, that you should cease to desire to be a priest, that there might spring up in your soul a love as great as that which is in my heart. Don Luis, tell me frankly, has Heaven been deaf to this prayer? Or is it, perchance, that to subjugate a soul as weak, as wretched, and as petty as mine, a petty love is sufficient, while to master yours, protected and guarded as it is by vigorous and lofty thoughts, a more powerful love than mine is necessary, a love that I am neither worthy of inspiring, nor capable of sharing, nor even able to understand?"

"Pepita," returned Don Luis, "it is not that your soul is less than mine, but that it is free from obligations, and mine is not. The love you have inspired me with is profound, but my obligations, my vows, the purpose of my whole life so near to its realization, contend against it.

68

Why should I not say it without fearing to offend you? If
you succeed in making me love you, you do not humiliate
yourself. If I succumb to your love, I humiliate and abase
myself. I leave the Creator for the creature. I renounce
the unwavering purpose of my life, I break the image of
Christ that was in my soul; and the new man, which I had
created in myself at such cost, disappears, that the old
man may come to life again. Instead of my lowering myself to the earth, to the impurity of the world that I have
hitherto despised, why do not you rather elevate yourself
to me by virtue of that very love you entertain for me,
freeing it from every earthly alloy? Why should we not
love each other then without shame, and without sin, and
without dishonor? God penetrates holy souls with the
pure and refulgent fire of His love, and so fills them with it
that, as metal fresh from the forge, without ceasing to be
a metal, shines and glitters and is all fire, these souls are
filled with joy, and see God, in all things penetrated by God
in every part, through the grace of the Divine love. These
souls then love and enjoy each other, as if they loved and
enjoyed God, loving and enjoying Him in truth because they
are God. Let us mount together in spirit this steep and
mystical ladder. Let our souls ascend, side by side, to this
bliss, which even in this mortal life is possible! But to do
this we must separate in the body; it is essential that I
should go whither I am called by my duty, my vow, and
the voice of the Most High, who disposes of His servant,
and has destined him to the service of His altar."

"Ah, Don Luis," replied Pepita, full of sorrow and con-
trition, "now indeed I see how vile is the metal I am made
of, and how unworthy I am that the Divine fire should
penetrate and transform me. I will confess everything,
casting away even shame: I am a vile sinner; my rude and
uncultured understanding cannot grasp these subtleties,
these distinctions, these refinements of love. My rebellious
will refuses what you propose. I cannot even conceive of
you but as yourself. For me you are your mouth, your
eyes, your dark locks that I desire to caress with my hands,

your sweet voice, the pleasing sound of your words that fall upon my ears and charm them through the senses; your whole person, in a word, which charms and seduces me, and through which, and only through which, I perceive the invisible spirit, vague and full of mystery. My soul, stubborn and incapable of these mystical raptures, will never be able to follow you to those regions whither you would take it.

"If you soar up to them, I shall remain alone, abandoned, plunged in the deepest affliction. I prefer to die; I deserve death; I desire it. It may be that after death my soul, loosening or breaking the vile bonds which chain it here, will be able to understand the love with which you desire we should be united. Kill me, then, in order that we may thus love each other; kill me, and my spirit, set free, will follow you whithersoever you may go, and will journey invisible by your side, watching over your steps, contemplating you with rapture, penetrating your most secret thoughts, beholding your soul as it is, without the intervention of the senses. But in this life it cannot be. I love in you, not only the soul, but the body, and the shadow cast by the body, and the reflection of the body in the mirror and in the water, and the Christian name, and the surname, and the blood, and all that goes to make you such as you are, Don Luis de Vargas; the sound of your voice, your gesture, your gait, and I know not what else besides. I repeat that you must kill me. Kill me without compassion. No, I am not a Christian; I am a material idolater."

Here Pepita made a long pause. Don Luis knew not what to say, and was silent. Tears bathed the cheeks of Pepita, who continued, sobbing:

"I know it; you despise me, and you are right to despise me. By this just contempt you will kill me more surely than with a dagger, and without staining either your hands or your conscience with blood. Farewell! I am about to free you from my odious presence. Farewell forever!"

Having said this, Pepita rose from her seat, and, without looking at Don Luis, her face bathed with tears, beside herself, rushed toward the door that led to the inner apartment. An unconquerable tenderness, a fatal pity, took possession of Don Luis. He feared Pepita would die. He started forward to detain her, but it was too late. Pepita had crossed the threshold. Her form disappeared in the obscurity within. Don Luis, impelled by a superhuman power, drawn as by an invisible hand, followed her into the darkened chamber.

The library remained deserted.

The servants' dance must have already terminated, for the only sound to be heard was the murmur of the fountain in the garden below.

Not even a breath of wind troubled the stillness of the night and the serenity of the air.

The perfume of the flowers and the light of the moon entered softly through the open window. After a long interval, Don Luis made his appearance, emerging from the darkness. Terror was depicted on his countenance, mingled with despair—such despair as Judas may have felt after he had betrayed his Master.

He dropped into a chair, and burying his face in his hands, with his elbows resting on his knees, he remained for more than half an hour plunged in a sea of bitter reflections.

To see him thus, one might have supposed that he had just assassinated Pepita.

Pepita, nevertheless, at last made her appearance. With a slow step, and an air of the deepest melancholy, with bent head, and eyes directed to the floor, she approached Don Luis, and spoke.

"Now, indeed," said she, "though, alas! too late, I know all the vileness of my heart and the iniquity of my conduct. I have nothing to say in my own defense, but I would not have you think me more wicked than I am. You must not think I have used any arts—that I have laid any plans for your destruction. Yes; it is true that I have been guilty of an atrocious crime, but an unpremeditated one; a crime inspired, perhaps, by the spirit of evil that possesses me. Do not abandon yourself to despair, do not torture yourself, for God's sake! You are responsible for nothing. It was a frenzy, a madness, that took possession of your noble spirit. Your sin is a light one; mine is flagrant, shameful, horrible. Now I am less worthy of you than ever. It is I who ask you now to leave this place. Go; do penance. God will pardon you. Go; a priest will give you absolution. Once cleansed from sin, carry out your purpose, and become a minister of the Most High.

"Then, through the holiness of your life, through your ceaseless labors, not only will you efface from your soul the last traces of this fall, but you will obtain for me, when you have pardoned me the evil I have done you, the pardon of Heaven also. You are bound to me by no tie, and even if you were I should loosen or break it. You are free. Let it suffice me that I have taken captive by surprise the star of the morning. It is not my desire—I neither can nor ought to seek to keep him in my power. I divine it, I read it in your gesture, I am convinced of it—you despise me more than before; and you are right in despising me. There is neither honor, nor virtue, nor shame in me!"

When she had thus spoken, Pepita, throwing herself on her knees, bowed her face till her forehead touched the floor. Don Luis continued in the same attitude as before. Thus, for some moments, they remained both silent with the silence of despair.

In a stifled voice, and without raising her face from the floor, Pepita after a time continued:

"Go now, Don Luis, and do not, through an insulting pity, remain any longer at the side of so despicable a wretch as I. I shall have courage to bear your indifference, your forgetfulness, your contempt, for I have deserved them all. I shall always be your slave—but far from you, very far from you, in order that nothing may recall to your memory the infamy of this night!"

Pepita's voice, as she ended, was choked with sobs.

Don Luis could restrain himself no longer. He arose, approached Pepita, and, raising her in his arms from the floor, pressed her to his heart; then, putting aside from her face the blond tresses that fell in disorder over it, he covered it with passionate kisses.

"Soul of my soul," he said at last, "life of my life, treasure of my heart, light of my eyes, raise up your dejected brow, and do not prostrate yourself any longer before me. The sinner, the vile wretch, he who has shown himself weak of purpose, who has made himself the butt of scorn and ridicule, is I, not you. Angels and devils alike must laugh at me and mock me. I have clothed myself with a false sanctity. I was not able to resist temptation, and to undeceive you in the beginning, as would have been right, and now I am equally unable to show myself a gentleman, a man of honor, or a tender lover who knows how to value the favors of his mistress. I cannot understand what it was you saw in me to attract you. There never was in me any solid virtue—nothing but vain show and the pedantry of a student who has read pious books as one reads a novel, and on this foundation has based his foolish romance of a future devoted to converting the heathen, and to pious meditations. If there had been in me any solid virtue I should have undeceived you in time, and neither you nor I would have sinned. True virtue is not so easily vanquished.

"Notwithstanding your beauty, notwithstanding your intelligence, notwithstanding your love for me, I should not have fallen if I had been in reality virtuous, if I had had a true vocation. God, to whom all things are possible, would have bestowed His grace upon me. It would have needed nothing less than a miracle, or some other supernatural event, to have enabled me to resist your love, but God would have wrought the miracle if I had been worthy of it, and a motive sufficient for its being wrought. You are wrong to counsel me to become a priest. I know my own unworthiness. It was only pride that actuated me. It was a worldly ambition, like any other. What do I say—

like any other? It was worse than any other; it was hypocritical, sacrilegious, simoniacal."

"Do not judge yourself so harshly," said Pepita, now more tranquil, and smiling through her tears. "I do not want you to judge yourself thus, not even for the purpose of making me appear less unworthy to be your companion. No; I would have you choose me through love—freely; not to repair a fault, not because you have fallen into the snares you perhaps think I have perfidiously spread for you. If you do not love me, if you distrust me, if you do not esteem me, then go. My lips shall not breathe a single complaint, if you should abandon me forever, and never think of me again."

To answer this fittingly, our poor and beggarly human speech was insufficient for Don Luis. He cut short Pepita's words by pressing his lips to hers, and again clasping her to his heart.

Some time afterward, with much previous coughing and shuffling of the feet, Antoñona entered the library with the words:

"What a long talk you must have had! The sermon our student has been preaching this time cannot have been that of the *seven words*—it came very near being that of the *forty hours*. It is time you should go now, Don Luis; it is almost two o'clock in the morning."

"Very well," answered Pepita, "he will go directly."

Antoñona left the library again, and waited outside.

Pepita was like one transformed. One might suppose that the joys she had missed in her childhood, the happiness and contentment she had failed to taste in her early youth, the gay activity and sprightliness that a harsh mother and an old husband had repressed, and, as it were, crushed within her, had suddenly burst into life in her soul, like the green leaves of the trees, whose germination has been retarded by the snows and frosts of a long and severe winter.

A city-bred lady, familiar with what we call social conventionalities, may find something strange, and even worthy of censure, in what I am about to relate of Pepita. But Pepita, although refined by instinct, was a being in whom every feeling was spontaneous, and in whose nature there was no room for the affected sedateness and circumspection that are customary in the great world. Thus it was that, seeing the obstacles removed that had stood in the way of her happiness, and Don Luis conquered, holding his voluntary promise that he would make her his wife, and believing herself, with justice, to be loved—nay, worshiped—by him whom she too loved and worshiped, she danced and laughed, and gave way to other manifestations of joy that had in them, after all, something childlike and innocent.

But it was necessary that Don Luis should now depart. Pepita took a comb and smoothed his hair lovingly, and kissed him. She then rearranged his necktie.

"Farewell, lord of my life," she said, "dear sovereign of my soul. I will tell your father everything if you fear to do so. He is good, and he will forgive us."

At last the lovers separated.

When Pepita found herself alone, her restless gayety disappeared, and her countenance assumed a grave and thoughtful expression.

Two thoughts now presented themselves to her mind, both equally serious; the one possessing a merely mundane interest, the other an interest of a higher nature. The first thought was that her conduct tonight—the delirium of passion once past—might prejudice her in the opinion of Don Luis; but, finding after a severe examination of her conscience, that neither premeditation nor artifice had had any part in her actions, which were the offspring of an irresistible love, and of impulses noble in themselves, she came to the conclusion that Don Luis could not despise her for it, and she therefore made her mind easy on that point. Nevertheless, although her frank confession that she was unable to comprehend a love that was purely spiritual, and her taking refuge afterwards in the obscurity of her chamber—without foreseeing consequences—were both the result of an impulse innocent enough in itself, Pepita did not seek

75

to deny in her own mind that she had sinned against God, and on this point she could find for herself no excuse. She commended herself, with all her heart, therefore, to the Virgin, entreating her forgiveness. She vowed to the image of Our Lady of Solitude, in the convent of the nuns, seven beautiful golden swords of the finest and most elaborate workmanship, to adorn her breast, and determined to go to confess herself on the following day to the vicar, and to submit herself to the harshest penance he should choose to impose upon her, in order to merit the absolution of those sins by means of which she had vanquished the obstinacy of Don Luis, who, but for them, would without doubt have become a priest.

While Pepita was engaged in these reflections, and while she was arranging with so much discretion the affairs of her soul, Don Luis had descended to the hall below, accompanied by Antoñona.

Before taking his leave, Don Luis, without preface or circumlocution, spoke thus:

" Antoñona, tell me, you who are acquainted with everything, who is the Count of Genazahar, and what has he had to do with your mistress? "

" You begin to be jealous very soon."

" It is not jealousy that makes me ask this; it is simply curiosity."

" So much the better. There is nothing more tiresome than jealousy. Well, I will try to satisfy your curiosity. This same count has given room enough for talk. He is a dissipated fellow, a gambler, and a man of no principle whatever, but he has more vanity than Don Roderick on the gallows. He made up his mind that my mistress should fall in love with him and marry him, and as she has refused him a thousand times he is mad with rage. This does not prevent him, however, from keeping in his money-chest more than a thousand dollars that Don Gumersindo lent him years ago, without any more security than a bit of paper, through the fault and at the entreaty of Pepita, who is better than bread. The fool of a count thought, no doubt, that

Pepita, who was so good to him as a wife that she persuaded
her husband to lend him money; would be so much better
to him as a widow that she would consent to marry him.
He was soon undeceived, however, and then he became
furious."

" Good-by, Antoñona," said Don Luis, as now, grave and
thoughtful, he left the house.

The lights of the shops and of the booths in the fair were
now extinguished, and everyone was going home to bed,
with the exception of the owners of the toy-shops and other
poor hucksters, who slept beside their wares in the open air.

Under some of the grated windows were still to be seen
lovers, wrapped in their cloaks, and chatting with their
sweethearts. Almost everyone else had disappeared.

Don Luis, once out of sight of Antoñona, gave a loose
rein to his thoughts. His resolution was taken, and all
his reflections tended to confirm this resolution. The sincerity and ardor of the passion with which he had inspired
Pepita, her beauty, the youthful grace of her person, and
the fresh exuberance of her soul, presented themselves to
his imagination and made him happy. . . .

Don Luis, in the middle of the street, at two o'clock in
the morning, was occupied with the thought that his life,
which until now, he had dreamed might be worthy of the
Golden Legend, was about to be converted into a sweet
and perpetual idyl. He had not been able to resist the lures
of earthly passion. He had proved false to his ideal; he
had been vanquished in the conflict. Those who have
no ideal, who have never had an ideal, would not distress
themselves on this account. Don Luis did distress himself;
but he presently came to the conclusion that he would substitute a more humble and easily attained ideal for his
former exalted one. And although the recollection of Don
Quixote's resolution to turn shepherd, on being vanquished
by the Knight of the White Moon, here crossed his mind
with ludicrous appositeness, he was in no way daunted by
it. He thought, in union with Pepita Jiménez, to renew, in

our prosaic and unbelieving time, the golden age, and to repeat the pious example of Philemon and Baucis, creating a model of patriarchal life in these pleasant fields, founding in the place where he was born a home presided over by religion, that should be at once the asylum of the needy, the center of culture and friendly conviviality, and the clear mirror in which the domestic virtues should be reflected; joining in one, finally, conjugal love and the love of God, in order that God might sanctify and be present in their dwelling, making it the temple in which both should be his ministers, until by the will of Heaven they should be called to a better life.

Two obstacles must first be removed, however, before all this could be realized, and Don Luis began to consider with himself how he might best remove them.

The one was the displeasure, perhaps the anger, of his father, whom he had defrauded of his dearest hopes. The other was of a very different and, in a certain sense, of a much more serious character. Don Luis, while he entertained the purpose of becoming a priest, was right in defending Pepita from the gross insults of the Count of Genazahar by the weapons of argument only, and in taking no vengeance for the scorn and contempt with which those arguments were listened to. But having now determined to lay aside the cassock, and obliged, as he was, to declare immediately that he was betrothed to Pepita and was going to marry her, Don Luis, notwithstanding his peaceable disposition, his dreams of human brotherhood, and his religious belief, all of which remained intact in his soul, and all of which were alike opposed to violent measures, could not succeed in reconciling it with his dignity to refrain from breaking the head of the insolent count. He knew well that dueling is a barbarous practice, that Pepita had no need of the blood of the count to wash from her name the stain of calumny, and even that the count himself had uttered the insults he had uttered, not because he believed them, nor perhaps through an excess of hatred, but through stupidity and want of breeding. Notwithstanding all these reflections, how-

78

ever, Don Luis was conscious that he would never again be able to respect himself, and, as a consequence, would never be able to perform to his taste the *rôle* of Philemon, if he did not begin with that of Fierabras, by giving the count his deserts; asking God, meantime, never again to place him in a similar position.

This matter, then, being decided upon, he resolved to bring it to an end as soon as possible. And as it appeared to him that it would be dangerous, as well as in bad taste, to arrange the affair through seconds, and thus make the honor of Pepita the subject of common talk, he determined to provoke a quarrel with the count under some other pretext.

Thinking that the count, being a stranger in the village and a confirmed gambler, might possibly be still engaged at play in the clubhouse, notwithstanding the lateness of the hour, Don Luis went straight there.

The clubhouse was still open, but both in the courtyard and the parlor the lights were nearly all extinguished. In one apartment only was there still a light. Thither Don Luis directed his steps, and on reaching it, he saw through the open door the Count of Genazahar engaged in playing *monte,* in which he acted as banker. Only five other persons were playing; two were strangers like the count; the others were the captain of cavalry in charge of the remount, Currito, and the doctor. Things could not have been better arranged to suit the purpose of Don Luis. So engrossed were the players in their game that they did not observe him, who, as soon as he saw the count, left the clubhouse and went rapidly homeward.

On reaching his house the door was opened for him by a servant. Don Luis inquired for his father, and finding that he was asleep, procured a light and went up to his own room, taking care to make no noise lest he should disturb him. There he took some three thousand reals in gold that he had laid by, and put them in his pocket. He then called the servant to open the door for him again, and returned to the clubhouse.

79

Arrived there, Don Luis entered the parlor in which the players were, walking noisily, and giving himself the airs of a fop. The players were struck with amazement at seeing him.

"You here at this hour!" said Currito.

"Where do you come from, little priest?" said the doctor.

"Have you come to preach me another sermon?" cried the count.

"I have done with sermons," returned Don Luis, calmly. "The bad success of the last one I preached has clearly convinced me that God does not call me to that path in life, and I have chosen another. You, count, have wrought my conversion. I have thrown aside the cassock. I wish to amuse myself; I am in the flower of my youth, and I want to enjoy it."

"Come, I am glad of that," returned the count; "but take care, my lad, for if the flower be a delicate one, it may wither and drop its leaves before their time."

"I shall take care of that," returned Don Luis. "I see you are playing; I feel inspired. You are dealing. Do you know, count, that it would be amusing if I should break your bank?"

"You think it would be amusing, eh? You have been dining liberally!"

"I have dined as I choose to dine."

"The youngster is learning to give an answer."

"I learn what it is my pleasure to learn."

"Damnation!" cried the count; and the storm was about to break when the captain, interposing, succeeded in re-establishing the peace.

"Come," said the count when he had recovered his temper, "out with your cash, and try your luck."

Don Luis seated himself at the table, and took out all his gold. At sight of it the count regained his serenity completely, for it must have exceeded in amount the sum he had in the bank, and he thought he should at once win it of this novice.

"There is no need to cudgel one's brains much in this

game," said Don Luis to the count; "I think I understand
it already. I put money on a card, and if the card turns up
I win; if not, you win."

"Just so, my young friend; you have a strong understanding."

"And the best of it is that I have not only a strong
understanding, but a strong will as well. But though I
may have the stubbornness of the donkey, I am not such a
donkey as many a one in these parts."

"What a witty mood you are in tonight, and how
anxious you are to display your wit!"

Don Luis was silent. He played a few deals, and was
so lucky as to win almost every time.

The count began to be annoyed.

"What if the youngster should pluck me?" he said to
himself. "Fortune favors the innocent."

While the count was troubling himself with this reflection, Don Luis, feeling fatigued, and weary now of the part
he was playing, determined to end the matter at once.

"The object of all this," he said, "is to see if I can win
all your gold, or if you can win mine. Is it not so, count?"

"Just so."

"Well, then, why should we remain here all night? It
is getting late, and according to your advice I ought to
retire early, so that the flower of my youth may not wither
before its time."

"How is this? Do you want to go away already? Do
you want to back out?"

"I have no desire to back out. Quite the contrary.
Currito, tell me, in this heap of gold is there not already
more than there is in the bank?"

Currito looked at the gold and answered:

"Without a doubt."

"How shall I explain," asked Don Luis, "that I wish to
stake on one card all that I have here, against what there
is in the bank?"

"You do that," responded Currito, "by saying, 'I play
banco!"

" Well, then, I play *banco*," said Don Luis, addressing himself to the count; " I play *banco* on this king of spades, whose companion will to a certainty turn up before his opponent the three does."

The count, whose whole cash capital was in the bank, began to be alarmed at the risk he ran; but there was nothing for it but to accept.

It is a common saying that those who are fortunate in love are unfortunate at play, but the reverse of this is often more nearly the truth. He who is fortunate in one thing is apt to be fortunate in everything; it is the same when one is unfortunate.

The count continued to draw cards, but no *three* turned up. His emotion, notwithstanding his efforts to conceal it, was great. Finally, he came to a card which he knew by certain lines at the top to be the king of hearts, and paused.

" Draw," said the captain.

" It is of no use! The king of hearts! Curses on it! The little priest has plucked me. Take up your money."

The count threw the cards angrily on the table.

Don Luis took up the money calmly, and with apparent indifference.

After a short silence the count said:

" My little priest, you must give me my revenge."

" I see no such necessity."

" It seems to me that between gentlemen——"

" According to that rule the game would have no end," said Don Luis, " and it would be better to save one's self the trouble of playing altogether."

" Give me my revenge," replied the count, without paying any attention to this argument.

" Be it so," returned Don Luis; " I wish to be generous."

The count took up the cards again, and proceeded to deal.

" Stop a moment," said Don Luis; " let us understand each other. Where is the money for your new bank? "

The count showed signs of confusion and disturbance.

PEPITA JIMÉNEZ

"I have no money here," he returned, "but it seems to me that my word is more than enough."

Don Luis answered, with grave and measured accent:

"Count, I should be willing to trust the word of a gentleman, and allow him to remain in my debt, if it were not that in doing so I should fear to lose your friendship, which I am now in a fair way to gain; but as I was a witness this morning to the cruelty with which you treated certain friends of mine to whom you are indebted, I do not wish to run the risk of becoming culpable in your eyes by means of the same fault. How ridiculous to suppose that I should voluntarily incur your enmity by lending you money which you would not repay me, as you have not repaid, except with insults, that which you owe Pepita Jiménez!"

From the fact that this accusation was true, the offense was all the greater. The count became livid with anger, and, by this time on his feet, ready to come to blows with the collegian.

"You lie, slanderer!" he exclaimed. "I shall tear you limb from limb, you——"

This last insult, which reflected on his birth and on the honor of her whose memory was most sacred to him, was never finished; its end never reached his ears. For, with marvelous quickness, dexterity, and force, he reached across the table which was between himself and the count, and with the light, flexible bamboo cane with which he had armed himself, struck his antagonist on the face, raising on it instantly a livid mark.

There was neither retort, outcry, nor uproar. When the hands come into play, the tongue is apt to be silent. The count was about to throw himself on Don Luis for the purpose of tearing him to pieces, if it were in his power. But opinion had changed greatly since yesterday morning, and was now on the side of Don Luis. The captain, the doctor, and even Currito, who now showed more courage than he had done on that occasion, all held back the count, who struggled and fought ferociously to release himself.

"Let me go!" he cried; "let me get at him and kill him!"

83

"I do not seek to prevent a duel," said the captain; "a duel is inevitable. I only seek to prevent your fighting here like two porters. I should be wanting in self-respect if I consented to be present at such a combat."

"Let weapons be brought!" said the count; "I do not wish to defer the affair for a single moment. At once—and here!"

"Will you fight with swords?" said the captain.

"Yes," responded Don Luis.

"Swords be it," said the count.

All this was said in a low voice, so that nothing might be heard in the street. Even the servants of the clubhouse, who slept on chairs in the kitchen and in the yard, were not awakened by the noise.

Don Luis chose as his seconds the captain and Currito; the count chose the two strangers. The doctor made ready to practice his art, and showed the flag of the Red Cross.

It was not yet daylight. It was agreed that the apartment in which they were should be the field of combat, the door being first closed. The captain went to his house for the swords, and returned soon afterward carrying them under the cloak which he had put on for the purpose of concealing them.

We already know that Don Luis had never wielded a weapon in his life. Fortunately, the count, although he had never studied theology, or entertained the purpose of becoming a priest, was not much more skilled than he in the art of fence.

The only rules laid down for the duel were that, their swords once in hand, each of the combatants should use his weapon as Heaven might best direct him.

The door of the apartment was closed. The tables and chairs were placed in a corner, to leave a free field for the combatants, and the lights were suitably disposed.

Don Luis and the count divested themselves of their coats and waistcoats, remaining in their shirt-sleeves, and selected, each one, his weapon. The seconds stood on one side. At a signal from the captain the combat began.

84

Between two persons who know neither how to parry a stroke nor how to put themselves on guard, a combat must of necessity be brief; and it was.

The fury of the count, restrained for some time past, now burst forth and blinded his reason. He was strong, and he had wrists of steel; and he showered down on Don Luis with his sword, a storm of strokes without order or sequence. Four times he succeeded in touching Don Luis— each time, fortunately, with the flat of his weapon. He bruised his shoulders, but did not wound him. The young theologian had need of all his strength to keep from falling to the floor, overcome by the force of the blows and the pain of his bruises. A fifth time the count hit Don Luis, on the left arm, and this time with the edge of the weapon, although aslant. The blood began to flow abundantly. Far from stopping, the count resumed the attack with renewed fury, in the hope of again wounding his antagonist. He almost placed himself under the weapon of Don Luis. The latter, instead of putting himself in position to parry, brought his sword down vigorously on his adversary, and succeeded in wounding the count in the head. The blood gushed forth, and ran down his forehead and into his eyes. Stunned by the blow, the count fell heavily to the floor.

The whole combat was a matter of a few seconds. Don Luis had remained tranquil throughout, like a Stoic philosopher who is obliged by the hard law of necessity to take part in a conflict opposed alike to his habits and his ways of thought. But no sooner did he see his antagonist extended on the floor, bathed in blood and looking as though he were dead, than he experienced the most poignant anguish, and feared for a moment that he should faint. He who, until within the last five or six hours, had held unwaveringly to his resolution of being a priest, a missionary, a minister, and a messenger of the Gospel, had committed, or accused himself of having committed, during those few hours, every crime, and of breaking all the commandments of God. There was now no mortal sin by which he was not contaminated. First, his purpose of leading a life of perfect and heroic holiness had been put to flight; then followed his purpose of leading a life of holiness of a more easy, comfortable, and *bourgeois* sort. The devil seemed to please himself in overthrowing his plans. He reflected that he could now no longer be even a Christian Philemon, for to lay his neighbor's head open with a stroke of a saber was not a very good beginning of his idyl.

Don Luis, after the agitations of the day, was now in a condition resembling that of a man who has brain-fever. Currito and the captain, one at each side, took hold of him and led him home.

Don Pedro de Vargas got out of bed in terror when he was told that his son had come home wounded. He ran to see him, examined his bruises and the wound in his arm, and saw that they were none of them attended with danger; but he broke out into threats of vengeance, and would not be pacified until he was made acquainted with the particulars of the affair, and learned that Don Luis had known how to avenge himself in spite of his theology.

The doctor came soon after to examine the wound, and was of opinion that in three or four days' time Don Luis would be able to go out again as if nothing had happened. With the count, on the other hand, it would be a matter of months. His life, however, was in no danger. He had returned to consciousness, and had asked to be taken to his own home, which was distant only a league from the village in which these events took place. A hired coach had been procured, and he had been conveyed thither, accompanied by his servant and the two strangers who had acted as his seconds.

Four days after the affair the doctor's opinion was justified by the result, and Don Luis, although sore from his bruises, and with his wound still unhealed, was in a condition to go out, and promised a complete recovery within a short time.

The first duty which Don Luis thought himself obliged to fulfil, as soon as he was off the sick list, was to confess to his father his love for Pepita, and his intention of marrying her.

Don Pedro had not gone out to the country, nor had he occupied himself in any other way than in taking care of his son during his sickness. He was constantly at his side, waiting on him and petting him with tender affection.

On the morning of the 27th of June, after the doctor had gone, Don Pedro being alone with his son, the confession, so difficult for Don Luis to make, took place in the following manner:

"Father," said Don Luis, "I ought not to deceive you any longer. Today I am going to confess my faults to you, and cast away hypocrisy."

"If it is a confession you are about to make, my boy, it would be better for you to send for the reverend vicar. My standard of morality is an indulgent one, and I shall give you absolution for everything, without my absolution being of much value to you, however. But if you wish to confide to me some weighty secret, as to your best friend, begin by all means; I am ready to listen to you."

"What I am about to confess to you is a very serious fault of which I have been guilty; and I am ashamed to——"

"You have no need to be ashamed before your father; speak frankly."

Here Don Luis, growing very red, and with visible confusion, said:

"My secret is, that I am in love with—Pepita Jiménez—and that she——"

Don Pedro interrupted his son with a burst of laughter, and finished the sentence for him:

"And that she is in love with you, and that on the night of St. John's Eve you were with her in tender conference until two o'clock in the morning, and that, for her sake, you sought a quarrel with the Count of Genazahar, whose head you have broken. A pretty secret to confide to me, truly! There isn't a cat or a dog in the village that is not fully acquainted with every detail of the business. The

87

only thing there seemed a possibility of being able to conceal was, that your interview lasted until just two o'clock in the morning; but some gypsy-cake women chanced to see you leave Pepita's house, and did not stop until they had told every living creature in the place of it. Pepita, besides, makes no great effort to conceal the truth, and in this she does well, for that would be only the concealment of Antequera. Since you have been wounded, Pepita comes here twice a day, and sends Antoñona two or three times more to inquire after you; and if they have not come in to see you, it is because I would not consent to their doing so, lest it should excite you."

The confusion and the distress of Don Luis reached their climax when he heard his father thus compendiously tell the whole story.

"How surprised," he said, "how astounded you must have been!"

"No, my boy, I was neither surprised nor astounded. The matter has been known in the village only for four days, and indeed, to tell the truth, your transformation did create some surprise. 'Oh, the sly-boots! the wolf in sheep's clothing! the hypocrite!' everyone exclaimed; 'how we have been deceived in him!' The reverend vicar, above all, is quite bewildered. He is still crossing himself at the thought of how you toiled in the vineyard of the Lord on the night of the 23d and on the morning of the 24th, and of the strange character of your labors. But there was nothing in these occurrences to surprise me, except your wound. We old people can hear the grass grow. It is not easy for the chickens to deceive the huckster."

"It is true, I sought to deceive you! I have been a hypocrite!"

"Do not be a fool; I do not say this to blame you. I say it in order to give myself an air of perspicacity. But let us speak with frankness. My boasting is, after all, without foundation. I knew, step by step, for more than two months past, the progress of your love affair with Pepita. . . ."

"DON PEDRO DANCED WITH PEPITA AS ALSO WITH THE MOST ATTRACTIVE AMONG HER MAIDS"

(From a sketch by John Lewis)

PEPITA JIMÉNEZ

Just a month from the date of this interview the wedding of Don Luis de Vargas and Pepita Jiménez took place.

The reverend dean—fearing the ridicule of his brother at the spiritual-mindedness of Don Luis having thus come to naught, and recognizing also that he would not play a very dignified *rôle* in the village, where everyone would say he was a poor hand at turning out saints—declined to be present, giving his occupation as an excuse; although he sent his blessing, and a magnificent pair of earrings as a present for Pepita.

The reverend vicar, therefore, had the pleasure of marrying her to Don Luis.

The bride, elegantly attired, was thought lovely by everyone, and was looked upon as a good exchange for the hair shirt and the scourge.

That night Don Pedro gave a magnificent ball in the courtyard of his house and the contiguous apartments. Servants and gentlemen, nobles and laborers, ladies and country-girls were present, and mingled together as if it were the ideal golden age—though why called golden I know not. Four skilful, or, if not skilful at least indefatigable, guitar-players played a fandango; two gypsies, a man and a woman, both famous singers, sang verses of a tender character and appropriate to the occasion; and the schoolmaster read an epithalamium in heroic verse.

There were tarts, fritters, jumbles, gingerbread, spongecake, and wine in abundance for the common people. The gentry regaled themselves with refreshments—chocolate, orange-cordial, honey, and various kinds of aromatic and delicate liqueurs.

Don Pedro was like a boy—sprightly, gallant, and full of jests. He danced the fandango with Pepita, as also with the most attractive among her maids, and with six or seven of the village girls. He gave each of them, on reconducting her tired out, to her seat, the prescribed embrace, and to the least demure a couple of pinches, though this latter forms no part of the ceremonial. He carried his gallantry to the extreme of dancing with Doña

Casilda, who could not refuse him; who, with her two hundred and fifty pounds of humanity, and the heat of July, perspired at every pore. Finally, Don Pedro stuffed Currito so full, and made him drink so often to the health of the newly married pair, that the muleteer Dientes was obliged to carry him home to sleep off the effect of his excesses, slung like a wine-skin across the back of an ass!

The ball lasted until three in the morning; but the young couple discreetly disappeared before eleven, and retired to the house of Pepita. There Don Luis reëntered, with light, pomp, and majesty, and as adored lord and master, the room which, little more than a month before, he had entered in darkness and filled with terror and confusion.

Although it is the unfailing use and custom of the village to treat every widow or widower who marries again to a terrible *charivari*, leaving them not a moment's rest from the cow-bells during the first night of marriage, Pepita was such a favorite, Don Pedro was so much respected, and Don Luis was so beloved, that there were no bells on this occasion, nor was there the least attempt made at ringing them—a singular circumstance, which is recorded as such in the annals of the village.

TALES FROM THE SPANISH

———

MARTA AND MARIA

BY

ARMANDO PALACIO VALDÉS

INTRODUCTION

THE foremost living Spanish novelist is best represented by *Marta y María*, one of his earlier works published so long ago as 1883. Says William Dean Howells, whom most people regard as the greatest of American novelists: " Armando Palacio Valdés delights me beyond words by his friendly and abundant humor, his feeling for character, and his subtle insight. . . . I think *Marta y María* one of the most truthful and profound fictions I have read."

One of the chief reasons for this is the beauty of the love story. No more lovely, sympathetic, and gratifying romance can be found in modern Spanish literature than the unconscious budding, unfolding, and blooming of love in the heart of Marta. To many not the least pleasing aspect will be the fact that it is not a fanciful picture, the dream of a poet concerning some land east of the sun and west of the moon, but an episode taken out of the actual life of a provincial Spanish town. Spanish youths and maidens do sometimes fall in love in this way, and when they have beautiful souls the story of their loves must be something like that of Marta and Ricardo.

To tell what a nation is like you must visit more than its large cities. It is the people and customs of the small towns that are really typical of a nation. Valdés allows you not only to observe the happenings of a provincial village, but he lets you live with the people. You attend their entertainments, you overhear their trivial chatter and their heated conversations, you learn their prejudices and preoccupations, you meet all the typical characters, you see the workings of political intrigue. Above all, you come to understand the hearts of these Spanish people, the things they love and hate, the qualities they admire and detest, the in-

93

tensity of their passions and the unswerving loyalty of their devotion.

Maria could never have lived out of Spain. A merely superficial acquaintance with Spanish history, the mention of a few names like the Inquisition and the Invincible Armada show how essential an element religion is in Spanish character. But to understand its power, to comprehend in their intimate workings those vague forces, Spanish mysticism and fanaticism, it is only necessary to follow the gradual transformation of Maria. For, with rare and masterful insight, Valdés has traced the subtle changes in a woman's soul that lead her to a lifelong spiritual communion with the Divine Master. Howells is quite correct in saying that the romance is one of the most truthful and profound fictions he has read.

Marta and Maria

CHAPTER I

IN THE STREET

WITHIN the arcade the people were crowding relentlessly; each and every one was performing prodigies
of skill to flout the physical law of the impenetrability
of bodies, by reducing his own to an imaginary quantity.
The night was unusually thick and dark. The feet of the
loungers found each other out in the darkness, and when
they met they indulged in somewhat expressive forms of
endearment; the elbows of some, by a secret and fatal impulse, went straight into the eyes of others; the passive
subject of such caresses instantly raised his hand to the
place of contact, and usually exclaimed with some asperity,
" You barbarian, you might at least——" but an energetic
" Sh—sh—sh " from the throng obliged him to nip his
discourse in the bud, and silence again began to reign.
Silence was at this time the most pressing necessity which
was felt by the inhabitants of Nieva who had gathered there.
The least noise was regarded as an act of sedition, and was
instantly punished by a threatening hiss. Coughs and
sneezes were prohibited, and still more condign punishment
was meted out to laughter and conversation. There was
profuse perspiration, although the night was not among the
mildest of autumn.

In the arcades of the houses opposite, more or less the
same state of things existed; but in the street itself there
were few people, because a very fine rain was slowly falling. Only a few people with umbrellas, and some others

who, not having them, sheltered themselves with their philosophy, maintained a firm footing in the midst of the gutter.

The balconied windows of the house of Elorza were thrown wide open, and through the embrasures streamed a bright and cheerful light which made the dark and misty night outside still more melancholy by contrast. Likewise there streamed forth from time to time torrents of musical notes let loose from a piano.

The house of Elorza was the principal one in a long, narrow street, adorned with an arcade on both sides, like almost all the rest in the town of Nieva. Its most important façade looked into this street, but it had another with balconies facing the town square, which was wide and handsome like that of a city. Though the darkness does not allow us to make out exactly the appearance of the house, yet we can prove that it is a building of faced stone and of one story, with spacious arcade, the elegant and stately arches of which instantly declare the rank of its owners. This arcade, which might be called a portico, makes a notable contrast with that of the succeeding houses, which is low and narrow and supported by round, rough pillars without any ornamentation. Likewise, the same difference is to be seen in the pavement. In the arcade of which we are speaking, it is of well-set flagging, while the others offer merely an inconvenient footway paved with cobblestones.

Without venturing, indeed, to call it a palace, it is not presumptuous to assert that this mansion had been built for the exclusive use and gratification of some person of importance; the fact that it had only one story very clearly decided this point. The truth demands that we set forth likewise the fact that the architect had given undeniable proofs of good taste in laying out the plan of the building, since its proportions could not be more elegant and correct. But what most struck the eye was a certain attractive and aristocratic thriftiness about it perfectly free from presumption, which, though calculated to inspire envy, certainly did not arouse in the minds of the people those hatreds and heartburnings always excited by overweening wealth. . . .

The darkness was dense in both arcades, for the town lanterns shed their pallid rays at respectable distances. Each served only to light up a sufficiently circumscribed area at wide intervals in the plaza, making melancholy reflections on the wet stones of the pavement. Amid the shadows now and then the light of a cigar flashed out for an instant, causing a ruddy glow on the smoker's *mustachios*. A little further away, on the corner, a variety shop still remained open; but the shopkeeper's shadow could be seen often crossing in front of the door as he was putting his wares in order before shutting up. On the principal floor of the same house the balconied windows were all thrown wide open; through them rang voices, coarse outbursts of laughter, and the clicking of billiard balls, sounds which fortunately reached the arcades greatly softened. This was the Café de la Estrella, frequented until the small hours of the night by a dozen indefatigable patrons.

At the moment when the present history begins, the vibrating tones of the piano were heard preluding the passionate *allegro* of the aria from *La Traviata: gran Dio, morir si giovine*. When the prelude was ended, a soft and appropriate accompaniment began. The expectation was intense. At last, above the accompaniment arose a clear and most dulcet voice, echoing through the whole plaza like a sound from heaven. The two groups of listeners were stirred as though they had touched their fingers to the knob of an electric machine, and a subdued murmur of satisfaction ran up and down among them.

" 'Tis Maria," said three or four, hoping that the ears of the walls would not overhear them.

"It was high time," remarked one, in a little louder voice.

"It is she that is singing now; hark! and not that beast of the canning factory!" exclaimed a third, still more impulsive.

"Have the goodness to keep quiet, gentlemen, so that we can hear!" cried a very angry voice.

"Let that man hold his tongue!"

"Out with him!"

"Silence!"

"Sh—sh—sh—shhh!"

"I have always insisted that there are no people more ill-bred than those of this place!" again cried the angry voice.

"Hold your tongue!"

"Don't be a fool, man!"

"Sh—sh—sh—shhh!"

Finally all became silent, and Verdi's passionate melody could be heard, interpreted with remarkable delicacy. The lovely, limpid voice, issuing from the open balconies, rent the saturated atmosphere out of doors, and vibrating with force, went the rounds of the plaza, and died away in the mazes of the town. The loneliness and gloom of the night increased the power and range of that lovely voice, lovely beyond all praise. The singer possessed a bewitching voice, of a passionate *timbre*, which penetrated to the very depths of the soul.

The loungers of both arcades, and likewise the philosophers of the gutter, gave unmistakable proofs of being moved. No one whispered, or moved a step from his place; with open mouths and far-away eyes, they followed ecstatically the course of that despairing melody, in which Violetta mourns that she must die after such sufferings undergone.

At some little distance from both groups, and near a column, were seen, not very distinctly, three small bodies, with whom we must bring the reader into contact for a few moments. One of them struck a match to light a cigar, and there appeared three fresh, laughing, mischievous faces of fourteen or fifteen years, which resolved into darkness again as the match went out.

"Say, Manolo," asked one, lowering his voice as much as possible, "who gave you that mouthpiece?"

"Suppose I ragged it of my brother!"

"Is it amber?"

"Amber and meerschaum; it cost three *duros* in Madrid."

"I pity you, if you should get caught by your——"

"Hush up, you fool you! What have we got a servant in the house for, if not to blame for such faults?"

A man who was standing nearer than the rest harshly bade them hold their tongues. The urchins obeyed. But after a moment Manolo said, in a barely perceptible voice, "See here, lads! would you like to have me break this all up in a jiffy?"

"Yes, yes, Manolo!" hastily replied the others, who evidently had great faith in the destructive powers of their companion.

"Then you just wait; stay quiet where you are."

And moving a little aside from them, he hid himself beside a door, and set up three extraordinary yelps, precisely like those emitted by dogs when they are beaten. A tremendous, furious, universal barking immediately resounded through the streets. All the dogs of the community, united and compact, like one single mastiff, protested energetically against the punishment inflicted upon one of their kind. Maria's singing was completely lost beneath that formidable yelping. The listening multitude experienced a painful shock, stirred tumultuously for some moments, uttered incoherent exclamations against the cursed animals, endeavored to bring them to silence by shouting at them, and at last, seeing the uselessness of their efforts, resigned themselves to the hope that they would cease of themselves. The howls, in fact, were gradually dying away, all the time becoming more and more infrequent and remote; only the dog belonging to the variety shop, which had just been closed, continued for some time barking furiously. At length even he ceased, though most unwillingly. The song of the dying Violetta was once again heard, pure and limpid as before, and once again the auditors began to experience the softening impressions which it had made upon them, although they were somewhat restless and nervous, as if fearing at any moment to be deprived of that pleasure.

Manolo, choking with amusement, rejoined his companions and was received with stifled laughter and applause.

" Come, Manolito, yelp once again."

" Wait, wait awhile; we want to take 'em by surprise."

After some little time had passed, Manolo once more cautiously crept away, and, skirting the group, stationed himself at the opposite extreme. From there he set up three more howls like the first, and the same thunderous barking filled the spaces, giving back kind for kind. The multitude underwent a new excess of vexation, but accompanied by far greater tumult; everybody was speaking at once, and uttering furious ejaculations.

" This is horrible! "

" Here's a concert for us given by those confounded dogs! "

" The dog that howled is the one to blame."

" Curse him! "

" Confound it! "

" Silence! silence! give us a chance to hear something! "

" What can you hear? "

" Deuced bad luck! "

" Silence! silence! "

" Sh—sh—sh—shh! "

The dogs one after another were beginning to quiet down, according to their own good pleasure, and little by little calm was reasserting its sway. Violetta's song reappeared, full of melancholy, sweetness, and passion. Maria's voice, in her interpretation of it, expressed such pathos that the heart was melted, and tears sprang into the eyes. One single dog, the one at the variety shop, kept on barking with a persistency that was in the highest degree exasperating, since it prevented the singer's voice from reaching the ears of the public with any clearness. A man with a cudgel in his hand detached himself from the throng, and braving the elements, crossed the plaza to stop his barking, but the dog immediately smelled the stick and took to flight.

The man came back into the arcade. At length perfect silence reigned in the plaza, and the music lovers could enjoy to their hearts' content the concert in the house of Elorza.

What had become of Manolo? His companions waited for him for some time so as to congratulate him on his praiseworthy conduct, but he did not put in an appearance. The smaller urchin at length timidly asked the other,

"Say! what would they do to him if they caught him yelping?"

"Why, nothing; they'd treat him to a little oil of birch."

He who had propounded the question trembled a little, and held his peace.

"But then," continued the other, "they haven't caught him, not a bit of it, he's too cute to let himself get caught."

At this instant Manolo raised two shrieks still more maddening in the opposite arcade, and with the same madness the dogs of the neighborhood, barking, took up the refrain. It is impossible to describe what happened thereupon in the multitude of listeners in both arcades. The tumult which ensued was in reality overpowering. A goodly number of hands flew about in the darkness, flourishing terrible canes and umbrellas, and from both the throngs arose a chorus of imprecations. The confusion and disorder took possession of all minds. Breasts breathed nothing but vengeance and extermination.

"Kill that beastly cur!" cried a voice above the tumult.

"Yes, yes, break his back for him!" replied another, instigating the fittest method of slaughter.

"That dog, that dog!"

"But where is that cursed beast?"

"Find him and break his back!"

"And if you can't find the dog, break his master's back!"

"That's the idea! his master's!"

"Thunder and lightning! kill 'em both!"

The disorder had increased to such a degree, and the shouting had become so loud, that some of the balconied windows in the vicinity emitted a sharp sound, and were cautiously opened; the inquisitive heads which were thrust forth, not being able to discover what had caused the disturbance, and fearing to catch cold, were incontinently withdrawn. In the house of Elorza three or four people likewise peered out and likewise hurriedly drew back, and oh! the grief of it! closed the windows as they went.

"Well now! we shall hear what we must hear."

"Have they shut the windows?"

"Yes, señor, they have, and shut 'em up tight."

From that multitude escaped a submissive sigh of weariness and rage. There was silence for a moment as a tribute rendered to their vanished hopes. No one moved from his place. At last some one said in a loud voice: "Señores, good-night, and good luck to you. I'm going home!"

This salutation shook them from their stupor. The groups began to dissolve slowly, not without uttering choleric exclamations. A few individuals walked off under the arcades. Others crossed the plaza with umbrellas spread. A few remained in the same place, making endless commentaries on what had just occurred. At last a half-dozen loafers remained, and these, tired of complaining in that locality, adjourned to the Café de la Estrella, to do the same.

CHAPTER II

THE SOIREE AT THE ELORZA MANSION

"WHAT a shame, Isidorito, that you did not study for a doctor! I don't know why it is I imagine you must have a keen eye for diseases."

The young man turned red with pleasure.

"Doña Gertrudis, you flatter me; I have no other desert than that of sticking fast to whatever I undertake, and this seems to me absolutely necessary in whatever career one devotes himself to."

"You are quite right. The main thing is to apply one's self to what lies before him, and not go wool-gathering.

Now, for example, take Don Maximo. It cannot be denied
that he has great knowledge, and I wish him well, but he
has the misfortune of not applying himself to anything that
is said to him, and therefore he scarcely ever hits the mark.
Please tell me, Isidorito, how is it possible for man to succeed in curing one, if when the invalid is telling him her
sufferings, he sets himself to work sharpening lead-pencils
or drumming with his fingers. You don't know how I have
suffered on account of him. I pray God may not set down
against him the harm he has done me. My husband is very
fond of him—and so am I too, you must believe me. In
spite of all, he is a good man, and it's twenty-four years since
he first entered this house; but I must tell the truth though
it is hard: the poor man has the misfortune of not applying
himself—of not applying himself little or much.

"Just so, just so. Don Maximo, in my opinion, lacks
those gifts of observation indispensable to the profession to
which he belongs. Perhaps it may surprise you to know
what qualifications are needed for the practice of medicine
from a scientific point of view; it is my own private opinion,
which I am ready to sustain anywhere, either in public or in
private. Medicine, in my judgment, is nothing else whatever than an empirical profession, purely empirical. I repeat that it is my private opinion, and that I expound it as
such, but I harbor the belief that very soon it will be a truth
universally accepted."

"The truth is, Isidorito, that he has simply not understood
me. Day before yesterday I spent the whole day with a
roaring in my head as though a lot of drums were beating
behind it. At the same time this left knee was so swollen
that I could not even walk from my room to the dining-
room. I sent a message to Don Maximo, and he did not
appear till it was dark. I assure you I passed a wretched
day, and if it had not been for some tallow plasters which
my daughter Marta put on my temples at midnight, I should
certainly have died, for Don Maximo did not think it necessary even to have a lamp lighted to see me."

"What you point out still more confirms my assertion.

You see how domestic remedies, administered without other judgment than that suggested by experience, by the results obtained in a long series of cases, sometimes operate on the organism in a more successful way than scientific medicine. Such a thing could not happen in our profession, señora, where all the chances that may occur are foreseen in advance by the laws, or by jurisprudence raised into the category of the law. There is not a single litigation which does not find its adequate solution in the civil codes, nor can any crime or misdeed whatsoever be committed, without provision being made for it in some article of the penal code. And in order that nothing may be wanting the free will of the tribunals (I except the *usual* interpretation), we have as a supplement the canonical law, which is an abundant source of rules for conduct, though these all are based principally on equity."

"Certainly, certainly, Isidorito. Doctors absolutely do not understand a single thing. If I could measure out into bottles, once for all, the medicine that I have taken, I could very easily open an apothecary shop. And yet here you see me just as I was at the very beginning,—at the very beginning,—without having made a single step in advance. God grants me great resignation, otherwise—— Just consider! yesterday I was as usual, but today, my fête-day too, what I suffer I'm sure will be the death of me, the death of me;—an uneasiness throughout my body,—a crawling up and down my legs like ants,—a rumbling in my ears. You who have so much talent, don't you know what it is to have a rumbling in the ears?"

"Señora, I think—ahem—that a purely nervous state is answerable for this infirmity,—nervous alterations are so varied and extraordinary—ahem—that it is not possible to reduce them to fixed principles, and so it is much better not to lay down any rule, but to study them in detail, or let each one stand separately."

It was hard work, but he had extricated himself from the difficulty. Isidorito was a lean, bashful young man, with deep precocious wrinkles in his cheeks, with thin hair and goggle eyes. He was regarded as one of the most serious-minded youths, or perhaps the most serious-minded youth of the town, and always served as a mirror for the fathers of families, to hold up before their rattlebrain sons. "Don't you see how well Isidorito behaves in society, and with what aplomb he talks on all sorts of subjects?" "Ah, if you were like Isidorito, what a happy old age you would make me spend!" "Shame on you for letting Isidorito be made doctor of laws these four years, while you have not succeeded in graduating as a licentiate yet, you block-head!"

Doña Gertrudis, wife of Don Mariano Elorza, the master of the house in which we find ourselves, was seated, or to speak more correctly, reclined, in an easy-chair at Isidorito's side. Although she had not yet passed her forty-fifth year, she appeared to be as old as her husband, who was now approaching his sixtieth. Not entirely lacking in her cadaverous and faded face were the lines of an exceptional beauty, which had given much to talk about there from 1846 to 1848, and which had redounded to her in a multitude of ballads, sonnets, and acrostics, by the most distinguished poets of the town, inserted in a weekly journal entitled *El Judió Errante,* which was published at that time in Nieva. Doña Gertrudis preserved with great care a gorgeously bound collection of *Judios Errantes,* and was in the habit of assuring her friends that if the young man who signed his acrostics with a V and three stars had not faded away with quick consumption, he would have been by this time the fashionable poet; and that if another lad, named Ulpiano Menéndez, who disguised himself under the pseudonym of *The Moor of Venice,* had not gone off to America to make his fortune in business, he would have been, at least, as great as Ayola, Campoamor, or Nuño de Arce. Don Mariano, her husband, shared the same conviction, although at another epoch the lyric poet, as well as the merchant, had caused him great anxieties, and not a few times had disturbed the peaceful course of his love; but he was a just man and fond of giving everyone his due.

Doña Gertrudis was wrapt up in a magnificent plush com-forter, and her head was covered with a net, underneath which appeared her hair turning from auburn to white. Her features were delicate and regular, and of a singularly faded pallor. Her eyes were blue and extremely melan-choly. The marks of close confinement rather than of ill-ness were to be seen in that face.

" This roaring in my ears is killing me, killing me. I cannot eat, I cannot sleep, I cannot get any rest anywhere."

" I think that you ought to stay in your room."

" That is worse, Isidorito, that is worse. In my room I cannot distract my thoughts. My mind begins to grind like a mill, and it ends by giving me a fever. I am much sicker than people give me credit for. They'll see how this will end. Today I am so nervous, so nervous. Feel my pulse, Isidorito, and tell me if I am not feverish."

As she drew out her thin hand and gave it to the young man, Don Mariano and Don Maximo, who were engaged in lively discussion in the recess of a balconied window, turned their faces in her direction and smiled. Doña Gertrudis blushed a little and hastened to hide her hand under her comforter.

" Your wife already has a new physician!" added Don Maximo, in a tone of irony.

" Bah, bah, bah! What cat or dog is there in town that my wife won't have taken into consultation? These days she is furious with you, and says that she is going to die without your paying any attention to her. I find her better than ever. But we shall see, Don Maximo. Do you really believe that we can accept the line from Miramar?"

" And why not?"

" Don't you comprehend that it would swamp us for-ever?"

" Don Mariano, it seems to me that you are blinded. What is of importance to Nieva is to have a railroad right away, right away, I say!"

" What is of importance to Nieva is to have a decent road, a decent road, I say. The line from Miramar would be our ruin, for it ties us to Sarrió, which, as you know very well, has far greater importance as a commercial town and a seaport town than we have. In a few years it would swallow us like a cherry-stone. Moreover, you must take into account that as it is fifteen kilometers from the junction to Nieva, and only twelve to Sarrió, trade would not fail to select the latter point for exportation, on account of the saving in the rate, for those three kilometers of difference. On the other hand, the line from Sotolongo offers the great advantage of uniting us to Pinarrubio, which can never enter into rivalry with us; and at the same time it decidedly shortens the distance to the junction, bringing it down to thirteen kilometers. The difference in the rates, therefore, is a mere trifle, not sufficient to induce trade to go to Sarrió. If you add to this the fact that sooner or later——"

A violent coughing fit cut short Don Mariano's discourse. He was a large, tall man, with white beard and hair, the beard very abundant. His black eyes gleamed like those of a boy, and in his ruddy cheeks time had not succeeded in plowing deep furrows. Doubtless he had been one of the most gallant young men of his day, and even as we find him now, he still attracted attention by his genial and venerable countenance, and by his noble, athletic figure. The violence of his cough had a powerful effect on his sanguine complexion, and he grew exceedingly red in the face. After he had stopped coughing, he resumed the thread of his discourse.

" If you add to the fact that sooner or later we shall have a good port, either in El Moral or in Nieva itself,—for the war isn't going to last forever, nor is the government going to leave us always in the condition of pariahs,—you will see at once what an impulse will be instantly given to the trade of the town and how soon we shall put Sarrió into the shade."

" Well, well, I agree that the line from Sotolongo offers certain advantages; but you very well know that neither at the present time, nor for many days to come, can we do anything but dream about that one, while the road from Miramar is in our very hands. The government is deeply interested in it because there is no other means of protecting our gun-factory. You certainly realize that if the Carlists succeeded in breaking the line of Somosierra, they would overrun us and make themselves at home; they would take the arms on hand, dismantle the factory, and without the slightest risk they could set out for the valley of Cañedo. At present there is no danger of their breaking the line; I grant that, but who can guarantee what the future may bring forth? Moreover, may not the day come when the Carlist element which we have here will raise its head? Then if there were a railroad, no matter from what point, nothing would be more easy than to set down here in a couple of hours four or five thousand men——"

"In the first place, Don Maximo, a military railroad, as you yourself confess that the one from Miramar is to be, is not such as we have the right to ask of the nation. We need a genuine railroad, suitable for the promotion of our interests, and not to serve merely for the protection of a factory. Just consider that it is a work to last for all time, and that if from its very inception it suffers from a gross mistake, this mistake will hang forever over our town. In the second place, the Carlists will never get beyond Somosierra. As to their raising their heads here, you understand perfectly well that it is impossible because they have very few elements to rely on—and, as to their doing this——"

"I have reason to believe that they are! We must be on the watch, and not be found napping. And, as a final reason, a sparrow in the hand is worth more than a hundred flying. But tell me, Don Mariano, to change the subject, have the stables been put in order yet?"

Don Mariano, instead of replying, felt in all the pockets of his coat with a distracted air, and not finding what he was looking for, turned towards a corner of the room.

"Martita, come here!"

A young girl who was seated at one end of a sofa, not talking to anybody, came running to him. She might have been thirteen or fourteen years old, but the proportions of a woman grown were very distinctly observable in her. Nevertheless, she wore short dresses. She had a light complexion, with black hair and eyes, but her countenance did not offer the exasperating expression so commonly met with in faces of that kind. The features could not have been more regular and their *tout ensemble* could not have been more harmonious; nevertheless, her beauty lacked animation. It was what is commonly called a cold face.

"Listen, daughter: go to my room, open the second drawer on the left-hand side of my writing-table, and bring me the cigar-case which you will find there."

The girl went off on the run, and quickly returned with the article.

"Let us go and have a smoke in the dining-room," said Don Mariano, taking Don Maximo by the arm.

And the two left the parlor by one of the side doors.

Marta sat down again in the same place. The ladies on one side were engaged in lively conversation, but she took no share in it. She kept her seat, casting her eyes indifferently from one part of the parlor to the other, now resting them on one group of bystanders, now on another, and more particularly dwelling on the pianist, who at that moment was *executing* an arrangement of *Semiramide*.

Scarcely ever had the parlors of the Elorza mansion presented a more brilliant appearance; all the sofas of flowered damask were occupied by richly dressed ladies with bare arms and bosoms. The chandelier suspended from the middle, reflected the light in beautiful hues which fell upon smooth skins, making them look like milk and roses. Those fair bosoms were infinitely multiplied by the mirrors on both sides: the severe bottle-green paper of the parlor brought out all their whiteness. Marta turned to look at the Señoras de Delgado: three sisters: one, a widow, the other two, old maids. All were upwards of forty; the old maids did not trust to their youthfulness, but they had absolute confidence in the power of their shining shoulders and their fat and unctuous arms. Near them was the Señorita de Morí, round-faced, sprightly, with mischievous eyes, an orphan and rich. At a little distance was the Señora de Ciudad, napping peacefully until the hour should come for her to collect the six daughters whom she had scattered about in different parts of the parlor. Yonder in a corner Marta's sister Maria was holding a confidential talk with a young man. The girl's eyes wandered slowly from one point to another. The music interested her very slightly. She seemed to be sure of not being noticed by anyone, and her face kept the icy expression of indifference of one alone in a room.

Doña Gertrudis according to her daily habit had gone sound asleep in her easy-chair. She asserted an invalid's right, and no one took it amiss. Isidorito, getting up noiselessly, went and stood by the library door. From that impregnable coigne of vantage he began to shoot long, deep, and passionate glances upon the Senorita de Morí, who received the fires of the battery with heroic calmness. Isidorito had been in love with the Señorita de Morí ever since he knew what dowry and *paraphernalia** meant, arousing the admiration of the whole town by his loyalty. This passion had taken such possession of his soul that never had he been known to exchange a word with or speed an incendiary look towards any other woman than the señorita aforesaid. But Isidorito, contrary to what might have been believed, considering his vast legal attainments and his gravity no less vast, met with a slight opposition in his love-making. Señorita de Morí was in the habit of lavishing fascinating smiles on everybody, of squandering warm and languishing glances on all the young men of the community; all—except Isidorito. This incomprehensible conduct did not fail to cause him some disquietude, compelling him to meditate often on the shrewdness of the Roman legislators who were always unwilling to grant women legal capacity. He had lately been appointed municipal attorney of the district, and this, by the authority conferred upon him, gave him great

* *Paraphernalia bona*, in Spanish *bienes parafernales*, are the goods and chattels brought by a wife independent of her dower.

prestige among his fellow citizens. But, indeed, the Señorita de Morí, far from allowing herself to be fascinated by her suitor's new position, seemed to regard his appointment as ridiculous, judging by the pains she took from that time forth to avoid all visual communication with him. Still our young friend was not going to be cast down by these clouds, which are so common among lovers, and he continued to lay siege to the restless damsel's chubby face and three thousand *duros* income, sometimes by means of learned discourses, and sometimes by languishing and romantic actions.

At one side of Marta a certain young engineer who had just arrived from Madrid, turned the listening circle gathered around him into an Eden by his wheedling and graceful conversation. It was tertulia, or *petit comité,* as the engineer called it, consisting exclusively of ladies, the nucleus of which was made up by three of the Ciudad girls.

" That's only one of your gallant speeches, Suárez," said one lady.

" Of course it is," echoed several.

" It is absolute truth, and whoever has lived here any length of time will say so. In Madrid there's no halfway about it; the women are either perfectly beautiful or perfectly hideous. That union of charming and attractive faces which I see here is not to be found there; and so don't let it surprise you when I tell you that the hideous are much more numerous than the beautiful."

" Oh, pshaw! Madrid is where the prettiest woman are to be seen, and especially the most elegant."

" Oh! that is quite a different matter; elegant, certainly; but pretty, I don't agree with you!"

" It is so, though you don't agree with us!"

" Ladies, there is one reason why you are more beautiful than the Madrileñas; it is a reason which can be better appreciated by those who, like myself, have devoted themselves to the fine arts: here there are color and form, and there they do not exist. By good fortune, this very evening, I have the opportunity of noticing it and of making comparisons, which show most favorably for you. Now that we are allowed to contemplate what is ordinarily draped with great care, I can take my oath that you have those beautiful forms which we admire so much in Grecian statues and Flemish paintings, soft, white, transparent; while if you enter a Madrid drawing-room, you don't stumble upon anything else than skeletons in ball dresses——"

The ladies broke into laughter, hiding their faces behind their fans.

" What a tongue, what a tongue you have, Suárez! "

" It only serves me to tell the truth. The Madrid girls have the effect upon me of shadow-pantomimes. In you I find visible, palpable, and even delectable beings——"

Marta noticed that the wax of a candelabrum was burning out, and that the glass socket was in danger of cracking. She got up and went to puff it out.

The pianist ended his fantasy without stumbling. The conversations stopped abruptly; some clapped their hands, and others said, " Very good, very good." No one had been listening to him, but the pianist felt himself rewarded for his fatigue, and raising his blushing face above the piano, he acknowledged his thanks to the company with a triumphant smile. A young fellow who wore his hair banged like the dandies of Madrid, profited by this blissful moment to beg him to play a waltz-polka.

At the very first chords an extraordinary commotion was observable among the young men near the doors, who were evidently suffering from lack of exercise. A few began to draw on their gloves hastily; others smoothed back their hair with their hands, and straightened their cravats. One asked with constrained voice,

" It's a mazurka, isn't it? "

" No, a waltz-polka."

" What! a waltz-polka? "

" Can't you tell by your ears? "

" Ah yes. You're right. But then, señor, this wretched fellow at the piano will prevent me from dancing with Rosario this evening."

All seemed restless and nervous, as though they were about to pass through the fire. The boldest crossed the drawing-room with rapid steps, and joined the young ladies, hiding their trepidation behind a supercilious smile. As soon as the señorita who had been invited stood up and took the proffered arm, they began to feel that they were masters of themselves. Others, less courageous, gave three or four long pulls to their cigars, puffing the smoke out toward the entry, and having keyed themselves up to the right pitch, slowly directed their steps to some young lady less fascinating than the others, receiving for their attention a smile full of tender promises. The more cowardly struggled a long while with their gloves, and finally had to ask some grave señor to fasten the buttons for them. When this operation was finished, and they were ready to dance, they discovered that there were no girls sitting down. Thereupon they resigned themselves to dance with some mamma.

One after another all the couples took the floor. Marta remained seated. Two or three very complaisant and patronizing young fellows came to invite her, but she replied that she did not know how to dance. The real motive of her refusal was that her father did not like to have her take part in society while she was so young. She sat, therefore, attentively watching how the others went round. Her great black eyes rested with placid expression on each one of the couples who went up and down before her. Some interested her more than others, and she followed them with her glance. Their ways, their movements, and their looks were so different, that they made a curious study. A tall, lean youth was bending his back as near double as possible, so as to put his arm around the waist of a diminutive señorita who was endeavoring to keep on her very tiptoes. An elderly and portly lady was leaning languidly over a boy's shoulder, besmearing his coat with Matilde Diez's wax-white.

Some, like Isidorito, did not succeed in steering, and frequently stepped on their partners, who soon declared that they were weary and asked to be excused. Others put down their heels with such force that they scratched the floor. Marta looked at these with considerable severity, like a true housewife. After a while the faces began to show signs of weariness, some becoming flushed, others pallid, according to the temperament of each. With mouths open, cheeks aglow, and brows bathed in perspiration, they gave evidence of no other expression than that of absolute stupidity. At first they smiled and even dropped from their lips a compliment or two; but very soon gallantries ceased, and the smile faded away; all ended by skipping about silent and solemn, as if some unseen hand were laying on the lash in order to make them to do so. Marta from time to time shut her eyes, and thus she avoided the dizziness which began to attack her.

At last the piano suddenly ceased to sound. The couples, in virtue of the momentum which they had acquired, gave three or four hops unaccompanied by the music, and this made Marta smile. Before they took their seats the girls walked around the drawing-room for a few moments arm in arm with their partners, engaged in lively and interesting discourse. The pianist accepted the effusive thanks of the smart young man with the bangs. At length the ladies were all seated in their respective places, and the gentlemen fell back once again to the doors, mopping their brows with their handkerchiefs. Those who had danced with the beauties of the drawing-room showed faces shining with beatitude, and smilingly received the jests of their friends, while those who had pressed the less favored to their bosoms, praised to the skies their partners' Terpsichorean skill.

The youth with the hair over his forehead conceived the idea of Don Serapio singing a song, and he went from group to group around the room, making an instantaneous and satisfactory propaganda with his happy thought.

"Yes, yes, Don Serapio must sing!"

"Don Serapio must sing! Don Serapio must sing!"

"Gentlemen, for Heaven's sake—I have a very bad cold!"

Copyright by the Hispanic Society of America.

DON SERAPIO NEVER TIRED OF OGLING THE LADIES

(From the painting, "The Old Boulevardier in Madrid," by Ignacio Zuloaga)

"No matter; you will sing well enough, Don Serapio!"

"A thousand thanks, ladies, a thousand thanks. I should wish at this moment that I had the voice of an angel, for angels only ought to sing to angels!"

This compliment produced an excellent impression upon the feminine element of the company. The masculine element received it with derisive smiles.

"We always enjoy great pleasure in listening to you; you know it very well."

"Because generosity ever goes in company with beauty. The face is the mirror of the soul, they say, and if that is true, how could you help being benevolent toward me?"

The second compliment was likewise received with a laugh of complacency by the ladies. The men continued to smile scornfully.

"Sing, sing, Don Serapio!"

"But supposing I am not in practice—I don't know how I can repay such kindness. Besides, I have lost my voice entirely."

Don Serapio let himself be urged for some time. At last he went toward the piano, escorted by a circle of ladies, to whom he addressed smiles and words full of honeyed sweetness, and managed to extract clandestinely a roll of music which he carried in the inner pocket of his coat. The pianist instantly saw through this maneuver, and came to his assistance by quietly taking the music from his hand.

"Don Serapio is going to sing—you are going to sing the romance *Lontano a te*," he said as he spread it out on the rack.

"Oh, for heaven's sake! It is too sentimental, and these ladies are not now in favor of romanticism——"

"On the contrary, Don Serapio!" exclaimed one of the Delgado girls; "we women in this age of selfishness and calculation are the very ones who ought to worship sentiment and heart."

"Always as graceful as you are felicitous!" declared the vocalist, bowing to the floor.

The pianoforte introduction began. Don Serapio, before he uttered a note, kept arching his eyebrows, and he stretched his neck as much as possible, as a token of his feeling. He was upwards of fifty, although pomades, dyes, and cosmetics gave him from a distance the appearance of a young man. Near at hand, his mustachios, though waxed to perfection, were not sufficient to make up for the crows' feet and wrinkles of every sort which lined his face. He was a manufacturer of canned goods, and a confirmed old bachelor; not because he failed to honor the fair sex and hold it in esteem, but because he thought that marriage was death to love and its illusions. Never was there a man more soft and honeyed in his conversation with ladies, and never was there a gallant who had a more abundant assortment of flatteries to lavish upon them. He made great use of such expressions as *the fire of passion, the loss of will power, perfumed breath, palpitations of the heart,* and other like elegancies, all sure of hitting the mark.

This was as regards society women. As for work-girls and serving-maids, Don Serapio's gallantries did not stop with compliments. He was regarded as one of the most formidable and successful of seducers among such, and it was a matter of common knowledge in Nieva that more than one, and more than two, had had seriously to complain of his behavior, so that it brought about his head a tremendous scandal which he had hastened to hush with the fullness of his locker. As a general thing he led a regular life, rising very early, going to his factory to attend to his accounts and to inspect the spicing of his fish and oysters, and coming home about five o'clock in the afternoon to wash himself and dress for his promenade or his calls, which were not few, and which always ended at eleven o'clock in the evening. The only reading for which he cared was that of detective stories.

Don Serapio's voice was a trifle disagreeable. As one of the young wags among those clustering about the door said, no one could tell for a certainty if it were tenor, baritone, or bass. In compensation, he sang with sentiment fit to melt the rocks, as could be judged by the infinite movements of his eyebrows, and by the expression of disconsolateness which came over his face as soon as he stood in front of the piano; no one ever saw a face so wrinkled, so long-drawn, so full of feeling. The romanza *Lontano a te,* more than any other, had the power of exciting his sensibility and giving his eyes an exceedingly hopeless expression.

While the proprietor of the canning factory was expressing in Italian his grief at finding himself far from his lady love, the elder daughter of the family was in the most retired part of the room still engaged in conversation with a youth of a pleasant, open countenance, with swarthy complexion, black eyes, and a young mustache.

" Enrique misunderstood my commission," said the youth. "I asked him to send me some jewelry worth something, but what he sent me is just about as commonplace as could be; so much so that I am thinking of sending it back tomorrow without showing it to you."

" Don't trouble about it any more; it's all the same one way or the other."

" What do you mean, ' all the same '? Since when, señorita, have you grown so indifferent to matters of the toilet? I am certain that if I were to bring you this jewelry, you would laugh me to scorn."

" Don't imagine such a thing."

" Perhaps you think I don't remember how you made fun of that hat that your aunt Carmen presented you a few days ago?"

" It was very wrong of me to make fun of it; but you are just as bad when you throw it in my face. The truth is that in the end one hat or one set of jewelry is as good as another."

" Be it so! Keep it up! I know you well, and you can't cheat me. The jewelry shall be sent back, and in its place we'll have another set to my taste and yours. But let's drop the subject. I had something to tell you, and I can't remember what it was. Oh yes! we must write to your uncle Rodrigo, for judging by the note I have just received from him, he doesn't know yet the day on which we are to be married. I think we ought to write him both of us in the same letter; doesn't it seem so to you?"

"Just as you like."

"All right; I'll come round tomorrow before dinner, and we'll write it."

Both remained silent a few moments and listened to the singing of Don Serapio, who was lamenting, always with a more and more pathetic accent, the solitude and sadness in which his mistress kept him. One of the Delgado señoritas lifted her handkerchief to her eyes, declaring in a low voice to those standing near that hitherto there had been few things that ever brought the tears into her eyes.

"What a bore that wretched Don Serapio is! he wrinkles up his forehead so that his wig is almost lifted off behind."

"Don't be so unkind. Have a little charity, and let the poor man enjoy himself without harming God or his neighbor."

"As far as I am concerned he may sing till doomsday. But I notice, lassie, that for some time you have been becoming a great preacher. Are you thinking of entering into competition with the *curé* of the parish?"

"What I am anxious for is that you shouldn't be a backbiter. If you love me as you say you do, my good advice ought not to make you vexed."

"It doesn't make me vexed, loveliest; quite the contrary. I always listen to it with pleasure and follow it—when I can. You surely are acquainted with my ways, and know that I can't help making fun. However, you'll have time enough to preach to me all you want, won't you? Not only time enough but space enough. You can go on giving me sermons from Nieva to Madrid, then from Madrid to Paris, and from Paris to Milan, and from Milan to Venice, and thence to Rome and Naples, and back by Geneva, Brussels, Paris, and Madrid, home again. With what delight I shall travel through all these foreign countries listening to a preacher so devoted! How do you like the itinerary of our journey?"

"Well enough."

"Well enough! That isn't saying anything. One would think the subject didn't interest you as much as it did me. I won't fix it definitely till you have made such changes as you like in it, or vary it entirely, if it seem good to you. I am just as much interested in going to Berlin or London as to Paris and Rome. You can imagine how much difference it makes to me, if I go with you, which way we travel!"

"Whatever you decide upon will be well."

"Let us have it decided. Do you like the plan I propose? Yes 'or no?"

"I have told you yes already."

"But, lassie, what is the matter with you? You have scarcely allowed yourself to smile this whole evening, and you haven't said a word more than was strictly necessary. What is the reason of such solemnity? Are you put out with me?"

"What reason should I have to be?"

"Then I'll ask you *why* you are. You must be, since there's no other way of explaining the curt way in which you have been answering me this long time."

"That's your own imagination. I answer you just as I always do."

Ricardo, without speaking, looked at his betrothed, who turned away her eyes, fixing them on Don Serapio.

"It must be so, but I don't understand it. If you are really angry with me, it would be very unkind of you not to tell me why, so that I could repair my mistake, if perchance I had committed any. My conscience does not accuse me of anything——"

"I tell you that I am not angry; don't be so tiresome!"

Maria said these words with evident asperity, not turning her face from the singer. Ricardo again looked at her for a long time.

" Very good—it is better so—still I thought———"

Both kept silence for some moments. Ricardo broke it, saying,

" When Don Serapio has finished, they are going to make you sing; I am sure—all get good out of it except me."

" Why ? "

" For two reasons: the first is, because much as I enjoy hearing you when we are alone, I don't like it when you sing before people; the second is, because they will take you away from me."

" I don't see why you should dislike it because I sing before people. I am the one not to like it—and I don't at all. As to the separation, that's nonsense, because we are together much more than we ought to be."

" It would be a long and difficult task for me to explain why I don't like you to sing in public. As to the separation which you call nonsense, it's the solemn truth. In spite of our being together several hours a day it seems to me very little. I could wish that we were together all the time. For a man who is going to be married inside of a month and a half, I don't think that such a wish is very extraordinary."

And lowering his voice, he added in a passionate tone,

" I am never satisfied, and never shall be satisfied, however much I am with you, my own life. In all the years since I have adored you, never for a single instant have I felt the shadow of satiety. When I am near you, I think I could not be more content, even in heaven; when I am away, I think how much happier I should be if I were with you. This is a guaranty that we should never get tired of each other's society; isn't it so? For my part, I give you my word that if we reach old age, I shall enjoy more being by your side than sitting in the sunshine! What a happy life is waiting for us, and how long it is that I have dreamed about it! Do you remember how one day in the big garden, when you were eight years old, and I was ten, my dear mamma made us take each other's hands, saying to us in a serious tone: ' Would you like to be husband and wife? Then kiss each other, and look out that you don't quarrel any more.' From that time forth I have never dreamed of the possibility of marrying any other woman than you."

Maria made no reply to this fervid declaration. She, kept looking at the proprietor of the canning factory, with a strange expression, as though her thoughts were far away.

" Do you know one thing? "

" What ? "

" That the chests have come with your clothes, but I have not opened them yet. Both of them have on the lid your cipher with the coronet of marchioness above. You may laugh at me, but I shall tell you, all the same, that it made my heart leap to see the coronet. I imagined that we were already married, and that I hadn't to wait these everlasting forty-five days. I don't know what I wouldn't give if today were the last day of December. Tell me, don't you feel any inclination to call yourself the *Marquesa de Peñalta*, to be mine, mine for ever? "

Maria arose from the sofa, and with a scornful gesture, nor deigning to look once at her lover, replied,

" Well enough."

And she went and sat down beside one of the De Ciudad girls. Ricardo remained for a few moments glued to his seat, without stirring a finger. Then he got up abruptly and hastened from the room.

Don Serapio at last ceased mourning his lady's absence, declaring in a finale that if such a state of things existed longer, he should die without delay. The pianist added force to this wail of woe by performing a noisy run in octaves. A great clapping of hands was heard, and affectionate smiles of approbation were lavished by the ladies upon the vocalist. The young fellows near the doors, always ready for fun, did their best to bring about a repetition of the romanza, but Don Serapio was shrewd enough to perceive that the plaudits of these boys were not in good faith, and he refused to grant the favor.

Then the stripling with the banged hair made the following little speech to the assembled audience:

"Ladies and gentlemen, I believe that now is the time for us to listen to the great *artiste*. We are all waiting impatiently for Maria to delight us—one of those happy moments—with which she has in days gone by delighted us. Isn't it a good idea?"

"That's it; Maria must sing!"

"Of course she will sing; she is very accommodating."

The spokesman offered his arm to the young señorita, and led her to the piano.

When Maria was left standing alone, facing the audience, a thrill of admiration was excited as usual. "How lovely, how lovely she is!" "That girl grows prettier every day!" "What exquisite taste she shows in her dress!" "She looks like a queen!" These and many other flattering phrases were whispered among the friends of the Elorza family.

Without being very tall Maria was of stately stature and presence. She was slender, lithe, and graceful as those beautiful dames of the Renaissance, whom the Italian painters chose as their models. The line of her soft lustrous neck reminded one of Grecian statues. This neck supported a shapely head; the face fair, the cheeks slightly rose-tinted, delicate, regular, transparent, with ruby lips and blue eyes. She bore a notable resemblance to Doña Gertrudis, but she had an attractive and fascinating expression which that celebrated lady never had, whatever may have been the persuasion of the lyric poet of the acrostics. Around her clear and brilliant eyes showed a slight violet circle, which gave her face a decided poetical look.

"Now, Suárez, you will see what kind of a singer this girl is," said one lady.

"I shall appreciate her, for this Señor Don Serapio has spoiled my ears for the time being."

"Oh! Maria is an artist."

"What I perceive just now is, that she has a stunning figure."

"You just wait till you hear her."

"That girl does everything well! If you could see how she draws!"

"Haven't the Elorzas any other daughters than this?"

"Yes, that other girl, who is sitting down over there; her name is Marta. She is going to be very handsome, too."

"Indeed, she is pretty; but she hasn't any expression at all. It's a common kind of beauty, while her sister——"

"Hush! she's going to begin."

Then ensued a silence in the company such as had always been Don Serapio's ideal—unrealizable like all ideals. Maria sang various operatic pieces which were asked for, and needed no urging. When she finished, the plaudits were so eager and long that it made her blush.

Suárez assured his circle of ladies that she had a voice which resembled Nantier Didier's, and that a short time at the conservatory would put her on an equality with the leading contraltos.

When the congratulations had ceased, and the looks of all had ceased to be fastened upon her, a shade of sadness came over Maria's lovely face. She went to Doña Gertrudis and whispered in her ear,

"Mamma, I have a very severe headache."

"Ay! daughter of my heart, I sympathize with you. I, too, am having my share of pain."

"I should like to go to bed."

"Then go, my daughter, go. I will say that you are feeling a trifle indisposed.'

"*Adios, mamita!* Good-night, and sleep well."

Maria kissed her mother's brow, and gradually, taking care not to be noticed, she left the parlor by the dining-room door. She stopped to get a drink of *eau sucré,* and stood a moment motionless, with her eyes fixed on vacancy. The shade of melancholy had greatly dulled the brilliancy of her face.

She passed out of the dining-room and crossed a long and pretty dark entry. At the end there was a door which led to a back stairway. She had mounted only four or five steps when she felt herself seized roughly by the arm, and uttered a cry of terror. Turning round, she saw with embarrassment the pale and troubled face of her betrothed.

" Ricardo! what are you doing here?"

" I saw that you left the dining-room, and I followed you."

" What for?"

" To hear for a second time from your lips the infamous words you said to me in the drawing-room. Do you think, perhaps, it isn't worth while to repeat them? Do you think, perhaps, that I can give up a whole past of love, a whole future of happiness, all the sweet dreams of my life, without calling you infamous, a hundred times infamous, a thousand times infamous, now right here, while we are together alone, afterwards in open society, and then before the whole world? Come, come back, you miserable girl—come back, and let me call you so before everybody!"

And Ricardo, pale and trembling like a gambler who has staked his last remaining money on a card, firmly grasped his sweetheart by the wrist and tried to drag her back to the parlor.

Maria hung her head and said not a word. Without offering any resistance she allowed him to pull her down the four or five steps of the staircase. But on reaching the passage-way, Ricardo felt on his cheek a warm kiss, which caused him to loose his captive and fall back with horror; instantly, Maria's arms were wound around his neck, and on his lips he felt the imprint of other lips.

" Ricardo *mio*, for heaven's sake don't put me to shame!"

These words, whispered in his ear with a passionate accent, were accompanied by a cloud of caresses. The young man pressed her close to his heart without answering a word; his emotion choked his utterance. When he became a little calmer, he asked her with trembling voice,

"Do you love me?"

"With all my soul."

"Was that nothing else but a moment of ill-humor?"

"That was all."

"Oh, what a wretched time you have made me have! Not for all the gold in the world would I go through it again!"

"Tell me, haven't I made up for it now?"

"Yes, loveliest."

"Let me go. I am going to lie down. I have such a headache!"

"Wait a minute. Let me kiss you on your forehead,—now another on your eyes,—now another on your lips,—now on your hands!"

"*Adios!*"

"*Adios!*"

"Let me go, Ricardo, let me go!"

The young fellow, laughing with happiness, still held her by the hand. Maria struggled to escape, though she also was laughing.

"Come, let me go, don't be foolish."

"It shows I'm not foolish because I don't let you go!"

"Think how my head aches!"

"All right, then, I'll let you go."

"Till tomorrow! Be careful whom you dance with now."

"Don't you worry. I am going immediately. Till tomorrow!"

Maria tore herself away. Ricardo tried to catch her again, leaping up the dark staircase, but he did not succeed. The girl said good-night with a merry laugh from the top of the stairs.

When Ricardo returned to the parlor he was smiling like a happy man. The light of the chandelier somewhat dazzled him, and he hastened to sit down.

Maria's room, when she entered it, was plunged in darkness. She groped about for the matches and lighted a lamp of burnished iron. The room was furnished with a luxury and good taste rarely to be found in provincial towns. The furniture was upholstered in blue satin; the curtains and paper were of the same color. In the recess between the windows was a mahogany wardrobe with a full-length mirror. The dressing-table loaded down under the weight of its bottles stood against the opposite wall; the carpet was white, with blue flowers. The exquisite niceness with which all these objects were put in place, the elegance and coquetry of the furniture, and the delicate fragrance perceptible on entering, clearly declared the sex and the station of the person who occupied the room.

When Maria lighted her lamp, her eyes met the eyes of an image of the Saviour which stood on the center of the table where the light burned. It was on wood, beautifully carved and painted, with a decidedly sad and meek expression of the face, and it was this which had led the young woman to buy it. When she caught sight of the sweet but icy face of the image, the happy smile which still hovered over her lips died away, leaving her motionless and deeply thoughtful. Little by little, doubtless under the influence of the ideas which came into her mind, her face lost its usual expression and assumed one as melancholy and humble as that of a Magdalene. At that moment the sound of the piano came vibrating through the dark stairway, telling of the first movement of a fascinating rigadoon. She fell on her knees and bent her head. Every now and then she sobbed. Her lips were pressed convulsively against the naked feet of the Saviour, and muttered unintelligible words.

After a long time she raised her face bathed in tears, and exclaimed in a tone of woe:

"My Jesus! what treachery! what treachery! How poorly do I repay the love which thou hast bestowed on me. Punish me, Lord, so that I may again have peace of mind!"

Arising from the floor, she took the lamp in her hand and went into her bedroom. It was tiny and warm as a nest, and it was ornamented with a profusion of engravings of Jesus and the Virgin. The bed, covered with satin curtains, was white and delightful as a baptismal altar. She placed the lamp on her dressing-table and with more tranquil face quickly undressed.

Then she took a traveling-mantle from the wardrobe, wrapped herself in it, blew out the lamp, made the sign of the cross time and again on her forehead, her mouth, and her breast, and lay down on the floor. The white bed, covered with satin and lawn, warm and perfumed, and full of sensuous delights, awaited her in vain all night. Thus she remained stretched on the floor till daylight dawned.

CHAPTER III

THE NINE DAYS' FESTIVAL OF THE SACRED HEART OF JESUS

DAY had hardly dawned, when our maiden arose suddenly from the floor. She stood motionless a moment with ear attent, but she did not catch the sound of the bells of San Felipe, which she thought she had heard in her dreams. She was mistaken; it was not yet six o'clock. She lighted her lamp, and going to her boudoir prostrated herself in humiliation before the image of Jesus and began to pray. As she wore nothing but a thin, cambric nightdress, she naturally felt the cold through it, and began to shiver, but she would not yield, and she kept on with her prayers until her teeth chattered. Only then she decided to quit the position which she had taken and dress herself. Thereupon, she opened the four windows of her boudoir and blew out the lamp.

A thin light, cold and chill, made its way into the Señorita de Elorza's room, giving the articles of furniture a lugubrious aspect quite different from what they usually bore. The morning chill also penetrated them as well as their mistress, and they stood silent and melancholy, doubtless hoping for the rays of the sun to show forth their beauty and splendor. Only in one spot or another, as the light fell on the varnish, there was a pale reflection which looked like the glassy, filmy eye of a dying person. The room was situated in a sort of square turret which was built in one of the rear angles of the mansion; it rose some yards above it, and was open to the light on all its four sides.

The tower held only two apartments,—Maria's, composed of boudoir and bedroom, and her maid Genoveva's chamber, which was single. They were the coldest but at the same time the most cheerful rooms in the house. The few times that the sun deigned to visit Nieva he went straight to lodge in them, entered without as much as asking leave, in the way of sovereign guests, and spent the day, shining in the mirrors, brightening up the satin of the chairs, dulling the varnish of the clothes-presses, and in a word disporting himself in a thousand different ways,—all this, it may be said, would have been, had not Genoveva taken the precaution to draw the curtains in time. They were likewise the quietest; the noises of the house did not reach them, and those from outside had no possibility of disturbing them, owing to their situation. Only the wind, which almost never ceased to blow heavily around the tower, made strange noises, especially at night, sometimes moaning, sometimes screaming, and constantly complaining because the windows were kept hermetically sealed. During the daytime it was neither melancholy nor petulant, but contented itself with a perpetual but very dignified murmur like seashells held to the ear.

Maria, still shivering though she was wrapped up in her shawl, went to one of the windows which looked down into the garden, the wall of which was close to the quay. From that window the whole length of the Nieva River could be seen down to El Moral, which was the place where it emptied into the sea.

The young girl looked for an instant at the sky, which was still profoundly dark towards the west, hiding and confusing the outline of the distant mountains. In the zenith she noticed that it was completely overcast, of an ashen color, which grew lighter as she turned her face toward the east. There the clouds were not as yet compacted into a solid mass as in the opposite quarter; they stood out against the sweep of the sky in monstrous, black piles, and opened sufficiently to let the few feeble, melancholy, ruddy rays pass through, which the sun, like a dying fire, was beginning to shed upon the earth. The tide was rising. The surface of the river absorbed the slender light of the sky, and gave forth nothing more than a tremulous metallic reflection in the far distance.

After watching the sunrise for a time, our maiden got a book which lay on the dressing-table in her room, and came back to the window to see if she could read; but it was not yet light enough. She laid the book on a chair and again went to the window, leaning her forehead against its panes. The sky kept growing brighter in the direction of El Moral; but it added no life or good cheer to the earth. The growing light seemed only to make more distinct its stern, forbidding face. A wretched and disagreeable day was in prospect, such as the natives of Nieva were accustomed to during the larger part of the year.

But soon the windows of the east were closed; the huge, thick clouds which had stood out separate, allowing the light to pass, once more made one unbroken mass by the impulse of some breath of air, and the rosy flush faded away. In their place remained a uniformly pallid light, which, little by little, spread over the heavens, lazily struggling with the shadows in the west. The far-away reflections on the river likewise died out, leaving it all a monotonous color, like unpolished steel. The boudoir slowly filled with light; the pretty articles of furniture, and the objects adorning it, emerged from the obscurity, graceful, dainty, and fascinating, like the dancers in the opera, when at an outburst from the orchestra they throw aside the spectral mantles in which they had wrapped themselves. The light, however, did not smile; all the time it grew more melancholy and forbidding. Across the mighty masses of dark violet cloud which were rising above the four or five houses of El Moral, others, small and white, began to fly like wisps of gauze—a sure sign of storm.

Maria quickly felt the pane against which she was leaning tremble. A gust of wind and rain had savagely lashed the window. She stepped back a little and saw that all the panes were weeping at once. For some little time she occupied herself in watching the more or less rapid and uneven course which the drops of water followed as they rolled down the smooth surface of the glass. The sharp, intermittent pattering of the rain brought back to her memory the many afternoons that she had spent near that same window listening to it with an open book in her hand. The book had always been a novel. For more than four months she had incessantly begged her father to let her have the use of the boudoir in the tower so that she might give herself up entirely to her favorite occupation without fear of anyone interrupting her. But Don Mariano had feared to give his permission, because the apartments in the tower were cold, and the girl's health was delicate. At last, overcome by her entreaties and caresses, he yielded, after having the rooms carefully carpeted, and exacting the condition that Genoveva should sleep near by.

It was a happy period for Maria. She was sixteen, and her mind was restless and high-spirited. Her music, in which she had made prodigious strides, had stimulated in her heart a decided tendency to melancholy and tears. She wept at the slightest provocation, sometimes without reason, and when it was least expected, but her tears were so sweet, and she experienced such intense pleasure in them, that on many occasions she fostered them artificially. How many times, gazing from that window upon the delicate clouds of the horizon tinted with rose or the last splendors of the dying sun, she felt her heart overcome by a depth of melancholy which found relief only in sobs! How many times she had pained her father with a storm of tears, the cause of which she could not tell, because she herself knew not! The knowledge of painting, in which she also excelled, turned her inclinations towards light and a wide outlook, and this equally contributed to make her long for the rooms in the tower.

When once she had taken her quarters there with her piano, her paints, and her novels, Maria looked upon herself as the most fortunate girl on earth. If at noon of some magnificent sunny day, under an effulgent azure sky, she opened all the windows of her boudoir and admitted the fresh, keen wind which toyed with her hair and scattered the papers from the table over the floor, she imagined with delight that she had mounted upon a star, and that she was in the midst of space, swimming through the air at the mercy of every chance. And this illusion, though it was hard for her to keep it up, made her happy. Sometimes at night she used to open the blinds and light not only her lamp, but all the candles in the candlesticks, so as to imagine that she was stationed in a lofty lighthouse. "From the river this tower must seem like a beacon, and my room the lamp which has just been lighted," was what she used to say, in childish delight. And then she began to peer through the panes to see if any ship were on its way down to El Moral, until, frightened by the darkness without and dazzled by the light within, she finally grew terror-stricken at such an illumination and hastened to extinguish the lights.

Don Mariano called that gay, aërial boudoir "Maria's bird-cage"; and in truth the name was admirably appropriate, for the girl was constantly flitting about in it, moving the furniture and changing the things from one place to another, nervous and restless as a bird. To make the resemblance more complete, it often happened that when the family were gathered in the dining-room they heard the distant trills of some cavatina or romanza which Maria was studying. Don Mariano never failed to exclaim, with his usual benignant smile, "Our little bird is singing." And all would likewise smile, full of content, for everybody in the house loved and admired the girl.

The blasts of wind fraught with rain, on the day of which we are speaking, lashed the panes of glass for a long time, until they had given them a thorough washing. Gradually the gusts became less frequent, and at last they completely ceased. The storm finally dissolved into a fine drizzle, which began to fall slowly, filling the atmosphere with an evanescent, tremulous veil, woven of watery threads.

Maria again took up her book, brought her chair to the window, and sitting down, began to read, it now being light enough to permit of this. It was the *Life of Saint Teresa*, written by herself,—a book bound in solid pasteboard covers, which were stamped with the gilt ornamentations characteristic of religious works.

As the young girl became absorbed in her reading, her face grew more and more serene, and the deep frown on her brow disappeared. She was reading the second chapter, in which the saint sets forth how in the years of her youth she was enamored with books of knight-errantry, and the vanities of the toilet, and hints at the love affairs which at the same time she had passed through. When Maria raised her eyes from the book, they shone with a peculiar delight of inward content.

The bells of San Felipe at last actually began to ring. Maria quickly threw down her book and opened her maid's chamber-door.

"Genoveva! Genoveva!"

"I am awake, señorita."

"Get up; San Felipe's bells are ringing!"

In a twinkling Genoveva was up, dressed, and on hand in her mistress' room. She was a woman of forty years, more or less, short, fat, swarthy, with puffy cheeks, with great, protuberant gray eyes which were expressionless, absolutely expressionless, and with thin hair waving on her

132

temples. She wore a plain, carmelite skirt, and the black merino cloak gathered at the shoulders, such as are used by all provincial serving-women. She had entered the household when Maria was not yet a year old, to be her nurse, and she had never left her, being a notable example of a faithful, steadfast servant.

"How long has my little dove been dressed?"

"About an hour already, Genoveva. I thought I heard the bells, but I was mistaken. Now they are ringing in earnest. Let us not lose any time; take the umbrellas, and let us go."

"Whenever you please, señorita; I am ready."

Both put on their mantillas, and trying not to make any noise, they went down to the entry, carefully unlocked and opened the door, and sallied forth into the street, which they crossed with open umbrellas until they reached the opposite arcade.

The little city of Nieva, as it seems to me I have already said, has almost all of its streets lined with an arcade on one side or the other, sometimes on both. As a general thing it is small, low, uneven, and supported by single round stone pillars, without ornamentation of any sort. Likewise, it is ill-paved. Only in occasional localities, where some house has been reconstructed, it is wider and has more comfortable pavement. If all the houses were to be rebuilt,—and there is no doubt that this will come in time,—the town, owing to this system of construction, would have a certain monumental aspect, making it well worthy of being seen. Even as it is now, though it does not boast of much beauty, it is very convenient for pedestrians, who need not get wet except when they may wish to pass from one sidewalk to the other. And certaintly its illustrious founders were far-sighted, for, as regards constant, ceaseless rain, there is no other place in Spain that can hold a candle to our town.

Protected from the rain, mistress and maid crossed through one corner of the Plaza, and entered a long, narrow, solitary street. The worthy inhabitants were sleeping the sweet sleep of morning. Only from time to time they met some sailor wrapped up in his rough waterproof capote, who, with fishing utensils in his hand, and making a great clatter with his enormous boots, was striding towards the quay.

"Are you well protected, señorita? See, there's been a frost; one would think it was already January."

"Yes; I put on a velvet waist, and besides, this sacque is well wadded."

"Well, well, sweetheart. If your papa knew that we were out so early, he would scold me for consenting to it. You are exceedingly virtuous, señorita. Few or none would lead such a saintly life at your age."

"Hush, hush, Genoveva! don't say such a thing. I am only a miserable sinner; much more miserable than you have any idea of."

"Señorita, for Heaven's sake—I am not the only one who says so; but everybody. Yesterday Doña Filomela told me that she was edified to see you go to mass, and take the Blessed Sacrament, and she would give anything if her daughters would do the same. And I don't wonder she wishes so, for one of 'em, the youngest, is the devil's own. Would you believe, the other day, señorita, she scratched her sister right in church because one was to confess before the other. Pretty kind of repentance! It's shameful, señorita, it's shameful to see how some women go to church! One would think that they were in their own houses Aye! the poor things don't realize that they are in the house of the Lord of heaven and earth, who will ask them to give account of their sins. Hasn't Doña Filomela shown you the rosary which her brother sent her from Havana? It is a marvel! all ivory and gold, with a great crucifix of solid gold. To say your prayers there's no need of such extravagance, is there, señorita?"

"To pray one needs only a pure and humble heart."

"Aye! señorita, how well you speak! It seems as if they were mistaken who say that you are not more than twenty years old. But when God wishes to pour out his

134

gifts on one of his creatures, it makes no difference whether she be young or old, rich or poor. Every day I pray the most Blessed Virgin to preserve your health, so that you may serve as an example for those who are in mortal sin!"

"What you ought to pray for, Genoveva, is that He will purify my soul and pardon the many sins that I have committed."

"God have mercy! If you need to be forgiven, you who are so pious and humble-minded, what would the rest of us need? Don't be so severe upon yourself. Fray Ignacio has so much esteem for you that he never wearies of sounding your praises; and that too, though he's not very indulgent, as you know. At this very moment I suppose that holy man is in the sacristy, listening to people confess! What a healthy man he is! It must be because God makes him so. He doesn't eat, he doesn't sleep, he doesn't rest a moment. And yet every day he grows stronger and stronger, and has greater and greater zeal in serving God. I don't see how he can spend so many hours in the confessional, without taking something to eat. Only the Lord can give him the power. Blessed be His name forever! Amen!"

"That's true; God works real miracles in him, because there is need in the world. O God! what would have become of my soul if these holy missioners had not come to open my eyes!"

"Though they have helped greatly in the way of salvation, still, before they came you were very good and used to attend the Sacraments."

"How little that amounts to, Genoveva, when the deepest nooks and corners of the conscience are not looked into!"

"Tell me, señorita, did you see in your dreams last night that beautiful bird with fiery feathers, with a cross in its bill, which you have seen lately?"

Maria stopped suddenly short and raised her hand to her breast as though she had received a blow. Then she began to walk on again, exclaiming in an undertone,

"Last night I was not allowed to see it!"

" Why not, sweetheart? "

She made no reply. She walked on a while, and a groan escaped her. Then she stopped once more, and throwing her arms around her maid's neck, she began to sob bitterly.

" I am very wicked, Genoveva, very wicked! My heart has not yet been freed from impurities; the flesh and the devil will hold me in their sway. If you knew what a sin I committed yesterday! "

" Hush, hush! don't be discouraged! What sin could you have committed, you lamb? "

" Yes, yes; I am more wicked than you imagine. The more light I receive from God, the deeper I seem to sink into the darkness; the more He heaps blessings upon me, the more ungrateful I am toward Him."

" God is infinitely merciful, señorita."

" But infinitely just, as well."

" Beseech the aid of Saint Joseph the blessed; there is no fault which the Lord does not forgive through his intercession. Come, stop crying now; you are going to confession, and all is going to be forgiven."

After the girl had calmed down a little, they proceeded on their way, till they reached a rather diminutive plaza, fronted by the stern, gray façade of a great church which attracted attention neither by its beauty nor by any other quality, good or bad. They crossed a portico, huge and gray like the façade, and entered the temple, which was likewise gray and enormous; these qualities were its only characteristics. It consisted of three naves, the central one broad and lofty like a cathedral; those on the sides narrow and low; all three had been whitewashed at some time very remote, but were now thick with dust, peeling off in various places and stained with wide-spread, mysterious spots. The altars, which were profusely adorned, presented a gray color, very distinct from the gilding which originally had covered them. Through its dirty glass could be seen the stiff image of some saint with metal aureole, or the sad anguished face of an Ecce-Homo.

MARTA AND MARIA

It was too early in the morning to find many people.
Nevertheless, scattered here and there, praying on bended
knees before the altars, a few women with covered heads
were to be seen; others pressed up to the latticed windows
of the confessional and held their mantillas on both sides of
their faces, while with a half-audible whispering they confided their misdeeds to the sacred tribunal of the Church.
A few priests, who kept the doors of the confessionals open,
could be seen in cassock and hood, bending forward, with
their ears to the window, reflecting in their frowning faces
and negligent attitude the weariness which they felt; others
kept theirs hermetically sealed, and scarcely could any one
in passing perceive the presence of a human being.

A few spots in the sanctuary were bathed in a melancholy light, but the corners and the hollows between the
pillars were left in almost perfect darkness. The huge
brazen lamps swung in the spaces on cords attached to the
roof. The leaded window of the two huge, open oriels,
high up in the walls of the great central nave, admitted a
sad sheet of light, extending like a pale altar-cloth before
the principal shrine. On one side of this, at some little distance, was another small portable altar, upon which was
raised an image of the Saviour with perforated breast,
wherein was seen a bleeding heart, wearing a crown of
thorns and haloed with flames; around the image were
a host of lighted candles, the hissing and crackling of
which sounded lugubriously in the immense, silent circuit of the church. It was a temporary altar set up because
of the Nine Days' Festival of the Sacred Heart of Jesus,
which was celebrated at that time.

Genoveva went to the sacristy to ask Fray Ignacio if
her señorita could make her confession. The latter remained kneeling near the confessional, waiting for the
priest. She felt a peculiar, timid impatience; a bit of fear
mingled with anxiety and desire. The sanctuary was filled
with a mingled odor of dampness and dust, of extinguished
candles and of faded flowers, which inspired her with
veneration. The moments preceding confession were filled.

with a delicious suspense for Maria. The circumstance and mystery which surrounded that intimate confidence, the most intimate in the world, exerted a certain fascination over her mind, and agitated her to the very depths of her being, without loathing. She felt slight chills run over her body, followed by flushes of heat, which mounted to her face and set it on fire. At that moment she thought not so much of her sins as of the way in which she should try to tell them.

Fray Ignacio's dark, resolute, and stern figure hastened up to the confessional, and without vouchsafing his penitent a single glance, took his place within it. Maria, tremulous and with melting heart, drew near the little window. When at the end of a half-hour she turned away, her eyes were red and her cheeks were pale.

The church, meantime, had been slowly filling, although almost exclusively with women. A few ventured as far as the center, making with their wooden shoes a real clatter as they walked on the tiled pavement; the most took them off at the door and carried them in their hands. The women of the people were in the majority, but there were a goodly number of señoras: men were few. The multitude for some time remained scattered about, kneeling at the altar-rails, all making their devotions. From time to time an acolyte in flesh-colored balandran and white surplice, with shaven head and crafty eyes, rang his bronze hand-bell, and a few women left their places and stationed themselves before some altar where a priest, decked with golden ornaments, was beginning the sacrifice of the mass. After consuming the elements, he would administer the communion to two or three sets of women.

Maria, with head bent on her bosom and hands devoutly crossed, joined them to receive the Holy Eucharist. When the priest placed on her tongue the consecrated particle, amid the dull, hushed murmur of the throng, she felt her cheeks slightly inflamed by the grandeur of the miracle which had taken place within her; then she withdrew three or four steps from the altar, overwhelmed with veneration, and without venturing to cast a look on either side, at the end of a short space she left her place and went to repeat the prayers imposed as her penance. An elderly clergyman in a surplice mounted the pulpit, which was covered with a cloth of gold tissue. The faithful came flocking from the remotest parts of the church towards the center, forming a dense throng about the pulpit. Maria and Genoveva stood in the midst of it. The priest made the sign of the cross, and began his *Ave Marias* and *Pater Nosters* in a loud voice. When the rosary was ended, he began the service, the *novena* of the Sacred Heart of Jesus. The clergyman put on an enormous pair of spectacles, and in a snuffling, doleful tone exclaimed:

" *O Heart (Corazón)* "—the multitude repeated after him with solemn acclaim, prolonging the words—" O Heart (*Corazoooón*)—*most lovable (amantísimo)*—most lovable (*amantísimooo*)—*most sacred (santísimo)*—most sacred (*santísimooo*)—*and honey-sweet (melífluo)*—and honey-sweet (*melífluoo*)—*of my divine Jesus*—of my divine Jesus—*full of flames*—full of flames—*of purest love (amor)*—of purest love (*amooor*)—*consume me entirely*—consume me entirely—*and grant me*—and grant me—*a new life*—a new life—*of love and of grace*—of love and of grace;—*kindle and consume*—kindle and consume—*my lukewarmness*—my lukewarmness. *O Heart (Corazón)*—O Heart (*Corazoooón*)—*most comfortable (dulcísimo)*—most comfortable (*dulcísimooo*)—*I adore thee*—I adore thee—*most profoundly*—most profoundly.—*Grant me grace*—Grant me grace—*O loving Heart (Corazón)*—O loving Heart (*Corazoooón*)—*to atone for*—to atone for—*the insults and ingratitudes*—the insults and ingratitudes—*done against thee (Vos)*—done against thee (*Vooos*)—*and what I pray thee for*—and what I pray thee for—*in this novena*—in this novena—*is for the greater glory of God (Dios)*—is for the greater glory of God (*Diooos*)—*and of my soul*—and of my soul—*Amen*—Amen."

Maria merely whispered the words of the orison and kept her eyes fastened on the ground. Genoveva repeated them aloud, looking straight into the priest's face. The multitude sighed after they said Amen.

When the orison was ended, the priest repeated three *Pater Nosters* and three *Ave Marias* in honor of the three marks of the passion with which the divine Heart of Jesus showed itself to the Blessed Mother Margarita of Alacoque. The faithful knelt in reply. Immediately began a new orison like the first, addressed to the Sacred Hearts of Jesus and Mary. Then the priest recommended all to beseech God through the mediation of the Sacred Hearts for whatever each most needed, and the congregation meditated silently for a few moments. Maria prayed fervently that God would make her a better woman. Genoveva spent some time in hesitation, without knowing what to ask for, and at last she asked for patience to endure the suffering of her influenza. The priest read with his snuffling voice, which drawled over the syllables like a lamentation, the following

ILLUSTRATION.

" In the city of Munich there lived not many years ago a lady of extraordinary beauty, who led such an exemplary life, that all gave her the name of saint. It happened that one day there came to her house a very lively young man to visit her, on the ground that she was one of his own cousins, and instantly the devil managed to get complete possession of him. His passion was so mad and wretched that at the end of some time she yielded to an impure sin, thus gravely offending God. After she fell into this sin she found herself sunk in a deep abyss of melancholy, for though the unhappy woman immediately sent away the one who had been the cause of her fault, she believed that she was doomed to hell. She began to lead an austere life, mortifying herself with fasting and penitence, and yet she could not escape the horrible thought. At length, by the advice of a pilgrim who happened to pass that way, she determined to make a *novena* to the Sacred Heart of Jesus. On the night of the fifth day of constant prayer, being in bed, she heard a great disturbance, and saw flying from her house a demon, horribly howling and leaving behind him an intolerably fetid odor. On the following morning she found herself cured of her melancholy, and very confident of the infinite mercy of God."

The faithful crowded closer around the pulpit to hear the illustration, and they took in with delight its romantic flavor. The *novena* ended with a sermon in Latin. The congregation repeated an *Ave Maria* and a *Credo*. The clergyman descended from the desk.

There was a loud and prolonged noise in the church. The throng of women spread out, dispersed, moved to and fro, gossiping and chattering all at once. The clattering of the wooden shoes again was heard on the damp and filthy blocks of the pavement. An acolyte began to snuff out the candles burning around the image of Jesus and, standing on the altar, with his shorn head and mischievous eyes, made profane grimaces at the other boys, whose mothers kept them on their knees saying their prayers. A few of the clergy issued from the confessionals and crossed over to the sacristy with long strides. One was detained in the center of the church by various ladies, and stood talking with them a long time, though with evident anxiety to escape from them. Through the leaded panes of the great oriels poured all the daylight dispelling the mystery of the temple, and making it seem melancholy, wretched, and dirty, as in reality it was. Two or three gay fellows, with coat-collars turned up and sleeves well pulled down, came in, casting quick glances of curiosity at all the places. A sacristan took it into his head to throw wide open the wooden screen at the door, and a restless, noisy multitude, who had not been early enough to take part in the *novena*, surged into the vast room to listen to the word of a missioner, who at that moment mounted the pulpit with a contemplative, zealous gesture.

When he stood up dominating the multitude, with the sacred dove made of painted wood above his head, the noise greatly subsided. The congregation, greatly increased, ag:.in crowded together beneath the lecturer. There were many men who came not out of pure devotion, but rather with the intention of judging the sermon from a literary point of view.

Meantime great throngs of people came pouring in through the door, disturbing the faithful, and preventing the attainment of silence. Maria and Genoveva were jostled hither and thither by the fluctuation of the multitude. The orator waited vainly for the bustle to cease. At last he extended his arm in academic style toward the door, and shouted emphatically, as though he were in the heart of his discourse,

" Close that screen ! "

The doors closed slowly, as though no one had touched them. The faithful were seating themselves in their places. For a time much coughing was heard; at last it ceased, and the church preserved a fragile, artificial silence, broken frequently by some stubborn cough or by the trumpet blast of some nose being blown. The jet and mother-of-pearl beads of the ladies' rosaries, clinking together,. made a soft, melancholy tintinnabulation.

The orator was young, tall, and slender, with great black deep-set eyes in a pale, classic face. He also wore a cassock with surplice and cowl. He inspired respect by his sweet, gentle gravity.

He took off his cowl, and said a few words in Latin which no one could hear. Then putting on his cowl again, and leaning far over the railing, he exclaimed in a loud voice,

" Beloved brethren in Jesus Christ ! "

He possessed a ringing voice, of a sweet and sympathetic quality, which lent a greater effect to the solemnity of the face. He began by showing an ironical astonishment that there were to be found any at all willing to abandon the vanities of the world to listen to the word of God, and he warmly congratulated the faithful who had come to take part in the Nine Days' Festival of the Sacred Heart of Jesus. Of all the forms of devotion invented by piety, the most grateful in the eyes of the Lord was this; for it summed up and included all the rest, since, "as the heart in the human body represents the sum and substance,—the very center of the physical life,—so in the same way the Sacred Heart of our Redeemer is the center of pious souls and the focus of light around which revolve our aspirations for immortal glory." He ended his exordium by invoking with impassioned phrases the aid of this Sacred Heart in letting his discourse bring forth fruit. He offered in behalf of all an *Ave Maria.* . . .

The sermon ended by exhorting the faithful, with lofty flights of eloquence rich in imagery, to devote themselves to the Sacred Heart of Jesus. "A quarter of an hour every day of loving discourse with this Sacred Heart brings to the soul the purest joy that it can have on earth. *Gustate, et videte quoniam suavis est Dominus.* Try to hold converse a while with the Lord, and ye will enjoy the delights of heaven and the rarest satisfactions, such as those who love have. All that is in this world is folly and deception: banquets, comedies, receptions, amusements, and all the rest that the world considers good are mingled with gall and sown with thorns. Doubt not that the Heart of Jesus gives greater delight and comfort to those souls which seek it with devotion and self-abnegation, than the world with all its pastimes and insipid pleasures. What delight to be speaking for one instant with the most lovable Jesus, forever ready to hearken to our prayers! To unbosom one's self to him alone as to a most intimate friend. To demand his grace, his love, and his glory! Oh, my dear friends, *gustate et videte, gustate et videte!*"

The orator ended the final clauses of his sermon always with those words, *gustate et videte, gustate et videte.* When he ended by expressing his wish that all might have eternal glory, he was pale with weariness. Drops of perspiration rolled down his noble brow. He had uttered the last part of his discourse with growing agitation and enthusiasm, which he succeeded in communicating to his hearers. Maria, after her first fit of weeping, remained comforted and almost happy. Genoveva whispered in her ear while the priest was descending from the pulpit,

"Señorita, I just saw Don César in the congregation."

The young girl's face changed slightly. The crowd began to dissolve, spreading out over the whole area of the church. The majority of the people crowded tumultuously to the door, struggling to get out. After some difficulty Maria and Genoveva succeeded in reaching the portico, and started on their homeward way. But the Señorita de Elorza kept frequently turning her head. An elderly gentleman, tall, slender, and pale, with goatee and long white mustachios, dressed in black from head to foot, was following them at a considerable distance. As they entered the arcade of a narrow and lonely street, the *caballero* hastened his steps, and the two women lingered for him, so that very soon they were together. The *caballero* turned to Maria and said in a low voice,

"Señorita, last night I returned from where you know."

"I have prayed God to bring you back in safety, Don César."

"Thanks, thanks. Have you finished embroidering the banner?"

"Yes, señor!"

"And the flannel hearts?"

"Those also."

"That is good, señorita; I shall not forget your diligence and enthusiasm."

Don César did not move a line of his vigorous face during this conversation. His eyes, which were of a strange intensity gleaming with ferocity, did not for a moment leave the girl's face. He said nothing for a time, having something in his mind, and then he broke the silence, speaking in the curt tone of command,—

"Tomorrow at this time be on hand again. We have some commissions to give you."

"I will not fail you."

Don César noticed that two young men had just turned

144

the corner and were coming toward them; thereupon, without saying farewell, he left the women, crossing to the opposite sidewalk.

CHAPTER IV

HOW THE MARQUIS OF PENALTA BECAME THE DUKE OF THURINGEN

A FEW days later Ricardo set forth from home as usual about ten o'clock in the morning and turned his steps toward the house of his betrothed. It was not love alone that impelled him to walk the street so early, but as much the melancholy solitude that reigned at the moment in the vast seignorial mansion where he lived; for our hero had been alone in the world a little more than a year. His father, the old Marquis de Peñalta, had died when he was under six, and he had scarcely more than a vague remembrance of his pale face between the sheets of the bed when they raised him up to give him a kiss a few hours before he died. He remembered also how on that same day everyone had hugged him and kissed him, with tears, and this had attracted his attention and made him ask, " Why are you all crying today? "

His mother had loved him with one of those concentrated and fierce affections which destroy by very reason of intensity. During his boyhood she had kept him tied to her apron-strings, never consenting for him to take part in the games of the other lads, lest he should hurt himself. Even when he was quite a youth, she always used to put him to bed, offering with him a series of innocent prayers, and sitting by his bedside with folded arms until he fell asleep, when she would silently leave his chamber on tiptoe. When he reached early manhood, she had nothing to do but think of her son's career, for the late marquis had insisted that he should follow one. Ricardo wanted to enter the artillery. How many tears the lad's resolute decision cost

145

TALES FROM THE SPANISH

the mother! The first time that he went to Segovia, the good lady thought she should die: she made up her mind not to leave the house until her son returned, and she carried out her intention. When he came home to spend his vacation, she could not be enough at his side, caressing him and reading in his eyes his slightest caprices, so as to carry them out instantly. Two or three days before it was time for him to return, she would begin to sob and cry: she held him close to her bosom for long moments and made him promise a thousand times to write her every day, to cover himself up warm during his journey, and not to go out nights. The only thing which served to divert her for a short time was the preparation of his cadet's chest, with which she took so much pains that it lacked nothing, from the more usual articles of dress, down to a piece of court plaster and a package of lint in case he was wounded.

Thanks to his genial, happy, and sympathetic nature, rather than by his application, the young Marquis de Peñalta finished his course. At college everybody loved him, students as well as professors. He was one of those frank and friendly young fellows with whom it is difficult to quarrel, and whom we all go to as a confidant worthy of sharing the secrets of our hearts in the bitter misfortunes of life. He was always found smiling and unreserved, bringing joy and confidence wherever he went, and rarely did a dispute arise between two cadets which he did not succeed in bringing to a friendly issue. In spite of his conciliatory temperament no one in college or out of it questioned his courage, much less the remarkable prowess of his fists. More than once, in the frequent quarrels between the cadets and the peasants, which generally broke out in candle-light balls, he had floored three or four stout fellows with as many blows, which attracted all the more attention from the crowd because there was nothing stout or athletic in his figure.

One day while encamped in the park at Seville, the colonel called him into his tent and asked him,

146

"Isn't it some time since you have had a letter from your mother, Peñalta?"

Ricardo grew as pale as death.

"What is it, colonel? what is it?"

"Don't be alarmed, child; I happened to learn that she wasn't very well."

Ricardo understood perfectly, and fell into the colonel's arms, shedding a flood of tears. That night he took the train for the north.

The dismal night spent in that journey remained deeply impressed upon his mind. When the engine whistled, and his comrades, who had come to see him off, standing on the platform, waved their *adios,* he went and sat in a corner of the carriage, wrapped up in his cloak, feigning to sleep, in order better to abandon himself to his painful, gloomy thoughts. Oh, how painful and gloomy these thoughts! He imagined the guardian angel of his infancy, the mother of his heart, dying alone, without receiving her son's last kiss, perhaps calling for him with yearning in the supreme moment of her agony. He remembered that when he had last left her, her health was rather feeble, and the embrace which she gave him was much longer than usual, and her kisses more numerous, as though the poor woman had felt a presentiment that she should never see him again. In her wide, moist eyes he read a fervent silent prayer that he would abandon his profession and not leave her. But he, pleased with the vanities of society, and seduced by the voice of selfishness, had paid no heed to this prayer which the unhappy woman had not dared to formulate with her lips. He felt deeply angry with himself, and called himself the most insulting and humiliating names. From time to time he put his head out of the window and breathed the cool night air, to prevent the sobs from choking him. The vague, mysterious outline of the undulating landscape, wrapt in shadows, transformed his despair into grief, which gradually changed into a solemn melancholy like the gloomy clouds hovering above the still more gloomy earth.

147

The silent majesty of inanimate nature calmed his agitation, but it made him think with cold chills of the great loneliness awaiting him. The tie that bound him to earth, and through which he felt that all human beings were his kin, was severed; now he had no one in the world whom he could call his own. The wind, stirred by the swift rush of the train, hummed in his ears and seemed to say to him, Alone! alone! The harsh noise of the wheels and engine violently excited his morbid state of mind, giving him a sensation almost of pain, like that caused by the thoughts rushing through his brain. The noisy, metallic rhythm of the wheels likewise seemed to say, with still more relentless accent, Alone! alone! His sad face followed the far-off line of the horizon, and this came back to him in quivering, prophetic reflections, which barely sufficed to cleave asunder the network of shadows, gloom upon gloom. The light from the engine cast a reddish gleam, tingeing as with blood the ground and the trees lining the track. Where there were no trees, the telegraph poles flew past him with bewildering rapidity like the happy hours of his youth. Above his head floated the huge black plume of the smoke, emitted by the smoke-stack of the engine, and this, as it disappeared in the atmosphere, in dying made a thousand strange and monstrous phantasms. These phantasms, as they fled away, rolling along just above the ground, seemed also to say mournfully, Alone! alone! Thereupon, being no longer able to endure the icy breath of the deserted landscape which penetrated his breast and parched his eyes, he shut the window and again returned to his corner and his tears.

In the car were four other people: an elderly señora and a young man of twenty or twenty-five, a girl of eighteen or twenty, and a little girl of five or six years,—all of whom seemed to be her children. The señora went to sleep, though she kept opening her eyes to watch the child, who was incessantly running from one side to the other; the two young people were chatting quietly and confidentially together. The sight of this mother surrounded by her children and often looking at them lovingly still more deeply affected Ricardo. The gentle murmur of the brother and sister's conversation, repeatedly broken by repressed laughter, roused in his heart a keen, melancholy envy. The young girl was beautiful, with a noble, fascinating face. Ricardo, without realizing it, watched her all night, but she seemed to give no heed to him. When the guard of the station shouted, " Cordoba! twenty minutes for refreshments!" all hastily got up and collected their things in preparation to leave the train. Then only the young lady gave him a long, sweet look, and as she went out, said with a sad, sympathetic smile, " Good-night, and a happy journey to you." There was no doubt that she had noticed his grief.

Ricardo felt deeply regretful to have them take their departure, as though some tide of affection bound him to that family, and he felt an inclination to say to the mamma, " Señora, I have just lost my mother; I am alone in the world, and I have no one to love me, and no one to love. Won't you take me home with you as your son? " The car door closed with a bang, the bell rang, the hoarse shriek of the engine was heard, and the train sped on its way with its metallic clatter, which ceaselessly cried in the silence of the night, Alone! alone! alone!

A few relatives and friends were waiting for him, and they went with him silently to his home, where they left him after a few meaningless words. During the days that followed he received many visits of condolence from people who extolled his mother's virtues and recommended great resignation. All called him Señor Marqués. Never did he suffer so much as at such times. The only person with whom he enjoyed talking was Don Mariano Elorza, who had been a good friend of his father's, and whose house he visited very familiarly whenever he came to Nieva during his vacations. Don Mariano, who was cordial and friendly to everybody, could not well help showing himself doubly affectionate to Ricardo on account of the sorrowful situation in which he was placed. His house during the period which followed the marquesa's death was a place of refuge for our young friend, where his grief was consoled, and he found a little of that family life which he so greatly missed.

On the other hand, it must be said that Ricardo had always felt toward Don Mariano's eldest daughter a strong admiration and affection, which easily changed into love when age and occasion offered, and frequency of intercourse stimulated it, and there was still greater reason for it since neither he nor she had ever been in love before. Long before they were formally engaged, the marriage of the young Marqués de Peñalta and the Señorita de Elorza used to be talked about in the city. It was a marriage desired and demanded by public opinion; for it must be remarked that the families of Peñalta and Elorza were the richest in town, and the public always consider it logical for wealth to seek wealth as rivers seek the sea. Accordingly, Ricardo and Maria were declared husband and wife not long after they were born, and the truth is, the gossips of the town would never have forgiven them if they had failed to carry out the edict passed by all the wiseacres of Nieva. We know on good authority that the young people had no thought of any such intention, and that they had accepted the sovereign decree with the greatest meekness.

Returning now to where we left off, it is sufficient for us to remark that Ricardo very quickly reached the porch of the house of Elorza, which was large and gloomy. From the great solid door, darkened by time and use, hung a bronze knocker, with which he rapped. He was immediately admitted into a rather large court, with a fountain in the center. A broad flight of stone steps with balustrade of the same material led from it. It was now somewhat the worse for wear, and needed repairs in many places. On the first landing this stairway divided into two arms, one of which led to the apartments of the owners, the other to those of the servants. The former ended in a wide corridor, or gallery, from which one looked through windows into the court.

The whole house presented the same elegance as that of the old palaces, although it was built at a comparatively modern period. It had the advantage over those old ancestral mansions, like the Marqués de Peñalta's, in that it had not been designed to minister so much to the vanity of its masters as to the suitable distribution of its rooms for the conveniences of daily life. It was not dark and gloomy, as those are apt to be; on the contrary, its whole interior spoke of joy, comfort, and elegance. It was, in fact, a great building, without being pretentious, and comfortable, without falling into the unpleasing vulgarity of many modern constructions. It held a conciliatory middle course between aristocratic and middle-class ideals, combining the proud lordliness of the one and the practical luxurious tendencies of the other.

The house in a certain way mirrored the position of its master and mistress. Both were children of the most important families not only in Nieva, but in the whole province in which the city is situated. The señora was sister of the Marqués de Revollar, who cut such a figure in Madrid a few years before by his incredible dissipation and prodigality, and who afterwards, being totally ruined and driven away by his creditors, had taken refuge in the army of the Pretender, whom he served as minister and adviser. Don Mariano came from a family less ancient and glorious but far more opulent. His grandfather had made an immense fortune in Mexico during the final years of the past century, and with it he had become the most important landowner in Nieva, and had built the house of which we are speaking. Not only himself, but his son and his son's son, had succeeded in giving luster to their millions by allying themselves with noble families.

Ricardo made his way through the various rooms of the house of Elorza with as much familiarity as though he had been at home, without even taking off his hat. When he entered Doña Gertrudis's boudoir, this señora, assisted by two waiting-women, was taking a dish of broth. On seeing our hero, she placed the cup on the little stand in front

of her, and pushing back her easy-chair, she exclaimed
in a doleful tone,

"Aye, my dear, you come at an evil hour."

"Why, what's the matter?"

"I'm dying, Ricardo, I'm dying."

"Do you feel worse?"

"Yes, my son, yes; I feel very ill; it is beyond the power
of words to say how ill I feel. If I don't die today, I
shall never die. I spent the whole night doing nothing
but groan, and then—and then—that tiger of a Don Maximo has not come yet, though I have sent him two messages.
May God forgive him! May God forgive him!"

Doña Gertrudis shut her eyes as though she were making
ready to die without either temporal or spiritual comfort.

Ricardo, accustomed to these vaporings, remained a long
time silent. At length he said in an indifferent tone,

"Did you know Enrique has succeeded in exchanging
the jewelry, and the new set came yesterday all right?"

"Indeed? thank God!" replied Doña Gertrudis, opening her eyes; "I certainly thought they wouldn't be willing
to exchange it."

"Why not?"

"Of course, because by selling the other they got rid of
an old thing, which I don't know how they will ever sell
now."

"Yes; but they would lose a customer who brings them
much gain. Don't you see, Enrique receives commissions
from the whole province?"

"That's true enough; but don't you know that these
traders are blinded by avarice? Umph! what wretched people. I tell you I can't bear to see tradesmen, Ricardo; I
can't bear to see them, nor painters either!"

After expressing this unfavorable opinion of commerce,
which, in the tribunal of her mind, she made co-extensive
with all industry and to the mechanical arts in general,
Doña Gertrudis again closed her eyes with a gesture of
woe, and continued in this strain:

"What I am sure of, my son, is that I am not going to

see you married, and that you will be obliged to postpone the wedding on my account. I feel very ill, very ill; my heart tells me that I am going to die before the day of your marriage; and the truth is, that it would be better for me to die if I have got to suffer so much."

"Come, Doña Gertrudis, don't say such things. Who is going to die? You must surely get better gradually; you will be cured, and you will be well and plump so that it will be a delight to see you."

Instead of brightening up at these words, Doña Gertrudis grew angry:

"That's nonsense, Ricardo; my illness is mortal, even if no one thinks so; my husband won't believe it, but very soon he will be convinced of it; I don't complain merely from habit, not at all. Aye! my dear, if you knew how I suffer, sitting in this easy-chair!"

It may be declared with certainty that from the day on which the priest had invoked the nuptial blessing on Doña Gertrudis, this noble señora had done nothing else but nurse her bodily woes and tribulations, dragging out a petty existence amid the strangest and obscurest ailments that were ever known. Before the birth of her eldest daughter, Maria, she had suffered from hemorrhage and consumption. Then for several years afterwards, until her second daughter, Marta, was born, she complained of a terrible pain in her heart, so sharp and cruel that many times she had fainted away. The symptoms of this disease, as related by the patient, would fill any one with terror. Sometimes she thought she felt her heart handled and squeezed to the last degree; at others she thought that it was freezing, and then they had her shivering so that all the furs and flannels which they put on her breast had not the slightest effect, until by an abrupt transition she went into a heated oven, where she was roasted to such a degree that her hands in her paroxysms tore into fragments whatever garments she had on; again, finally, she was conscious of some animal gnawing it with his teeth, and of causing

such exquisite agony that she could not refrain from shriek-
ing.

Don Maximo, the young graduate in medicine, was
absolutely nonplussed by this pathological case, and at each
visit he prophesied the immediate death of his patient unless the remedy for spasms which he prescribed should
instantly restore her safe and sound. As Doña Gertrudis
did not make haste to die, nor did her extraordinary malady disappear, Don Maximo came to lose all faith in her.
He kept up his visits to the house, but always at his regular
hour, from which he rarely deviated even though Doña
Gertrudis often sent for him by messengers, begging him
to play the old farce over again in her sick-room. Don
Maximo ended by having the greatest contempt for his
noble client's infirmities, and he went so far as to characterize them publicly in the apothecary shop, where he was
an assistant, as woman's *cajigalinas*. The exact meaning
of the word *cajigalinas* was never known by the public or
anybody else, nor can it be decided whether it was a private invention of Don Maximo's, or whether it was derived
from some very ancient, even some dead, language which
the licentiate had studied. The word, from its root, seems
to be of Semitic origin, but I do not venture to settle this
question offhand. Let the wise men decide. What is in-
dubitable is that Don Maximo intended thereby to mean
something that was insignificant, mean, or of little account;
and this is enough for us to know what to make of the
opinion of science in regard to Doña Gertrudis's ills.

After Marta's birth Doña Gertrudis's sufferings did not
disappear, but they returned in a new form. Her heart
was considerably calmed down, but instead, all the afflicted
señora's muscles and tendons began to suffer contraction,
causing powerful pains, preventing her for some months
from using her limbs at all, and finally leaving her, though
greatly improved, yet obliged when she walked to lean on
her husband or one of her daughters. Don Maximo at the
beginning of this new phase showed himself preoccupied
and captious to the last degree; he studied with watchful

eye all the symptoms and causes, prescribed remedies for spasms by the gallon, made use, in a word, of all the resources which science (that is, Don Maximo's science) offers for such emergencies, but without reaching any satisfactory results. At length the word *cajigalinas,* of Semitic origin, once more appeared on his lips, and from that time on he never entered the señora's room without a slight smile of incredulity hovering on his dark face.

Ricardo still remained a while at Doña Gertrudis's side, and then he left her to scour the house in search of the girls. He found Marta in the kitchen busily engaged in making pastry for pies.

"Where's Maria, *ma petite ménagère?*"

"She's in her room, dressing; she'll be down soon."

"If I disturb you in your work, I'm going; if not, I'll stay."

"You don't disturb me, if you'll only stand out of the light a little—there, that'll do!"

"All right! I'll stay and learn how to make—what is it you're making?"

"Pork pies."

"Well, then, to make pork pies."

The girl raised her head, smiling at her future brother-in-law, and then she resumed her work. She was standing at a low table which, judging from its shining surface, was meant for the operation now going on. She wore an enormous white apron like the kitchen girls, and on her head a cap no less white. Her great bright black eyes made a more brilliant contrast with this costume, and so did her jetty hair. She had rolled up the sleeves of her dress and bared a pair of soft arms, which were more fully rounded than might have been expected at her age. Her arms bespoke a woman in full possession of all the physical attractions, all the graceful curves of her sex; they were the smooth white arms of a Flemish maiden, but solid and well-knit like those of a working-girl; they might have served as a model for a sculptor, or to keep a room in daintiest order. With them she rolled from side to side, on the top of the table, a great lump of yellowish dough, manipulating it and doubling it over and over constantly without thought of rest. The dough spread out softly over the table because of the lard which shortened it, making a slight noise like the rustle of silk. A few maidservants were bustling about the kitchen, attending to their duties. Ricardo watched the operation for an instant without speaking, but before long he exclaimed with signs of astonishment,

"What an extraordinary thing! what an extraordinary thing!"

The maidservants turned their heads around. Marta likewise looked up.

"Why, what's the matter?"

"But, child, where did you get those plump arms of yours?"

The young girl blushed, and half laughing, half vexed, raised her hand and pulled down her sleeve a little.

"Come! will you begin now? See here, I did not tell you that you might stay to behave like this."

"Then I deserve the punishment of staying, though you should demand the opposite."

"Well, do what you please, but let me work in peace."

"I will let you work, but I must say it never entered into my calculations that the Señorita Marta had such arms. I knew that she was pretty, comely, round, and solid—but how could I suspect such a thing?—Come now, I tell you that no one would believe it without the evidence of his eyes."

The servants laughed. Marta went on industriously kneading her dough, making a gesture of resignation as one who has made up her mind to endure a jest to the end. Ricardo kept on:

"And that, too, though I have heard Maria speak of them—but vaguely. Her information wasn't definite. The best way in these matters, if one wants to know about a thing, is to see for himself. - Look here, lassie, supposing one were to quarrel with you, I wouldn't answer for the consequences! And the beauty of it is, that their strength doesn't injure their elegance; they are muscular but well-shaped. They taper gracefully down to the wrist, which is slender and dainty. The truth is, that all things considered, a girl only fourteen has no right to have such arms as those!"

Marta suspended her work and burst into a merry peal of laughter.

"What a plague you are, Ricardo! there's no resisting you!"

Then her face once more resumed the placid, grave expression which characterized it, and she resumed her work, plunging again and again her firm, rosy fists into the pliant dough. The paste kept taking different forms under the steady pressure of the girl's small but strong hands. Sometimes it made a thick, short roll or cylinder, which, little by little, as it was worked over the table, kept growing longer and slenderer; again, it assumed the fashion of a great ball, the roundness of which Marta brought carefully to greater and greater perfection, until she suddenly fell upon it with both hands and flattened it out; at other times it presented the appearance of a thin sheet taking up half of the surface of the table, and which kept spreading more and more, until she began to double it over with repeated folds as one does with a garment; again, she built it up like a pyramid on the slopes of which the graceful little baker bestowed soft pats, as though she were caressing it, but not hesitating fiercely to beat it in pieces in order to give it immediately some new and capricious figure. When it seemed to her that the paste was sufficiently kneaded, she cut it into a number of lumps with a knife, and taking a wooden rolling-pin, she began to shape them with great care. Ricardo asked timidly,

"Will you let me help you, Martita?"

"You don't know how."

"You can tell me what to do, and under your direction it will go first-rate."

"Now, you flatter me! All right. I'm willing; but you must wash your hands first."

Nothing was left for Ricardo but to go and wash his hands.

"That's good. Now take this rolling-pin and flatten out this lump of dough till you make it into a thin, round piece."

The new baker applied himself to his work with ardor; with too much ardor, for the dough was sometimes rolled so extremely thin that it was nothing but holes. The servants looked on with broad smiles of admiration, while Marta kept gravely intent upon her task. In the kitchen the atmosphere was suffocating, as it was heated by the red-hot iron covers of the oven, and impregnated with the heavy odors of cooking viands, which disturb and revolt the stomach when it is surfeited, but excite and stimulate it when it is empty.

Ricardo could not keep his tongue still a single instant. While he was passing the rolling-pin over the dough with greater circumspection than if he had been engaged in preparing a magic philter, he did not cease to ask questions and make remarks of all sorts to Marta, principally in regard to the pie which they had undertaken to make: "How many eggs did you put in the flour? How much lard? Who taught you to make pies? How long does it have to stay in the oven?" etc., etc. Marta gave laconic answers, and did not lift her face to all his questions, allowing a vague smile of condescending superiority to hover over her lips.

"Aye! Marta, what would Manolito Lopez say, if he were to see us at this moment?"

"What has he to say? It's nothing to him," replied the girl, slightly blushing.

"Wouldn't he be jealous, to see us so near together?"

"Why?"

"Oh, I know! I know he's in love with you, according to what they say."

"Why do you wish to plague me so?"

"Lassie, everybody is talking about it; it's no invention of mine."

"Very well; then keep it up, as you say."

"I will, so far as I see it."

"Come, don't be foolish!"

Marta's tone in saying this showed some signs of vexation. It was evident that she did not quite relish the joke.
Ricardo's ground for making it was slight enough, as is
almost always the case with children; but it was true to a
certain degree. Little urchins of fourteen or fifteen,
called, in popular language, *pipiolos,* run after the small
girls of the same age; and they establish, for the most
part tacitly, certain relations with them which resemble or
imitate the love affairs of their seniors. It is said for
example, among them that Fulanito is Fulanita's sweetheart, without any reason why; and Fulanito, merely from
this fact, without Fulanita meaning much to him, goes to
wait for her, with other friends, at the schoolroom door,
and follows her home, greatly to the vexation of the tend-
ing maid; at the little parties which are given from house
to house he takes her out to dance more frequently than
the others.

If he be somewhat daring, he is apt to offer her candy
in cones of gilt paper; and he passes in front of her
house several times a day, when he begins to wear new
clothes or a new hat; he manages, when he walks behind
her, to speak loud and distinctly for her to hear, and plumes
himself on his clever talk; and he is quick to roll up his
sleeves for the most insignificant thing, so as to exhibit in
her presence a boldness and courage which he would not
have if she were absent; he spends the pennies which he
possesses on pomade or scented oil, and comes to mass
when she is present, his hair brushed and as shiny as a
cat just out of water; in the afternoon, when his heart is
sore because she does not take any notice of him, he follows behind her with some of his friends, indulging in
naughty words and stupid laughter; and sometimes, coming close up to her, he pulls her by the hair-ribbon,
until, with these and other trickeries, he succeeds in
making her cry.

Fulanita's conduct is generally of a piece. In reality she doesn't care a fig for Fulanito; but as they say he is her sweetheart, she does all she can to carry out the idea, and so she keeps turning her head to look for him when she comes out of school; at the german she selects him as a partner more times than the others; she hurries to the window when he passes, and blushes when they joke her about him. But these pseudo-affections are almost never lasting, and rarely become real. They begin silently, they live their day silently, and silently they pass away when the girl puts on long dresses. The reason for such fickleness is very obvious. Fulanito has as yet attained the age, not of love affairs but of the gymnasium, *suspensos,* and sage cigars. Fulanita is already far more perfectly developed as far as the life of the heart is concerned, and in her inmost soul she has a profound scorn for Fulanito, who does not know how to descant on affinity and love, is incapable of kissing a fan fallen from the hand, and hasn't a sign of a mustache.

Of this sort, though with slight variations, was our Marta's friendship with Manolito Lopez. To the general causes which tend to wither and nip in the bud such predilections must be added in this case the very slight similarity of their characters. Manolito, though he had an expressive and even handsome face, was mischievous, obstreperous, quarrelsome, and saucy; one good quality was observable in him: he was not inclined to be spiteful. Marta was placid, taciturn, and reserved; the fault which they found with her at home was that she was somewhat obstinate. It was not possible, therefore, to have a more complete antithesis. If this had not been so, Marta would have come to love Manolito, for her temperament was opposed to change not only in the furniture of her room, but in the sentiments of her heart.

When they had finished molding various thin covers of pastry, Marta went to work to put some of them on top of others in copper baking-dishes, which made the bottom of the pie. Then one of the maids put in the pork, neatly

trimmed and cut into small bits. The lard, well seasoned
with spices, exhaled a stimulating, appetizing odor, which
made the mouth water. When once the bits were laid on
the bottom crust in the most accurate order, the girl went
to spreading new covers of pastry which she laid over the
pork. Ricardo no longer helped her; he was evidently
tired of it. But when it came to making the ornaments for
the top, he once more hastened to offer his services, and
he took great delight in designing in the dough a thousand
kinds of mosaics, arabesques, and figures of every species
that was ever seen. Marta put an end to such dilettante
labors by taking the pastry from his hand, for he was never
done. When the pie was made, the girl herself put it in
the oven, and following a pious custom traditional in that
part of the country, she made the sign of the cross over it,
and repeated a *Pater Noster* so as to obtain a happy
result.

" Do you know one thing, Martita? "

" What is that? "

" That kitchen odors and the labor on these pies have
given me an abnormal appetite! "

" Really? "

" It's the honest truth! "

" Then something to eat will cure it. Come with me."

She drew him to the dining-room near by and seated
him at the table. Then she took out of a sideboard a nap-
kin, bread, wine, a plate of cold turkey, and a jar of pre-
serves, and put them down one after the other with the
carefulness and system which characterized all her movements.

" Eat, Señor Marqués, eat."

To call Ricardo " Señor Marqués " was one of the most
audacious jests which Marta allowed herself to indulge in
toward her future brother. It was not in accordance with
her nature to make jokes and epigrams about anyone.
Those that occasionally came from her lips were meant to
disguise a tenderness which her reserved nature prevented
her from showing openly to anyone, even to her own sister.

Ricardo proceeded to despatch a slice of turkey with all solemnity, occasionally washing it down with draughts of Valdepeñas, while the girl, smiling and happy, stood enjoying her friend's voracious appetite, and looking out to fill his glass with wine and change his plate when there was need.

"You are a fine woman, Martita," said Ricardo, with his mouth full. "You're worth your weight in gold, and certainly you would not weigh a little, judging by the signs which I won't mention for fear you would call me a bore. When I see Manolito Lopez, I shall tell him not to think of any other woman if he wants to get fat and plump; and that's what he very much needs. If you take such good care of me, what care you would take of him! That's enough, that's enough, Martita! don't give me so much preserve. One would think that you wanted to give me dyspepsia here, on the sly. This turkey is excellent; it deserves the honors which I have done it; a little more wine, please!"

Marta poured out the wine, and looked at him out of her great, calm eyes, in which gleamed an evanescent smile of comfortable satisfaction. It seemed as if it were she who was feasting.

"See here, lassie! do me the favor to eat something too, because it grieves me to see you so abstemious. I should think you were being punished."

The girl was not hungry, and she refused to take the plate which Ricardo offered her. However, she cut a small piece of bread, and began to devour it solemnly with her little white teeth.

"I prophesy that it won't be long before you dispose of this saucer of preserve, Martita. The thing is to begin. The worst of it is, it's now twelve o'clock, and at dinnertime I shan't have any appetite. Yet I don't know how far that's certain, for my stomach is a good one! Martita, don't be foolish, but eat this preserve, which you will find appetizing."

While Ricardo was bringing his task of feasting and

chattering to an end, Genoveva came into the dining-room,
saying,

"The Señorita Maria has a little headache and is resting
in her room."

"I'll go to her," cried Marta, hurrying away.

"And I bring you this message from her, señorito,"
added the maid, handing him a note.

But seeing that the young man was about to break the
seal, she said,

"The señorita wanted you not to read it till after you
had left the house."

"Very good," muttered Ricardo, somewhat disturbed.

And taking his hat, and without saying farewell to anyone, he hurried home devoured by impatience, and tearing
open the envelope with trembling hand, he read the following letter:

"Mio queridisimo Ricardo,—

"For some time I have been anxious to tell you a thought
that has filled my mind, but I have not had the courage.
I know your nature well: you are extremely impetuous,
and thus many times, instead of reflecting on my words and
trying to understand their meaning, you would flare up like
gunpowder, spoil everything, and frighten me terribly, as
on the evening when we celebrated mamma's fête-day.
Accordingly, after much vacillation, I have decided to tell
you by letter and not by word of mouth.

"The thought that disturbs me of late is to ask you to
postpone our wedding still a little longer. Don't get angry,
Ricardo mio, and read on calmly. I am sure that the first
thought that will occur to your mind is that I don't love
you. How mistaken you would be to think such a thing!
If you could read in my soul, you would see that love holds
my conscience in its sway, and this I deplore bitterly. But
that is not the question now.

"Are you sure, Ricardo, that you and I are properly
trained to enter upon a state which entails so many and
such serious responsibilities? Have you thought well of

what the sacrament of marriage means? Is there not in our hearts rather an unreflecting inclination, mixed, perhaps, with carnal impulses, than a serious desire to undertake an austere, religious life, becoming in a Christian family, educating our children in the fear of God and in the practice of virtue? If you reflect a little on how frivolous hitherto our love has been, and on the sins which we are constantly committing, you cannot but agree with me that two young people, so wanting in gravity and genuine virtue, are not authorized by God to bring up and direct a family. I should feel a great smiting of the conscience if I were married now (and you ought to feel the same), and I believe that God could not bless or make our union happy. If it is to be blessed, we must make ourselves worthy of celebrating it, by leaving forever behind us our frivolous, worldly manner of loving, for another, more lofty and spiritual, by refraining absolutely from certain earthly manifestations to which we are impelled by our great love, and by making preparations for it, during a few months at least, by a virtuous and devout life, by performing a few sacrifices and works of charity, and by constantly imploring God to illumine our minds, and give us power to fulfil the duties imposed upon us by the new state.

"There is an example in history which ought to encourage us greatly in doing what I propose. The beloved Saint Isabel of Hungary had been betrothed from early youth to the Duke Luis of Thuringen, but the nuptials were not celebrated until both reached the proper age. After the betrothal was celebrated, Isabel and Luis did not separate, but lived in the same palace, as though they had been brother and sister, until, by the will of God, they became husband and wife. The pious sentiments of the lovers, together with the austere education which was given them, made their affection always pure and upright, founding the unchangeable union of their hearts, not on the ephemeral sentiments of a purely human attraction, but on a common faith and the stern observance of all the virtues inculcated by this faith. Until they were united by the indissoluble

bond of matrimony, they always called each other brother
and sister; and even after they were married, they frequently used to apply this sweet name to each other.

"I confess, Ricardo, that the spectacle of those noble and
holy young people has an unspeakable attraction for me.
Love sanctified in such a way is a thousand times more
beautiful, and bestows upon the heart purer and loftier
pleasures. Why should we not follow, as far as possible,
the steps of that illustrious husband and wife, the pattern
of abnegation and tenderness, as well as of purity and
fidelity? Why should you not imitate, my beloved Ricardo,
the stern virtue of the young Duke of Thuringen, the noble-
ness and dignity of all his actions, the innocence and modesty of his soul, never found guilty of falsehood,—virtues
which in no respect were opposed to the valor and boldness
of which he always gave eminent proofs? For my part,
I promise you to imitate, according to the measure of my
feeble strength, the tenderness, the obedience, and the faith-
fulness of his saintly spouse Isabel, living subject to the
law of God, within the affection which I profess for you.

"This is what I propose to you, and desire to do. Don't
get angry, for God's sake, dear Ricardo. Reflect over what
I have just said, and you will see how right I am. Doubt
not that I love you much, much,—I, who am, for the time
being,

"Your sister,

"MARIA."

CHAPTER V

THE ROAD TO PERFECTION

THE letter which we have just read led to a very important crisis in the lives of our lovers. Ricardo at first
was furious, and wrote a long answer to his betrothed, announcing the end of their acquaintance, but he did not
send it. Then he held a consultation with her in which

he overwhelmed her with recriminations and insults, saying that all she had written in her letter was nothing but a tissue of follies and absurdities, manufactured on purpose to hide her treachery; that she might have dismissed him in some way not so grotesque; that although he had no claim upon her love, at least he might and ought to demand the frankness and loyalty which he had always shown; that for a long time back he had noticed her coldness and indifference, but he could never have believed that she would make use of a pretext so ridiculous and so absurd for breaking the tie that united them, etc., etc. Maria received this storm of contumely with great humility, assuring him with gentle words of persuasion, when he left her a moment's chance to speak, that she still loved him with all her soul; that he might put her love to the test as often as he pleased, since she was ready to make whatever sacrifice he demanded, except what went against her conscience; that his suspicions of her untruth and treachery cut her to the heart, but she forgave him because she was aware of his excited state of mind; that she likewise felt it keenly that he should call the motives of her resolution grotesque and ridiculous when she found them so worthy; and, in fine, that she begged him to calm himself.

After the young marquis had thoroughly vented his ill-feeling without result, he began to get off his high horse and try the effect of skilful reasoning, and then he changed to entreaties, but without any better results. He employed all the devices of genius and all the tender and expressive words dictated by his honorable heart, in order to convince her that neither of them was fortunately under the necessity of mourning for their sins like two criminals; since if they were not better than the average of humanity, they were at least as good; and as for their skill and judgment in governing themselves and their children in matrimony, he believed that they were no less fitted than the rest, and that in the end they would come out as well as other people. All was useless. The young woman met argument with argument, and her lover's prayers, sprinkled with endearments, with a firm and obstinate silence. Ricardo, in a state of tribulation which Father Rivadeneira does not take account of as a matter of merit in his treatise, went straight to Don Mariano, whom he loved like a father, to tell him the state of things, and ask his aid and advice. The latter was highly surprised and disturbed when he read his daughter's letter. He read it over many times as though he could not get the key of it, and at each new reading he found it more obscure and inexplicable. Finally he handed it back with a gesture of dismay, signifying that his daughter must have lost her wits, for he could not understand any such nonsense.

In point of fact, Don Mariano was a sincere believer, fulfilling scrupulously the moral precepts of religion, but he looked upon the things which relate to worship with some coolness, if not with scorn. He had never doubted the religious truths learned in his childhood, but he had never made much account of masses and sermons, and he never went to church more than was strictly necessary. He could make a distinction, when these subjects were up for discussion, between religion and the priests, professing for these latter a decided Voltairian hostility, which came from inheritance, according to Doña Gertrudis, since his grandfather, the Mexican, had kept up friendly relations and a voluminous correspondence with a member of the French Convention. He had an insuperable faith in modern progress, and he made use of the inventions constantly realized by human industry, in order to combat and crush the fragile arguments of his constant enemies, the partisans of tradition, among whom not the least obstinate and vexatious was his wife. If, for example, a telegram from any relation or friend was received in the house, Don Mariano, after reading it, would hold it out to his wife with a triumphal smile, saying,

" Here, this miserable modern invention brings us word that your brother has reached Paris safely."

He delighted in making humorous conjectures on the fright that would seize our forefathers if they were suddenly put in a railroad car, or were told that they could communicate whenever they pleased with a friend residing in Havana. Whenever he found in the papers a notice of any wonderful invention, the audacious man hastened to read it to his wife, and he kept the paper so as to read it also to the many conservatives who frequented his house. If the invention was not costly, he had the machine sent him, although it was not of the slightest use to him; and so he kept the house stored with curious manufactures, almost all of them covered with dust, and out of order by want of use,—ice-making machines, churns, cider-mills, organs, etc., parlor telegraphs, stereopticons, pans for cooking meat with a piece of paper, life-preservers, canes with chairs and guns, waterproof umbrellas with tent arrangement, and an array of other strange articles. When the machine did not work, Don Mariano was disgusted and felt humiliated, and fearing lest the glory of modern science should be diminished in consequence, he did not speak of the apparatus before his señora; or if he were obliged to do so, he escaped the difficulty on a tangent, as he used to say, by always attributing the unfortunate result to his own stupidity, and not the quality of the machine. This eager love which he professed for the incredible advances of the present age, and the struggle which he waged both in his house and out of it with the friends of tradition, occasionally impelled him to employ forbidden weapons, as for example to exaggerate the power of modern industry, giving fictitious accounts of the beginning of stupendous new enterprises which had never as yet entered into the mind of man.

One day he startled his friends by assuring them that it was seriously intended to establish a floating bridge between Europe and America, over which one could travel by rail to the New World; another time he astonished them by declaring that a telescope was in construction, which would bring the moon within half a league of the earth, so that we could discover whether that satellite had inhabitants. Again, he filled them with wonder by informing

MARTA AND MARIA

them that in the United States a whole cathedral had been
moved at once from one town to another by means of
hydraulic pressure. In regard to mechanical advances,
Don Mariano had more imagination than Shakspere.
National politics engaged his attention little in comparison
with the incessant and sublime progress realized by humanity, and he detested the exaggerations which in his view
tended to hinder it. His affiliations were with the liberal-
conservative party.

With these peculiarities, it is easy to imagine the effect
made upon him by his daughter's letter. He looked upon
it as one of those many extravagant hobbies which she
had passed through in her life, and he solemnly promised
Ricardo to make her desist from such folly. But after he
had called her to his room and spent about two hours
closeted with her, he began to suspect that the thing was
not so easy as it appeared at first sight. Neither by turning her austere plan into ridicule by his jests, nor by showing that he was annoyed, nor by descending to entreaties,
was our worthy *caballero* able to accomplish anything.
Maria met these attacks like her lover's, with a humble but
resolute attitude impossible to overcome. No other way
was left them but to resign themselves, and this they both
did perforce with the secret hope that the girl would very
soon change of her own accord when once her caprice was
satisfied. Accordingly the wedding was indefinitely post-
poned, and poor Ricardo began to play his part as Duke
of Thuringen almost as ill as a Spanish actor.

From that time forth his interviews with Maria became
less frequent and familiar. The girl seemed to shun him
and to avoid opportunities of talking confidentially with
him as she used. Ricardo eagerly sought them, sometimes
employing them in bitter expostulations, at others in softly
whispering a thousand passionate phrases. She always
appeared sweet and affectionate, but endeavored to turn
the conversation to serious subjects. Ricardo still caressed
her whenever he had an opportunity, but he no longer
obtained from her the usual reciprocation in spite of the

incredible efforts which he made to obtain it. And not only he did not obtain this grace, but little by little the girl came to avoid his familiarities by always talking with him in the presence of others. One day when he found her alone in the dining-room, he said to himself with inward delight, "She is mine." And creeping up behind her carefully, he gave her a ringing kiss on her neck. Maria sprang suddenly from her chair and said, with a certain sweetness not free from severity,

"Ricardo, don't do that again!"

"Why not?"

"Because I don't like it."

"How long since?"

"I never did; don't be foolish." She said these words with asperity, and another unpleasant stage in Ricardo's love was signalized. Almost absolutely ceased those happy moments of fond raptures, sweet and delicious as the pleasures of the angels in which the poesy of spirit and matter is indistinguishable, the prospect of which kindles and stirs the deepest roots of our being, and their remembrance throws over all our lives, even for the most prosaic of men, a vague and poetic melancholy helping us to endure the rebuffs of existence and to contemplate without envy the felicity of others. The most that the young marquis obtained grudgingly from his sweetheart was the permission to give her a brotherly kiss on the forehead from time to time. And there is no need of telling my experienced readers, for they must be able to imagine it, that with this enforced fast the young man's love far from growing less, increased and became violent beyond all power of words

Maria was able fully to devote herself to the life of perfection toward which she had felt such vehement aspiration. The hours of the day seemed to her too few for her prayers, both at church and at home, and for the repentance of her sins. She attended the sacraments more and more, and she was present and assisted with her sympathy and money in all the religious solemnities which were celebrated in the town. The time left free from her prayers she spent in reading books of devotion, which, in a short time, formed a library almost as numerous as her novels. The lives of the saints pleased her above all, and she soon devoured a multitude of them, paying most attention, as was logical, to the lives of those who reached the greatest glory and brought the greatest splendor to the Church,—the life of Saint Teresa, that of Saint Catarina of Siena, of Saint Gertrudis, of Saint Isabel, Saint Eulalia, Saint Monica, and many others who, without having been canonized, were celebrated for their piety and for the spiritual graces which God bestowed upon them, like the holy Margarita of Alacoque, Mademoiselle de Melun, and others. These works made a very profound impression on our young lady's ardent and enthusiastic mind, driving her farther and farther along the road to perfection. The incredible and marvelous powers of those heroic souls, who, through love and charity, succeeded in lifting themselves to heaven, and in enjoying through anticipation, while still on earth, the delights reserved for the blessed, filled her with deep, fervent admiration. She felt an ecstasy over the most insignificant incidents in the lives of the saints, where God often showed them that He held them as His chosen ones, and would not let the world entice them away, as, for example, the scene of the miraculous toad which Saint Teresa saw talking in the garden with a *caballero* toward whom she felt a drawing; the sudden death of Buenaventura, Saint Catalina's sister, who was leading that holy woman along the worldly path of bodily adornments and pleasures; and many others which filled the books aforesaid. Maria regarded these notable heroines of religion with the same emotion and astonishment as one regards the phenomena and marvels of Nature. A long time passed before she dared to lift her eyes toward them in the way of imitation; she contented herself with beseeching them, through interminable prayers, to intercede with God to pardon her sins. She bought the finest effigies that she found and, when she had caused them to be richly framed, she hung them up on the walls of her room. To do this she had to take down Malec-Kadel and many other warriors of the Middle Ages which had invaded them. She was especially carried away by the scenes of their infancy, and by the first steps which these blessed women had taken along the road to perfection; but when she reached that part of their lives which marked the apogee of their glory on earth, when God, overcome by their steadfast love, their fidelity, and the wonderful penances imposed upon themselves, began to grant them favors and spiritual gifts by means of ecstasies and visions, she remained somewhat disturbed and even cast down. She did not as yet comprehend the mystic delight of direct communication through the senses between the soul and God, and she confessed with great compunction that if one of these miraculous visions were to be vouchsafed her, she should feel much greater fear than pleasure.

Nevertheless, before long, the desire to imitate them sprang up in her heart. It is always a short step from admiration to imitation. She began where it was proper, that is, by imitating their humility. Hitherto she had been modest, but not to such a degree as not to enjoy being flattered and applauded; but from this time forth she not only carefully avoided all praise, but she repelled those who offered it, and even tried to hide her talents so as to give her friends no chance to praise her. She began to talk as little as possible with friends or members of the family, and to do on the instant whatever they asked her to, lamenting in her heart that they did not give her harsh commands. She managed to have the servants help her at table after all the rest, and always give her stale bread instead of fresh. To conquer the natural impulses of selfishness she showed those who had offended her more affability than others, and anyone had only to offend her pride more or less for her immediately to overwhelm them with attentions, as though she owed them gratitude. On the other hand, to those who, as she knew, loved and admired her, she took delight in seeming peevish, so that they might not think her better than she really was.

Having started out on this pious path, which has been traveled by all the saints for the glory of God and of the human race, since the virtue of humility raises man above his own nature, conquering the passions deepest rooted in the human heart, and, of all virtues is the one that best proves the power of the spirit, and inspires respect even in the most unbelieving of men; having started out, I say on this pious path, and being aided by vivid imagination, she performed a number of strange deeds, well-nigh incomprehensible to those whose attention is turned to the world and not to religious things, deeds which the illustrious biographers of Saint Isabel call *secret and holy fancies,* serving as the mystic steps whereby the soul mounts to perfection and communicates with God. One day, for example, it came into her mind to eat humbly with the servants as though she were one of them. In order to do this, when dinner-time came, she pretended to have a headache, and kept in her chamber; but when the family were gathered in the dining-room, she softly ran downstairs to the kitchen, and there she stayed all through the dinner-hour, helping herself to the remains of the food, to the surprise and admiration of the servants. Another day, when it seemed to her that she had not answered her father with sufficient respect, she suddenly presented herself in his office, fell on her knees, and begged his pardon. Don Mariano lifted her from the floor, with startled eyes:

" But, my daughter, suppose you have not offended me or committed any fault? And even if you had, there is no need of going to these extremes. What nonsense! Come, give me a kiss, and go and sew with your sister, and don't frighten me again with such absurdities! "

Maria did not meet with the contrarieties in the bosom of her family that she would have liked, in the way of test. Her father and sister, though they did not encourage her in her devotions, said nothing to oppose her; and each day they showed her more and more affection, which was the natural consequence of the growing sweetness and gentleness of her character. Her mother adored her with foolish frenzy, blindly applauded all her acts of piety, and never wearied of praising to the skies the virtue and talent of her first-born. The servants, and particularly Genoveva, likewise joined their voices in a chorus of flatteries, spreading all over town the fame of her virtues, and crowning her with a halo of respect and sanctity. As far as such things influenced her salvation, our maiden would have preferred a cruel, tyrannical father, who laid harsh commands upon her, or a disagreeable mother or an envious sister, who would not let her live in peace, since, according to the biographies which she read, no saint had been free from suffering persecutions in her own family. She grieved inwardly at the ease and comfort which she enjoyed at home, and she thought that she suffered nothing for the God who had redeemed us with His blood. She would have liked it had a calumny been breathed about her, such as Palmerina caused Saint Catalina of Siena to suffer, so that she might be scorned and maltreated; but no one in the house or out of it dreamed of doing such a thing.

To compensate for this absence of persecutions, she mortified her flesh with fasting and penances, always performing those which were most unpleasant to her. Some dish on the table was distasteful to her; then she imposed upon herself the penance of eating it, leaving others, of which she was extremely fond, untouched. She went so far as to put aloes in some, in imitation of what was done by Saint Nicolas of Tolentino. On Fridays she fasted rigorously on bread and water, performing miracles of shrewdness to prevent her father from discovering it; for she felt certain that if he knew it, he would not give his consent.

She always wore a locket around her neck, containing the picture of her betrothed. One day, when he had suc-

ceeded in having a moment's conversation alone with her,
she said to him,

" Listen, Ricardo; if you would not be vexed, I would
tell you something."

" What is it?" hastily asked the young man, with the
sudden alarm of one who is always afraid of some misfortune.

" I see that I am going to offend you—but I will tell you.
I have taken your picture out of the locket."

Ricardo's face expressed amazement.

" And the worst is, that I have put another in its place."

The expression of amazement changed into one of such
pain, that Maria, on looking in his contracted and grief-
stricken face, could not refrain from breaking out into a
fresh, ringing peal of merry laughter, such as in former
times used to ripple from her lips all the time, and which
little by little had decreased, as though the fire of light
and joy from which they came had died down.

" Good heavens! what a long face! Wait! Now I'll
show your substitute, so as to make you suffer more."

. And taking the locket from her neck she showed it to
him. It held the effigy of Jesus crowned with thorns.
Ricardo, half satisfied and half vexed, answered with a
smile.

" Now kiss it!"

The young man obeyed instantly, placing his lips on
the picture of the Lord, and at the same time touching the
rosy fingers that held it out to him. Maria withdrew them
and ran away.

Equally as she schooled herself in humility, so she gave
much heed to that other virtue, which is, so to speak, the
foundation of our religion and the chief crown of glory
that the creature can offer to God,—the virtue of charity.
Our maiden's excellent heart and the example of her parents were sufficient reason for her to alleviate as far as
possible the miseries of her neighbors, but besides this there
was now the continual inducement in the incredible powers
of abnegation and charity shown by the saints, whom she

175

worshipped with the greatest fervor, particularly the holy Duchess of Thuringen, who bore the name of Mother of the Poor. And so she visited her compassion on all the wretched, and lost no opportunity to supply their needs with lavish hand. All the money which her father gave her she employed in almsgiving. In company with Genoveva she visited the houses of many poor people, whom she assisted not only with money but also with words of counsel, on the ground that man lives not by bread alone. In order to school herself in humility in the same way that was practiced by Margaret, the sainted queen of Scotland, she had some beggars brought secretly to her room, and washed their feet with the greatest scrupulousness.

Each one of these pious deeds filled her with a holy inward joy such as she had never before experienced. She practiced the habit of never allowing any poor person who asked alms to go without receiving them, since in addition to the dictates of her heart she remembered the multitude of cases in which our Lord or the Virgin had appeared to many saints in the disguise of beggars. Her desire, mixed with fear, that something of this sort might happen in her case, impelled her to scrutinize with considerable care the faces of the poor. But as her own resources did not suffice for her attention to such numerous charities, she had to scheme in order to obtain money from her father, using a thousand innocent devices: one day asking it for a parasol, another for a clock, another for a case of scissors, etc., etc. She went to such extremes, however, that Don Mariano began to suspect the truth, and put a limit to his munificence. His daughter had impoverished him with the greatest innocence.

Carried away by her ardent charity, she likewise wanted to put herself to the test by caring for the sick; above all, for those who were suffering from disgusting diseases. She heard that a woman near her house was suffering from a sore breast, and she made the resolution to go every morning and dress it, and this she instantly put into practice; but at the very first visit, wishing to add what she had read

176

in the history of Saint Catalina, that is, wishing to kiss the sick woman's sore, the loathing and horror which overcame her were so great that she grew faint, became very ill, and Genoveva had to take her in her arms and carry her home.

The poor girl attributed her misfortune not to the feebleness of her stomach, but to her lack of virtue, and she applied herself with increased anxiety to better her life.

Genoveva took part in all these exercises of piety, but rather as her companion and confidential friend than as her maid. She aided her, oftentimes without understanding where she was going to stop, absolutely persuaded that she could not go on the wrong track, for she had blind faith in her señorita's discretion. It was not so much affection which she felt for her, as a species of idolatry in which were mingled admiration for her beauty, respect for her talent, and pride in having seen the birth of a prodigy in the creation of which she had had a share. Maria was unable to arouse in her the mystic enthusiasm which possessed herself, for Genoveva was not of an inflammable nature, and a supine ignorance shielded her from all sorts of enthusiasms; but she succeeded through her acts and religious discourses in awakening in her the fanaticism which is always dormant in the depths of vulgar, ignorant souls.

One night after Maria had retired from the family circle, and Genoveva had left the kitchen, they found themselves in the boudoir in the tower. Maria was reading by the light of her polished iron lamp, while Genoveva was seated in another chair in front of her, engaged in knitting stockings. They often spent an hour or two in this way before going to bed, since the señorita was accustomed of old to read till the small hours of the night.

She did not seem so absorbed in her reading as usual. She often laid the book on the table and remained a long while thoughtful, with her cheek resting in her hand. Then she took it up again, only to lay it down very hastily. She was nervous, judging by the creaking of the chair.

177

From time to time she fastened a long gaze on Genoveva in which gleamed a timid, restless desire and a sort of inner struggle with some thought preoccupying her. Genoveva, on the other hand, was more than ever absorbed in her stocking, doubtless mixing with her stitches a crowd of more or less philosophical considerations, which obliged her, from time to time, to lean forward towards her hands just as if she were asleep.

At last the señorita decided to break the silence.

"Genoveva, don't you want to read this passage from the life of Saint Isabel?" she asked, handing her the book.

"With all my heart, señorita."

"Look here where it says: 'When her husband.'"

Genoveva began to read the paragraph to herself, but very soon Maria interrupted her, saying,

"No, no; read it aloud!"

Whereupon she obeyed, reading what follows:-

"When her husband was absent, she spent the whole night watching with Jesus, the spouse of her soul. But the penances which the innocent young princess imposed upon herself were not limited to this alone. Under her most splendid garments she always wore a haircloth cilicium next her flesh. Every Friday she let herself be severely whipped in secret in memory of the dolorous passion of our Lord, and daily during Lent (in order, says a biographer, to requite the Lord in some measure for the punishment of the lash), coming thereafter to Court, her face full of joy and serenity. As time went on she carried this austerity into the small hours of the night, and entering into an apartment next the chamber where she slept with her husband, she caused her damsels to inflict a severe scourging upon her, thence returning to her husband's side more joyful and amiable than ever, having gained comfort from these severities practiced on herself and against her own weakness. Thus it was, as a contemporary poet says, she succeeded in drawing near to God and breaking the bonds of

the prison of the flesh like a brave warrior of the love of the Lord."

" That'll do; don't read any more. What do you think about it?"

" I have often read that same thing before."

" That's true; but what should you think if I decided to do the same?" she asked impetuously, like one who determines to propose something long thought about.

Genoveva stared at her with wide-open eyes, failing to understand her.

" Don't you understand?"

" No, señorita."

Maria got up, and throwing her arms around her neck, she whispered, her face aflame,

" I mean, silly one, that if you would be willing to do the office of Saint Isabel's damsels, I would imitate the saint tonight."

Genoveva vaguely understood, but still she asked,—

" What office?"

" Oh! you stupid and more than stupid, that of giving me a few blows with the lash in memory of those which our Lord received, and all the saints in example of him."

" Señorita, what are you saying? How did such a thing ever enter into your head?"

" It entered my head because I wish to mortify and humiliate myself at one and the same time. That is the true penance and the most pleasing in the eyes of the Lord, for the reason that he himself suffered it for us. I intended to inflict it upon myself, but I could not; and besides, it is not so efficacious as to suffer the humiliation of receiving it from the hands of another. And so you won't be willing to do this for me?"

" No, señorita, not for anything. I couldn't do it——"

" Why not, *tonta?* Don't you see that it is for my good? If I should fail of freeing myself from a few days of purgatory because you did not do what I ask you, wouldn't you feel remorse?"

" But, my heart's dove, how could you want me to mal-treat you even though it were for your good?"

" Why, you have nothing left but to do it because it is a vow, and I must fulfil it; you have helped me hitherto in the road to virtue. Don't abandon me when I least expect it. You won't, Genoveva? You won't, will you?"

" Señorita, for God's sake don't make me do this!"

" Come, Genoveva, I beg of you by the love that you bear me——"

" No! no! no! don't ask me to do it——"

" Come, you old darling, do this favor for me. You don't know how bad I shall feel if you don't do it. I shall believe that you have ceased to love me."

Maria exhausted all the resources of her genius to con-vince her. She sat on her lap and overwhelmed her with caresses; she fondled her, now getting vexed, now entreat-ing her, and always fixing her eyes upon her in a wheedling way impossible to resist. She was like a child asking for a forbidden toy. When she saw that her maid was soften-ing a little, or rather was very tired of refusing, she said, with fascinating volubility:—

" Truly, *tonta*, don't believe that it is a thing of such great consequence. A bad toothache is much worse, and you know that I have had them often enough. Your imag-ination makes you think that it is terrible, when in reality it is a trifling thing. It all comes from the fact that it isn't done nowadays because virtue is vanished from the world, but in the good old days of religion it was a common, every-day occurrence, and no one who claimed to be a good Chris-tian failed to perform this penance. Come, make up your mind to grant me this favor, and at the same time to do a good work. Wait a moment, I will find what we need."

And running to the bureau, she opened a drawer, and took out a scourge, a genuine scourge, with round wooden handle and leather cords. Then, all excited and nervous, with her cheeks on fire, she brought it to Genoveva, and thrust it into her hand. The maid took it mechanically, not knowing what she did. She was perfectly stupefied. The girl began to caress her again, encouraging her with persuasive accents; but she did not answer a word. Then the Señorita de Elorza, with trembling hand, began to unloose the blue silk dress which she wore. On her face glowed the excited, anxious joy of a caprice about to be gratified. Her eyes shone with unwonted light, hinting at keen, mysterious joys; her lips were dry, as one athirst; the violet circle around her eyes was larger than usual, and bright crimson spots burned in her cheeks. She breathed excitedly through her nostrils, which were more than ordinarily dilated. Her white, aristocratic hands, with their slender fingers and rosy nails, loosed with strange haste the buttons of her dress. With a quick movement she freed herself from it.

"You shall see; I have on only my chemise and under-waist. I am all ready."

In truth she took off, or rather tore off, her underwaist and a skirt or two, and was left only in her chemise. She stood an instant, glanced at the instrument in Genoveva's hand, and over her body ran a tremor of chill, of pleasure, of anguish, of terror, and of eagerness, all at once. In a low voice, changed by emotion, she said, "Papa must not know this."

And her linen chemise slipped down on her body, catching for an instant on her hips, and then falling slowly to the floor. She was now entirely naked. Genoveva looked at her with ecstatic eyes, and the girl felt somewhat abashed.

"You won't be angry with me, Genoveva?" she asked, smiling.

The serving woman could only say,

"Señorita, for God's sake!"

"The sooner, the better, for I shall get cold."

In this way she wished to bring still greater pressure to bear on her servant. With a nervous movement she snatched the scourge from her left hand, thrust it into her right; again threw her arms around her neck, and giving her a kiss, whispered very softly, in a joyous tone,

"You must ply it vigorously, for so I have promised God."

A violent trembling took possession of her body, as she said these words; but it was a delicious trembling, which penetrated to the very depths of her being. Then, taking Genoveva by the hand, she pulled her toward the table where the Saviour's image stood.

"Here it must be,—kneeling before our Lord."

Her voice choked in her throat. She was pale. She bent humbly before the image, rapidly made the sign of the cross, folded her hands over her breast, and turning her face toward her maid, said with a sweet smile,

"Now you can begin."

"Señorita, for God's sake!" exclaimed Genoveva, in perfect trepidation.

Through the señorita's eyes flashed a gleam of anger, which instantly died away; but she said, in a tone of considerable irritation:

"Do we believe in this? Obey me, and don't be obstinate."

The woman, overawed, and persuaded that she was aiding in a work of piety, obeyed, laying the scourge gently enough on the señorita's naked shoulders.

The first blows struck by the maid were so soft and gentle that they left no sign on that precious skin. But Maria was excited; she desired them to be heavier.

"No, not like that; but with force—but wait a moment; let me take off these jewels, which are out of place at such a moment."

And hastily she tore off all the rings from her fingers, pulled out her earrings, and laid the handful of gold and precious stones at the feet of Jesus. In that same way Saint Isabel, when she prayed in church, laid her ducal crown at the foot of the altar.

She resumed her humble posture, and Genoveva, seeing that there was no escape, began relentlessly to bruise her pious mistress's flesh. The lamp shed a soft, diffused light, bathing the little boudoir in subdued brilliancy; only as it touched the jewels lying at the Redeemer's feet, it broke into beautiful fleeting sparkles. The silence at this moment was absolute; not even the mournful voice of the wind in the casements was to be heard. The room breathed an atmosphere of mystery and seclusion, which enraptured Maria and filled her with an intoxicating pleasure. Her lovely body, bared, shuddered every time that the straps of the scourge curled around it with a pang not without voluptuous pleasure. She pressed her brow to the Redeemer's feet, breathing quickly and with a certain oppression, and she felt the blood beating in her temples with strange violence, while the light golden hair at the back of the neck rose slightly under the impulse of the emotion which filled her. From time to time her pale, trembling lips said softly,

" Go on, go on."

The lashes had already raised many rose-colored weals in her shining skin, and she did not ask for a truce. But at last the barbarous instrument brought a drop of blood. Genoveva could not restrain herself; she threw the scourge far from her, and hastened to embrace her señorita, covering her with caresses and begging her by the salvation of her soul not to make her do such an atrocious thing again. Maria consoled her, assuring her that the flagellation had hurt her very little; and now that her ardor was somewhat cooled, and her ascetic impulses calmed, she said good-night and went to her bedroom to lie down.

CHAPTER VI

IN SEARCH OF A CANARY

"I KNOW it's you, Ricardo; let me go!"

Ricardo did not reply.

" Come, let me go; you see I must hurry and carry the broth to mamma."

Ricardo still blinded her eyes from behind without saying a word.

"For pity's sake let me go, Ricardo! It isn't fair, after I have told you who you are."

"In punishment for your not taking the joke gracefully, I won't let you go," said Ricardo, still clasping her eyes.

"All right, then; I admit that it's perfectly fair."

"Ah, that's another thing! if you submit, I will let you go. But you must pay a forfeit."

Marta, as soon as she found herself free, ran behind him with uplifted broom, so that he could not get hold of her; thereupon she went back and again began her task of brushing up the dining-room. She had not dressed for the day. She wore a loose red gown somewhat the worse for wear, and her hair was put up in a white redicilla. But there was one very strange thing about this girl; in an old morning dress, sometimes even ripped, and with her hair in disorder, she was prettier than when she put on her fine clothes. It may have been because her peculiar style of beauty was not best brought out by rich and splendid dresses as her sister's was, or because she was not used to wearing them (for it was rare for her to put on those which were bought for her), so that she appeared awkward and constrained when she went out; but at all events, on the street and at the theater, Marta certainly attracted little attention, and remained entirely overshadowed by her sister's proud and splendid beauty. On the other hand, at home her graces were greatly increased; her motions were easy and unembarrassed; her eyes gained brilliancy and animation, and her whole body acquired a freedom which it lost as soon as she set foot in the street.

She swept without haste, firmly and easily, like one who always expects to finish in time, and she kept humming a march very softly. She had no voice for singing or any great love for music, and all the exertions of her teachers and her liking for study struggled with this lack of musical ability. The masterpieces of music, and even the *fantasias, réveries,* and nocturnes, which Maria played on the piano left her cold and incapable of understanding their worth. On the other hand, she confessed with shame that certain operatic airs and many popular songs delighted her. Another thing she did not confess, though it was no less true: the bands which sometimes accompany funerals, and are, as a general rule, of the very worst sort, composed almost entirely of brass instruments, moved her deeply, even to tears. She almost never sang, but she was apt to hum softly when she was doing any work as now. From time to time she stopped to take breath, leaning for a moment on her broom, and after brushing back one or two curls which fell on her forehead, she went on with her task.

Ricardo appeared again in the door.

" Martita, are you still vexed with me? "

" If I am," she replied, between a frown and a smile, " you had better make your escape, *señor marqués*, quick, before I dust you with the broomstick."

" But are you really vexed? "

" Certainly I am."

" Very well, then; I humbly ask your pardon," said Ricardo, getting down on his knees. " Give me all the blows you want, for I have no idea of moving."

" Come, get up, and don't be foolish! See how you are soiling your trousers! "

" Though I should soil the very collar of my shirt, I wouldn't move until you pardoned me! "

" What a boor you are, Ricardo! "

" Many thanks! "

" Will you get up, child? "

" No; not till you pardon me."

" You must be serious, Ricardo! "

" We will speak of that by and by. Do you pardon me? "

" Yes; bother! yes; get up! "

Ricardo arose, went up to Marta, and taking her by the arms and shaking her violently, exclaimed,

" How very pretty you are, little one! I don't wonder that Manolito—of course you understand me."

"This is a great way of trying to be serious!"

"I shall be in time. Don't you worry!"

"Very well; then let me have a chance to carry mamma's broth to her."

"Do you know, I have searched the whole house and not found a soul?"

"Mamma has not left her room yet, and papa and Maria are out."

"Maria is at church as usual, isn't she?"

"She only went to mass; she will be back soon."

"Of course," replied the young man, becoming suddenly serious and silent.

Marta finished her work under her future brother's grave and not very careful inspection.

"Will you wait for me? I'm coming right back."

Ricardo nodded assent; and while the girl was gone, he went to one of the balconied windows and began to drum with his fingers on the glass, casting a vacant, absent look at the neighboring houses.

Marta came hurrying in again.

"Come, go with me; I am going to put the linen away."

Ricardo followed the girl like a lamb into a bright room full of clothes-presses. It looked into the garden. In the center of it was a table on which stood a great basket heaped up with white clothes just from the wash.

"Will you help me take down this basket and put it there, near that clothes-press?"

"Why didn't you put it a little further off?"

The basket was a huge one, and it was a tug to carry it to the place designated: while they were carrying it, they got into such a frolic that more than once they had to set it down. Ricardo with his efforts grew very red in the face, and this made the girl laugh until she had no strength left. She rarely laughed; but when the flood-gates were opened, nobody could stop it. Ricardo, with his inclination to make fun, puffed out his cheeks and grew

186

·redder yet. All ill humor had completely disappeared. The basket made very little progress, and both stood bending over it and struggling with it, being unable to lift it an inch from the ground, the one shaking with laughter, and the other affecting a comic desperation.

" What a valiant soldier, to be vanquished by a basket of clothes! " exclaimed the girl, in the height of glee.

" I should like to see Prim or Espartero or even Napoleon himself here! This isn't a basket at all! There is linen enough here for an army ! "

" Let go, then! If you didn't make me laugh, I could lift it by myself."

After much laughter, and no little bantering, the basket reached its destination. Marta opened the clothes-press, from which came the distinctive, fresh, penetrating odor of fresh linen. The girl for several moments breathed it in with delight, while she was transferring the pieces from one shelf to another in order to make room for the clean clothes that she was going to put away. Then she started to call Carmen—one of the maids—to help her, but Ricardo asked timidly,

" Listen, child, couldn't I help to do it? "

" Oh! if you would like——"

" But it isn't for me to like. Pure gold though I were, *preciosa*, it is for you to command me, as queen and mistress."

" It won't do at all."

" It's no condescension on my part; you can put me to the test."

" Well, then, this time I command you to take the two corners of this sheet and stretch them out in that direction hard—not so hard, man, how you pull me! That's the way! that's the way! Now double it as I do—so—one corner over the other—good!—now stretch it out again— more, ever so much more—that's it! Now fold it again; pull it out once more! There, that'll do. Now come towards me,—let me have it; I can manage it now. Here's another. Take the two corners—shake it well and stretch

187

it out. Be careful, for this one has a ruffle—don't tear it!
These are mamma's and Maria's sheets."

"How it would shock Maria if she knew I were folding
her sheets!" cried Ricardo, laughing.

"Why, yes; the sheets themselves are shocked. Mamma
and she like very fine ones, and have theirs made of batiste;
but papa and I like them coarser. I can't bear fine sheets;
I slip about in them and can't get settled. We are careful
not to put any kind of ruffles on papa's, for the touch of
starch tries his nerves, and the rustling keeps him awake.
It's a hobby of his. Just imagine when he is traveling,
· and at some house they put on sheets with trimmings, he
takes the trouble to pull the bed to pieces and put the ruf-
fling under the mattress at his feet. I don't like them
either, but if I find them on, I put up with them. Papa has
a good many hobbies. Every night he has to go asleep with
a cigar in his mouth. I walk up and down near his room
until I see that he is asleep, and then I go in very gently
and take the cigar from his mouth and put out the light.
Don't pull so hard, for my arms ache already. The truth
is, I make you do very improper things for a military man;
isn't that so?"

"Don't you believe it! At college, and even after we
left, at boarding-houses we had to do much worse things.
How many buttons have I sewed on in my life? And
how many times I have patched my trousers when they
were worn through!"

"Really?"

"Certainly!"

Marta was sincerely astonished. She could not understand that a man should have to descend to such duties
when there are so many women in the world, and she
asked particularly about his college life,—how they were
treated, what they ate, at what time they went to bed, who
attended to their rooms, who did their washing and ironing, were their mattresses hard or soft, did they drink wine,
how many times a week they gave them clean towels, etc.,
etc. Ricardo answered all her questions, giving a circum-

stantial account of his college habits with the fulness of
one who has very fresh recollections, and is not bored in
recounting them.

From college customs he passed to his adventures, relating those which might be told to a young girl, and amusing
himself above all in painting in the darkest colors the tribulations of freshman year and the cruelties practiced upon
them by the seniors, who compelled them to spend whole
nights making cigarettes of sand so as to learn to make
better ones of tobacco; in the street they would make them
sit down on the stone seats and not let them get up till they
gave them permission; they seated them at table, even
though they had dined, just for the fun of the thing; those
who were weakest would vomit or faint; one fellow who
ventured to rebel against a *galonista* they kept for six
months face to face with a stone wall, during all play
hours, until he was taken ill with jaundice and almost died.
One Sunday afternoon, while he was in the hall with five
other freshmen reading a novel, two seniors came in and
beat them furiously with cudgels until they were tired out,
and gave him a painful cut near his eye.

Marta listened with profound attention, showing in her
face all the phases of indignation. She pulled with greater
and greater force on the sheets, and folded them any way,
without taking her eyes from the narrator's. From time to
time she exclaimed:

"But, good heavens, that is abominable! Those men
are crazy; why didn't you tell the president about such
cruelties?"

Ricardo could not persuade her that it would have been
useless to rebel or tell the colonel, since hazing was a
traditional custom in the college which the officers did not
care to root out. To all his reasonings she replied:

"Well, I would have gone to the colonel, and if he had
not made it right for me, I would have run away from
college."

"Come, don't be excited, Marta, over what I went
through. The men who suffer this way do the same thing.

189

TALES FROM THE SPANISH

Now I am going to tell you something that took place between me and the colonel. After I became lieutenant——"

And changing his tack, he began to tell amusing adventures and jolly incidents, which smoothed out the frowns on the girl's face, and finally made her laugh heartily. Gradually the basket was emptied, and its contents were transferred to the clothes-press, which still exhaled its fresh and somewhat pungent odor of newly washed clothes. This odor filled the whole room, and gave it a refreshing perfume of health and cleanliness pleasanter than any perfumery or pomade. It was the perfume which always clung about Marta, as her father said, and seemed especially created for her. When she went alone to open the cloth-presses, she took a great delight in putting her head into them, and burying it in the clothes, enjoying the coolness of the linen against her face, and breathing with keen pleasure its healthful aroma. The light pouring through the white tulle of the curtains, the ceaseless chatter and the merry laughter of the young people filled the room with joy and animation. It was called the "ironing-room," for all the linen of the house was ironed there. The walls not occupied by the clothes-presses were painted a plain white.

Carmen burst into the room like a hurricane, crying,

"Señorita Marta, Señorita Marta!"

"What's the matter?" asked Marta, in alarm.

"Menino has got out, señorita!"

Marta dropped the sheet which she had in her hands, and exclaimed in astonishment,

"Has got out?"

"Yes, señorita; as I was just going through the gallery, I looked at the cage and found the door open and the bird gone!"

"Come along, come along!"

And all three rushed to the gallery. Indeed, Menino had flown away. By an incredible piece of carelessness Marta, when she fed him and hung him up to enjoy the view of the garden and the singing of the other birds, had left the cage door open. For three years Menino had been under the young maiden's care, and during all this time he had showed no sign of cherishing plans of escape; on the contrary, hitherto the little hypocrite had always shown, as far as possible, that he did not care a straw for liberty, and that he had renounced it willingly for the sake of his dearly beloved mistress. For a long time he had been in the habit of coming out of his cage to eat chocolate with her. He would perch on her shoulder, peck softly at her hand to show his affection, hop about here and there over the furniture, and when it was time to retire, he would go back into the cage, meek as a lamb. By every presumption he was a happy canary, who regarded the loss of liberty as compensated by the care and attention of such a lovely girl, and by the permission to peck her rosy cheeks whenever he pleased.

And aside from these more or less spiritual enjoyments, for which more than one lad in the town would have made stupendous sacrifices, and looking only at the material aspect of existence or bodily comforts, it must be laid down as a fact that Menino lived in his cage like an archbishop, with every want satisfied, supplied with hemp-seed on one side, with canary-seed on the other, at one time treated to lettuce, at others to lumps of chocolate, at others to crumbs soaked in milk; indeed, to ask more was to offend God. And as for neatness and cleanliness of habitation, he had just as little cause for envying anyone. Every morning Marta herself cleaned it out, leaving the cage like a mirror. But contrary to the general belief that he found himself perfectly satisfied, and would not change places even with the director of the mint, Menino was certainly waiting impatiently for a chance to escape; he had allowed himself to be overwhelmed with melancholy, his character had been soured, and his bile excited by lack of exercise. If he had not gone out to breathe the fresh air on the day least expected, he would have dashed the top of his head against the bars of his cage.

As our young people stood under the cage, they deliberated briefly what to do. Marta was heart-broken. It was decided that Carmen, with the laundress and the gardener should scour the garden, for they thought that from lack of practice he would not fly very far at first; meanwhile Marta and Ricardo should make a thorough search through the house in case he had remained inside, flying through the halls as he had done once before. Marta acted as guide, and they immediately began to look through the suite of rooms next the corridor, a great square chamber with two sleeping-rooms leading from it, in which she and Maria, when they were children, had slept with their respective nurses.

Then they passed through several rooms designed for the guests who visited the house; they inspected the girls' rooms, they went down into the kitchen, which was in an entresol, and returned upstairs without any success. Then they visited Don Mariano's library, which was a magnificent room with two balconied windows facing the plaza, decorated in severe classic taste; great leather armchairs, rich tapestries, an ebony writing-desk, and bookcases of the same wood; on the walls hung a few family portraits, painted in oil. Marta always felt in this library a sensation of happiness and well-being which she did not enjoy in the other parts of the house. In this sensation there was a delicious union of reverence and tenderness wherein were blended all her childish recollections, which overflowed with this exclusive, eager, and absorbing love, such as cause the unreasonable anger of children when the nurse tears them from the paternal arms, and the yearning to go to them when they are held out to invite them. As soon as she had strength and skill enough to put his room in order, she never allowed anyone else to do it. In the morning she always spent half an hour of delicious ease and comfort, dusting the huge chairs, which cost her a great effort to move from their places, and making Don Mariano's huge bed. She felt happy in that solemn patriarchal chamber. The colossal bookcases, the table, the chairs, the pictures, and the dignified figures of the tapestries fixed on her a

silent, benevolent gaze in which she felt as it were alive,
her father's great, protecting shadow.

Ricardo halted lazily before a portrait.

"Is that your aunt? How much you resemble her!
What a pity she died so young! She was a very fascinating woman."

"I should like to resemble her. She was very tall, and
I am short."

"What difference does that make? You are like her,
very much like her. And that is natural, after all, for
you are like your father, and you are an Elorza from head
to foot. What huge bookcases Don Mariano has! there's
enough here to keep one busy a good while."

"Still, Maria has read the most of them."

"And you?"

"Oh, I don't read very much. I am very lazy," replied
the girl, with her frank smile, and looking a little ashamed;
then she added: "But look, Ricardo, it isn't absolutely
true, what papa says; though I don't care much for books,
some of them please me; but one doesn't get time to take
them up. I don't know how I manage not to have an hour
for myself. Sometimes it's one thing, sometimes another."

"Confess, little one, that you don't like them, and I
won't say any more!"

"If you like, I will confess it; but it isn't true. I like
some of them."

"How about Menino?"

"Aye! yes! come, come!"

They went to the next room, which was Doña Gertrudis's, and this alone was proof positive that no sign of
Menino was there, though occasionally she had in her head
such a singing, as of a whole nest of birds, that it prevented
her from resting. Therefore they went to the next room,
which was Marta's. It was a room which seemed lined
with mirrors, since everything in it was polished, from
the wooden floors to the railing of the balconies; whatever
was not varnished by the cabinet-maker was rubbed bright
with cloths. Marta's great hobby, which gave her the most

joy and the most trouble, was keeping things bright. Her exaggerated love for cleanliness had quickly brought her to the point of trying to put a shine on all the articles of furniture in the house, and more especially those in her own room. Every day, aided by the maid, she rubbed them with a dry flannel, polishing them with unwearied zeal, until you could see your face in them. Then, all out of breath, sometimes dripping with perspiration, her hair in disorder, and her cheeks ablaze, she lifted the flannel and stood awhile contemplating her work, the lovely scintillations made by the light in the polished surface, with a genuine inward satisfaction, with almost mystic enthusiasm. The household made much fun of her, which caused her to hide herself while performing this task, and induced her to lock her room to everybody. Ricardo had never been in it. And so without any thought of Menino he began to inspect it with bold, inquisitive attention; he gazed at the pictures, halted in front of the toilet-table, opened the bottles, felt of the curtains, and even went into the bedroom to see the bed, uttering exclamations of astonishment at the perfect order which he found everywhere, and especially at the wonderful polish of all the furniture.

"What a pretty room you have, child! It's like a silver cup! What a lovely white little bed!"

"Ricardo, don't be inquisitive. Go away; come, Menino isn't here!"

The girl felt annoyed by the young man's curiosity. Every woman of gentle birth feels a certain modesty, if we may say so, in regard to her room, for the reason that there clings about it something like the essence of her very self which she hesitates to let a man approach; but in Marta's case, in addition to this modesty, there was a sense of shame in having her stubborn, childish fancies brought to light, like that of keeping things bright, that of placing the bottles of her dressing-table in a sort of symmetry worthy of an altar, and other such things which served her family as subjects for merriment at dinner time. Consequently she tried to push him out by main force.

"Come, Ricardo; there's nothing to see here. Come along, come along!"

"Do let me, *niña,* do let me have a look at this charming room! How exquisite!" And putting his nose to the bed, he said with great seriousness, "It smells like Marta!"

"Will you be quiet, you foolish fellow?"

"It may not give you any trouble to keep your room in this way, but let me tell you, child, I couldn't keep it so if my life depended on it. If you were to see my room, Martita!"

"Yes, yes, it must be fine! You always were a disorderly fellow. But come, dear, come; let us go!"

"We'll go whenever you please. My room is a stable compared with this. But just consider that it's open to dogs and cats, the gardener, with his dirty feet, the coachman, with the smell of the stable, and, in fact, to every living creature. It is not my fault."

From Marta's room they passed through various other apartments, the dining-room, the parlor, the gallery of the court, another private room, and a few others, without finding Menino anywhere. As they were standing in the midst of a passage-way without knowing whither to turn, an idea suddenly struck Marta, and she said,

"Let's go to the terrace; we haven't been there yet."

The terrace was now only a large hall tiled with marble and covered over with stained glass. It was called the terrace because it had been one in former times; but Don Mariano had had it closed in with glass a few years before, transforming it into a handsome, fantastic room in Moorish style, where he went to drink coffee on summer evenings with his daughters and friends. It was for the most part unfurnished, having only in one corner three or four small marquetry tables and a few rocking-chairs. When our young people reached this hall, they found it flooded with light: the sun, that morning leaving his long seclusion, came forth bright and warm, resolved on visiting all the corners of the city; and when he found the thousand crystals of the Elorza terrace, not caring to see anything better, he passed through them and reveled inside with a lively eager pandiculation which occupied the whole circuit of the room. It was a magical sight. Thousands of rose, green, yellow, purple, gray, and blue lights burned within it, pouring over the floor, the ceiling, and the walls, and dissolving into an infinity of tints, delighting and dazzling the eyes. Over the mosaic pavement fell a shower of blinding rays, reflecting up in a delicate, many-colored vapor; and these rays were crossed and interwoven in the air, making a flame-bearing web, subtle and beautiful, through the interstices of which passed the intangible scintillations of other rays more diaphanous, from which arose a vapor still more aërial. And these veils of dust, of rays, of scintillations, and of colors, stretching one behind the other, in spite of their transparency scarcely allowed you to see with vague indefiniteness, as through a mist, the crystals and arabesques of the windows. The sun squandered his treasures of light and color like a Turkish pasha within the walls of some chamber in the East, proving once more that when he endeavors to make a brilliant and fanciful decoration with them, there is no stage director with all his spangles, bengolas, and curtains who can equal him.

Our young people, entirely forgetting Menino, stopped an instant in surprise at the whimsical, magical work of the light; and without saying a word they entered the hall and went to the center with the slow, uncertain step of one who goes into a bath. In point of fact they stood submerged and inundated in a luminous vapor wherein all possible colors were floating.

"How beautiful the terrace is today!" said Marta at last.

"It seems like a room in an enchanted palace. It would be more appropriate if, instead of us, a Moor in a white turban stood here, and an odalisque covered with brocade and precious stones. How many capricious effects of light! Wait a moment, Martita; step into this ray of rosy light. If you could see what a peculiar expression it gives your face now! You look like a gypsy,—a daughter of the desert."

Indeed, that light turned the girl's fair complexion to
brown, kindled it with a sunset tinge, and animated it with
the ardent, cruel expression of southern natures. All the
innocence of her eyes, all the purity of her maidenly form
were lost under the power of that perverse, luxuriant flame,
which transformed her into another being, fiery, and at the
same time voluptuous, and certainly far from her own
true nature. Ricardo understood this, and said,-

" No! that color does not suit you. Come into this one!"
And he drew her under a ray of greenish light.

"Heavens! you look like a dead person! No, no; that's
just as bad! Here, try the yellow color; that goes well,
but it makes you ruddy, and brunettes ought to stay brunettes,—I mean dark-haired people,—for of course we
know that your complexion is light; come, try the blue.
Oh, superb! wonderful! How beautiful you are, child!"

The young marquis was right. Blue, which is the most
spiritual, the purest, and the sublimest of colors, was admirably adapted for Marta's bright face. The sun-ray
fell on it like a caress from heaven, bathing it sweetly in
a diaphanous light. Her long black hair assumed a pur-
plish tint, while the adorable oval of her face and her firm,
mellow neck were softly tinged with a heavenly blue. The
delicate line of her regular features acquired an ideal perfection, and her whole countenance was transfigured with
an angelic expression of beatitude.

Nevertheless, there was a certain exaggeration not in
good taste in that rapturous, celestial expression given by
the blue light. It was not the true Marta, ingenuous and
modest in her looks as in her features, but a different
Marta, affected, theatrical, and fantastic. Ricardo finally
declared that no light was so becoming to her as the natural.

The girl suddenly exclaimed,-

" And Menino!"

" It's true; we had forgotten him. But where shall we
go now? we have looked everywhere."

" Let us go to Maria's room; perhaps he has flown up
there."

"It does not seem to me likely; however, let's go there."

They mounted to the tower, but without any better success; neither in Maria's room nor in Genoveva's did they find any sign of the canary-bird. Ricardo felt a peculiar emotion in entering his lady-love's room, and Marta did not fail to notice it. He became graver and more silent, and began to examine with interest everything there, moving the articles, opening the scent-bottles, and even pulling out the drawers, so that the girl felt obliged to interfere.

" Don't meddle with her things. When Maria comes and sees her things tumbled up, she will be angry."

" And what if she is? " replied the young man, with a touch of asperity.

" The blame will be thrown on me."

"All right; then tell her that it was mine, and that'll settle the matter."

He stepped into the bedroom, lifted the bed-curtains, took up the books from the dressing-table, laid them down again, and finally pulled out the table drawer. In it were a number of articles laid away, but he thrust in his hand, pulling out one more extraordinary than the rest. It was a large leather cross, full of brass brads on one side, and with a cord to attach it to the neck.

" What is this? " he asked, turning it over and over in his hand, with amazement.

Marta guessed what it was.

" Put it back, put it back! for God's sake, Ricardo! Maria will be very angry."

" Horrors! What an abominable thing! This must be a cilicium."

" It may be; but put it back, put it back for Heaven's sake! "

The young man threw it violently into the drawer again, with a gesture of scorn and disgust.

" Maria has become crazy. It is an abomination, and there's no good in it."

" Don't say that; it's wrong. Maria is very religious."

"Religious! religious!" muttered the young fellow, angrily. "So are you, and you don't have to perform these penances——"

"Don't compare me with Maria!"

Ricardo began to pace up and down the room excitedly and without speaking. Then he returned to the chamber, and pulled out the leather cross once more, examining it with more care.

"It seems to me that these nails form letters. Look! Can you make out what they say?"

"No; I don't see anything; it's your imagination."

"Yes, yes; there is an inscription on it. But, however, I don't care to bother with deciphering it. All these things are only absurdities. Come, child, come along! Let every fool have his folly!"

And shutting the drawer angrily he left the chamber, followed by Marta. As they were passing by one of the windows of the boudoir, the girl uttered a cry of surprise and joy.

"Look! look! Ricardo! Look! there's Menino!"

The young man hurried to the window, and saw, on the roof of the house, not very far away, Menino himself, hopping about with delight, and full of pride and stateliness.

"What a rascal! And so that's where he's gone! We must catch him. Where do you get out on the roof?"

"Not here; we must go down to the house first, and climb up through the skylight."

"Come on, then!"

They left the tower, and after crossing several rooms, they mounted the garret stairs leading from one of them. It was extremely dark, and the young man met with much difficulty. On the second step he received a tremendous knock.

"Oh, of course you aren't used to it. You'll hurt yourself; give me your hand and I'll guide you."

He took the girl's hand, which was small but firm and solid like an Amazon's. It was not so satiny as Maria's, for her work about the house had hardened it somewhat; in compensation it had the lovely smoothness which testifies to health and good blood. It was not feverish either like Maria's, but was always cool and moist and ready for any emergency, like the hand of a daughter of the people.

The young marquis did not think of making these observations, for he was going along, intent only on not falling. They reached the garret,—feebly lighted here and there by a few very tenuous rays of sunlight which filtered through the cracks in the tiles. After they had gone quite a distance, Marta dropped his hand, saying,

"Wait here; I am going to open the window."

And nimbly hurrying ahead, she ran up a half-dozen steps which led to the skylight, and threw open the door. A burst of intense, bright, comforting sunshine suddenly invaded the whole garret, dazzling our young hero.

"Here is Menino! Here's Menino!" cried Marta, enthusiastically, as she stood on the top step. He's very near! Menino! Menino! Come, *tonto*, here! here! Don't you know me?"

Menino, who was only six or eight steps away when he heard his mistress's voice, bent his head gracefully, as if to listen. The sunlight, falling full on him, bathed his yellow plumage, making him contrast so vividly with the red-colored roof that he seemed like a bit of living gold. He hopped three or four times, as though he were going to Marta, and said, *Pii, pii.*

"Do you want me to try to get him?" asked Ricardo.

"No; hold still a moment; he seems to be coming of his own accord. Menino, Menino! come here, pretty one; come here, come!"

Menino came two or three hops nearer, and seemed to be cocking his head to listen. What could then have passed through his brain? Something low, and base, and shameful, it must have been, according to the morality of his species, for, forgetting his mistress's tender attentions, her ceaseless caresses, the many bits of chocolate shared with her, the feasts of biscuits, and his overflowing dishes of canary-seed, he cleaned his feathers in her presence with perfect indifference, several times repeated his *pii, pii,* with affected laziness, and spreading his wings, he launched into space, flying out of sight amid the foliage of the neighboring gardens.

Marta uttered a cry of grief.

" My stars, he has gone! "

" Has gone? "

" Yes! "

" Very far? "

" Out of sight."

" Then, you may be sure, he's gone for good! "

Ricardo mounted to the window, and following the direction indicated by the girl's finger, he looked and looked again, until his eyes pained him, without seeing the slightest sign of anything resembling a canary-bird. When he looked at Marta again, he saw a tear rolling down her cheeks.

" Aren't you ashamed to cry for a bird, *tonta!* "

" You are right! " replied the girl, trying to laugh, and wiping away the tear with her handkerchief.

" But I felt as much affection for him as for a person. Yes, indeed, for three years I have been taking care of him! "

CHAPTER VII

HUSBAND OR SOUL

THE dew of grace kept falling copiously on the soul of the eldest daughter of the Elorzas. The Christian virtues flourished in her like mystical roses replete with fragrance, and with the impatience and ardor which characterized all her actions she continued to mount one by one the rounds on the ladder of perfection leading to heaven. Her deeds of charity and humility not only filled those who lived near her with astonishment, but were bruited about the whole town, serving as an edifying example for young and old, and as a theme of conversation among the clergy. Her fasts and penances, always growing more frequent and severe, increased the enthusiasm and seraphic joy of her soul; but at last they had a naturally weakening effect upon her health.

Her delicate constitution began to rebel against so much mortification of the flesh, and to protest at every instant by pains, sometimes in her heart, at others in her stomach, at others in her head, and yet she endured it all with enviable resignation, and did not let it discourage her saintly endeavors. She suffered frequently from fainting fits in which she remained long unconscious, and from severe convulsions; some days she could not retain the food that she ate, and on others she complained of acute headaches. Don Maximo began to prescribe preparations of iron, sea-baths, and wine of quinine, and this treatment brought about some improvement, but not much; the doctor finally declared that unless she entirely changed her mode of life, these attacks would not cease. But it was impossible to persuade her.

Maria began to notice with a secret pride, of which she tearfully accused herself to her father confessor, that she inspired admiration and something more than respect among the people; that when she went along the street, many saluted her with words of praise, and when she was at church, all the faithful gazed at her with peculiar persistence. Through the mouths of the servants many such flattering phrases came to her ears, as that her virtues were worthy of the most venerable priests and the most pious souls of the community, and, as she perceived a certain sweet savor in them, she forbade their being repeated to her. Many ladies consulted with her on matters concerning their consciences, and she was appointed teacher of a Sunday-school for adult women, to whom she began to explain the doctrine and moral precepts of Christianity with so much clearness and eloquence that nothing else was talked about. On the second Sunday the hall granted by the board of magistrates in an old convent was crowded not only with servants and working-girls, for whom the institution had been founded, but also with the most distinguished ladies in town, desirous of seeing for themselves what was reported of the young woman. And indeed they had to agree that she had decided gifts for teaching,—an artless, animated discourse, manners free from conceit and unwearied patience. The girls made notable progress under her direction. Not satisfied with this, she asked and obtained from her father permission to use a pavilion which he had in his garden, and there she gathered every day a dozen orphan children, whom she taught to read, write, and say their prayers, giving them an education suitable to their sex and social position. The extreme gentleness with which she treated her scholars soon won their love, and even their adoration.

From every side our virtuous heroine received unimpeachable evidence of the great regard in which she was held, but more especially in the society of the devout and saintly, among whom she was considered as a brilliant beacon kindled for the advantage of religion. In the age of unbelief, whereunto we have attained, the spectacle of such a beautiful, well-educated, and illustrious maiden, consecrating herself exclusively to the practice of the virtues and religious deeds, could not fail to have a deep influence on the morals of the town.

One morning, as she was leaving the steps of the altar, where she had just received holy communion, her face presented such a sanctified expression that a woman left the throng, and, kneeling before her, asked for her blessing. Maria, disturbed and perplexed, would have refused, but finally she had no other escape than by yielding to her entreaties. On another occasion, as she was going through one of the suburbs with Genoveva, a poor woman, who was standing at the door of a wretched hovel with a dying child in her arms, begged her to take him into hers and offer a *Pater Noster* for him; Maria did so to satisfy her, but protested that she was a miserable sinner, to whom God could not listen. The child, however, had scarcely felt the tender caress of her lovely hand before it began to smile, and in a few days was entirely restored to health. This miraculous cure, proclaimed by the grateful mother, made a great noise among the people; whereupon the house of Elorza was besieged by a throng of women who came with their sick children to ask Maria to take them in her arms and bless them. As this partook of the nature of wonder-working, according to report, Maria hastened to consult her confessor whether she ought to continue yielding to the entreaties of these afflicted mothers; and the priest, after taking a day to reflect, replied that he saw no harm in it, but, on the other hand, believed that it might redound to the advantage of the faith.

"How is it possible," asked Maria, "for God to be willing to perform miraculous deeds through the medium of such a low and sinful creature as I am?"

And the confessor replied that it showed great audacity to think of searching the high purposes of God, and that she should abstain from making such irreverent remarks; that God chose whomever He pleased to manifest His sacred will, and that, at all events, even though no miracle took place, it was never wrong to attribute to the power of the Almighty the blessings which we experience both in soul and body. Maria accepted this reasoning, and endeavored, by all the means at her command—by prayer, humility, and penance—to make herself worthy of these incredible favors which God gave into her hand.

Gradually, through the renunciation to which she was compelled by her pious life, all the ties that bound her soul to things earthly began to be relaxed. At first she shunned all worldly recreation and amusement, such as balls, theaters, and promenades, where she used to shine by her beauty and elegance, and she came to the point of abhorring them. Then she abstained from certain proper recreation, such as singing and playing secular music, taking part in games of cards, walking in the garden, being present at tertulias at her home; in her craze for crucifying the flesh, she went to the extreme of not gazing often at the landscape from the windows of her room, and of depriving herself of breathing the scent of the flowers and

the perfume of her colognes. Still, however, and for
some time, she took pleasure in dressing elegantly; this
arose from a reflection that she had read in a French de-
votional book, counseling young people not to neglect the
neatness and adornment of the body, since God took delight in seeing them beautiful and knowing that they
adorned themselves for Him alone. At the same time
that she grew more and more to hate the pleasures of
this world, she crushed out in her heart the sentiment of
love towards human beings, even towards those who were
nearest and dearest to her. Understanding that if one
would love God, he must free himself from earthly affections, since no other is worthy of entering into a heart
consecrated to the Creator, she constantly struggled against
her love not only for her betrothed but also that for her
parents and sister. She ceased those frequent outbursts
of affection which she used to lavish on them all and
which had always proved the tenderness of her affectionate
spirit; when she met her father in the morning, she no
longer threw her arms around his neck and covered him
with caresses; she no longer revealed to her sister the
secrets and sorrows of her heart; she kept everybody at a
distance by a cautious reserve veiled in sweetness and
humility. The Señorita de Elorza compelled herself to follow literally the solemn words of Jesus: "*If any man come
to me, and hate not his father, and mother, and wife, and
children, and brethren, and sisters, yea, and his own life
also, he cannot b my disciple.*"

The fervor which constantly died away, as far as human
beings were concerned, burned like a sweet-smelling incense on a lofty altar, to an object infinitely more worthy
of it. Her heart could not remain inactive; she had to
love, for it was the law of her being; she had to overflow
with enthusiasm for something on which she should en-
gage her thoughts every instant of her life, and offer continual sacrifices. Maria could not desire anything or love
anything, without feeling herself stirred by a consuming
fervor. When she was a child, she had loved another

little girl of her own age, a child of dark complexion, with great, cruel, black eyes, and she loved her so passionately that she became her willing slave; the little black-eyed girl, the daughter of a poor mechanic, treated her with the authority of a queen and mistress, demanded from her all the playthings that she possessed, compelled her to submit to all her caprices, humiliated her whenever she felt like it, and oftentimes abused her in word and deed, without the affection of her enthusiastic friend being diminished in the least. On one occasion, when the two were ironing a doll's skirt, the cruel little girl said, in a disagreeable tone of mockery, " If you love me so dearly, why don't you put this hot iron on your arm for me? " Maria, without a moment's hesitation, pulled up the sleeve of her dress, and laid the heated iron on her arm, making a terrible burn. On account of other such actions as these, which had attracted Don Mariano's attention, he drove this unworthy friend out into the street, and forbade her ever darkening the door of his house again, a prohibition which broke his daughter's heart with grief.

When a heart is to this degree inflammable, its constant tendency is to take fire and be consumed with some extraordinary love; and if the object is not at hand, it seeks for it as one athirst seeks the fountain of crystalline water. Maria had sought hard for it and found it,—a love pure and immortal, sublime and marvelous; love for a God who crushes the stars to powder and enters the enamored soul like a gentle lamb. This love, which took more and more violent possession of her soul, was not only manifested in almost incomprehensible deeds of humility and mortification, but also escaped continually from her lips in passionate phrases, which winged themselves away like timid birdlings to take refuge in the sacred heart of Jesus. At first she had prayed with respectful worship, with soul and body prostrate, terrified rather than melted, like one who makes a declaration of love; but according as she understood, by a thousand manifest signs, that Jesus replied to her passionate affection and returned it with increase, she found greater freedom and eloquence in her words and a more enduring felicity in her whole being.

The happiest moments of her life were those which she consecrated to prayer, which in her case was a sweet colloquy of two lovers, incomprehensible for those who have never fathomed the secret depths of the divine love or tasted the delights of the mystical union. By dint of holding converse with God, of communicating to Him her most occult thoughts and feelings, of confessing with tears each day the most trivial spots on her conscience, she succeeded in bringing about with the Almighty a sacred familiarity, full of joy and consolation. At the twilight hour, after she had ceased from the pious tasks which kept her busy all the day, she was in the habit of retiring to her room to enjoy at her ease the sweet delights which Jesus granted to her fervent prayers as a recompense for the labors and humiliations of the day.

One calm, quiet evening, toward the end of winter, Maria found herself in her room, prostrate in prayer, before the image of Jesus. All the blinds were open to let in the slowly fading light. From the one that looked inland could be seen the wide stretch of level meadows, and the gentle hills on the horizon bathed in a purple vapor, which grew thicker and thicker till it changed to mist. From the one facing the river could be seen its tranquil surface, motionless as though all that sheet of water had been suddenly changed to stone; near El Moral were four or five low sandhills called appropriately Los Arenales, which, struck by the last rays of the setting sun, gleamed like mighty topazes. Not the slightest sound disturbed the silence of the boudoir, which at that moment, by reason of its gloom and loneliness, was like a great confessional.

For a long hour the young woman had been communing with the Beloved of her heart, and no earthly thought had made its way into her enraptured spirit. Never had she felt herself so abstracted and lifted above the flesh, above mundane interests. All the life of her body had gone to her heart, which beat with unwonted violence. She kept her eyes closed. After she had repeated all the prayers that she could remember, some of them composed purposely for her, she allowed her lips to rest, and abandoned herself to a delicious meditation in which her imagination wandered away as if in a boundless field enameled with flowers. Both her confessor and her books of devotion counseled her to think often on the bloody passion and death of the Redeemer, and so she had done until she was filled with grief and burdened with tears. In her mind she saw that agonized, grief-stricken face of Jesus nailed upon the cross, those dying eyes lifted, wherein still burned the eternal love and compassion of a God. When she saw him going toward Calvary, laden with the heavy cross and stumbling, once, again, and yet again, overcome by fatigue, not finding in the bloodthirsty faces of those who surrounded him one look of sympathy, she felt her throat contract and her breast choke with sobs. She had been present at all the agonies of Christ, one after the other, from the memorable night in the garden until the moment when he closed his mortal eyes between the two thieves, the victim of the perfidy of men. The sublime words of pardon which he uttered as he died rang in her ears like a promise of heaven and a hope of seeing him once more, haloed with glory, in the other life.

But at this moment her thought shunned the death scenes. Around her floated smiling, glorious forms, which filled her with a delicious joy such as she had but few times experienced before, accompanied by an unspeakable physical comfort. It seemed to her that she felt a most delicious sensation of warmth radiating from her heart even to her hands and feet, as though she were plunged in a bath of warm milk. At the same time soft fragrant hands held her eyelids closed, while a gentle breeze cooled her brow. The boudoir in the tower was filled with vague, subtle sounds, which her imagination transformed into mysterious harmonies. She was so beside herself that she could not tell whether she was in reality awake, although she had possession of all her faculties.

MARTA AND MARIA

Little by little, she began to lose her power of volition. She tried to open her eyes and could not; she tried to separate her hands, which she kept folded, and she had no better success. A superior power held her in its sway, but so gently that for nothing in the world would she have broken those bands; it was a celestial swooning of her whole being, which carried her away into ecstasies such as she had never known before. Tears streamed down over her face like an exquisite ichor, bathing her lips with sweetness, and flowing from her lips into the very center of her being, filling her heart as with a most gentle unction, as with a mighty perfume. This ichor intoxicated her and strengthened her at once, and she did not weary of drinking it. Its salubrious strength penetrated her emaciated body, bestowing on it an incomprehensible force. She entered into a life full and divine, where no pains existed; into an ecstatic lethargy full of soft delight, from which was born a throng of vague longings, like flowers opening for an instant and shedding perfume from their calyxes. The longings of her soul likewise spread and were quenched in the immense joy which took hold of her.

While her body was sleeping in this sweet hallucination of the senses, her mind was attent with a marvelous activity. Her memory was bathed in brilliancy, and her imagination, in precipitate flight, darted out into the universe. Instead of meditating on the death of the Lord, she thought with deep delight about his adorable life, and, completely enchanted, she reviewed all its occurrences, representing them with as much accuracy as though she had really been present at the time. First, she beheld Jesus at his birth in the grotto near Bethlehem, embracing with his sweet arms the Virgin's neck, and smiling at the shepherds and the Magi, who came from far-distant countries to adore him. She beheld him secretly transported to Egypt, crossing the deserts of Arabia, sleeping on his mother's lap under some tree or in the depths of some cavern.

Then she found him in the porticos of the Temple of

Jerusalem, seated in the midst of the doctors, though he was only twelve years of age, with his long golden hair curling in ringlets over his shoulders, and his white tunic falling in graceful folds till it hid his feet, astonishing them all by his more than human beauty as well as by the profound wisdom of his words. She contemplated him in his modest dwelling in Nazareth in the peace of an obscure and contemplative life, nourishing his divine spirit with the sublime truths which the Eternal Father vouchsafed him during his frequent solitary walks. Then she was present at his first ministrations through Galilee, and at the first miracle, with which he manifested his infinite power at the wedding of Cana. She accompanied him to Capernaum when, as he stood in a fishing-boat gently rocking on the waves, he addressed to the multitude gathered on the shore his discourse, clearer than the sun which shone upon them, sweeter than the evening breeze. She returned with him to Nazareth, where his stubborn, ungrateful countrymen were unmoved by his gentleness and power of speech and rejected him. She went to Bethany, where her name-saint Mary Magdalene and Martha her sister had the blessedness of giving him hospitality, and the former of sitting long at his feet and listening to his words.

She saw him everywhere serene and beautiful, as he is represented by tradition, with his blue eyes of wonderful sweetness, his skin rosy and transparent, his beard pointed, and his golden hair parted in the middle, and falling in waves on his shoulders. The numerous pictures which she had seen, not only of his divine person, but of the country where his ministrations had taken place, united to her powerful imagination, carried her back to the time of the Redeemer's life more vividly than one could conceive. But where her imagination most revelled was in seeing his entrance into Jerusalem followed by a multitude carried away by enthusiasm, amid hosannas and shouts of welcome; then his beautiful face, which almost disappeared amid the foliage of the palm-branches, assumed an expression of divinity, his eyes so gentle flashed with the effulgence of omnipotence, and he spread out his hands toward the city, granting it pardon in advance for its barbarous deed. Oh, how her soul delighted in this fine, poetic scene where Jesus was given on earth a little of the adoration which was his due! If she had been in those happy places, she would have taken part in the cortège of the King of kings, and raised her voice in acclamation. The union in him of power and humility, of force and gentleness, filled her with enthusiasm and admiration.

She knew, however, that Jesus' triumphal entrance into Jerusalem was repeated daily in a mystic sense; that the divine Lord takes more pleasure in entering into the soul of his elect than into the ungrateful daughter of Zion; that love was efficacious against the absolute master of all things, and took pleasure in receiving whoever professed his name. But for this it was necessary to love him much, to love him in such a manner as to prefer pain and torment coming from his hand to the most exquisite delight of earth, to love him even to fainting and dying in his presence and falling prone at his feet under the majesty of his gaze. It was necessary to spend long hours watching for him in the depths of the sky, in the calm of the eventide, in the beauty of flowers, of birds, and of all creatures, at the bedside of the sick and dying, in the midst of sorrows and penances; it was necessary to let the hours pass in ecstatic prayer, feeling the tears stealing down, and the cheeks on fire; it was necessary to be obedient to all men, the humble servant of all men, to turn the mind from accepting all favors, even from one's parents, and to despise one's self, to be the beloved of Jesus.

Thus, thus she loved him! How many hours of the day and night she had spent thinking of him! How many tears she had shed for his sake! How many times in the silence of the night had her soul gone forth, fired with sickness of love, like the bride of the mystic Song of Solomon, in search for the Lord and Master of her heart! And when she had, in this manner, sought for him, kindled with amorous yearning, she never failed to find him. On one occasion, having spent the whole day ministering to the sick in the hospital, she had felt at the hour of retiring such keen delight in her soul and body that she almost fell in a swoon. When she humbled herself before anyone, she felt an exquisite delight; in crucifying her flesh with sharp cruelties she had felt more pleasure than the world with its harassing joys had ever given. In this way Jesus began to return a thousandfold the love which she professed for him, transforming in her case into comfort what to others was pain and penance.

This last consideration pierced so sharply into her spirit that it caused her to indulge in an infinitude of thanksgivings and blessings, which remained locked in her heart without issuing from her lips. Her lips were silent, motionless as those of the sphinx; for she did not dare to reproduce by the medium of sounds the ineffable thoughts that passed through her mind. She heard within herself a thousand sweet voices speaking to her, but she could not understand what they said; she felt as though she were lifted up by gentle arms which ceaselessly lavished caresses upon her, and she was conscious, though not by visual proof, of the presence of a supernatural being, consoling her with its power. Then she became suddenly convinced that the Lord loved her; she saw clearly with the eyes of the Spirit that the Bridegroom listened to the voice of the bride, and had no deeper desire than to take her to himself, to pour out upon her all riches and joys forevermore.

Even now he was near at hand; she felt him at her side, and she was melted with desire to look upon him; but he showed himself not; he refused to yield to her warm, affectionate entreaties. As one who shows a dainty to a child and then hides it, and again brings it forth and once more hides it in order to stir his appetite, so the heavenly Bridegroom kept her in suspense and ravishment, kindling more and more her desire. The impassioned stanza of San Juan de la Cruz came into her mind:

MARTA AND MARIA

"Aye! who else has power to mend me!
Prithee deign to make my humble heart thy dwelling;
I beseech thee now to send me
Faithful angels not incapable of telling
Truly all the longing in me welling!"

And a thousand times she repeated it mentally, with a sublime solicitude, in which it seemed as though her soul were going to burst forth through her lips. But her lips remained speechless; she wished to cry out, to break into praises of Jesus, to give vent to the passionate impulses of her breast, and it was impossible. She felt a strange oppression, torturing her with celestial death, which she would not exchange for a hundred lives.

A keen, eager, resistless desire suddenly took possession of her heart. Jesus, the King of souls, had granted to more than one favors which were terrible by their very grandeur and incomprehensibility. He had appeared to Saint Isabel after her prodigious deeds of charity and penance, and had said, "Isabel, if thou art willing to be mine, I also am willing to be thine and will never leave thee." Frequently he had come to Saint Catalina of Siena in her convent cell, had conversed with her, had walked with and many times had helped her offer up her prayers. He had taken Saint Teresa in his arms so that she could not move, and had lavished caresses and kisses upon her. If she might only win such regalement! Scarcely had this overweening thought been born in her mind before she was filled with fear, and felt such shame that she would gladly have had the earth open and swallow her up.

"Oh, no, my God! Who am I to receive such a favor, granted only to the martyrs of charity and the seraphic virgins who shine in heaven like bright stars. Pardon me, Jesus mine, pardon me!"

But her audacious thought would not depart from her mind; it kept following her in spite of her strongest efforts to shake it off. She was unworthy of such glory, she knew well, but her yearning was the child of the love with which the divine Jesus had filled her heart to overflowing; thus not she but Jesus himself was the author of this desire. If he had not kindled in her his celestial love, and had not begun to pour out upon her favors as sweet as they were undeserved, such an absurd idea would never have entered her head. No; she asked not so great a grace, so great a consolation; it was enough for her that Jesus was willing to give himself to her, that she had a few particles of his immortal love. She should consider herself the most blessed among the virgin daughters of heaven, if at the end of long years of prayer and penance, of bitterness and tribulations, Jesus should allow her once only to touch her lips to his divine face.

"O Jesus mine, is it sinful to ask this? Could such a base worm as I ever deserve a joy so infinite?"

She opened her eyes. Jesus, with his golden aureole shining amid the shadows, as it reflected the last melancholy light that came through the window, lifted his hands towards her, at the same time fastening upon her a profound, sweet gaze. Through her veins ran a sensation of chill, as though she were near to death; but instantly this was supplanted by another of such intense heat that it made the perspiration start from all the pores of her body. She comprehended vaguely that an adorable mystery was taking place in her presence, and a holy fear seized her. The boudoir was wrapt in shadow: the windows seemed like great, colorless eyes gazing through the walls. A sweet, languid delectation took possession of her whole being, and overwhelmed her with bliss. Her fear vanished. She was filled with the certainty that she was loved by Jesus, that she was the bride-elect of a God. Tenderness, worship, joy, welled up in her bosom, and she could not take her eyes from the eyes of the Lord, drinking from them the mysterious, ineffable delight of glory.

Once more the desire came back to her mind. This time she promulgated it with words, the warm breath of which stole through her hands crossed before her face.

MARTA AND MARIA

"Jesus mine, wouldst thou permit thy servant to touch her lips to thy divine person?"

Jesus bent forward still more graciously. Maria felt her hair stand on end, and her heart wanted to leap from her breast. His voice like music penetrated into the soul of the young girl, who believed that she was dead and translated to heaven.

Jesus had said,

"*Arise, my beloved, my fair one, and come.*"

"Lord, I am not worthy!" exclaimed Maria, with a cry at once of anguish and of joy.

Again Jesus said,

"*Thou art all beautiful, my beloved; there is no blemish in thee.*"

"My Jesus, thee I love above all things!"

"*My dove, show me thy face, let thy voice sound in mine ears, for thy voice is sweet, and thy face is beautiful,*" replied Jesus, bending still nearer.

Then the girl, carried away by glory and enthusiasm, threw her arms about the knees of the Lord, and flooded them with her tears, saying, between her sobs, like the bride in the sacred book,

"*My soul melted within me when my beloved spake.*"

And little by little, her arms clinging to the body of Jesus, stole slowly, slowly upwards, till they were fastened around his neck. Her breath failed her, and she felt her memory, her imagination, and all her powers give way, fading into an immense, eager bliss, in which her whole being was plunged as in the purest ether. Her face drew near the Lord's. She touched with her cheeks the cheeks of the Bridegroom; she put her lips to the whiteness of his brow, to the effulgence of his eyes, to the coral of his lips.

And in the chief room of the tower, silent, buried in darkness, was long heard the sound of sobs and subdued kisses. At last, a human body, the body of the Señorita de Elorza, senseless, fell heavily at full length upon the floor. Genoveva, when she came in with a light, found her there still in the swoon, with eyes open and fixed, reflecting in her face a celestial joy.

CHAPTER VIII

AS YOU LIKE IT

THE spring came. The northeast winds, like a gigantic besom swung by the hand of some god with a .passion for cleanliness, constantly swept away the dust and ashes of the firmament. The sailors who put out at daybreak after fish, as they set foot on the quay, often saw above the distant houses of El Moral a wide strip of azure sky, which went on slowly spreading to the four points of the compass, leaving a few tenuous shreds of violet cloud like great eyebrows overhanging the horizon. The vast sheet of the river now gave forth lovely blue sparkles in place of the melancholy, metallic reflections of the winter; and the wooden hulks, called *barcos* by a misnomer, pitched in the dock like colts impatient to be off. But in the afternoon winter still clung to its rights; now spreading over town and river a thick mantle of fog which quickly changed into storm; now furiously driving across the sky colossal black clouds which discharged their freight as they flew inland. Some days, however, at sunset a breath of genial air came from the land, and brought the delightful tidings to the peaceful inhabitants of Nieva that the most lovely and coquettish of the seasons was present in that jurisdiction; and this breath of air laden with perfumes, reaching by the medium of the nostrils to the brains of those inhabitants who were most inclined to poesy and sweet expansions of the heart, manifested itself as the avowed enemy of tranquillity in feminine minds, and as the infamous disturber of peace in families. The town slept placidly like a sultana, receiving the adulatory caresses of this breeze.

Nevertheless, the calm underneath the roofs was more apparent than real; a large part of the inhabitants slept the sleep of the righteous as before, but another no less numerous and estimable, without knowing any reason for it, awoke more than once in the course of the night, and occasionally spent an hour unsuccessfully wooing sleep by lighting the lamp, and reading the articles in *The Times.* They drank great goblets of water; they dreamed fifty thousand absurd dreams, which, when they remembered them in the morning, made the worthy natives smile, and more than one, and more than two, caught colds on their lungs by getting uncovered at night. In the two apothecary shops of the town a prodigious quantity of pearl barley was disposed of; some banished wine from the table to the astonishment of their wives; and the behavior of young men toward the girls became extremely dulcified. The Market Street bookseller sent to Madrid for a quantity of novels by Paul de Kock and Adolphe Belot on commission for his customers, and the professor of the piano made a similar demand on the music publishers, for various sentimental romanzas with erotic titles, such as *Vorrei morir, Tutto per te, Non posso vivere,* and others of like quality, at the request of his pupils.

The swallows began to take possession of the corridors, and after making love for a few days, chasing each other through the air with obstreperous chirpings and then retiring couple by couple to the most remote corners of the gardens, without any thought of Mrs. Grundy or of due formality; they celebrated their nuptials with the same freedom, without consulting the desires of papas or asking for a special dispensation, or by publishing the banns through the office of the parochial priest, or by ordering a trousseau from Paris, or by receiving a miserable coffee service from relatives, or sending cards to friends and acquaintances, announcing their indissoluble union; or even by having a notice inserted in the *Correspondencia de España,* saying: " Yesterday, before a numerous and select assemblage, in which were included the most illustrious

members of the nobility and the world of politics and literature, were celebrated in the house of the bride the long
announced nuptials of the most beautiful and distinguished
dame swallow, Lady Such an One, to the wealthy sir swallow, Lord Somebody or Other. After enjoying a splendid
collation, the newly married couple departed to their noble
domain of Robledales in Aragon." And whoever speaks
of the swallows may clearly say the same thing of the whole
throng of birds which had encamped both in the gardens
of Nieva and in the immense pine groves which lined the
banks of its river.

   To be reckoned among the people most manifestly influenced by this spring breeze (leaving aside, of course,
the Señorita de Delgado, with whom no one would dare
to maintain any rivalry in the matter of sensations, sentiments, emotions, and all that refers to the life of the heart),
was our acquaintance, Manolito Lopez. His worthy family
noticed with grateful surprise, not only that the lad's character was manifestly softening, but likewise that the habits
of orderliness and an inclination toward sedateness had
sprung up, and were growing in him with unusual rapidity.
This praiseworthy inclination was manifested in everything that pertained to the adornment of his person, but
most particularly to that of his feet; a box of superior
blacking every fortnight was not sufficient for the demands
of his shoes, and he spent a large part of the morning and
of his physical powers in making them shine like a looking-
glass. Even then he was not content. Manolito would
not have been satisfied if anything less than the brilliancy
of a Brazilian diamond, of all the jewels of the royal
crowns of Europe, of the seas and the stars had been put
into them. After giving the last finishing touch to his
hair, Manolito always sallied forth in the amiable company
of his glistening boots to promenade in front of the house
of Elorza, and up the street and down the street he went
all the time allowed him by his occupations, and also a good
part of the time when he had no business to be there.

   The balconies of the house, as a rule, remained hermetically sealed; but Manolito, judging by the graceful gait which he affected as he passed, must have suspected that a pair of steady, love-stricken eyes were always observing him through the cracks. Once in a while the balconies were thrown open, giving a glimpse of Carmen, of Genoveva, of Adela, or some other servant, who looked at him without sufficient respect considering our young lad's age (fifteen years and three months) and his character. Very, very rarely likewise appeared Marta's pretty head. She looked out for an instant with an expression of indifference which, be it said for the sake of the truth, did not change into one of affection and tenderness at sight of Manolito, but certainly remained exactly as calm and serene as though our youth had no more personality than a column of the arcade, or the clock on the townhouse, or the sign of the Café de la Estrella, or any other of the inanimate objects whereon the girl's eyes rested.

Manolito, for a few moments, felt as much disturbed as one who, sailing through the Arctic Ocean, should suddenly see an enormous iceberg coming down upon him; but soon he recovered his spirits, saying, for the encouragement of his heart, "What a sly one she is!" And though the balconies were immediately shut with a scornful creak, and remained closed all the day, yet Manolito did not cease to promenade back and promenade forth, fortified always in his conviction that through the interstices of the curtains a pair of ecstatic, love-softened eyes were launching at him a thousand passionate darts.

But where the spring held a more absolute and even despotic sway (always excepting, of course, the Señorita de Delgado's poetical soul) was the Elorza garden. There, without consulting in the slightest degree the will of the flexible mimosas or of the round acacias or of the dignified catalpas or of any other tree or shrub, flower or plant, however respectable, she began to clothe them all in green, carefully variegating their garments, making this one deep and dark, that one, bright and dazzling, and the other pale and yellow, playing with them a sort of gay, original masquerade delightful for those to see who still persist in feeling affection for the works of Nature. Above this habiliment there shone like decorations of honor many flowers, yellow, white, blue, or pink, quick to fill the ambient air with the sweet perfume stored up in their hearts.

The garden was unusually extensive, stretching out from the plaza where Don Mariano's mansion was built to the quay on one side, and on the other to the farthest houses of the town. And whether because it was not very easy to take the most perfect care of such a large piece of ground, or because Don Mariano as a man of taste did not wish to impose upon Nature his own law, by establishing in her demesne a tyrannical system of geometrical crosses and lines, at any rate it offered all the lawless vigor, the exuberance, and the spontaneity, which it is not customary to find any longer except in provincial gardens managed according to a broad and tolerant Spanish fashion. The paths, though originally laid out in straight lines according to the style in vogue at the time when they were first designed, were now fluctuating, thanks to the flourishing or disappearance of quince-tree, boxwood, or rose hedges. The trees in many places enclosed these paths with a thicket, giving them an air of long mystery, which, according to amateurs, is the greatest charm of gardens, and I appeal to the testimony of all ardent and elevated souls, particularly to the Señorita de Delgado. Back of the trees, through the hedges, could be seen a stone faun or satyr, discolored by great green spots on the muscular shoulders, spurting water from mouth and nostrils; in this agreeable occupation its whole life had been spent.

Flowers in the Elorza garden did not possess those inordinate privileges which they are wont to obtain in flashy parks of modern times, but a number of succulent vegetables had established themselves on a footing of equality with them. At the side of a group or clump of dahlias grew an asparagus-bed, and within sight of a splendid bunch of *canna indica* and *calladium* flourished a thicket of artichokes and a bed of Alsatian cabbages. And why not?

MARTA AND MARIA

However indisputable the superiority of flowers may be, we must not deny to vegetables esthetic qualities worthy of the consideration and respect of French gardeners, who at the present time have declared a merciless war upon them. Perhaps they consider that if vegetables are banished from parks, they bury prose forever and have poetry only left, according to the example of those ancient novelists who did not dare to show their heroes and heroines in the act of eating for fear of soiling or tarnishing them.

In one of the angles there was a great storehouse where were piled old furniture from the house, a number of broken-down carriages, the gardening utensils, and other things. The whole garden was surrounded by a wall of considerable thickness and elevation, over which climbed ivy and honeysuckle cautiously letting their leaves peer over the top, like two rogues coming in to rob fruit and get away before they should be discovered by the gardener. Over one of the faces of the wall arose the masts of the vessels at the quay, which with their multitudinous cordage enlacing and crossing in every direction, looked from a distance like monstrous spiders. A great gate barred with iron led from the garden to the quay.

The younger daughter of the proprietor of this garden found herself in it one morning culling flowers with the aid of a pair of shears suspended from her belt, and then placing them very daintily in a small osier basket. She went about taking them now from this side and now from that, seeming at times to ponder before some, leaving them untouched to go straightway to others, and then coming back to them, thus endlessly meandering in every direction with hesitating step. She was so immersed in the depths of some combination for her bouquet that she allowed herself to be pitilessly burned by the sun, more splendid in his anger and pride than was his wont.

Since we last saw her, a slight change not easy to define had taken place in her figure. She had just finished her fourteenth year. Her physical development, always exuberant and vigorous, had taken a sudden start during the last three months, not causing her to grow at once tall and thin, as is apt to be the case with girls at this age, but bringing her beauty to a more ideal perfection. Marta was destined to be rather stout. Nature had been giving the last touches to her figure, strengthening the line of her hips, rounding her arms, filling out her virginal bosom, and perfecting the oval of her face, without being willing, on any consideration, to grant her three inches more of stature, though she really needed them. On this account an Andalusian cavalry lieutenant, while saying something in her praise and dispraise in a game of forfeits, recently declared:

"You are very charming, but your roundness is alarming."

And this had given occasion for the friends of the house to call her in fun *la redondita* (the round), and to plague her continually with the Andalusian rhyme. The expression of her face was as placid, grave, and as gentle as before. Nevertheless, her great black eyes, calm and liquid, which, as we have said, used to present a certain strange immobility, acquired a movement so gentle and sweet that one of the De Ciudad girls, the very one who had pointed her out to the engineer Suárez, could not help exclaiming on one occasion,

"Don't you see how sweet Martita is looking!"

"Certainly," replied the engineer, "that girl seems to caress you with her eyes when she looks."

At the same time they inclined to grow liquid, which still more increased their brilliancy and gentleness. At this particular moment she wore a dark violet dress, extremely snug and well fitted to her body, and, although at her earnest request it had been made a little longer than before, still, as she stooped over to cut the flowers, it allowed more than a glimpse to be seen of a pair of beautiful, well rounded ankles, comparable with the arms which Ricardo had admired.

After she had cut as many flowers as she wanted, she sat on a stone bench in the shade, and placing the basket by her side and taking out a ball of thread, proceeded, with great calmness, to make a nosegay. First, she took a magnificent white tea-rose, and pulled off all its thorns, tying around it instead some leaves of althea. As she reached this stage in her operation, Ricardo made his appearance. Marta raised her head, hearing his steps, and quickly dropped it again, continuing her work.

"I have been hunting for you, Martita."

"What for?"

"Nothing—only to see you.—Is that a little thing?"

"If that's all, it seems to me a very little thing; yes!"

"Perhaps you don't want me to see you?"

"I didn't say that—but it hasn't been twenty-four hours since you got home."

"Well, at any rate I wanted to see you."

Marta said nothing, and kept on with her task, placing around the rose and in the althea three pansies. Ricardo also had changed a little since the last time that we saw him. His face had grown somewhat thinner, and in place of its ordinary expression of contentment had come another as of fatigue sometimes approximating to gloom and bitterness. Unquestionably he had not been very happy during the last months, and we know very well that he had no good reason for being so. The perpetual struggle which he had to sustain with Maria's scruples, and the sincere or simulated coldness which he saw in her, caused a steady, dull discomfort which embittered his existence. The brief moments when he succeeded in talking with his beloved, instead of being brightened by the sweet expressions of love, were generally spent in bickerings and recriminations, or at least in long exhortations on one side and the other,— Ricardo trying to prove to Maria that her pious practices were an exaggeration incompatible with human nature; Maria urging Ricardo to abandon the frivolities of the world and enter upon the road of virtue, which is that of salvation.

After he had silently watched Marta's work a moment, he asked her,

223

"Whom is that bouquet for?"

"For Maria, who wants to collect her flowers for the Virgin this evening. She asked me to make two, and I keep one in the house."

A flash of joy passed through the young man's eyes at the mention of his sweetheart's name, and he began to take an interest in the formation of the nosegay. Marta noticed particularly her future brother's joy and interest. Between the three pansies she placed three pinks,—one red, one rose-colored, and the other white. Then she took a number of leaves of sweet marjoram and rose, and tied up with them the growing bouquet; thereupon she placed all around it a row of marguerites, alternating the colors,— purple, white, blue, and mottled.

"Now, you ought to put in some pinks," added Ricardo, with the boldness of ignorance.

"Hush, Ricardo, you don't know what you are talking about.—Now you want a filling of sweet marjoram and althea, so that the marguerites may have a background. —Flowers must be loose and not touch each other, so that each may preserve its form in the bunch.—Do you see?—Now a row of roses can be added without fear of crushing the marguerites—a white one, then a red one— a white one—another red one—there! that'll do!"

The thread unrolled between her fingers, gently binding the flowers together; the nosegay went on assuming a pyramidal form very well proportioned. Ricardo, looking into the basket, saw some extremely bright-colored geraniums, and cried out,

"Oh, how lovely those geraniums are!—Such a bright color ought to become you, Martita; put one in your hair."

The girl, without more ado, took the one that he offered her, and stuck it in her dark locks above her ear. This combination of red and black, which is vulgar, as all girls know, appeared more harmonious than ordinarily, through the exceptional intensity not only of the black, but of the red. The geranium, on being translated to that position, seemed to have fulfilled its destiny on earth, or to have realized its essence, as my friend Homobono Pereda, shining with more beauty and satisfaction than ever, would say. Ricardo contemplated Marta's head with genuine admiration, while an innocent smile of triumph hovered over her lips and in her eyes.

Around the roses she placed, instead of the green setting of sweet marjoram and althea, another of white and blue violets, and next a row of geraniums of all colors, combining them exquisitely. The bouquet was finished. To add a crowning grace she put in a few handfuls of thyme, arranging them in such a way that they might serve as a support. The flowers, all artistically combined, appeared loose, each one showing its own individuality, or, as my friend Homobono would add, perfectly united in the whole.

Marta lifted the nosegay up, saying, with childish delight,

"Isn't that fine!—isn't that fine!"

"Admirable!—admirable!" cried Ricardo, and in the height of his enthusiasm he took the nosegay, waved it several times, and then laying it down in the basket, seized the girl's hand and lifted it to his lips.

Marta grew as scarlet as the geranium that she wore in her hair, and snatched her hand away. Ricardo looked at her with a mischievous smile, and said:

"What does this mean, señorita, what does this mean? You are ashamed to have anyone kiss your hand, when it isn't four months since we all kissed you on the cheek? This won't do—this won't do at all."

And forcibly seizing her two hands he began to shower kisses on them without stopping, until he thought he felt something strange on his head, and lifted it. Marta was in tears. The young man's surprise was so great that he dropped her hands without saying a word. The girl hid her face in them, and began to sob with keen pain.

"Martita, what is it? What is the matter with you?" he asked, thoroughly terrified, stooping down to look into her face.

"Nothing! nothing!—Leave me."

225

"But what are you crying about?—Have I hurt you? Have I offended you?"

"No, no!—Leave me, Ricardo—leave me, for Heaven's sake!"

And jumping from the bench, she started to run toward the house, wiping her eyes. Ricardo grew more and more surprised, as he saw her disappearing, and he stayed some time at the bench, trying in vain to explain the girl's behavior. Then he got up, and began to promenade in the garden. In a short time he had entirely forgotten Marta's tears; more painful memories came to disturb his mind and absorb his attention. An hour, at least, he spent in walking up and down the park, thinking about them, until at last, as he passed in front of the bench where he had been sitting with the girl, he noticed that her bouquet still remained in the basket, as she had left it, and thinking that it was not good for it to be there, he started with it to the house. He asked the first servant whom he met where the señorita was to be found.

"I think she is in the señora's room."

He turned his steps thither. At Doña Gertrudis's room he met Marta, who was doubtless bound on some errand for her mother. The girl, who still wore the red geranium in her hair, as soon as she saw him, gave him a sweet smile, and showed signs of being somewhat confused.

"Are you still vexed, Martita?" asked Ricardo, in a whisper.

"I wasn't vexed at all, Ricardo."

"But those tears?"

"I myself don't know what made me.—I have not been quite well for a few days,—and I cry without any reason."

"Then I am relieved in my heart, *preciosa*. You can't imagine how I felt at having caused you any pain!"

"Bah!"

"And how violently you wept! I believed that something really serious had occurred.—Has anything happened to grieve you today?"

"No, no; nothing at all.—I shall be right back. Good-by."

The Marquis of Peñalta went into Doña Gertrudis's room, where at that time Don Mariano and Don Maximo were conversing together, neither of them showing in their faces any of the painful anguish, the pallor, and the fear of those who are witnessing the last agony of the dying; and this irritated Doña Gertrudis to such a degree that she would almost have taken delight in dying at that moment, for the sake of giving them a fright. She was reclining, as usual, in her easy-chair, her feet and legs wrapt up in a magnificent mountain-goat skin, casting looks of bitter desolation, now at the ceiling, and now at a cup of milk which she held in her hand. From time to time she carried it to her lips, and swallowed a portion of its contents, thereupon lifting her eyes, and exclaiming inwardly, "My God, may this cup pass from me!" Again and again she looked at her persecutors with ineffable serenity, saying, in a touching manner, that if God forgave their cruelty, she, for her part, did not find it hard to grant them a full and generous pardon, though she greatly doubted whether the Supreme Creator would grant it.

Ricardo sat down near her persecutors, without any ceremony, for that very morning he had had the opportunity of spending a good hour over Doña Gertrudis's nerves. She, considering that whoever has to do with sinners is prone to fall into sin, included him in advance in the universal and liberal amnesty which she had declared in favor of those who offended her.

"I would never permit either traitorous periodicals, like *La Tradición*, or magistrates who would not obey the government punctually and unconditionally, Don Maximo."

"I agree with you up to a certain point; yet we find ourselves in a time of conflict, and it is necessary to proceed by exceptional measures. But you will not deny that, in a normal state of things, liberty."

"Liberty and not license!—Liberty to work—that's the only kind that we need. Roads, bridges, factories, land improvements, railways, and ports, that is all that our unfortunate nation asks for.—The liberty that you progressives are ambitious to get is liberty to starve to death.—When I consider that, if it had not been for *la gloriosa,* our railway would have been at point of completion, such desperation seizes me that——"

"This is only a passing conclusion, Don Maximo.—You will see how very soon the rainbow of peace will shine!"

"Yes, yes—it is certainly raining now.—Have you read the leading article in *La Tradición?* [*La Tradición* was a Carlist journal, published in Nieva every Thursday.] Then, when you read it, you will see what rainbows the partisans of the Church and the throne are getting ready for us."

"Is it very strong?"

"It's a trifling thing!—It says that all good Catholics ought to take arms to exterminate the horde of the impious and ruffianly who govern us today."

At this moment Marta entered the room. As she passed in front of Ricardo, he took her by the hand, and obliged her to sit on his knees, giving her a speechless look of tenderness with his eyes, without losing any of the conversation. The girl sat down without resistance, and likewise listened in silence.

"But does it really say that?" asked Don Maximo.

"It certainly does.—Read it for yourself, and you will be edified.—In my opinion the Carlists are meditating and even plotting some *coup de main.* The general commander is taking too little care of this region, and is carrying off all the forces to drive the guerrillas from the highlands.—The factory always requires a strong garrison for what might happen.—It is a prize coveted by them."

"I don't believe that they would ever dare to make any attempt in that direction. And except that the *señor marqués* says——"

Ricardo did not catch Don Maximo's last words, for, with an affectionate smile, he was saluting Maria, who at that moment came in. After she had sat down near Doña Gertrudis, and exchanged a look or two with him, he remembered the remark that had been directed to him.

"What did you say, Don Maximo?"

"That I don't believe the Carlists have any intentions against the factory.—It would be a ridiculous undertaking."

"Oh, no indeed! Not so ridiculous as you imagine, Don Maximo.—This very day, with the small garrison which we have there, it would not be impossible or very difficult to take it by surprise.—How many times I have thought, when on guard at night, that thirty decided men might get the better of me! If they succeeded in procuring a foothold inside, the thirty would be settled, you may believe."

"Do you hear what he says, you stubborn man? do you hear him? Now you shall see how we must look out for our powder magazine, now that thunderbolts and meteors are falling. But listen to one thing, Ricardo: why don't you utilize for the defense of the factory the last advances made in electric lighting?"

"How?"

"I should suggest that if a number of electric lamps were put in different parts of it, which the officer on guard could set going by simply pressing a button, all danger of a surprise could easily be avoided; and if at the same time a goodly number of heavy bells were set up, likewise worked by electricity, which would give an instant alarm in the city and wake the workmen, who for the most part live near.—Martita, what's the matter?" he exclaimed, suddenly breaking off the thread of his discourse.

All hastened to her assistance. The girl, who was still seated on Ricardo's knees, had grown pale without anyone noticing it. When Don Mariano casually glanced at her, she was white as a sheet of paper.

"What is it, my daughter?"

"What is the matter, Martita?"

"I don't feel quite well. Give me a glass of water."

Maria ran to get it for her. Don Maximo felt of her pulse and said,

"It's only a little giddiness, which water will cure."

In point of fact, as soon as she drank the water, and had sat down on the sofa, she began to feel better, and in a few moments was perfectly well. The conversation went on.

CHAPTER IX

EXCURSION TO EL MORAL AND THE ISLAND

FOR a fortnight at least there had been talk of an excursion to El Moral and the island. During the spring the young ladies who went to the parties at the house of the Elorzas had been anxious to save a sum with the products of the tax and lottery to defray the expenses. Don Mariano allowed them to do so, smiling roguishly every time that he was told the state of the funds; but when the time came which was fixed for the excursion, in presence of the whole *tertulia*, he took the handful of silver from the little box in which it was kept and handed it to the parish priest of Nieva to divide among the parishioners who most needed it.

"Why!" exclaimed the noble *caballero* at the same time, "is it not a hundredfold better to spend this money in alleviating the hunger of one or two poor people than in a frivolous and unnecessary amusement?"

"Certainly, certainly," said the girls, putting on an expression which in truth did not give evidence of the purest delights of virtue and the joys of the righteous.

That evening there was very little talking, singing, or dancing at the Elorza *tertulia*. Virtue, stern by nature, does not approve of noisy demonstrations. The young people of both sexes expressed the deep, pure satisfaction with which their sacrifice had inspired them by an ineffable severity, making them demure and silent the most of the time, as though they were meditating deeply on some Gospel text. Great, therefore, must have been the displeasure felt by all when Don Mariano said to them at the last moment:

"Ladies and gentlemen, Thursday, at eight o'clock in the morning, I should be greatly pleased to have you meet at the quay, properly provided with hats, parasols, wraps, and so forth and so forth. Nothing is more likely than that the sailors of my *falúa* will be anxious to take us down to El Moral, and, as you well know, it wouldn't be polite to disappoint them."

The *tertulia* deplored this determination which deprived them of making a sacrifice for the universal brotherhood, and manifested it with a running fire of laughter, remarks, and disorderly movements: "What a man Don Mariano is!" "He always has to be playing these jokes!" "Thursday, Thursday!" "What engagement have I for Thursday? Oh, none, I believe." "Must we take waterproofs?" "I think cloaks will be enough." And so on.

And in fact, on Thursday at eight o'clock in the morning, Don Mariano's launch and the quarantine boat, both clean and adorned like damsels on a fête-day, were impatiently waiting for the people, tossing side by side in the slip by the quay. Four sailors in each were making the final arrangements, from time to time casting inquiring glances now at the river, now at the streets which led from the quay. The passengers were not in sight, and the tide had already gone down two feet and a half. One of the sailors expressed his dislike of tardiness in a rough voice which was far from being considerate. At last a variegated group of women and men appeared, among whom straw hats and red cloaks predominated, and the old sea-dog who had just been swearing like a pirate blasphemed once more out of pure satisfaction, and put down a gang-plank between the dock and the *falúa* for the people to cross on.

The first to leap on board was Don Mariano. The boat gently tipped on one side when she received her master's weight, as though making him a loving bow. All the young ladies, including, of course, the Delgados, next came tripping on board, leaning on Don Mariano's strong hand. The gentlemen followed. When the first *falúa* was full, they began to load the second, and this was quickly accomplished. In the first, among other people of distinction, were the two Señoritas de Delgado with their sister, the widow, who chaperoned them; the De Merinos with their brother Bonifacio, the most self-satisfied of all brothers; three or four officials from the factory, Don Mariano, Don Maximo, Martita, and Ricardo. Maria did not go because she would not break her vow to refrain from all recreation. Likewise Doña Gertrudis's indisposition prevented her from taking part in the excursion. In the second boat excellent accommodation was found by our friend, the fascinating, sprightly Señorita de Morí, under the watchful goggle eyes of the illustrious Isidorito. Likewise, we can distinguished among others a very pretty young girl named Rosario with whom the young swell at her side was not able to dance on the evening of the Elorza *soirée*, on account of the war proclaimed by the pianist against the german. The sailors were just going to cast off the lines for starting when from one of the *falúas* came a voice, asking,

" But the De Ciudads? "

The De Ciudads were missing. Don Mariano and the quarantine doctor were in consternation at the mention of this name, which was such a guaranty of respectability. Before they had recovered from their consternation, there appeared at the end of one of the streets leading to the quay the six señoritas accompanied by their papa, their mamma, their engineer Suárez, and two small brothers. It was impossible to accommodate so many people in the two *falúas;* they had to hunt up another, and man it with the first sailors they could find, and thus precious time was lost. But at last, as everything in this world can be managed except death, the De Ciudads and their friends were well stowed in a fishing-boat, and the captain of the quarantine gave the signal for the start. The twelve oars of the *falúas* began to strike the water in time with a gentle splash, like the arms of one stretching.

The level of the river was smooth, motionless, and bright as a mirror; the sun cast upon it wide, silvery spots towards the center, and darker ones near the edges. The sky was covered by a delicate veil of clouds, making a splendid rival for the ladies' hats and parasols. Only a gentle breeze laden with the keen odor of pines on the shore came timidly kissing the soft back of the waters, and the no less soft and fresh necks of the ladies. It was not as yet a legitimate sea-breeze, but a hybrid kind with the characteristics both of sea and land. The oars now put out all their agility, and with the blades lifted the crystal of the waters, causing fleeting, foamy whirlpools; all faces showed the healthful joy which is always caused by motion and the ever new and beautiful spectacle of Nature. The girls, bending over the gunwale of the boat, delighted in taking off their rings and plunging their hands into the water, letting it flow with a murmur through their white fingers; they talked, they screamed, they laughed, and they exchanged greetings from one boat to the other. The young fellows spattered their faces with their canes or suddenly leaned to one side to scare them, taking great pleasure in their cries of desperation. All was noise and hubbub in the little squadron.

As they came near El Moral the marine qualities of the breeze began to get the upper hand of the inland ones; it grew stronger, sometimes even blowing violently as when the *falúas* passed by some glen made through the hills or sloping banks which shut in the river valley. The ribbons on the hats, the pennants on the mast-heads, handkerchiefs and neckties began to flutter violently. A few aquatic birds flew out from one shore and went flapping above the *falúas*, which was sufficient cause for Don Serapio, in a fit of enthusiasm for the sea, to get upon deck and, leaning over the flagstaff like one possessed, to sing the song which begins:

233

TALES FROM THE SPANISH

" Al ver en la immensa llanura del mar.

When o'er the mighty prairie of the sea,
I watch the sea-gulls in their rapid flight,
My soul is filled with envious thoughts," etc.

If the river could blush, it would not have failed to do so on hearing itself called so hyperbolically the *mighty prairie;* but it took it in bad part, believing that there was some joke intended, and was seriously angry. At all events, the wind undertook to wreak vengeance for it by suddenly snatching off the inspired singer's sombrero and cutting short the current, not to say the torrent, of his voice. The *falúa* in the wake picked up the hat and restored it in a very water-soaked condition to its owner, who showed no more desire for the time being to continue apostrophizing the sea-gulls.

The little squadron stood nearer and nearer to the handful of houses at El Moral, distant from Nieva about a league and a half. The town kept growing more distant from our voyagers, offering them a beautiful spectacle. It was situated under the brow of a not very lofty mountain, decorated with green gardens and groups of laurel and orange trees on all sides; its white-walled houses seemed to have been placed in such a situation by the hand of an artist who believed in combining the advantages of Nature so as to produce the esthetic emotion, as a stage manager would say; the dazzling whiteness of the town stood out against the dark green of the mountain like a great patch of snow stretching down from the top; the silvery sheet of the river extending at its feet waited motionless and humble till it should melt into its bosom. The gentle, pine-clad hills, which bordered the shores, and which our voyagers left one after the other, seemed like the bristling backs of huge, fantastic monsters.

The remarks made by one *falúa* to another gradually ceased. Each of the boats recovered self-jurisdiction,

234

living for itself alone. Let us listen to what is said in them. . . .

On Board of " La Sanidad "

" Last night I slept splendidly, after a number of nights when I didn't close my eyes hardly at all," said the Señorita de Morí to her friend Rosario, who was seated near her.—" I don't know what has been ailing me this long time.—I feel nervous.—My head aches when I get up. —I think I need a tonic."

" Sometimes you need to give the heart a tonic, señorita," said Isidorito, boldly, with his face frightfully contracted by a smile.

" I didn't know that the apothecary shops furnished tonics for the heart," replied the young lady, with a scornful gesture, directing her words to Rosario.

' Oh, no, señorita; not in the apothecary shops; the heart is not cured by the preparations of ordinary therapeutics, nor by any formulas of the pharmacopœia, for it has apart from its physical nature, which is not unlike the rest of the viscera, another nature purely spiritual as we are generally accustomed to speak of it, and this cannot be treated except by moral medicaments. When I said that sometimes you need to give your heart a tonic, I meant to indicate that possibly it would be good for you to drive away certain preoccupations of an amorous character, which often are wont to affect it."

" I am not troubled by these *preoccupations* of which you speak, nor do I intend to have them at present, God helping me," replied the señorita with the same air of dissatisfaction as before, and addressing herself only to Rosario.

" You cannot affirm that in such a categorical manner."

" And why not? "

" For in the state in which you find yourself it is very difficult, not to say impossible, to fathom all the profundities of the spirit and scrutinize all of its hiding-places.

Frequently impressions make their way into our souls in a surreptitious manner without our taking note of it; they begin by being vague and fugitive, and for that very reason pass without being observed; but slowly they go on taking shape, growing in strength, and finally they conquer the individual and rule him at their will. Then they pass into the category of the passions."

" But I know perfectly well what I feel and what I. don't feel."

" Oh, no, señorita; allow me to contradict you. You cannot know."

" Man, for goodness' sake! Can't I know what I feel?"

" Why, then, you must know that——"

" Perhaps I know better than you do.

" Self-observation, according to all the philosophers and moralists, is more difficult than to observe others, and there are very few who are able to reach to it. On the other hand, youth is little prone to reflection, and above all, women are incapable of taking perfect account of their inclinations and of the vague emotions passing through their hearts."

" Look you! women are as God created them, and so are men."

" I don't doubt it; but God has so created them, with a sensitive capacity (if I may express myself in this way) more quick and delicate than that of men. It may be said that they are born exclusively for love, and that love ought to fill the measure of their existence. Love and the consequences which arise from love constitute the first end of conjugal union or, in other words, matrimony. Thus it has been established in all legislative codes, and particularly in the canonical, which is the purest fountain of all. Woman consequently works more under the impulse of fancy and sentiment than of reason——"

" Heavens! how much Isidorito knows about us poor women!" exclaimed the Señorito de Morí, in a tone between anger and jest.

The learned attorney was somewhat crushed, but at

length he went on with his remarks, without ceasing the pseudo-smile which afflicted his face.

"Love being, for the reason above given, the most powerful, not to say the only, motive of a woman's life, there is nothing wonderful in the supposition that a young lady like you may find herself agitated by this omnipotent feeling, and paying tribute to what constitutes an inevitable law of life. You may now see how I was not out of the way when I affirmed that sometimes it is necessary for you to give your heart a tonic or—and this is the same thing—alleviate it of some too grievous impression."

"Oh my, what a bore!" said the Señorita de Morí, in a whisper; but she replied aloud, " Why, you are absolutely mistaken, Isidorito; nothing grieves me or disturbs me at present!"

"Allow me to doubt it."

"You are welcome to doubt it; but I assure you that I have the best reason for knowing."

"Certainly, according to all logic, although you may declare the contrary, yet there is no possibility of sustaining such an opinion; not only reason and good sense oppose it, but from the most superficial observation of the facts it results, first, that love is a natural and constant sentiment in young ladies; second, that you have no reasons for escaping from it; and third, that the fact of sleeping little and uneasily makes the supposition that you are in love a very reasonable one."

The Señorita de Morí shrugged her shoulders, made a scornful grimace with her lips, and without deigning to reply, resumed her conversation with her friend Rosario.

Isidorito had triumphed over his opponent as usual; for always the woman with whom he was conversing was in his eyes his opponent, and he believed in the necessity of involving her in the meshes of his logic, and of getting her close in his grasp, until he subdued her like a rebellious rival in the law. Thus he expected to win the admiration and respect of the feminine sex. But the feminine sex (be it said to its dishonor) not only did not admire Isidorito for his belligerent logic, for his sedateness, and for his vast legal knowledge, but it looked upon him with marked disfavor, and avoided his conversation as though it were a disgusting clatter. The Señorita de Morí, with whom he had carried on the most pugnacious argument on the nature of love and friendship, the sweets of remembrance, the bitterness of forgetfulness, sympathy, and all else relating to the heart, in which he always came out instantly victorious, had learned to hate him like death. Consequently our wise youth was really more than a hundred leagues from the lovely heiress's three thousand *duros* income, while he believed that he could touch them with his fingertips. His never-failing sedateness, his self-possessed and serene eloquence, his long-tailed coats, his ideas of order, and his legal diction had aroused against him a prejudice as cruel as it was unjustified.

In the De Ciudad Falua

" Maria, Julia, Consuelo, just see how lovely the water feels when you put your hand in ! "

" How lovely ! how lovely."

" You'll wet your clothes, Amparo ! "

" See what cunning white feathers the water makes between the fingers, Suárez ! "

" Splendid !—but you'll wet the sleeve of your dress."

" Wait a moment.—I am going to tuck it up.—There, that's good.—Look, look ! "

" It still seems to me as though it would get wet.—Tuck it up a little more."

" More ? "

" Yes."

" But I shall show my whole arm ! "

" What difference does that make ? "

" Be sensible ; it isn't the time to give one a cold.—Now it seems to me all right.—Uf ! how cold this water is !—It isn't noticeable on the hands, but on your arms ! Look ! Look how it jumps up !—If you put your palm flat against the current, it runs clear up your arm. Don't you see how beautiful and clear it is today?"

"Speaking frankly, I will tell you," whispered the engineer in Amparo's ear, "that at this moment my attention is attracted more by your fair arm!"

"If you don't hush, you rogue, I shall spatter the water in your face," replied the girl, threatening him with her chaste vengeance.

"Though you should throw me into the river, I should still say so.—I am an artist, above all things, as you well know.—There is nothing so beautiful as the human form,—when it is beautiful; and that arm of yours stands comparison with the most perfect models of the sculptor's art."

"Come, come! don't be absurd!—My arm is like anyone else's. The main thing is, that it is beginning to feel cold.—Whew! what water. It seemed so warm at first!—And how it keeps on growing colder and colder, till at last it chills one to the bone!"

"Take it out, take it out—we must dry it!"

And Amparito obeyed, taking her arm out of the water, and innocently holding it towards the engineer, who began to wipe it with his handkerchief, lavishing upon it delicate attentions, and saying, at the same time:

"But what a lovely arm you have, Amparito! How white! what soft skin! and how round it is, above all!—A woman's arm ought to be so,—round and slender, like that of the Venus de Medici—the arm ought to diminish gradually and symmetrically to the wrist.—The truth is, with such an arm you ought to be worthy of being a sculptor's model.—Well-formed women are scarce enough nowadays. To this is due the decay of sculpture, according to some critics.—If there were many like you, this certainly could not be said.—What an arm! what a lovely arm!—You can't imagine the pleasure I feel in touching it with my hand."—The engineer, as he said this, suited the action to the word, and rubbed it so hard that Señor de Ciudad, who, with grim eyes, was watching the operation from the bow, could not help exclaiming, in an angry tone,

TALES FROM THE SPANISH

"Amparo, please pull down your sleeve.—You most
foolish girl!"

The girl blushed, and pulled down her sleeve. The
engineer, not being able to evolve his artistic theories without his model in sight, renounced, for some time, the use
of speech.

The *falúas* were now over against Los Arenales. The
sun had succeeded in making a few rifts in the veil of cloud,
and was threatening, sooner or later, to rend it in pieces.
The pencil of rays which penetrated through these rifts,
and fell on the sand-hills, made them gleam like enormous
flakes of gold, shedding their splendors over the whole
breadth of the watery sheet; occasionally, when the sunbeams were cut off a moment by the interposition of some
cloud, the splendors paled, and the sand assumed the grayish or gilded shades of webs of yellow silk. The voyagers
all agreed that those sand wastes gave a very good idea
of the deserts of Africa; and Don Mariano expressed his
opinion that it would be very easy to control the sand by
means of feather-grass and other suitable vegetation, and
soon convert them into magnificent groves of pines.

The valley, which in the midst of the way opened out
till it acquired considerable breadth, became narrower again
as it neared El Moral. The waters became more restless,
revealing the proximity of the sea; the hills, protecting the
village with their stony slopes and their bare, melancholy
tops, likewise made it evident. The breath of the monster
began to be felt, blowing freshly and proudly through the
narrow mouth of the river; and far away could be heard
the low, portentous beating of his heart. The *falúas* now
and then pitched upon patches of foam, which came rolling
over the water, like tatters torn from the mantle of some
god who had been battling all the night with the monsters
of the ocean.

They reached El Moral. Don Mariano had prepared for
them a delicious luncheon in a large warehouse, which he
owned there, and the numerous •company gave one more
proof that the sea-breezes are the most excellent stimulant

240

for the appetite. When they had done good justice to it, and rested a little while, they re-embarked to continue their excursion. A short distance from El Moral was the mouth of the harbor from which they put out to sea, leaving on the starboard quarter the lighthouse tower set on a bluff. The sailors dropped their oars and hoisted the sails to take advantage of the fresh northeast wind which forced them ahead. It was eleven o'clock in the forenoon. The cloud veil had entirely vanished down the horizon, leaving in view a beautiful, diaphanous blue sky wherein the sun swam haughty and brilliant as never before. The sea stretched out before our voyagers' eyes like one enormous, measureless blue plain, shutting in on all sides the celestial vault to collect its light and its harmony.

Above this azure plain the luminous disk of the sun made a wide path of shining silver peopled with tremulous, sparkling gleams and extending in a direct line towards the east. In each one of the crests which the breeze raised on the water the sunbeams left a fugitive, vivid light which, on mingling and joining with the rest in an incessant dance, seemed like the monstrous, fantastic ebullition of the treasures hidden in the depths of the ocean. The voyagers followed that silvery path with their gaze and did not open their lips for a long time, enjoying the deeply fine and solemn impression which the sea always makes on the mind. The outlines of the island, dimmed and confused by the excess of light, stood out opposite the very mouth of the river, about five miles from the coast. Around it could be seen great flocculent shreds of foam which alternately grew and narrowed down again, girdling it with a white belt of lace-work. The wind blew strong, but with generous benignity, for it had plenty of room to exercise its powers. The three *falúas*, with sails spread, cut through the water, one behind the other, like so many sea-gulls chasing them. The cordage whistled, the masts creaked in the holes imprisoning them, and the sails bellied under the breath of the breeze which tipped the boats more than was relished by the ladies. The water, as it passed, broke into foam, making a musical murmur against the bow, and sliding along on both sides with a rustle like the unrolling of silk.

Don Serapio felt himself attacked by a maritime ecstasy, and, holding his hat in one hand and gesticulating dramatically with the other, he sang:—

> *" How blessed that man who can number*
> *His joys on the ocean;*
> *For the billows rock him to slumber*
> *With somnolent motion."*

The almost imperceptible voice of the proprietor of the canning-factory had the honor of joining in with the eternal concert of the seas, like one of so many noises of tumbling billows or rattling pebbles. The wind would not deign to carry it twenty yards away.

The *falúas,* as they glided out on the swelling breasts of the waves, mounted and fell with a gentle, lazy motion which at first was delightful to the passengers. They began to sway, softly closing their eyes with a smile of delicious content, surrendering themselves in full to the vague, poetic dreams awakened in their hearts by the sea. Who would have said, alas! that those who were dreaming so comfortably, and rejoicing in a smiling world of gentle fancies and gilded illusions, would be seen in a few minutes with heads sadly bent over the sea, necks leaning on the gunwale, as though it were a chopping-block, faces livid and eyes fixed upon the water, as though they were trying to sound the secret arcana of the ocean! Oh, terrible fickleness of human affairs!

But what was taking place in the quarantine boat that she should come about and leave her companions? An unforeseen contingency, and certainly one most annoying. Isidorito's breakfast had played him false. Hardly were they clear of El Moral when he began to be pale and silent, though no one noticed it; but at last the pallor increased to such a degree that he really looked like a corpse. Then

242

it was suspected that he was seasick, and they advised him
to put his fingers in his mouth; but the learned attorney,
very thoroughly acquainted with the tragedy at that moment enacting in his stomach, would not do any such thing,
and begged humbly that, if it were possible, they should
turn about and leave him on shore. All were stupefied at
this proposition, and the *falúa* continued on her swift
course, as though she had not heard. But, after a time,
Isidorito propounded it in a still more energetic manner,
and the sailors were obliged to reply that, though it was
not impossible, still, to return to shore would cost them
an hour's time. Another interval passed. Isidorito got
up suddenly, with his face convulsed, and, extending his
right hand toward the shore, he exclaimed with a voice of
mighty anguish, " Turn around, turn around for God's
sake, or I shall jump into the water!" Then the *falúa*,
not wanting to be an accomplice in a suicide, veered around,
dropped sail, and, putting out oars, began to make its way,
as quickly as possible, to the nearest point on the shore.
There are reasons, however, for believing that the distinguished legal gentleman did not reach land in sufficient
time. The Señorita de Morí felt sufficiently avenged for
the many annoyances which his inflexible logic had occa-
sioned her.

CHAPTER X

THE EXCURSION CONTINUED

MEANTIME the ocean, indifferent to the laughter and
the discomfort of those petty insects which skim
over its burnished surface, reflected the fire of the sun over
all its immensity, enjoying this lofty pleasure with the same
calmness as in the first days of the world. The light could
wander freely over its humid surface, running leagues
upon leagues in a second, shooting its blazes to the furthest
confines of the horizon, or gathering them in a splendid

bundle. It could sport over the foamy crests of its waves, or timidly kiss the diaphanous mirror of the waters, or spatter it with fine silver powder, or fall in a swoon with languid, voluptuous tremors, losing themselves amid the folds of the billows: nothing could change the solemn peace of his heart or cause him to utter a note lower or a note higher in the grandiose air in basso profundo which he has sung since the beginning of the world.

The outlines of the island now stood out with clearness, black and burnt as though they had just emerged from a fire. As they came nearer, the white belt, which from a distance seemed to girdle it, broke into a thousand separate pieces, a considerable distance from one another. The formidable roar as of multitudes fighting, chains dragging, and rocks crashing, came from that direction, announcing to our voyagers that they were approaching their destination. At the end of an hour they succeeded, not without difficulty, in effecting a landing on its rock-bound shore; then they had to climb up by a narrow, perilous footway hollowed out of the rock, before they reached the solid, level land. The island did not deserve a bad name. It was an islet two or three kilometers long, belonging to Don Mariano Elorza, who made use of it only for occasional hunting excursions, and for collecting a few hundred gulls' eggs from it every year. It was covered here and there with pines, but for the most part it was clad in furze, where hares and rabbits had their warrens: on nearly all sides it presented perpendicular cliffs to the sea, which beat incessantly against it, furiously rushing in and out of the hollows in the rocks everywhere abounding. Don Mariano had built in the center a small house as a hunting-box which, little by little, he had provided with many conveniences. It contained only a large parlor, a dining-room, a few bedrooms, and the kitchen; but it was quite well furnished, and was surrounded by a small garden where a few shade-trees grew reluctantly.

While the dinner was in preparation and they were waiting for the quarantine *falúa*, which had gone to de-

posit Isidorito like a melancholy exile on a barren coast,
the ladies and gentlemen scattered about, devoting themselves to hunting and fishing, according to the taste and
disposition of each. Shots began to be heard here and
there, showing that the rabbits, which had multiplied in
geometrical progression, suffered the law of repression discovered by Malthus. The voyagers who had not bloodthirsty instincts made themselves comfortable on the moss
at the edge of the cliffs, contemplating the horizon from
quarter to quarter, where the sail of some bark was often
seen. Others · studied the flora, plucking flowers and
entering into long discussions about the cultivation which
would suit that soil and the products which it might give.
When everything was arranged, Don Mariano sent word
by his servants, and one after the other the guests made
their way back to the house and entered the parlor, where
a splendid table had been improvised, loaded with viands
and flowers. It took much labor and sufficient noise to
seat so many people, but at last it was accomplished, thanks
to the activity of the master of the house, greatly aided by
the young man with the banged hair, whom we had the
honor of meeting on the evening of the *soirée* celebrated
in honor of Doña Gertrudis.

The feast was worthy of Amphitryon. No gastronomic
refinement was lacking; everything was wisely provided
by an imagination familiar with culinary subjects and, as
someone at the table was moved to say with truth, " life
on a desert island was not so unhappy as it was pictured
in Robinson Crusoe and other books." Each plate had
before it five or six glasses which two servants were com-
missioned to keep filling successively with different kinds
of wine according to the courses served. No one will be
surprised, therefore, that after dinner was over there were
enthusiastic toasts preceded by most eloquent speeches and
accompanied by shouts, bravos, and congratulations of all
sorts to the orator. Don Maximo cut them short by a few
phrases, ill enough expressed but very touching, referring
to the brevity of human life, to the vanity of pleasures, to

the recompense which we shall have for our sorrows in another world, and other supernal subjects. The orator ended by shedding copious tears stirred by such funereal thoughts. Nevertheless, there were some who said in an undertone that Don Maximo's *papatina* was the least diverting that they had ever known.

Then the engineer, Suárez, made a speech elegantly phrased and ornate, directed to emphasizing the importance enjoyed by woman in our civilization and the salutary changes which, thanks to her influence, had obtained in the manners of modern nations. He made a eulogy, as brilliant as it was finished, of her artistic abilities, declaring them to be much superior to man's. He likewise spoke of her physical perfections, enumerating them with great satisfaction, and he ended by toasting her unconditionally as the most beautiful and exquisite work of creation, as the eternal and sweet companion of man. The Señoritas de Ciudad clapped their hands. Thereupon Don Serapio got up and with rather unctuous speech proposed in concrete terms that the brilliant assemblage who was hearkening to him should settle for good in the island, in order to populate it, and invited each and all of those present to select as quickly as possible their partners. The fact that at the end of his invitation he tipped a mischievous and impudent wink at one of the maid-servants who was helping at table raised against him a tempest of hisses and interruptions. Not being able satisfactorily to explain his behavior, Don Serapio grew very angry and went out into the kitchen, where, after a short time, was heard a ringing box on his ears.

Next followed the toasts, growing constantly more fiery and tempestuous, so that nothing that was said could be heard. One of the most famous was Martita's. By the advice of Ricardo, who sat by her side, she had drunk three glasses of champagne and did not know what was going on. The poor girl, so reserved and silent by temperament, began to let her tongue have free course, directing very facetious sallies at all present, who received them with rejoicing and applause. When a lady said that she was a little tipsy, she grew very serious and declared that she was only rather happy, which was nothing very strange considering that she was young. This repartee caused great laughter among the picnickers. When she was speaking, she kept fanning herself with her handkerchief. Her eyes, ordinarily so steady and serene, had acquired a strange loveliness and a malicious brilliancy which attracted the attention of Suárez, the engineer. The very timbre of her voice had notably altered, making it deeper and firmer. For the time being, she seemed like a woman in all the plenitude of her powers.

When they were tired of talking nonsense, Don Mariano had the tables removed from the parlor, so that the young people might dance. A piano, which had reached a dignified old age in that cloistered retreat, was called upon to mark the time of a mazurka with its cracked voice. As was to be expected, the dance from the first instant lost all ceremony and was converted into a whirlwind of hops, screams, and laughter. Marta, who was dancing with Ricardo, quickly said,

"I can't endure this heat! Don't you want to go out into the fresh air for a little?"

"Let us go; I, too, am almost suffocated."

When they were in the garden, she said to him,

"If you will come with me, I will take you to a place which no one here knows anything about except papa and me; it is a beach hidden among the rocks; you don't see it until you are on it—it is a lovely place."

"If I like! you know well enough the love I have for landscapes, and above all for seascapes! How do you get to it?"

"Follow me—you shall see."

Marta started out toward a clump of pines situated not far from the house, and Ricardo followed her. The girl wore a marine blue dress with white lace trimmings, and she had on her head a straw hat with a wreath of red convolvulus.

"After we reach that grove, you are going to enjoy a surprise."

"Indeed?"

"Just wait and see!"

In fact, after they had reached the grove and had been walking some time in it, they came upon a grotto half covered up with trees and underbrush. Marta, without saying a word, entered it, and in two seconds disappeared from sight. Ricardo waited an instant in uncertainty and deep surprise; but a gay peal of laughter echoing from within startled him from his stupor.

"What does this mean? Don't you dare to come in, coward?"

"But, child, don't you see, you might get hurt!"

"Come in, come in, brave warrior!"

"Very well—seeing that you have set the example."

When he joined Marta, he found that the grotto was quite large and had a sandy floor.

"Oh, I didn't suppose it was so large and comfortable."

"Good; now follow me."

"Where?"

"How inquisitive you are!—You shall see, man, you shall see for yourself."

She entered further into the cave, which kept growing darker and darker, and Ricardo followed, not taking his eyes from her for fear she should fall or stumble upon some obstacle. After some little time the girl's silhouette vanished in the gloomy depths of the cavern, and Ricardo found himself in real darkness.

"Don't be worried; follow me, and nothing will happen to you. I will be talking all the time, so you can walk in the direction of my voice.—If you want me to give you my hand, I will.—No?—very well, but don't fall far behind.—In a very short time you will begin to descend, but it is a gentle slope.—Do you see?—Don't grumble against the footing.—Still, if one should fall, it would not do much harm.—We shall be in the light soon.—Be careful; turn to

248

the right, for the path here makes a bend.—There, we have light at last!"

A luminous point was, in fact, visible below our young friend's feet a hundred yards distant. Marta's silhouette again emerged from the darkness and stood out against the niggardly light which entered through the aperture.

A long, dull murmur was audible in the cave, hinting at the proximity of the ocean. In a few moments they came out into the light.

Ricardo was in ecstasies over the sight which met his eyes. They stood facing the sea in the midst of a beach surrounded by very high, jagged crags. It seemed impossible to issue from it without getting wet by the waves, which came in, majestic and sonorous, spreading out over its golden sands, festooning them with wreaths of foam. Our young people advanced toward the center in silence, overcome with emotion, watching that mysterious retreat of the ocean, which seemed like a lovely hidden trysting-place where he came to tell his deepest secrets to the earth. The sky of the clearest azure reflected on the sandy floor which sloped toward the sea with a gentle incline; months and years often passed without the foot of man leaving its imprint upon it. The lofty, black, eroded walls, shutting in the beach with their semicircle, threw a melancholy silence upon it; only the cry of some sea-bird flitting from one crag to another, disturbed the eternal, mysterious monologue of the ocean.

Ricardo and Marta continued slowly drawing nearer the water, still under the spell of reverence and admiration. As they advanced, the sand grew smoother and smoother; the prints of their feet immediately filled with water. Coming still nearer, they noticed that the waves increased, and that their curling volutes at the moment of breaking would cover them up if they could get them in their power. They came in toward them solid, stately, imposing, as though they were certain to carry them off and bury them forever amid their folds; but five or six yards away they fell to the ground, expressing their disappointment with a tremendous, prolonged roar; the torrents of foam which issued from their destruction came spreading up and leaping on the sand to kiss their feet.

After some time spent in silent contemplation, Marta began to feel disturbed. She imagined that she noticed in them a constantly increasing desire to get hold of her, and that they expressed their longing with angry, desperate cries. She stepped back a little and seized Ricardo's hand, without confessing to him the foolish fear that had taken possession of her. She imagined that the sheet of foam sent up by the waves, instead of kissing her feet, was trying to bite them; that as it gathered itself up again with gigantic eagerness, it attracted her against her will, to carry her away no one knows whither.

"Doesn't it seem to you that we are going too close to the waves, Ricardo?"

"Do you think perhaps they'll come up as far as where you are?"

"I don't know—but it seems to me as though we were sliding down insensibly—and that they would get hold of us at last."

"Don't you be alarmed, *preciosa*," said he, throwing his arm around her shoulder and gently drawing her to him; "neither are the waves coming up to us, nor are we going down to them.—Are you afraid to die?"

"Oh, no, not now!" exclaimed the girl, in a voice scarcely audible, and pressing closer to her friend.

Ricardo did not hear this exclamation. He was attentively watching the passage of a steamboat which was moving down the horizon, belching forth its black column of smoke.

After a time he felt like renewing the theme.

"Are you really afraid of death? Oh, you are well off. —Today the world has in store for you its most seductive smiles—not a single cloud obscures the heaven of your life. God grant you may never come to desire it!"

"And are you afraid to die? tell me!"

"Sometimes I am, and sometimes I am not."

MARTA AND MARIA

" At this moment are you? "

" Oh! how funny you are! " exclaimed the young fellow, turning his smiling face towards her. " No, not at this moment, certainly not."

" Why not? "

" Because, if the sea should carry us away, we two should die together; and going in such charming company, what would it matter to me leaving this world? "

The girl looked at him steadily for a moment. Over the young man's lips hovered a gallant but somewhat condescending smile. She abruptly tore herself from him, and turning her back, began to walk up and down on the beach skirting the dominions of the waves.

The steamship was just hiding behind one of the headlands like a fantastic warrior, walking through the water until only the plume of his helmet was visible. When it had disappeared, Ricardo joined his future sister, who seemed not to notice his presence, so absorbed was she in contemplation of the ocean; yet after a moment she suddenly turned around, and said,

" Do you dare to go with me to the point which extends out there at the right? "

" I have no objection, but I warn you that it's flood tide, and that that point will be surrounded by water before the end of an hour."

" No matter; we have time enough to go to it."

Leaping and balancing over the rocks along the shore, which were full of pools and lined with seaweed, whereon they ran great risk of slipping, they reached the point far out in the sea.

" Let us sit down," said Marta. " Sometimes the sea comes up as far as this, doesn't it? "

Ricardo sat beside her, and both looked at the humid plain extending at their feet. Near them it was dark green in color; farther away it was blue; then in the center the great silvery spot was still resplendent with vivid scintillations reflecting the fiery disk of the sun. From the liquid bosom of the boundless deep arose a solemn but seductive

251

music, which began to sound like a paternal caress in the ears of our young friends. The great desert of water sang and vibrated in its spaces like the eternal instrument of the Creator. The breeze coming from the waves brought a refreshing coolness to their temples and cheeks; it was a keen, powerful breath, swelling their hearts and filling them with vague, exalted feelings.

Neither of them spoke. They enjoyed the contemplation of ocean's majesty and grandeur, with a humble sense of their own insignificance, and with a vague longing to share in its divine, immortal power. Their eyes followed again and again unweariedly along the fluctuating line of the horizon which revealed to them other spaces, endless and luminous. Without noticing it, by an instinctive movement they had again drawn nearer to each other as though they had some fear of the monster roaring at their feet. Ricardo had laid one arm around the young girl's waist, and held her gently as if to defend her from some danger.

At the end of a long time, Marta turned her kindled face toward him and said, with trembling voice,

"Ricardo, will you let me lean my head on your breast? I feel like weeping!"

Ricardo looked at her in surprise, and drawing her gently toward him, laid her head on his knee. The girl thanked him with a smile.

The waters beat upon the point where they were, spattering them with spray, and ceaselessly pouring in and out of the deep caves of the rocks, which seemed hollow, like a house. The rivers tumbling over them awoke strange, confused murmurs within, seeming sometimes like the far-off echoes of a thunder-clap, again like the deep rumbling of an organ.

Marta, with her head resting on the young man's knee and her face turned to the sky, allowed her great, liquid eyes to roam around the azure vault, with ears attent to the deep murmurs sounding beneath her. The fresh sea-breeze had not yet succeeded in cooling her burning cheeks.

"Hark!" she said, after a little; "don't you hear it?"

"What?"

"Don't you hear, amid the roar of the water, something like a lament?"

Ricardo listened a moment.

"I don't hear anything."

"No; now it has stopped; wait a while.—Now don't you hear it?—Yes, yes, there's no doubt about it—there's someone weeping in the hollows of this rock."

"Don't be worried, *tonta;* it's the surf that makes those strange noises.—Do you want me to go down and see if there's anyone in there?"

"No! no!" she exclaimed, eagerly; "stay quiet.—If you should move, it would disturb me greatly."

The great spot of silver kept extending further over the circuit of the ocean, but it began to grow pale. The sun was rapidly journeying toward the horizon, in majestic calm, without a cloud to accompany him, wrapt in a gold and red vapor, which gradually melted, till it was entirely lost in the clear blue of the sky. The point where they were, likewise stretched its shadow over the water, the dark green of which, little by little, grew into black. The roaring of the waves became muffled, and the breeze blew softly, like the indolent breathing of one about to go to sleep. An august, soul-stirring silence began to come up from the bosom of the waters. In the caverns of the rock Marta no longer perceived the mournful cry which had frightened her; and the thunders and mumblings had been slowly changing into a soft and languid *glu glu.*

"Are you going to sleep?" asked Ricardo again.

"I have told you once that I don't care to go to sleep—I am so happy to be awake!—He who sleeps doesn't suffer, but neither does he enjoy.—It is good to sleep only when one has sweet dreams, and I almost never have them.— Look, Ricardo; it seems to be now that I am asleep and dreaming.—You look so strange to me! I see the sky below, and the sea above; your head is bathed in a blue mist; —when you move, it seems as though the vault covering us swung to and fro; when you speak, your voice seems to come

out of the depths of the sea.—Don't shut your eyes, for
pity's sake! how it makes me suffer! I imagine that you
are dead, and have left me here alone. Don't you see how
wide open mine are! Never did I want less to sleep than
now.—Hark! put down your face a little nearer; should you
suffer much, if the sea were to rise slowly, and finally cover
us up?"

Ricardo trembled a little; he cast a look about him, and
saw that the water was ready to cut off the isthmus uniting
them to the shore.

"Come, we are almost surrounded by water already."

"Wait just a little.—I have something to tell you.—I am
going to whisper it very low, so that no one shall hear it—
no one but you.—Ricardo, I should be glad if the sea would
come up now, and bury us forever.—Thus we should be
eternally in the depths of the water; you sitting, and I with
my head on your lap, with eyes wide open.—Then,—yes, I
would dream at my ease; and you would watch my sleep,
would you not? The waves would pass over our heads,
and would come to tell us what is going on in the world.—
Those white and purple fishes, which sailors catch with
hooks, would come noiselessly to visit us, and would let us
smooth their silver scales with our hands. The seaweed
would entwine at our feet, making soft cushions; and when
the sun rose, we should see him through the glassy water,
larger and more beautiful, filtering his thousand-colored
beams through it, and dazzling us with his splendor!—Tell
me, doesn't it tempt you?—doesn't it tempt you?"

"Be quiet, Martita; you are delirious.—Come along, the
tide is rising."

"Wait a moment.—We have been here an hour, and the
wind hasn't cooled my cheeks—they are hotter than ever.—
No matter—I am comfortable.—Do you want to do me a
favor?—Listen! I must ask your forgiveness."

"What for?"

"For the scare I gave you the other day. Do you remember when we were making a nosegay together in the
garden?—You wanted to kiss my hand, and I was so stupid

254

that I took it in bad part, and began to cry.—How surprised and disgusted you must have been!—I confess that I am a goose, and don't deserve to have anyone love me.—However, you may believe me that I was not offended with you—I wept from sentiment—without knowing why.—What reason had I to weep? You did not want to do any harm—all you wanted was to kiss my hands; isn't that so?"

"That was all, my beauty!"

"Then I take great pleasure in having you kiss them, Ricardo.—Take them!"

The young girl lifted up her gentle hands, and waved them in the air, fair and white as two doves just flying from the nest. Ricardo kissed them gallantly.

"That doesn't suit me," continued the girl, laughing; "you always used to kiss my face whenever you met me or said good-by.—Why have you ceased to do so?—Are you afraid of me?—I am not a woman—I am still only a child. —Until I grow up you have the right to kiss me—then it will be another thing.—Come, give me a kiss on the forehead."—

The young man bent over and gave her a kiss on the forehead.

"If you would not be angry, I would ask for another here;" and she touched her moist, rosy lips.

The young marquis grew red in the face; he remained an instant motionless; then bending down his head, he gave the girl a prolonged kiss on her lips.

A strong gust of wind waked the ocean just as he was getting ready to sleep; he stirred an instant in his immense bed of sand, as though he were going to change his position, and uttered a low murmur of discontent. The waves in the distance began to roll in, big and blue; on the beach they clamored with strong voices. The lights which had shone on their crests were gone, and the magnificent ebullition of the submarine treasure had ceased. The silver spot was fast taking on the melancholy reflections of burnished steel.

When Ricardo raised his head, the first thing he did was to cast an anxious glance along the line of the point. The water already surrounded them. He sprang up hastily, and, without saying a word, seized Marta in his arms as easily as though she had been a fawn, and making a tremendous leap, he fell headlong on the nearest point, slightly cutting his hand. Marta was entirely unharmed, and she looked at the young man's wound; then taking out her delicate linen handkerchief she silently bound it around it, and started off with rapid steps. Ricardo followed her. They both walked in perfect silence. The distance between them grew greater and greater; for Marta no longer walked; she ran. The young marquis felt a vague discomfort, and a strange uneasiness which caused him to deliberate as he walked; he was angry with himself. When they entered the mouth of the tunnel leading to the pine grove, he entirely lost sight of his friend, and could not even hear the noise of her boots on the ground. When he reached the middle of the cave where it was perfectly dark, he thought he heard, very confusedly, the echo of a sob, and his heart was still more oppressed. After he got out into the light he felt better.

When they got to the house they found that a number of servants had been sent out in search of them, as everything had been long ready for the return. The afternoon was wearing on, and the ladies would not find it much to their liking should night catch them on the sea. They were welcomed back therefore with signs of satisfaction, and all hands hastened to settle themselves again in the *falúas*, which, on account of the swell, were as restless as horses harnessed and waiting for their master at the stable door.

Their sails were raised, and making long tacks to get advantage of the wind, they bore away to El Moral. Marta, when she entered the yawl, had lost the bright color from her cheeks.

The sun constantly hastened toward the horizon. The ladies looked with foreboding as the shadows crept over the sky and the sea, and they cast anxious looks at the sailors. The frequent tacks made by the yawls delayed them extraordinarily, and at last they had to furl the sails and follow the direct course by oars. There was nothing strange in this, and it is the most usual way when the wind is not astern; but it happened that Rosarito, the Señorita de Morí's friend, took it into her head that the change from sails to oars signified imminent danger of shipwreck, and this she represented in her imagination with all the horrors by which it is surrounded in magazine stories,—the pitchy darkness of the night, the waves rising like mountains to the sky, the cries of the sailors mingling with the roaring of the sea, etc., etc. And being unable to control herself, she began to clutch her friend with nervous hands and to utter exclamations of anguish and fear.

"Alas! O God! we are going to perish, we are going to perish!"

"There is nothing wrong; calm yourself, Rosario."

"Yes, yes! we are going to perish—we are going to be drowned.—O God, what a terrible death!—Why should I have gone to the island?—What will my papa say when he learns that his daughter is dead?—Papa! my heart's papa!"

"But, child alive, there's absolutely nothing to be afraid of!"

"Don't tell me so, for God's sake; because can't I see that they have lowered the sails. Alas! what a death! what a frightful death!—To die without confession!—To die away from my papa!—And to be buried right here in these awful black depths!—And be eaten by the fishes! and by crabs!—It's horrible!"

The Señorita de Morí's efforts to calm her friend were useless. It added no little to her fright to hear the shouts of the sailors, who in order to encourage each other and overcome the resistance of the waves, at each stroke of the oars shouted in chorus, *yo-heave-oh!—yo-heave-oh!* Every time that this exclamation rang through the air with its brutal rhythm, Rosario breathed a shriek of anguish; till the vivacious Señorita de Morí, fearing that she was getting ill, said to the sailors,

"Gentlemen, will you have the goodness not to say *yo-heave-oh!* for it greatly frightens this young lady."

But Rosario, quite irritated and shedding a sea of tears, instantly exclaimed,

" No, no; let them say *yo-heave-oh!* but let us perish quickly if we are going to! "

Little by little, however, and seeing that the tremendous catastrophe did not take place, her nerves grew calmer, and before long she was laughing, giddy girl that she was, at her ridiculous fears.

In the Elorza *falúa* there was little talking. Don Mariano and Don Maximo were too full of medoc to feel like indulging in an animated conversation. The Señorita de Delgado, seconded by her sisters, admired the sunset with lively transports of enthusiasm, and with much opening and shutting of eyes. The Marquis of Peñalta had closed his, and seemed to be dozing with his cheek in his hand. One or two couples were whispering together.

What was Marta thinking about at that moment, her gaze fastened on the sea, serious, motionless, and pale as a statue? What black phantasms rose before her from the depths of the waters to trace in her fair brow the deep furrows with which it was corrugated? What deathly secrets whispered the breeze in her ear?

Ah! easier were it to unriddle the mystery in the murmurs of the ocean and the secrets of the breeze than the vague thoughts hidden behind a maiden's brow!

The sea once more tried to dispose itself for slumber; the crests of its waves no longer gleamed white from afar with their crown of foam; the horizon withdrew its indefinite line, which faded away in the twilight shadow. The smooth, swelling billows rose and fell like the indolent, tranquil breathing of a gigantic bosom. One by one, with lovely ease and confidence, the *falúas*, leaving them behind, swept onward to the port. The coast with its dark, undulating line girdled the luminous plain. Far in the distance inland, the peaks of the mountains could be seen bathed in a transparent violet haze.

Marta's thought broke through the heavy cloud which girt it in with a sea of confusions and vaguenesses, and in

her soul arose all at once a host of sweet and ineffable recollections like so many luminous points with which the serene
sky of her life was sown. She amused herself a long time
in recounting them, taking new delight in each. How bright
and beautiful they burned in her memory! What a gentle
light they cast over the monotonous, laborious days of her
existence! They were surrounded by silence and mystery;
no one had enjoyed them, no one had known them except
herself; the very hand which had dropped into her heart
the balm of joy was absolutely ignorant of its beneficent
influence. This thought filled her with a secret delight
which brought a smile to her pale lips.

One by one, however, and without her knowing why,
those luminous points vanished away, were blotted out and
lost in the deep, black abyss of an idea. Her imagination
began to fly about like a bewildered bird within this sad and
desperate idea where not the slightest ray of light could
penetrate. Why was she in the world? The happiness
which she had discovered was another's, and there was
nothing else left to do but to look upon it without grief
and without envy, for envy in this case would be a terrible
sin. And was she sure of not falling into it at any moment, or what was worse, was she sure of not raising her
hand against that happiness? The hidden beach on the
island came instantly into her memory, with its golden sands
and its foaming waves flinging their foam flakes upon her.
A great remorse, a keen, cruel remorse, began to make its
way into her innocent heart like the sharp point of a dagger,
causing her such anguish that she uttered a muffled groan
heard only by herself. Confusion and dizziness tormented
her brain; her head burned like a volcano. She raised her
hand to her brow, and it was as cold as though made of
marble. This gave her a shock of surprise. So much heat
within and so cold without!

The ocean at that moment seemed full of peace and gentleness. The sun was just about submerging his heated
face in the crystal of the waters, but still lighted up a few
places in the vast plain with a fantastic, gilded light, leav-

ing others in the shade. The murmurs were heavier and deeper, of an infinite melancholy; that measureless mass of water was slowly losing its azure hue and changing to another, of very opaque green, sown here and there with fleeting reflections. The melancholy ease with which the sea took leave of the light made a deep impression upon Marta. With her head leaned over the water, and with dreamy eyes, she watched the most delicate tints which the light was awakening in it, and listened to the murmurs which resounded in the depths.

The sun was entirely sunken. The ocean gave one immense, colossal sob. In this sob was so much compassion that Marta thought she felt the ambient air vibrate with a movement of sympathy and wonder. Never had she seen the sea so grand and so sublime, so strong and so generous at once. That august silence, that momentary repose of the great athlete, moved her to the depths of her soul, filled her turbulent spirit with an ardent desire for peace. Who had told her that the sea was terrible? What small heart had spoken to her of his cruel treacheries? Ah, no! The sea was noble and generous, as the strong always are, and his wrath, though fearful, was quickly over: in his tranquil depths lived happily pearls and corals, the white sea-nymphs, the purple fishes.

The *falúa*, when it pressed up against his humid shoulder, made between bow and stern a broad, comfortable couch, with foamy edges, a couch where one might sleep eternally with face turned toward the sky, watching through the transparent bosom of the water the flashing of the stars.

" Heavens!—What was that?"

" Who has fallen overboard?"

" Daughter of my heart!—Marta!—Marta! Let go of me!—Let me save my daughter!"

" She is already safe, Don Mariano; there is no need of your wetting yourself."

" Back water! Back water! Steady!—" said the captain's rough voice. " Fling that line, Manuel.—Don't be alarmed, ladies; it is nothing at all.—Back water! Weigh all—Lay hold, all of you, on that line. There is nothing to worry about."

At first the confusion was great. Ricardo and one of the sailors had leaped into the water and were swimming powerfully to make up the short distance which the *falúa* had gone before the alarm was given. Ricardo, who was ahead, dived, and in a few seconds reappeared with the girl on his arm. The *falúa* was near them, and he could clutch the rope which they had flung him, and then the gunwale of the yawl, finding himself suspended by a number of arms which lifted them on deck. Don Mariano, in the short moments that this lasted, struggled with Don Maximo and others, trying to leap into the water. When he saw his daughter on board, it took him but a moment to press her to his heart.

Marta had fainted away. Various ladies hastened to loosen her clothing and shake her violently to rid her of the water which she had swallowed. Then they laid her down on one of the seats on the deck, and Ricardo, taking a bottle of salts which Don Maximo had brought with him, applied it to her nostrils. She soon opened her eyes and, on seeing the young man's solicitous face leaning over her, she smiled sweetly, and said to him, so that no one else could hear:

"Thanks, *señor marqués!*—It is not so bad down below there."

When they reached El Moral, they dried themselves at the house of some friends who were taking baths there, and they donned the first clothes that came to hand. Then they once more took up their homeward way, and reached the quay at one o'clock, finding each of their respective families was beginning to feel anxious over their late arrival.

CHAPTER XI

A STRANGE CIRCUMSTANCE

DON MARIANO'S guests were amusing themselves with the game of forfeits. The evening was thoroughly disagreeable, and only the most courageous h..d ventured out. When this happened (and it was not very infrequent) music and dancing were forbidden and games of cards, of commerce, or of forfeits were substituted, or at times merely a pleasant, bright conversation. On the evening of which we are speaking, the feminine sex was represented by three Señoritas de Ciudad, two Delgados, the Señorita de Morí, and one more, together with the family. In the masculine part figured the family physician, Señor de Ciudad, Don Serapio, the engineer Suárez, and four or five other young fellows who, being simple and insignificant, deserve no special mention. The *tertulia* occupied only one corner of the parlor, although on occasions when the game required, it was scattered about over the whole of it. Don Mariano walked up and down, and enjoyed his discussions, frequently stopping to lay down some intricate logic, and then continuing his walk with hands behind his back.

It fell to Don Serapio's lot to say *yes* and *no* three times each, and consequently he retired to one of the corners, gazing at the wall. The ladies and gentlemen once more gathered together in one group, and began to whisper with the greatest animation, each one proposing some question. At last they agreed to ask him if he enjoyed *bisogné*.

"Eeeeeh?" shouted the chorus, dwelling on the vowel.

"Yes," replied the unhappy Don Serapio.

The reply was received with tumult and delight, making the proprietor of the canning factory tremble in his shoes. Next they agreed upon asking him if he had any intention of getting married. "No," was his unhesitating reply.

"Bravo, bravo!" shouted the men.

" What a stony-hearted man ! " cried the women.

One of the young fellows proposed that they should ask him if he still had a fondness for chamber-maids. The ladies wanted to oppose this, but there was no remedy.

" Eeeeeh ? "

" Yes."

Great laughter and applause in the group. The same malevolent young fellow proposed something even worse: " to ask him if he intended to give any of his children a profession." The ladies seriously objected to this question, and another was given in its place. And thus they continued until he had said the three *yeses* and the three *noes* required by the game, and then, greatly despondent, he came to find out what the questions had been.

It came next to Amparito Ciudad to give a favor to all the gentlemen of the party, and she began to perform the duty with the greatest discretion and grace, beginning with the young fellows, except the engineer Suárez, who roundly declared that he was not satisfied with any of her propositions, and whispered to her very softly what the only thing was that would satisfy him. Amparito blushed a little, and replied with a gentle look of reproach, at the same time casting a glance at her father, who fortunately had his back turned while promenading with Don Mariano.

Isidorito's turn came next, and it unfortunately fell to him to be put " in Berlina " ; and what a chance this was for the Señorita de Morí ! Isidorito, though not attractive at all, inspired general respect on account of his reputation as a studious, sensible young man : thus the majority of the girls and boys contented themselves with criticising him as " too studious," as " having too little hair," as " dancing very badly," as " studying to excess," as " wearing too long coat tails," etc., etc. ; but when it came to the Señorita de Morí, who was impatiently waiting her turn, she put him *in Berlin,* with unconcealed satisfaction as " very heavy in brain and light in stomach." Isidorito, noticing the reasons for their criticisms, recognized with grief the source of that envenomed dart ; but he did not care to show that he did, and preferred to preserve in this respect a noble, and at the same time, a prudent silence.

The eldest daughter of the family, as usual, took no share in the game. She was sitting by her mother's side, totally oblivious of all that was going on around her, with her eyes fixed on vacancy. A strange, intense pallor covered her somewhat emaciated but always lovely face, and her whole body showed signs of uneasiness and anxiety. She scarcely answered the questions which Doña Gertrudis asked her from time to time, and if she did, it was with such curtness that it took away all the worthy lady's desire to repeat them. Four or five times already she had got up from her chair and gone to the balcony, remaining a long time there with her forehead leaning on the glass, without anyone knowing what she was looking at. The plaza of Nieva, just as on the first night when we saw it, was dark and checkered with pools of water, wherein were reflected the melancholy beams from the kerosene lamps burning in the corners. Not a soul was crossing it that night. Maria strained her eyes in vain to penetrate the darkness under the arcades: the neighbors had all withdrawn into their houses, perfectly convinced that dampness is the cause of many infirmities. The windows of the Café de la Estrella were the only ones that were lighted. The air was filled with a gentle murmur of rain which barely made itself audible through the panes to the young girl's ears.

It came Rosarito's turn to act the sultana. The dandified young fellow with the hair over his forehead placed a chair in the middle of the room and seated her in it; then he spread before her a velvet cushion. The young men of the *tertulia*, like genuine Moors, began to march before her, bending their knees in her presence and waiting humbly for her choice. Rosarito, with the notable ability which all women have for playing queen, rejected them one after the other with a gesture of sovereign disdain. Only when the young fellow of the mazurkas came by, and tremblingly bent low at her feet, the beautiful but ferocious sultana deigned to hand him the handkerchief which she held in her hand

and to select him as her lover, as a just reward for his most distinguished neckties and his no less exceptional *chaquets!* Then the two marched in a triumphal procession to the harem; or, what amounts to the same thing, they walked twice around the parlor, and sat down on the sofa where they had been before.

The little *tertulia,* after exhausting the not very varied resources of the game of forfeits, remained inactive and comfortable in the corner of the parlor, engaging in a low but very lively conversation, broken by bursts of laughter and exclamations, as the brilliant young men of the party found occasion to amuse them at the expense of some unfortunate, whom they flayed pitilessly. Those who had not this talent contented themselves with smiling and stupidly applauding the others' repartee, and occasionally trying to put their fingers in the pie with little success. They made interminable jokes on the girls about their suitors, and the girls defended themselves as usual with the classic replies: " I don't know why you should say so." " You have been very ill-informed." " He comes to see me as a friend and nothing more," etc., etc. The mischievous smiles and the expression of something hidden accompanying these replies, told very clearly that the girls did not object to be chaffed in that way.

Doña Gertrudis had gone to sleep. Don Mariano and his proselytes were still promenading from one end of the parlor to the other, involved in deep disquisitions on the probable fall of real estate. Maria was again standing with her forehead leaning against the panes, apparently absorbed in one of her long and frequent meditations to which her household were accustomed, but in reality exploring with anxious eyes the shadows which enveloped the plaza of Nieva. She paid little heed to the frivolous conversation kept up by the guests. She soon heard a strange noise in the distance and trembled. She abstracted herself as much as possible from the confusion in the room, and lent a deep and uneasy attention to that distant rumble which gradually grew louder and louder in the silence of the night, each moment becoming clearer and more definite. It was not a confused, fantastic noise, like that caused by the wind or the sea, but solid and well-defined, perfectly clear in Maria's ears. Soon it grew into the measured and characteristic sound of a multitude marching in step. The young woman's astonished eyes could distinguish by the street lamps the points of bayonets and the varnished caps of the soldiery. All the guests on hearing the noise hurried to the balconies, and saw with surprise two companies marching by the house, crossing the plaza, and disappearing from sight in the cross-streets of the town.

Don Mariano's friends looked at each other in amazement.

"What are those soldiers going to do at this time o' day?" asked one lady.

"I don't understand where they are going," replied Don Mariano. "To get to the interior of the province, even though they came from the West, there is no need of their going through here; they have the valley of Cañedo, and that is a much shorter road."

"This very day I was calling on the captain," said Don Maximo, "and he did not say a single word to me of the coming of these companies."

"I didn't know it either," said the Señor de Ciudad. "The most likely thing is that they are on the march, and are only going to spend the night here, and start off again in the morning."

"It's a strange thing," added Don Mariano, "but of course it may be—it may be."

The young people returned to their places, and quickly forgot the incident, as they gayly took up the broken thread of conversation. Their elders continued their promenade, making interminable comments and endless hypotheses about the unexpected visitation. Maria still stayed obstinately at the window, shielded from the eyes of her friends by the great damask curtains.

A very heated discussion about music had been set on foot in the group of young people, among whom figured the sensitive Señorita de Delgado, in spite of the vehemently expressed protests of Rosarito, who declared on her word that the said señorita had often held her in her arms, and that, when she as a child was going to confession, and the Señorita de Delgado was at her house, she had kissed her hand, as an elderly person. One of the most elegant of young men, who had been educated in Madrid for five different professions in succession, upheld the superiority of the German composers, declaring that there were no operas like *Roberto, Les Huguenots*, and *Le Prophète*, and that no symphonies could be compared with those of Beethoven and Mozart. The ladies, powerfully supported by the rest of the men, stood up for the advantages of Italian music.

"Don't nauseate us with your Germans, Severino! What kind of music do they make? It sounds to me like a pack of dogs barking."

"That is only at first; if you should continue to hear it, you would acquire the taste for it; the same thing happens with olives and ale."

"Then if one has to go through such wretched moments to get used to it, surely the thing isn't worth the trouble, you see! This does not happen with Italian music; you enjoy it from the very first."

"Of course, for the most part of Italian music is only a melody accompanied by four guitars."

"Silence, man, silence! Don't speak blasphemies. Would you think of comparing rubbish, which they themselves don't understand, with the sublime finale of *Lucia*, or with the soprano aria of *La Favorita* which begins, *Oh mioooo— Ferna—a—a—an—do—riii — raaa — ri — ro — ra — riii — ira——*"

"Ah, if you had heard the fourth act of *Les Huguenots!* What dramatic music! How expressive! It makes the hair stand on end! How magnificent this duet is:—*La— sciami—paar—tiiir—la—sciami—paar—tiiir—riira — riri— riri—ra—rooo—riri—ra—roo—laaa—to—rii—ro—ra——*"

"But could you ever hear anything sweeter than the concerted piece in *Somnambula* beginning, *Tooo—ra—ri—ro*

—ra—roooo—laa—riii—roo—raa—rora—rooo,—rii—ra—ri —roo " ?

" Impossible! impossible! " said several at once.

" Above all, Italian music stirs the heart, while German music only deafens you," added the Señorita de Delgado.

" That's true," affirmed her sister, the widow.

" I believe," continued the señorita, " that the object of music is to move—to elevate the soul—to cause us to shed tears—to transport us to ideal regions far away from the prosaic world in which we live.—For the truth is that prose is getting such control over society that soon it will seen ridiculous to speak of things which are not material and sordid."

" Certainly," affirmed the widow again.

" Music follows the road of prose like everything else.— Don't you hear what silly things they sing nowadays? what insipid, popular airs? And you are lucky if it isn't some indecent piece from some *opera bouffe!* In songs love is not mentioned; there are only phrases with double meanings hiding some nastiness."

" I believe that you know some very pretty romantic ballads, and sing them admirably," said the youth with the banged hair, ready, as always, to provide the *tertulia* with a new enjoyment.

" No, señor—don't you believe it.—In days gone by I used to sing some—but I have forgotten them."—

" For my part," persisted the youth, with a deeply diplomatic smile,—" and I think the same may be said of all these people,—it would give the greatest pleasure if you would search into your memory and let us listen to some.— Isn't it so, friends? "

" Yes, yes, Margarita, sing something, for Heaven's sake! "

" But supposing I don't remember anything! "

" Nonsense! it will come back to you.—If you once begin, you will find yourself gradually remembering it."

" It seems to me impossible.—Besides I always accompanied myself with the guitar."

268

"Isn't there a guitar in the house?" quickly asked the youth, jumping up from his chair.

The guitar which Marta brought lacked two or three strings, and they had to be put on, in which operation some time was lost. Then there was delay in getting them in tune. When it was once tuned the Señorita de Delgado declared up and down that she would not sing, for she did not remember anything. The *tertulia* was deeply grieved, and with reiterated entreaties endeavored to inspire her to recollect some delicious melody. But as the singer did not put up the instrument, and continued to thumb the strings softly, all became silent and waited eagerly for the song. However, just as the sensitive señorita was about to utter the first note, she made a fresh and categorical protestation to the same effect as before, and this so grieved the *tertulia* and particularly the youth with the banged hair, that they would gladly have granted the singer all the memory at their disposal, on condition that she would not leave it in any bad place. At last the señorita fixed her eyes on the ceiling, and in a quite dulcet though quavering voice, she struck up the following song, the music of which I would transfer to paper with great pleasure, if I knew how to write the score. Unfortunately, in my philharmonic studies I never went beyond the key of G with even moderate success:

" *Hope that art so flattering to my inmost feeling,*
    Thou dost all my bitter sorrow calm.
    Ay! thou art no creature of imagination.
    To the heart thou bringest welcome balm.
    If a cruel fate remove me from the presence
    Of my loved one many leagues away,
    Then 'tis Hope alone that soothes my deep affliction,
    Promising a brighter, happier day."

" Bravo, bravo!"—" How pretty!"—" How sweet!"—" How melancholy!"—" Go on, Margarita, do go on!" The Señorita de Delgado continued in this way:

269

TALES FROM THE SPANISH

" If at solitary midnight I am thinking
Of my sweetheart's ever blessed name,
And before my spellbound memory slowly rises
Her enchanting features limned in flame,—
Then 'tis thou, O Hope, that softly prophesyest
That my loved one will not say me nay;
Then 'tis Hope alone that soothes my deep affliction,
Promising a brighter, happier day."

Just as this point was reached, and when the audience
was getting ready to enjoy the unspeakable sweetness of
a new strophe, even more passionate and more pathetic than
the last, when the Señorita de Delgado was languorously
laying her pudgy fingers on the strings of the instrument,
and drooping her head still more languorously on her bosom
in testimony of her bitter grief, there occurred one of those
strange and terrible events, more terrible still from being
unexpected, and therefore overwhelming, that suspend and
for the time being cut short the use of speech: an extraordinary scene, occurring with such rapidity that it
allowed no time for reflection, and left the spectators in the
deepest consternation without power of interference.

The parlor door was thrown violently open, and the eyes
of the bystanders turned toward it, saw with surprise the
pale face of a servant, who addressed his master, saying,—
" Señor ! Señor ! "

" What is the trouble ? " asked Don Mariano, in the energetic tone customary to high-strung natures, when they
suspect danger.

" The soldiers are here ! "

" And what have I to do with soldiers, you dolt ! " replied
the master in an angry voice.

" Th-they're c-come to arrest you ! "

" It isn't true ! " cried a voice from the hall.

And at the same time six or eight figures filled the door-
way behind the servant. The first to be seen were a very
young officer in undress uniform, and a *caballero,* not very
well-favored, in a tight-buttoned greatcoat, and holding in

his hand a staff with tassels. Behind them were seen the caps and the muskets of several soldiers. The man with the staff, who was apparently the one who had spoken, advanced two steps into the parlor, and without removing his hat asked Don Mariano sharply,

"Are you Don Mariano Elorza?"

The old gentleman's eyes sparkled with indignation.

"First of all, take off your hat!"

The man with the staff, somewhat bluffed by Don Mariano's attitude and the looks of the company, took off his sombrero.

"Now, what is your business?"

"Are you Don Mariano Elorza?"

"No! I am the *excelentísimo señor* Don Mariano Elorza!"

"It's the same thing."

"It is not the same thing!"

"Well, let us drop discussions; I have orders to arrest your daughter, Doña Maria."

All the Señor de Elorza's energy suddenly vanished like a shadow, at hearing those portentous words. He stood a few moments bewildered and petrified, with his face crestfallen, like one who has just beheld a miracle and has no faith in his own eyes. Then suddenly recovering himself, he sprang at the man with the staff, and shaking him violently by the lapel of his coat, he said to him in a voice of thunder,

"And who are you, insolent man, to dare think of such a thing?"

"I am the chief of police for this province, and I warn you that if you offer the least resistance I shall make use of the force which I have with me."

"Are you perfectly sure that it is my daughter whom you come to arrest?"

"Yes, sir; I have orders to arrest the Señorita Doña Maria Elorza. I request you to hand her over to me without delay."

"Here I am," said Maria, issuing from the hollow of the

balconied window, and advancing toward the chief of police.

"But it cannot be," thundered Don Mariano again, holding his daughter back. "This man is crazy or has come to the wrong place."

"Are you ready to go with me?" asked the *comisario* of the young woman.

"Yes, señor," was her firm reply.

"Then come along."

Don Mariano hid his face in his hands, and exclaimed with a cry of agony:

"Daughter of my heart, what have you been doing?"

"Nothing that dishonors me or dishonors you," replied the girl proudly, lifting her lovely face and hastening from the room. Don Mariano was held back by all his friends, who clustered around him, but quickly finding himself alone, as all, warned by a cry from Marta, hastened to the assistance of Doña Gertrudis, who had fainted, he darted like a flash from the room.

CHAPTER XII

GATHERED THREADS

SOME time before the events which we have just related, the loves of Ricardo and Maria, which had been going on in a gradual *diminuendo* like the notes of a beautiful melody, until Ricardo himself knew not whether they really existed or had completely died away; whether he was the lover of the first-born daughter of the Elorzas, or whether he had other rights over her heart than those granted to an old valued friend—these loves, I say, had suddenly and unexpectedly gained, without anyone knowing a reason for it, a new lease of life, just as a light about to die from lack of oil is renewed by being given a good quantity of this combustible. Everyone was surprised to see them together, talking as before in one corner of the parlor, during long interviews, oblivious of everything around them, dwelling in that nook of heaven which lovers find as easily in crowds as in solitude.

Satisfaction followed surprise in their friends, and this in turn was followed by hypotheses as to the approach of the wedding-day, and conjectures about the motives serving to make such a change in the conduct of the lovers. The mischievous ones, winking as they said it, declared that of the three enemies of the soul, the flesh was the most to be feared, and that God had said, *Crescite et multiplicamini,* and that it was folly to fight against the laws of nature. The ladies, casting down their eyes, declared that in all states one could well serve God, and that not the easiest of penances were imposed by the care and education of children and the rule of the house. But at all events, the fact was that things had changed without anyone knowing why, and that ladies and gentlemen were delighted, hoping that the illustrious partners would soon vouchsafe them a happy day. Don Mariano's delight was so great that it shone through his eyes every time that he turned them toward the handsome couple, and a thousand lovely dreams in which figured a swarm of rosy, frolicsome grandchildren, just as his daughter had been, came at night to caress him in the solitudes of his feudal couch. Doña Gertrudis, as usual, thoroughly approved of Maria's conduct. Learn now how this state of things came about.

One morning when the young Marqués de Peñalta awoke earlier than usual, noticing from the window of his room that the sky was clear (contrary to its time-honored custom), he felt an inclination to take a walk in the suburbs of the town, and making the thought father to the act, he hastily dressed and went down into the street in search of pure air; but before he left the inner town, as he was passing the Elorza mansion, he accidentally met Maria going to church with her maid. His heart gave a leap, and, somewhat agitated, he stopped to salute her. The girl met him with that gay, blithesome gesture, full at once of mischievousness and candor, which was peculiar to her nature, and therefore impossible to overcome by any force.

"You have arisen early—to hear mass, I suppose?"

"Oh no," replied Ricardo with a smile; "I was going to take a walk in the country, as it must be very lovely now."

"Very well; but today you must not go to walk: I claim you, and am going to take you to mass," said the girl in a tone of resolution, and with a decidedly adorable inflection of voice; and suiting the action to the word, she took him by the hand and led him captive this way for some distance.

Lucky Ricardo! what better could he desire at that moment than to see himself captured in such a lovely way? He could not say a word during the first few moments. Emotion overmastered him, and a tear slipped down his honest, manly face.

"Oh, Maria, if you knew how happy you make me!" he said to her in a low, trembling voice. "If you wanted to take me with you, where would I not go? You cannot comprehend how I long for you to speak with me, to smile on me, to lead me. I try eagerly to find ways to please you, and I don't find them. Tell me how I can cause you any pleasure, how I can melt the ice which is destroying our love, and I will try to do it, even if it should cost me my life. If I did not love you more than any other being in this world, and also as the blessed remembrance of my mother, how long ago I should have left you forever!— But my love is of such a nature, it is so strong, so eager, so absorbing, that it has succeeded in disarming all my pride—and I fear that it has got the better of my dignity," he added in a low tone.

The young woman looked at him steadily, full of delight and admiration of such sincere affection, and she replied gayly,

"At present you can please me by going to mass with me; will you?"

"Yes, dear."

"Will you come tomorrow also and every other day?"

" Yes, loveliest, I ask nothing better."

" You don't know how you rejoice me, Ricardo ! "

" Truly ? "

"Yes, I love you dearly, but I want you to be good
and religious, because, before everything else we ought to
think of our salvation, and make it our richest possession
in this world."

The young man at that moment felt his heart melt within
him, as he drank in the drops of affection which his sweetheart let fall upon his lips.   There is nothing that can so
quickly change our most deeply rooted ideas and our
firmest judgments as the voice of the woman whom we
love.   Ricardo was a lukewarm believer, like most men
of our day, and he detested exaggerations, and looked with
decided repugnance upon religious practices.   Accordingly,
then, by the work of enchantment, that is, by the work of
that sweet voice and those still sweeter eyes, which gazed
upon him with eloquent expression, he was stripped of his
anti-clerical opinions, and was transformed into a decided
champion of the altar and a fervid devotee of the saints,
male and female, of the celestial court.   He took delight in
thinking that what his betrothed was doing was, after all,
not blameworthy; that her piety and mysticism were the
reflection of a noble and lofty spirit; that this same piety
was the sweet pledge of her conjugal happiness, since it
would cause her to refrain from the vanities to which other
women after marriage devote themselves; that there was
nothing strange in the poor girl desiring her betrothed to
be a believer and devout, when her ideas about eternal
salvation were taken into consideration, and that in this
regard he had done very wrong to oppose her so obstinately,
striking her in the very heart of her sensitive and admirable
faith.   Finally he came to the conclusion that he was a barbarian, incapable of enjoying the sacraments or of understanding the adorable mysteries which a heart consecrated
to God might take in, and that Maria was a saint who
had borne with him with too much patience.   Moved,
partly by this thought, and infinitely more by the emotion

caused by his sweetheart's unexpected favor, he replied with accents of tenderness:

"Listen, Maria—You know well that I am not, and have never been an unbeliever.—It is true I have looked with a certain coolness on religious practices, but you ought to know just as well that this is a common fault among young men, and particularly among the military.— As for the rest, I tell you with all the sincerity of my soul, I have never abandoned the faith which my sainted mother taught me in childhood.—Even now ring in my ears her counsels, and still I can repeat without mistake the multitude of prayers which she made me say on my knees on the bed when I retired.—That cannot be forgotten, Maria.—It would be infamous if one forgot it! Today the same counsels are repeated by lips that I worship.—How could you think that a religion always inculcated by the beings whom I have most loved and respected in my life, should not be sweet!—Yes, my loveliest, I am religious by birth and by conviction, and I hope to be still more fervently so by your aid.—Tell me what you desire me to do in this regard, and I will do it.—Tell me what thoughts you wish me to think, and I will think them!—I am all yours, body and soul."—

"Thus, thus I love you.—But you must not be religious for the sake of my love, for then it has no merit in it, but for the sake of God. The ties which are made in this world,—what are they worth in comparison with that existing eternally between the Creator and His creatures? If you love me much, love me in God and for God, as I love you. In any other way it is a sin to fix our attention and our love on any creature."

Ricardo's emotion and ardor received from these words a dash of cold water, but they were strong enough to persist without diminution, and they still kept control of his heart until they reached the portico of the church. Then Maria, taking the holy water, and offering it to him with the tips of her fingers, said:

"Now you must stay under the choir to hear the mass;

I am going up to the altar. Be careful not to look for me
a single time! You must understand that this would be
to profane the sanctuary, and in such a case it would be
better for you not to come in."

" No, I will not look at you, though it will be very hard
work."

" Give me your word that you won't."

" I give it."

' Well, then, *adios,*—it won't be long—wait for me at
the entrance."

After she had gone several steps away, she turned around
to say in a very subdued tone,

" Be sure to do as I said,—and be reverent, will
you ? "

Ricardo gave a sigh of assent, while a happy smile brightened his face.

From that time forth the Marqués de Peñalta every
morning escorted the eldest daughter of the Elorzas to
mass, leaving her at the church door and joining her again
when service was over. Maria evidently felt great pleasure
in having his company, and as for Ricardo, it is not easy
to exaggerate the joy which suddenly fell upon him through
the change brought about in the behavior of his betrothed.
Gradually her influence began to have such weight upon
his spirit, that before long, as he himself had already
suspected would be the case, his ideas began notably to
modify, and not only his ideas but likewise his habits and
manner of life, causing him to be more circumspect in
nature, more careful in his speech, more gentle, and more
religious. Anxious to please his betrothed, who did not
cease to urge him with entreaties and advice, he began to
give up the noisy amusements and even the company of
the other officers of the gun factory, going home early,
frequenting churches, and spending many afternoons with
some of the clergymen; he became a member of several
pious confraternities, among them that of Saint Vincent
de Paul, visiting the poor in company with the *beatos* of
the town, and spending no little money in contributions

for worship; finally, after many heartfelt prayers he made general confession to Fray Ignacio, Maria's confessor.

However strange it may seem, we must declare that Ricardo, far from feeling repugnance or discomfort in this new life, found deep, mysterious pleasures, which till then he had never enjoyed. The pomp and circumstance of the Catholic religion, to which he had hitherto paid little attention, began to fascinate him; the sweet seclusion of the church at eventide, when it is peopled with shadows and murmurs, filled him with a gentle perturbation, with a certain peculiar longing for a lofty secret something; the odors of the incense and wax were for him like a pleasant poison, which put him to sleep, carrying him away to glorious regions of immortal bliss; his frequent deeds of charity produced in him an agreeable aftertaste and a great sense of comfort, increasing his faith; the humiliation of the sacrament of penance, which at first had been so distasteful to him, came to be a fountain of delights; he himself did not know whence they proceeded or how they took possession of his soul. . . .

The afternoon when he made general confession, he felt more deeply than ever the singular consolation and the lively delights to be enjoyed in the depths of humility. It was a clear, beautiful spring afternoon. Fray Ignacio, forewarned by Maria, was waiting for him in the sacristy of San Felipe, and received him with a certain familiar solemnity not free from condescension. He confessed in the sacristy itself, Fray Ignacio being seated in a wooden chair blackened and polished by use, while he knelt at his feet with the diffidence and emotion such as he used to feel as a boy when his mother led him by the hand to the same confessional. The shame of announcing his sins soon passed away, giving place to a gentle tenderness full of unspeakable sweetness, which was so overpowering that he was constrained to tears. The spacious room in which he found himself, its lofty ceiling, its dusty walls set with black shelves and gloomy paintings, gave a melancholy echo to the murmured words of his confession; the sunlight made its way in through the leaded panes of the two windows, making in the wide spaces lines of floating, luminous dust.

The priest threw one arm around his neck and brought his ear close to his lips, gradually probing with many leading questions the inmost nooks and corners of his conscience and the deepest secrets of his soul, sometimes severely chiding him, sometimes giving him sweet counsels, sometimes entertaining him with exemplary anecdotes which agreeably occupied for a few moments the intervals of the pious proceeding. He stopped to speak long of Ricardo's love and its advantages and of Maria's splendid character. Ricardo felt a lively pleasure in these words. He looked with admiration and reverence on that man who was the absolute master of his loved one's secrets, and he determined to put his soul into his hands, that he might guide it just as she had done. The priest continued with a final exhortation full of fire, wherein he eloquently united Maria's name with all the acts of virtue which he expected from him henceforth, so as to stir him to the highest pitch and kindle in his spirit sincere repentance and an irresistible desire to live piously and rejoice his betrothed. When they were done, and Fray Ignacio, assuming a certain solemnity, drew back a little and let fall upon him a full and generous absolution, the lines of the floating luminous dust had vanished and the sacristy was half enveloped in shadows. On the following day, when he went to mass with Maria, instead of waiting under the choir, he went with her to the great altar and received in her presence and to her great joy the holy wafer.

"You have given me the greatest pleasure of my life, Ricardo," she said as they went out of the church.

The young marquis smiled beatifically, and replied in a whisper,

"Do you love me more now?"

"I don't care to answer you," replied the girl with a sweet expression of face. "After communion one ought not to speak of such things.—Let us wait till tomorrow."

They waited till the morrow, and then Maria told him without hesitation that his virtuous conduct inspired her with more and more love, and that he must not faint in the way if he desired to see himself always loved. Ricardo had no other thought than this, and he found so much to delight him in this new state of affairs that for no earthly advantage would he consent to change it. Thus, then, each day he kept on with greater resolution in the path which his betrothed laid out for him, and paid no heed to the chaffing of his companions of the factory, since it was difficult to catch sight of him anywhere else except at home, at Don Mariano's, or at church.

"You have converted me into a *beato!*" he said sometimes to Maria, as a sort of affectionate reproach.

"Why? are you getting tired of it, you rogue?"

"No, dear, no; I am happy enough because thus I have conquered your love——"

"Is that the only reason?"

"—And because I like to lead this better regulated and sober life."

"That is a different thing!"

Let us say here (though the reader will not have failed to perceive it) that in imagination, and even intelligence, Maria was the young Marqués de Peñalta's superior, and that in this regard, and taking into account the deep affection which he professed for her, it was nothing strange that he should yield to his mistress and her counsels in matters wherein men of greater learning and talent frequently give way to their mothers and wives. Maria, aside from her vivid imagination, stimulated and kindled by continual reading, had a special gift for persuading. Her language was always easy and picturesque, and she took especial delight in moving her friends to compassion, when she wanted to entice from them money for the poor or for church services. The rare facility with which she passed from the serious and pathetic to the humorous, and mingled with an earnest entreaty the salt of a witty saying, made her irresistible. The religious confraternities and societies of Nieva had no more active and influential member, and they relied upon her in emergencies as upon a guardian angel who would be able to rescue them from their difficulties. As may be supposed, this lofty estimation was supported, not only by the young lady's splendid moral and physical qualities, but also in no small degree by the fact that she was the daughter of the richest and most respected gentleman in town.

Let us say also that at the period when these events occurred, the clergy and the religious tendencies of our people were suffering a mild sort of persecution on the part of the government, which was then under the control of liberals most extreme in their views and notorious for their heretical ideas, and this, as was to be expected, had greatly excited the consciences of the God-fearing, and had kindled in the Northern provinces, naturally more religious and more tenacious of tradition, an obstinate and bloody civil war which threatened to overthrow the body politic, and, at the same time, our wealth and prestige. All people of greater or less piety who loved our Catholic traditions, everyone who detested the persecution suffered by the Church, and yearned for the kingdom of Jesus on earth under the mediation of his ministers, awaited eagerly the result of this formidable war, in which were at stake not only the more or less genuine rights of a claimant to the throne, but likewise the dearest and most august interests of religion. Those who frequented the churches and were on terms of intimacy with the clergy, took a tacit stand together against the heretics in power, receiving joyfully and quickly spreading all intelligence favorable to the royal-Catholic cause, and falling into anxiety and melancholy when bad news came. In the houses of the richest landed proprietors, in the sacristies and in the back shops of many an absolutist merchant was read on the sly the *Cuartet Real*, the official journal of the Pretender, which came from time to time between pieces of cretonne or packages of macaroni.

Festivals in honor of the Virgin were celebrated with

great pomp as an atonement for the manifold impieties of the Congress of Deputies, and these festivals on more than one occasion ended violently by the interference of drunken Republicans. There was a great increase in attention to religious worship, especially to that of the Sacred Hearts of Jesus and Mary, and many pious people went on pilgrimages to the sanctuary of Lourdes, on their return telling their friends about the fine arrangement and the solid organization of the Catholic hosts in the Basque provinces. A number of young men of the best known families of Nieva had not been seen over night, concealing the real purpose of their absence.

From this to open, resolute conspiracy is but a step, and in Nieva this preparatory step had already been taken. There was formed in the town a Carlist committee, which held its meetings with a certain mystery and kept up close relations with the Central Committee, whose orders it obeyed, and a lively correspondence with the army of the Pretender. As in the country, though not to such a degree as in the Basque provinces, there existed sufficient elements for the service of the Catholic-monarchical cause, to bring about, provided they were well managed, if not a formal war, at least a serious agitation. The committee of Nieva, instigated by that of the capital, decided, after much vacillation and no few discussions, to raise a company within the territory. The preparations were very extensive; they began early in the winter, and did not terminate until the beginning of the spring. There were reports emanating from Bayonne, there came orders and plans of action, there were numberless secret meetings, a few women were enlisted, muskets were surreptitiously abstracted from the factory by a few Carlist workmen, a quantity of white caps and spatterdashes were made; finally, one night there went out to camp some thirty young men, for the most part students and seminarists, at whose head marched the president of the committee, Don César Pardo, whom we had the honor of meeting at the end of the preceding chapter of this narration.

MARTA AND MARIA

Those who had sworn to go forth that night were more than three hundred, but only that handful of braves were on hand, and Don César, giving proofs of what he was, that is, a bold, heroic *caballero*, did not hesitate to take command of them, hoping by his example to carry along the timid. They made their way to the mountain by the valley of Cañedo. But on the next day a dozen policemen, who immediately started in pursuit of them, took them by surprise just as they were dining in camp, and brought them back to the city, bound, without being able to make the least resistance. The people, hearing of the incident, hastened in great numbers to await them on the highway, and saw them filing toward the jail, melancholy but dignified and stern, showing in their haughty eyes that if they had not been victims of a surprise, much blood would have been shed.

The eldest daughter of the house of Elorza was a most ardent devotee of religion, enlisted body and soul in the divine mission of sanctifying her spirit and saving it from the clutches of sin. An unwearied worker in the field of evangelical virtue, ever aspiring to greater perfection, and a zealous propagator of the faith, she could not fail to share in the indignation burning in the breast of the people with whom she had most to do. To her ears came, greatly exaggerated, the rumor of the revolutionary excesses, and the blasphemies daily uttered by the newspapers at the capital, though of course she never ventured to read them. Her confessors commanded her to implore God in her prayers, that the Church might triumph and its enemies be brought to confusion and repentance; her friends and companions in the confraternities asked her to join them in special *novenas* for the consolation of the Virgin; not a few times they asked alms of her for some priest who was lying in misery, and at other times for the unfortunate nuns of some convent, cruelly torn from it that it might be turned into barracks.

All these things, along with a fervid affection for the holy institutions thus persecuted, continually fomented in her

ardent, enthusiastic soul a deep aversion for the persecutors
and the impious men who governed contrary to the law of
God. Sometimes, carried away by her impressionable
temperament, she felt powerful impulses to follow the
example of Judith, making some villain expiate such horrible deeds of sacrilege. She would have liked to hold in
her power the persecutors of Jesus, to destroy them and
crush them to powder. When these cruel impulses passed
away, they left her always with a warm compassion for the
innocent victims of the madness of impiety, and a vague
desire to contribute with her blood to the reign of Jesus
and Mary over all the powers of the earth. She felt that
a something was born in her heart spurring her toward
active life, persuading her to leave for a time the joys of
contemplation for the pains of struggle, repose for labor,
the enchantment of solitude for tumult; she heard, like the
bride of the Sacred Song, a voice saying:

"*Open to me, my sister, my love, my dove, my undefiled,
for my head is filled with dew and my locks with the drops
of the night.*"

She saw clearly that her Jesus suffered for the injustices
of men, and that he demanded her aid; that he asked a new
proof of love by tearing her away from the comfort which
she enjoyed and casting her amid the hurricanes of the
world. But the beautiful young girl at the same time saw
the enormous difficulties rising before her at the first step
which she should make, the persecutions which would come
upon her, and the certainty that those who loved her would
regard her conduct as absurd. She understood her weakness, was afraid of the bitter griefs in store for her, and
she replied, like the bride:

"*I have put off my coat; how shall I put it on? I have
washed my feet; how shall I defile them?*"

Long she struggled with herself to quench the voice calling her to active life, and convince herself that she could
not do anything for the cause of the Lord; but it was in
vain. All her specious arguments were answered victori-
ously by the voice, putting it before her that she ought not

to question whether her aid would or would not be valuable,
but simply to consider the will with which she offered it;
that God was pleased oftentimes to show his power by en-
trusting the execution of great deeds to humble and frail
creatures, as was proved by the renowned Jeanne d'Arc,
Saint Catarina of Siena, Saint Teresa, and other excellent
virgins who accomplished mighty works in spite of the
high powers of the earth.

An insignificant incident brought Maria to a decision.
Her uncle Rodrigo, Marqués de Revollar, who was one of
the most important magnates of the court of the Pretender,
learning of her enkindled faith and the relations which she
maintained with the partisans of Catholic monarchy in
Nieva, wrote her from Bayonne, asking her if she were
ready to serve as intermediary for the correspondence between him and Don César Pardo, president of the Carlist
committee. Maria hastened to reply that she should be delighted to do so, and from that time she began frequently
to receive letters from her uncle, inclosed in which came
others for Don César. These were doubtless the thread by
which the Carlist conspiracy of Nieva was connected with
the lofty spheres whence the orders emanated. And, without her knowing how, she found herself compromised—
and she was not troubled by it—in the cause of the good
Christians who, as she frequently heard from the lips of
Don César and others, were endeavouring to restore Jesus
to his sacred throne, and to rescue him from pride and
heresy.

Far, as I said, from feeling fear or trouble by it, her
courage increased from the danger that she ran, and this
was for her a manifest sign that the favor of Heaven accompanied her, and she constantly entangled herself more and
more in the designs of the conspirators, being present at
their meetings and serving them with zeal and enthusiasm
to the best of her ability. At the time of Don César's armed
expedition she it was who embroidered the standard and
the flannel hearts which the defenders of the faith wore
sewed on their waistcoats. The conspirators felt toward

her the greatest respect on account of her reputation for sanctity, and they professed for her deep affection for the enthusiasm with which she burned for the cause. In some of these meetings she was invited to give her opinion, and she did so with such talent and eloquence, she showed so much fire, and at the same time so much discretion in her language, that the conspirators saw in the beautiful young girl an angel sent from God to sustain their faith and cause them to hold firm in their mighty schemes.

After Don César's abortive attempt the Carlists of Nieva were quite cast down. Maria shed many tears, and besought God earnestly that He would not allow iniquity and falsehood to prevail against His holy law, and that He would have compassion on His good soldiers, now banished and persecuted. And, in fact, God had compassion, and allowed Don César and the larger part of the young men, who with him had been banished to the Canary Islands, to escape in a foreign steamship, and return *incognito* to their fatherland, where they hid in the houses of their faithful and valorous friends. Thereupon the partisans of tradition recovered their energy and began once more to plot, though it was vaguely and without definite object. The object did not appear for some time, until the heroic and determined Don César suggested the idea of striking an audacious blow which would suddenly give them the means of struggling advantageously with the few troops in the province. This stroke, proposed by the valiant ringleader, was nothing less than to seize the gun factory of Nieva. At first all thought the project a crazy one, but gradually, by dint of thinking the idea over and over, they came to look upon it as less unreasonable, and even began quietly, and with great enthusiasm, to prepare the means for carrying it out. Such being the state of things, Maria, one afternoon, went to the house where Don César was concealed, and asked to speak with him in private. What the damsel said must have been exceedingly important and flattering, for the old ringleader, offering her his hand, and giving her a kiss upon the forehead, replied with trembling voice:

" My daughter, you are going to be our salvation. God desires to submit the lot of many brave men to such dainty hands, and who knows if not also the triumph of His cause? "

The young woman retired to her room, where she engaged in prayer for a long time, and then she went down to her mother's apartment. Ricardo soon came in, according to his habit. After a few moments of conversation, Doña Gertrudis went off to sleep, and the two young people retired to a nook in the wnidow to tell each other the sweet every-day secrets, which are sweeter and more delicious the more they are repeated. Maria was preoccupied; her betrothed, with the quickness of one who truly loves, instantly noticed it.

" What ails you today?—it seems to me that you are troubled——"

" I feel sad, Ricardo—I feel sad, as though some misfortune were hurrying on me."

" It's your nerves, which are overtaxed, dear.—Fasts greatly weaken you. You ought to stop them for a while, as well as so many hours of prayer.—You are weakening yourself very much——"

" On the contrary, I have never felt so well as I have lately. It is not my nerves, but a genuine sadness.—It is my soul that suffers, and not my body."

" But have you any reason for being melancholy? "

" I have a presentiment."

" But who cares for presentiments? "

Maria kept silent, and Ricardo also. It was the twilight hour. Both gazed steadily out of the window, upon the great plaza of Nieva, surrounded by its arcades, where the boys who had been let out of school were amusing themselves, running and shouting. The sun was already down, leaving above the tiled roof of the town-hall a wide stretch of sky slightly tinted with rose, which took bluish shades toward the zenith, and yellow toward the horizon. The people of the town were hurrying through the streets, attending to the last duties of the day, and enjoying the sweet

gloaming. Such an evening was rare. The balconies of the
Café de la Estrella were occupied by a few customers, who
were casting their restless eyes around the plaza. On the
balcony of the opposite house a little boy, with blue eyes
and light, curly hair, was having a good time with a wooden
pipe, blowing soap-bubbles. Several ragamuffins below,
with no little chatter, caught them as they floated down,
bursting them with their hats and handkerchiefs.

After a while, Maria turned to her betrothed, and fixing
upon him an intense, anxious look, said, with trembling
voice,

" Ricardo, do you love me much?"

" Why do you ask me that question?—Don't you know
that I do?"

" Yes, I know that you love me.—You have already given
me proof of it—but in love, as in everything not transitory
in this world, there is always a more and less.—Only divine
love is infinite.—The love that you bear me has stood certain proofs; who knows if it could stand others?"

" The love which I have for thee," said the young marquis, placing his hand on his heart, " has power to stand
all proofs."

" All?"

" All."

" Even if I were to ask you your life?"

" Bah! bah!" replied the young man, shrugging his
shoulders with gesture of disdain, " that would be to ask
very little."

Maria smiled with satisfaction, and after a pause, demanded timidly,

" And if I asked your honor—or what you men understand by honor?—" she added, correcting herself.

Ricardo, slightly pale, arose to his feet, and hesitated
some time before he replied. At last he said in a low
tone, calmly:

" Honor, my love, is not our own possession; it is a
trust which Heaven places in our hands at birth, demanding account of it when we die."

A flash of indignation and scorn passed through Maria's eyes as she heard those words.

"And who has told you what Heaven grants you or asks of you, and why do you mix Heaven with things that oftentimes pertain to hell?"

But calming herself in an instant, and giving her words a sweet, persuasive tone, she added:

"What Heaven confides to man at birth nothing can reveal except religion, and religion tells us that man not seldom counts his honor in what he ought to look upon as his ruin and destruction.—Generally what the world most appreciates and thirsts for goes against God's law.— Therefore we ought to make very little account of this pretended honor with which pride and haughtiness are cloaked. The true honor of the Christian consists only in serving God, and obeying His holy commands.—Listen, Ricardo—I asked you if you loved me much for the reason that it was imperative for me to know—to know with absolute and entire certainty.—I am going to make you a confession, after which, if you are as noble and have as much faith as I may demand of you, perhaps you will love me more than ever;—but if your faith is frail and vacillating, and you pay tribute to the frivolous considerations of the world, you will surely love me less, and possibly you will even desert me——"

"Never that!"

"Wait a moment.—Imagine that your betrothed, neglecting and even violating certain rules laid down by society, and overstepping the limits always set for women, especially when she is an unmarried girl, mingles in actions that are purely masculine;—for example, in politics,—and not only mingles in them with thought and word, but actually takes an active part in them. Imagine her to enter into a conspiracy, and work with ardor for the triumph of her cause,—and put her life or her liberty at stake to accomplish it——"

"What, you?"

"Yes," replied Maria, with resolution. "I have entered

with all my heart into a conspiracy.—I am working with all my might and main for the triumph of the cause of the righteous.—God knows well that it makes no difference to me whether one set of men or another rule over us, and that no earthly consideration has tempted me to such a step. But I have seen, and I still see religion and the ministry of religion, abused; I see the salvation of many souls endangered, I see every day the divine Jesus and his sweet name made a mockery by the impious men who chance to rule in Spain, wearing a crown of thorns a thousand times more grievous than what he bore at Jerusalem—and I feel that his eyes implore me and I hear his celestial voice begging me to lift that terrible-crown a little.—Do you think that I can weigh against the sublime interests of religion, the safety of my soul, and the glory of Jesus, the childish fear of displeasing the world?"

"I know nothing about it," replied Ricardo, in a dull voice, buried in deep thought.

"You see how I was right! Now that I have confessed to you and told you my secret, your love already grows dim, and you certainly will soon drift away from me and abandon me!"

The young girl's last word caused Ricardo to lift his head quickly. He had a presentiment that something serious was at hand, and he replied in a tone of ill-humor,

"And what is it that has moved you to confide to me all these things, which you have kept so secret till now?"

"Before all, forgive me for not having confided in you before.—They were secrets that did not belong to me.— Besides, I imagined that you would not think as I did, and would raise some objection to my plans.—But now you have greatly changed; you are more religious, and you love the name of Christian which you bear.—Therefore, I decided to open my soul entirely before you, and to put into your trusty, honest hands the lives of many noble-souled men.—I am very weak, Ricardo *mio;* I am only a poor girl, incapable of struggling and resisting;—a

shadow makes me tremble,—a word startles me and moves
me to the very depths of my being.—My eyes are more
accustomed to shed tears than to direct imperious glances,
and my hands are folded with more pleasure than they are
raised in anger.—I have no cunning to avoid impositions,
or fortitude to endure pain.—I can do nothing,—nothing,—
and I am filled with despair; but you are brave, you are
noble, and you are generous.—I can rely on you as the
bird in the air, and thanks to you, win heaven.—These moments are supreme for me.—I feel as though I was near the
abyss, and I have no power to stay my steps.—If you do
not reach me out your hand, you will very soon see me
plunging into it.—Ricardo *mio,* do not abandon me,—for
God's sake, do not abandon me!"

The young man felt that the danger was nearer than
ever, and exclaimed,

"Let us have it done with at once, Maria. Let us know
what it is all about."

"It is about a great act of merit that you can accomplish
toward your salvation if you will abandon the wicked suggestions of the world and listen to the invitation of Heaven.
—In this town there is a mighty weapon which, instead of
serving God, as everything in this world ought to serve
Him, is an awful auxiliary of the devil. This weapon is
the gun factory—— " Maria stopped a moment, and then,
casting a frightened look at her lover, continued in a trembling voice: "You can snatch this weapon from the evil
one and restore it into the hands of God by delivering it
over to the defenders of religion and——"

Maria stopped a second time, and looked with horror at
the livid, contracted face of the young marquis, who
grasped her by the arm, and shaking her violently, roared,
rather than spoke:

"Who suggested to you the idea of proposing *that* to
me?—Answer me.—Who was the vile, low wretch who
advised you to do it?—I'll go myself this very instant and
tear out his tongue for him! Tell me, tell me, Maria!—
This thought never originated with you.—You couldn't

have supposed that your lover, the Marquis of Peñalta, the descendant of so many noble gentlemen, a soldier of honor and loyalty, could calmly listen to such a proposition!—You could not have imagined that the man who adored you was a cowardly traitor, whom his comrades would justly laugh to scorn!—Only thus can I pardon the horrible words which you have just spoken.—Listen, for God's sake, Maria.

"Just now my brain is on fire and my heart is frozen.—I hear within me a voice which prophesies a great misfortune.—Yet still, at this moment, I tell you that I love you with all my soul.—Even to the point of giving my life for you gladly;—but if this love which I have for you were multiplied a thousandfold, and were not to be gratified in this world, I would crush it, I would blot it out as a light is blotted out,—with a breath,—and I would remain all my life long in darkness sooner than consent to such villainy.—What am I saying?—If God himself came down to propose that to me, and threatened me with the eternal torments of hell, I would refuse.—I would prefer to be damned with the loyal than be saved with traitors."

Maria hung her head in consternation. After some little time she succeeded in saying in a weak voice:

"You do not understand me, Ricardo, nor do I understand you any better. In judging of the things of this world we put ourselves at very opposite points of view; you look through the glass of the conventions established by men, and I only through that of the law of God. For you the renown of bravery, the reputation of being loyal and noble, is the first thing; for me the main thing is the salvation of my soul.—Pardon me if I have offended you, and let this *honor* which you worship so fervently serve you to forget forever what we have been talking about."

Ricardo gave the girl a long, sad look. He had just learned once and for all that this woman could never be his; that he held only a very subordinate place in this idolatrous heart, so full of mysterious sentiments, grand and sublime perhaps, but incomprehensible for him. A tear sprang into his eyes and rolled tremblingly down his cheeks.

"You are right, Maria.—I don't understand you.—My father was a man of honor, and he also could not have understood you.—My grandfather was a soldier who lost his life in the defense of his country, and he, too, would not have understood you any better.—But my father and my grandfather would have felt insulted, as I feel insulted,. that anyone should remind them that they ought to keep secrets confided to them."

Both maintained a protracted silence, gazing sadly through the panes upon the great plaza of Nieva, which began to be concealed under the gathering shades of night. The passers-by were going to their homes with slow and lazy gait. A few lights were already burning in the depths of the houses. The ragamuffins, who had been laboriously catching the soap-bubbles sent out to them by the boy in the opposite house, had disappeared, and he, tired of blowing through his pipe, finally flung it to the ground together with his bowl of soap-suds, and set himself making faces at Ricardo and Maria; but they, solemn and motionless, paid no attention, as on other occasions, and the child, surprised to find them so serious, likewise remained motionless, staring at them with his bright, beautiful, cherub eyes.

CHAPTER XIII

IN WHICH ARE TOLD THE LABORS OF A CHRISTIAN VIRGIN

THE general commander kept by the fickle Spanish republic in the province of —— was a good deal of a barbarian,—be it said without intention of hitting him too hard, for every man has the right to be as much of a barbarian as he finds consistent with sound morals and good habits. The first thing that he did, as soon as it was breathed to him that the Carlists of Nieva were getting ready for a surprise (*algarada*, battering-ram, was what he called it), and intended nothing less than to get possession of the gun factory, was to summon the commandant Ramírez and say to him:

"Within an hour you must start for Nieva with two companies, together with the inspector of police, and as soon as you get there, you arrest and bring to me lashed arm to arm—do you understand?—lashed arm to arm, all the individuals who are put down on this paper."

" 'Tis well, my brigadier!"

"It will not need more than half a company to guard them. You, with the rest of the force, put yourselves under command of the colonel-director until I make other arrangements."

" 'Tis well, my brigadier!"

As the commandant Ramírez, having made his salute, was going out of the office door, the brigadier called him back,—

"Harkee, Ramírez, how did I tell you to bring the prisoners?"

"Lashed arm to arm, my brigadier."

"Correct; God go with you!"

The night on which the two companies reached Nieva was the one chosen by Don César's friend to sound the battle-cry and seize the factory. The conspiracy was well planned. At one o'clock in the morning fifty men were to meet in the garden of a rich Carlist proprietor, and fifty more in the wine-cellar of another, to arm and equip themselves. At two precisely they were all to march against the factory, the guard of which, at this time under command of the young Marqués de Peñalta, did not exceed twenty-five men, and attack it ostensibly at the doors, while others should scale the walls in the rear. Once inside they would quickly seize upon the arms already manufactured, loading them upon mules which were in readiness, set fire to the workshops, and haste away from the town. In case they should be attacked, they expected to raise easily five or six hundred men well provided with arms and ammunition. Don César had no doubt of the success of his enterprise, but the cursed bird traditional in all conspiracies, past and to come, upset the brave *caballero's* project.

At eleven o'clock that evening the commandant Ramírez and the inspector of police had possession of all the individuals of the committee, and ten or a dozen of the most outspoken Carlists of Nieva, who, tied together and under the guard of half of a company, according to the orders of the general commander, were under the arcade of the town-hall, waiting the order of march. The only woman among these was Maria. In vain did Don Mariano, with tears in his eyes, beg the leader of the force to let him take her in a carriage. The commandant Ramírez declared that he was deeply grieved at not being able to gratify him, and that the only thing that he could do, out of respect for him, was to give her parole-leave and wait a few moments until she procured thick footwear and suitable outside garments, though to do this exposed him to the wrath of the brigadier who—(and here the commandant Ramírez employed the term which we have already had the honor of applying to him).

At last the order was given, and the lieutenant set out on the march with the prisoners. Don Mariano would not leave his daughter. Though it did not rain at that particular moment, the night was very damp and the roads truly abominable, as was proved by the spatterdashes of the soldiers. In the town almost everybody was aware of what was going on, and many dark, silent forms filled the balconies, straining their eyes to see the prisoners pass by. As they went through a certain street, an angry female voice cried from a balcony,

" Villains, you will pay for all these things in hell ! "

The soldiers lifted their heads and dropped them again, silently proceeding on their march, the measured sound of which inspired melancholy and fear. They all felt on their caps a steady broadside of looks of hatred, which, notwithstanding their innocence, they received with the resignation of those accustomed to suffering injustice. They soon left the last houses of the town and entered the high-road, the first stretches of which were adorned with lofty poplars. The sky was still dark and thick, wrapping the earth in darkness. Scarcely could they see the trunks of the neighboring trees, or the shapes of the houses or farm buildings along the roadside. The feet of the company no longer produced the sharp clatter which they made when they were walking over the paved streets, but a muffled sound still more sad.

The lieutenant, a pretty good-natured young fellow of twenty, ordered the soldiers to march in parallel column, with the prisoners in the middle. Then he approached the latter, and asking them if he could do anything for them, apologized courteously for taking them bound together, but they must understand that the brigadier was somewhat of a—(the young lieutenant made use of the same expression which his commandant, and we as well, has already applied to him). The prisoners muttered their thanks and relapsed into a dignified silence. Soon it began to rain furiously. Don Mariano, who had not exchanged a word with his daughter, hastily spread his umbrella to shelter her, and held her long pressed to his heart, whispering in her ear: ·

"My daughter, what a bitter trial you are giving me!—Wrap yourself up well!—Are you cold? oh, that obstinate brute shall answer me for this!—I will go to Madrid and see the Minister of War, and have him sent to prison!—Does the rain reach you anywhere, sweetheart mine? Do you want my waterproof?—To send and have my daughter pinioned!—Oh, the confounded pig! in what sty did this farcical government find him!—If you get sick, I will kill him without a moment's hesitation.—But you, silly girl, who inveigled you into this pack of conspirators without my permission?—If I had not let you wander about so much among these churches, you would not at this time be suffering such trials.—What have you to do with Carlists or with Republicans?—A well-educated girl stays quietly at home, looking after her father's shirts and knitting stockings.—Do you hear?—knitting stockings!—The beast!

wretch! to send and take my daughter pinioned!—If I see him, I won't promise not to seize him by the throat——"

"Calm yourself, papa,—calm yourself, for Heaven's sake. I am perfectly comfortable.—When one suffers for God the suffering is turned into pleasure.—Never did I feel better than at this moment—and it is because I feel in my soul the consolation of having done something to restore Jesus to His holy kingdom.—The only thing that makes me suffer, is to see you unhappy.—Ay! papa, what wouldn't I give to have your faith as living and ardent as mine, so that you would despise all the pains of earth, and march calm and content, as I am marching, whither God may wish to take me!"

Don Mariano felt a torrent of sharp, angry words choking him, but he could not give them utterance. All that he did was to wrap his waterproof around his daughter, emitting a sort of grunt significantly eloquent.

It ceased to rain at last. A slight breath of southwest wind made itself felt, and the thick mantle over the sky began to thin away, letting through a slender, feeble light which brought out the silhouettes of the soldiers, and the trees, and the enormous forms of the mountains girding the valley. The silence in the band was sepulchral. The prisoners exchanged not a single word, devouring their rage and grief. In the country, likewise, was heard none of those pleasant sounds that increase the mystery of the night, and fill the soul with soft melancholy. Only as they passed in front of some house, they heard within the threatening bark of a dog, protesting against the march of troops at such an unusual hour, and, now and then, the no less gentle muttering of Sergeant Alcarez as he cursed the night, and his luck, and the mother who bore him.

The wind kept blowing stronger and stronger, a soft, moist wind which the prisoners took to be of sufficiently evil import. The trees, lining the sides of the road, twisted, as though in agony, scattering all the rain drops with which they were laden. In the feeble light of the sky the forms of the huge, black clouds began to appear, rushing swiftly through the air, as though closely pursued by some monster of the night. Back of these clouds the faint blue of the firmament could not be seen, but a thick mantle of gray, seemingly impenetrable. Nevertheless, the wind, still increasing in violence, began at last to rupture it in a few places, making beautiful rifts, in the depths of which could be seen the soft lightning of some star. The great, black clouds swept over them, and blotted them out, but the mantle was constantly rifted again in other places, and the little stars once more tipped friendly winks to the earth.

At last a great burst of silvery light suddenly bathed the whole landscape: the moon had come out between two clouds, fair and splendid as a virgin who opens the windows of her apartment. But hardly had she cast one look of curiosity at our band, when the rude clouds drew together, binding a fillet over her eyes, and leaving the earth gloomy and dark. Again she appeared on high, and once more she was hidden, as she saw a hurrying legion of clouds of every form and shape, flying to unknown regions, pass before her face. In the space of half an hour, she presented and hid herself an incredible number of times, seeming to the eyes of the pilgrims like a ship ready to sink in some restless, stormy ocean.

Finally the tempest of the sky grew calm. Slowly the thick cloud masses, which spotted the face of the sky, had disappeared behind the mountains. A few, which still remained, and at long intervals, passing across the moon, left the earth in darkness, likewise hid the mountain-peaks. And the sky was left clear and bright, spreading out its dark mantle adorned with stars. The moon traced a luminous circle around her, in which, like a haughty queen, she let no other star shed his light. The wide valley seemed to quiver gently with joy at feeling the kiss of her silvery beams, and sent forth from the orange groves, and the quiet streams, and the white hamlets scattered here and there, millions of reflections vanishing with gentle mystery in the air. In some places great, luminous sheets stretched out,

298

where could be seen with wonderful clearness the outlines of trees and fences; in others, clustered shadows, guarding the dreams of flowers. The broad valley, when thus illumined, had the semblance of a sleeping lake.

After tramping along for a considerable time through the midst of the valley, our band struck into the mountains circling it. It was necessary to cross them to reach the plain surrounding ——. The highway followed the most accessible places, skirting the side of one of the mountains with a pretty decided slope. The horizon widened wonderfully. As they began to climb, the lieutenant commanded a halt before a huge tavern, situated near the highway, and sending to the landlord, obliged him to arise and provide his people with food. The prisoners went into the house and rested some time. Then they set forth once more, calmly climbing the sharp declivity.

The exuberant vegetation of the valley had been passed. The mountains, which constantly shut them in closer, leaving barely room for the highway, were clad only in ferns. From time to time they came upon the opening of some coal mine, dug near the road. Don Mariano could not resist the temptation of talking about the railway to Nieva, and he approached the lieutenant and showed him where the line from Sotolonga was going, explaining in full the advantages which it had over the line from Miramar. The pathway was now considerably drier on account of the hillside, and the moon from on high still lighted up the way, and fixed her sweet, calm gaze on the pilgrims. The notes of a guitar were heard. When did the guitar ever cease to sound during a march of Spanish soldiers? And a voice of heroic timbre sang in the accents of the South:

> " *Como cosita propria*
> *Te miraba yo;*
> *Te miraba yo;*
> *Pero quererte como te quería*
> *Eso se acabó,*
> *Eso se acabó.*"

299

Four or five soldiers scattered here and there likewise showed their southern origin by shouting at the end of the strophe, *Olé, olé!* That song, born in the warm soil of Andalusia, was a magic wand which banished sadness from all hearts. The stern mountains, as though possessed by a sudden sympathy, re-echoed the soldier's voice, carrying it far away across the gorges and ravines. Lively conversation arose in the company, stopping every time that the Andalusian soldier struck up a new verse. The prisoners persisted in their obstinate silence. All marched negligently, with mouths open, instinctively enjoying the favorable change which the night had undergone. Suddenly, as they were doubling one of the numerous turns in the road, in the roughest part of the divide, the report of a musket was heard. A soldier dropped to the ground. Almost at the same time the portentous cry of *¡ Viva Carlos Septimo!* was hurled into space. Lifting their heads, all saw at no great distance, standing on one of the rocks commanding the road, a man with long, white mustachios, dressed in a sheepskin *zamarra* and Basque cap. The prisoners instantly recognized in him the president of the committee, Don César Pardo. The lieutenant ordered the men to close up, fearing an ambuscade, and gave the command to fire; but the volley had no result. When the smoke cleared away Don César was still seen calmly reloading his gun. As he fired it, he cried again, with still more fury,

" *¡ Viva Carlos Septimo!* "

" May the lightning strike you, you old fox; you have spoiled my arm for me," exclaimed Sergeant Alcarez, raising his hand to the wound.

" Second column, aim! fire! " shouted the lieutenant.

This time there was no better result. Don César fired again, crying,

" *¡ Viva la religión!* "

Then the lieutenant angrily gave the command,

" Fire as you please! "

An incessant crackling of musketry followed from the half company, drawn up in battle array; but the solitary enemy neither retreated nor fell. Standing on the rock, without even deigning to shelter himself 'behind it, he steadily loaded and fired his musket, always repeating in a terrible voice,

"*¡ Viva Carlos Septimo! ¡ Viva la religión!*"

He rarely fired without causing some loss in the company. The moon illuminated his proud, fierce face loaded with wrinkles, giving it a fantastic appearance. His eyes gleamed like those of a madman, and his tall, lusty frame stood forth in the luminous atmosphere, like that of a supernatural being who had come down to punish offences committed against heaven.

"Do you know me, republicans, do you know me?" he cried, without ceasing to fire. "I am Don César Pardo, an old Christian and a Carlist from head to foot."

"You're a scoundrel," replied a soldier.

"Harkee, little fellow, you're all of a tremble, and the balls you shoot go wide of the mark."

"Try this one, then!"

"No, sir!—It didn't hit.—If I had ten men with me, how you would all scatter, you lapdogs!"

"Do what you please, boys!—Kill that whelp!" cried the lieutenant at the height of irritation.

The soldiers broke for the mountain, and began to climb it with the agility of wildcats. The rage which possessed them redoubled their powers. But at the same time the lieutenant, snatching a musket from one of the soldiers, leveled at Don César and brought him down.

"That'll do, boys!—Come back!—the hawk is winged at last," he cried in triumphant accents.

"It only wounded my leg;—my bill is whole yet," replied the ringleader, with hoarse voice.

And in truth, though his hip was shot through, he managed to raise himself up and load his musket, which he instantly fired at those who were coming up against him. They roared with rage as they pulled themselves up by the ferns, or dug their fingers into the moss to climb faster.

"Come, come, you cowards," screamed Don César, like-

wise maddened with rage. "Come and learn how to fight!
—You see how a Carlist officer makes war!—You see how
he is equal to fifty republicans!—Tomorrow tell your ex-
ploit to General Bum Bum who sent you!—Let 'em give
you the laurel wreath, you heroes! Now here goes a shot
for Don Carlos!—Ah! I know how you are taking off a
girl as prisoner, you brave warriors of the republic!—Here
goes another for Doña Margarita!—Did the pill taste bad,
eh, fellow?—Oh, how glad I am to see you! *¡ Viva
Carlos!*"

He was not allowed to finish. A soldier who had reached
the summit put the muzzle of his gun to his forehead and
blew off his head, saying,

"Die, you hog!"

He killed him without heeding the voices of his comrades, who said, "Leave him for me! Leave him for
me!"

As they reached him, with pale cheeks and bloodshot
eyes, they all discharged their guns at the lifeless body of
the terrible ringleader, quickly destroying it in the most
horrible manner. When that act of barbarism, inspired
by wrath, was accomplished, the soldiers remained silent.
Their irritation being calmed, they began to realize how
they had been fighting with one single man, and they were
dissatisfied with themselves. In spite of themselves they
felt stirred to admiration.

"The old man had nerve," said one, as he wiped off a
few drops of blood which had spattered into his face.

"He was well quit of his life," declared a second.

"The truth is, that taking them one at a time, that old
man would have swallowed this whole division, uniform
and all," said a third, finally; and no one uttered a protest.

In the company there were one killed and five wounded,
as the result of the skirmish. They placed them all, as
well as they could, on improvised stretchers, and again took
up the line of march. Not only the soldiers, but the prisoners, plodded on in silence and melancholy, profoundly
impressed by the tragic event which had just occurred.

The night was still as calm and bright as before, and in the zenith the moon, which had just been lighting that unequal combat with her soft poetic beams, still shed them upon the company slowly ascending the highway, and upon the livid, dismembered corpse which they had left behind on the crag. The struggles, the joys, the griefs of us poor devils who creep on the earth, what worth have they? what do they signify before the august serenity of the heavens? For them the fall of an empire and the fall of a leaf are of equal consequence; for them the sigh of a maiden in love and the groan of a dying man are alike in sound. "Nature is deaf," said the great Leopardi, "and cannot pity."

But Maria walked along with her eyes fixed on the sky, regarding it with far different thoughts. There where the poet found nothing but a blind will, incapable of good, the pious girl saw a foreseeing and merciful God, as merciful as terrible, who received the good into his bosom, and sent the wicked to eternal torment—a God, who, like ourselves, was appeased by prayers and tears. She felt stirred as she thought of the fate which the soul of him who had just died would meet in presence of divine justice, and by a quick, spontaneous movement of her heart, she said in a loud, clear voice:

"For the soul of the departed Don César Pardo: Our Father, who art in heaven, hallowed be thy name; thy kingdom come; thy will be done on earth as it is in heaven." The prisoners began to pray with fervor. Some of the soldiers did the same. Then they relapsed into silence as they marched along, and nothing was heard but the sound of labored breathing, and occasionally the complaints of the wounded, not very well accommodated in their litters. At last they crossed the highest point of the watershed, and began to descend toward the wide valley of ——. The dawn was already appearing in the confines of the east. The dull blue of the sky in that quarter was fading into a pale, melancholy light, which at the same time blotted out the sparkling stars. The travelers felt a chill, unpleasant breath of wind which turned their noses and hands purple.

Very soon a great, golden fringe spread over the eastern hills, and the band could regard at their pleasure the valley stretching out at their feet, where the green of the meadows and the yellow of the plowed lands shone in variegated tones, coarse or soft, like a rich mantle of brocade. A few tufts of cloud were slowly rising from the depths of the streamlets which furrowed it; and yonder, in the west, a great curtain of black mountains, on whose summits the snow still gleamed white, shut it in abruptly, casting across it a great mantle of shadow. In spite of this shadow, the eyes of the travelers who knew the region could distinguish in the very edge of the black curtain the spire of the proud tower of the cathedral of ——. The prisoners and their guards reached the plain, and crossed the valley from one end to the other, expending much time in the transit, principally because of the care required by the wounded. Finally, at eight o'clock in the morning, they reached the first houses of the suburb of ——.

The inhabitants of the capital had heard of the sudden blow struck by the military governor against the Carlists of Nieva, and a great throng, collected in the streets, was impatiently waiting to see the prisoners pass by. It was composed almost entirely of what, during the revolutionary period, was called the sovereign people; that is, of all the ragamuffins and rough-scuff of the city, together with quite a number of respectable people, though loungers, and almost all the *ladies* of the suburbs.

On seeing the band from afar, the multitude was stirred tempestuously, and there arose a dull, universal clamor.

" There they are now! There they are now!"—" I was told that they intended to assassinate all the liberals of Nieva last night."—" Ah! the rascals! Fortunate they fell beforehand into the trap!"

" They must be undeceived," declared a fat and highly colored *caballero,* with a good-natured face; " all the Carlists are either rascals or fools. I would not employ any

other means with them than extermination.—Fire and
sword!"

"Let us sing them *El trágala* when they pass," said a
ragged lad to two other swells accompanying him.

The people pressed close as the band approached, those
who could finding standing-room on the street-walls and the
trees along the way. On seeing the wounded, and learning through the curt account of some soldier about the incident of Don César, the inquisitive citizens felt justified in
manifesting their indignation, and though at first they contented themselves with giving each other the benefit of their
hostile thoughts, finally they began to belch forth against
the prisoners furious insults, apostrophizing them in loud
tones, as though they had all received some wrong at
their hands. Thus they continued escorting them through
the streets of the city, their fury and indignation ever on
the increase, until words were not enough to satisfy them.
The prisoners marched with sunken heads and flushed
faces.

"Oh, you hypocrites! saint-killers!" shouted one at
them; "may the day soon come when we shall see you
strung up!"

"See how those cursed rascals hang their heads! If
they had us in their fists the meanest of them would be
happier."

"Now cry 'Long live Carlos Seventh,' you rubbish!"
But the popular fury was most madly excited against
Maria. Neither her youth, nor her beauty, nor her weak-
ness, served to spare her from ferocious, filthy insults.

"Who is that woman with 'em? They say she's a saint."
—"Yes, a saint, but she's a loose character!"—"See here,
wench, if you're hunting for a husband, you'll find one
here!"—"That one needs a few dozen lashes!"—"See
what hypocritical eyes the harridan has!"

It is easy to appreciate the state of disturbance, wrath,
anguish, and excitement which overmastered Don Mariano
Elorza, at being obliged to listen to these rude remarks. In
his impotent rage he bit his hands and stopped his ears,

fearing that his blood would boil over and lead him to do something endangering his daughter's life.

As we have already said, the crowd, not content with flinging insults, took it into their heads to indulge in brutal treatment of them. One rough youth gave the example by hurling a piece of orange. Many others followed his example, and there fell on the unfortunate prisoners a hailstorm of projectiles, more disgusting, it must be confessed, than deadly. However, a cabbage-stalk thrown violently, hit Maria in the face and made her lips bleed.

Oh! then the unhappy Don Mariano's fury burst forth, terrible and resistless, as the sea in its moments of tempests, as a volcano in eruption. His athletic figure fell upon the group of loungers nearest him, and he annihilated it with his onslaught, scattering the men on the ground as though they had been made of straw; those who were left on their feet fled without awaiting a second attack. The Señor de Elorza would have made his way through the whole crowd, but meeting with resistance in the serried ranks, he grasped the throat of the first ruffian at hand and would have surely choked him to death, had not the soldiers come to his aid and pushed back the angry father. His wrath then broke out in a storm of frenzied words, which brought the throng to silence.

"Guttersnipes! vile guttersnipes! cowards! beasts!—If they had not prevented me, I would have pulled your tongues out, one at a time.—You have wounded my daughter.—Didn't you know she was my daughter, you rascals? Here you showed your valor, you bullies! why don't you go to Navarra to fight with armed men, instead of attacking the defenseless!—Because you are cowards!—An indecent rabble that ought to be scattered with whips! If there be among you anyone worthy of meeting me, let him come out so that I can spit in his face.—Let go of me, let go of me, for God's sake! Let me kill one of these scamps who have wounded my daughter. Let me go, señores, let me go!"

Don Mariano struggled to tear himself from the arms of
the soldiers. The rabble who had fallen back before his
attack, seeing him in custody, recovered from their alarm,
and crowded back again like basilisks, foaming at the
mouth with rage.

" This old coxcomb insults the people! "—" He's a crazy
fool! "—" It's a shame for the people to be so insulted! "
—" Why don't you kill this knave! "—" Kill him, yes, kill
him! "—" Kill him! "—" Kill him! "

And the throng pressed up to the band closer and closer,
though slowly, like an ocean of waves swelling and threatening, and would soon have put an end to Don Mariano
and the prisoners, had not the lieutenant prevented such
an act of barbarism by shouting at the top of his
voice,

" Attention, company—ready—aim! "

Then the swelling waves subsided as by magic. The
lieutenant's voice was Neptune's *sed motos prestat compo-
nere fluctus*. The sovereign people turned tail, and saying
in their hearts " escape if you can," started to run in all
directions, tripping up here, and scrambling to feet again
there. And it is reported that his majesty ran so fast
and so far, that in less than three minutes he disappeared
from before the guns of the military.

Thanks to this, the prisoners were left in peace until
they reached the prison, where they were lodged in a great
hall, filthy enough, with a wooden floor, filled with rat-
holes in many places. Maria was assigned a separate room,
comparatively clean and comfortable.

The hour set for the hearing before the council of war
was twelve o'clock; and when the clock struck, the prisoners, securely guarded, were transferred to a handsomely
decorated salon in the building where it met. The officers
composing it were seated behind a long table, covered with
red damask trimmed with gold lace, under a velvet canopy
which, in other times, before we had the republic, had
served to give regality and prestige to the portrait of the
king. The presiding officer was the military governor, who

was anxious to have done with the business in a rapid and violent manner. He wished to inflict exemplary punishment upon all of the conspirators, or, what is the same thing, "not to leave a mannikin with his head on," to use his own words. He was a chubby man, with great blub-cheeks and a thin mustache; a perfect image of what we, and likewise the Commandant Ramírez, and the lieutenant of the convoy, have already called him. The other officers had absolutely nothing remarkable in their faces; coarse features, black eyes, twisted mustachios, sharp-pointed goatees, commonplace faces, on the whole, though, manly. At first sight, it was evident that they wore their togas broad. When the prisoners entered, the doors and the standing-room of the building were invaded by a great crowd, not so rude and low as that of the morning; it was made up of people of more respectability,—students for the most part, *hidalgos,* and officeholders. This throng preserved a thoughtful, compassionate silence at seeing them enter.

They were introduced one at a time in the great hall of state. The captain, who acted as prosecutor, took their depositions, having before him documents in proof of the crime. The members of the Carlist committee of Nieva gave their testimony as best suited their ideas of propriety, denying the majority of the counts, astutely pleading guilty to others, and, in fine, doing all in their power to be let off easily. The fat-cheeked brigadier lost his temper not a few times during the course of the hearing, interrupting the prosecutor to launch harsh apostrophes at the prisoners, and threatening to have them shot in the interim, if they did not reveal all the minutiæ and ramifications of the conspiracy; but he accomplished little by his intimidations. When Maria's turn came, he smiled sarcastically, and said with rough irony,

"Have the goodness to draw near, señorita, and to reply to the questions which this *caballero capitán* will put to you."

"What is your name?" asked the prosecutor.

" Maria de Elorza y Valcárcel."

" *De, dee, dee,*" snorted the brigadier, " always the same aristocratic pretensions ! ".

" You are accused of serving as intermediary in the cor-respondence between the Marqués de Revollar, Don Carlos's minister and counsellor, and the ringleader, Don César Pardo, lately exiled by virtue of sentence of the council of war, which met on the 14th of March. More-over, you are accused of having been present as an active participant at various meetings held by the conspirators of Nieva, with the assistance of the same ringleaders who escaped, and various other political criminals. In these meetings you have indulged in speech fomenting rebellion, and making suggestions to help its success. It is said that you embroidered the banner for the rebels, and have hidden hats and spatterdashes in your house, and likewise have procured money for the conspirators."

The prosecutor stopped speaking. There were a few moments of silence. The brigadier impatiently said,

" Come.—Reply ! Are the deeds of which you stand ac-cused true ? "

Maria, with her clear gaze fastened on the president's supercilious face, replied in firm, calm accents:

" All that the Señor Fiscal has just set forth is pure truth, and I take the warmest pride in it. It is true that I have served as intermediary in the correspondence between my noble uncle, the Marqués de Revollar, and the brave Don César Pardo (whom may God take to glory!). It is certain that I have been present at the meetings, where a conspiracy was planned against the impious government now existing, and that I have endeavored, with my feeble speech, to stir the conspirators to the combat, and it is equally certain that I embroidered the banner and other articles for the defenders of the faith. It is likewise true that I have furnished all the money that I could, but it is not enough to say that I hid in my father's house hats and spatterdashes: I have also hidden arms, muskets, and their bayonets and ammunition."

The officers of the council were stupefied. The brigadier himself, in spite of his choleric temper, remained for some moments dumb before the girl's audacity. But if they had known her as we know her, it is certain that they would not have had reason to be surprised. The eldest daughter of the Elorzas had entered into the Carlist conspiracy, completely persuaded that she was accomplishing a work very grateful in the eyes of God, and she had firmly determined not to turn back before any danger. Her ardent, all-powerful faith was eager to find means to serve Him, and moreover the longing for imitation, for which we have already given her credit, impelled her to imitate the conduct of those sainted virgins who fought against the power of the cruelest tyrants, and gave a glorious example of constancy in times of persecution. She knew by heart the lives of Saint Leocadia, Saint Barbara, Saint Julia, Saint Eulalia, and other illustrious martyrs of the Christian faith, and their steadfastness was for her an example and further incentive in the road to sanctity upon which she had entered. Countless times she had imagined scenes of martyrdom in which she was the principal personage, and in which she had always come forth conqueror; just as many men fond of battles, dream that they are fighting with a dozen champions and making them run ignominiously, and others enamored of oratory represent themselves as speaking before multitudes, moving them and carrying them away by their eloquence. With what admiration had she read about the flight of the sainted maiden of Merida, from the battlefield of her fathers to the city where she presented herself voluntarily before the governor Calfurniano to confess her faith, and ask a martyr's death! In the march which she had just made from Nieva, she had many times recalled the details of that memorable flight, gladly seeing in it a certain analogy with that of the saint. Now that she saw herself in the presence of stern, angry judges, she found the resemblance still more striking, and this encouraged her, in no small degree, in her determination to stand firm in spite of danger.

The brigadier, who was not very well informed in regard to what had happened to Saint Eulalia at the hands of Calfurniano, believed honestly that the silly girl was ridiculing him, and, giving a tremendous rap on the table with his fist, he shouted:

" Listen, señorita, do you know with whom you are talking? Do you know that I am the military governor of the province, and that I have never had any decided fondness for jests? Do you know what risk you run at making sport of this most dignified council of war, over which at this moment I preside? Do you know that I have a mind to send you to prison, and shut you up in a cell, and keep you there on bread and water for the rest of your life? Do you know it? heh?—Do you know it? heh?—heh?—heh?"

" I know perfectly," replied Maria in steady, but modest tone, " that I am in the presence of a council of war; but, though I were facing a battalion of soldiers, aiming at me with their guns, I should say the same thing without dropping or adding a letter. I am not accustomed to telling falsehoods, and when it concerns acts which may be of some service to the cause of God, I should be unworthy of calling myself a Christian, if I denied them in the presence of anyone."

" And what is it that you call the cause of God, my beautiful señorita?" asked the brigadier with apparent calmness, while his eyes flashed lightnings of wrath.

" I call the cause of God that which is at the present time represented by the legitimate and Catholic king, around whom are collected all those who feel scandalized to see religion persecuted and its ministers molested; those who mourn at seeing the infamous blasphemies uttered in Congress, and daily spread broadcast by the journals; those who do not wish to see impiety enthroned in Spain, the Catholic land, above all others, granted by God one single faith and one single worship."

The brigadier grew redder than a guindilla pepper; his lips trembled with wrath; he was about to make some shocking remark, but at last he controlled himself, and said to the prosecuting officer,

"Continue your examination, Señor Capitán."

For the first time in his life the brigadier smothered his barbarous words. The fiscal, over whom the force of attraction for the opposite sex had not yet lost its influence, perhaps from the reason that he was younger, continued, all the time softening his voice and sweetening the smile that distorted his countenance:

"Very well; since you have the candor to confess that you have been a party to the conspiracy, let us hope that you will continue to be frank, and tell us all its details and the names of the persons connected with it."

"Oh, no,—that cannot be. I declare and confess my acts, but I cannot those of the others. Even if they granted me permission, be very sure that I would not do it, since it seems to me a sin to put into the hands of the impious arms to murder good Christians——"

"This cannot be allowed," vociferated the brigadier, overcome by wrath. "Let us see, señorita; do you believe that I have not the means to make you tell the whole story? Let us have the session in peace, and do you tell mighty quick what you know, for otherwise there'll be trouble—there'll be trrrouble—there'll be trrrrrouble."

"Señor Presidente, I am not willing to say a single word that might compromise my friends, the pious and loyal defenders of the faith of Jesus Christ. Do with me whatsoever you will, but you must know that I shall accept with delight any chance to suffer something for Him who suffered so much for us."

"Heavens and earth!" screamed the brigadier, giving another terrible pound to the table. "This child has put an end to my patience!—Orderly, see that this girl is instantly conducted to prison, and keep her in solitary confinement until further orders." The officials of the council, understanding that this would make a scandal without any result, put it before the governor in a whisper, and he became a little calmer. He himself understood it.

"You are right," he said aloud; "all the information that this girl can give is already known to us, and more too. I don't wish these scrubby Carlist newspapers to be saying that we lost our temper with a woman.—Harkee, orderly! see if this young woman's father is anywhere about, and have him brought in."

In a few moments Don Mariano entered.

"I find myself obliged to tell you, Señor de Elorzá," said the brigadier, addressing him, "that you have a very ill-educated daughter, and that thanks to the fact of your not figuring as a Carlist and to our own benevolence, we do not adopt in her case the rigorous measures which she deserves for her boldness. You can take her home whenever you please, pledging yourself to us that she shall not directly or indirectly enter into any conspiracy or into anything of the like.—Do we agree?—Have a little more care of her if you don't want to expose her to greater tribulations, and don't let her go so free and easy as hitherto."

Don Mariano almost spoiled everything by hurling an insult in that rough soldier's face; but the sorrows which he had been undergoing since the night before kept him very humble. Besides, he feared to compromise his daughter's situation, and seeing her free he had no wish to lose her again. Reserving, then, *in pectore* for more favorable times, the right of demanding of the governor full satisfaction for his impudent words, he gave the promise demanded, and immediately passed from the hall and from the building with Maria, and went to call upon one of his relatives. In the afternoon they set out for Nieva, reaching home just at nightfall.

CHAPTER XIV

PALLIDA MORS

WHEN the carriage stopped, Don Mariano perceived by the face of the servant who came to open the door that nothing very delightful had occurred during his absence.

" The *señora?* " he asked in alarm.

" The *señora* is in bed."

" Oh, I might have known it! How could the poor soul have had strength to resist this blow!"

The faces of the other servants whom they met on the way had the same expression of silent solemnity, and this greatly increased his agitation. Maria followed him. When they reached Doña Gertrudis's room, they saw that there were a number of people in it who, on catching sight of them, came toward them with a warning gesture.

"What! Is she so ill?" exclaimed the unhappy Don Mariano, in a hoarse, trembling voice.

" She is not very ill," said an officious lady; " but it is better that you should not enter so suddenly, for a powerful excitement might be bad for her. She has had a number of attacks since last night, and finds herself rather weak.—Let me prepare her."

The lady, in fact, went to tell Doña Gertrudis that her daughter was at liberty, and would soon be back to Nieva.

" My daughter is here!" cried the invalid, with that wonderful instinct of mothers and hysterical women.— " Yes, she is here!—I know she is!—I see her.—Come, my daughter, come!"

And at the same time she made a desperate effort to sit up in bed. Maria entered her bedchamber, and kneeling beside the bed, respectfully kissed the hands which her mother extended to her.

" Forgive me, mamma! forgive me for the anxiety which I caused you.—You were made ill because of me, but the Lord will soon make you well."

" No, my daughter, you have done nothing that needs my forgiveness; you have done what God commanded.— It made me ill—that is true—but it is because I have not virtue enough, as you' have, to suffer the trials God imposes upon us.—You are a saint.—I shall be well.—Don't worry about me.—What frightens me now is, that I did not die when I saw you marching off that way, among soldiers.— My poor daughter.—Come, give me a kiss!"

When Maria entered the bedroom, Ricardo and Marta were there; the girl seated near the pillow, and Ricardo at the foot of the bed. The young marquis, on learning at the factory that Maria was arrested, had asked the colonel to be relieved that night of guard duty, and his request being granted, he hastened to the Elorza mansion just as Don Mariano and his daughter were outside of the town. Doña Gertrudis was in the midst of a very severe fit, from which it was feared that she would not recover; she came to herself but only to fall immediately into another.

What an anxious night! Don Maximo and the Señora de Ciudad remained with poor little Marta to watch by the sick woman. Ricardo likewise was unwilling to leave the house. The girl appreciating that her mother's health and life depended on her behavior, kept up her courage, and did not cease to busy herself about the bed, entering and leaving the room hundreds of times. As soon as Don Maximo gave an order she fulfilled it with admirable exactness. A multitude of remedies requiring much skill and some practice were taken; mustard poultices, leaches, asafœtida washes, various applications to the temples, etc., etc. Marta would not consent for any servant to touch her mother; she did everything without bustle, without noise, as though all her life she had done nothing else. During the intervals of rest she sat by the bedside and watched the invalid's face with anxious eyes.

The bedroom was feebly lighted by a lamp half turned down in the hall; a strong smell of drugs and medicines arose from the vials accumulated on the dressing-table; but Marta was not nauseated by any of the odors; her head was steady and her never-failing health was the envy of all the household. Ricardo likewise sometimes sat at the invalid's feet. The girl scarcely saw more than his silhouette outlined against the brighter opening of the door, but this was a great comfort to her. She was not alone; Ricardo was not a stranger. Sometimes when the invalid asked for something and both arose in haste to give it to her, if their hands met, Marta withdrew hers hurriedly, as though she had touched something cold, and she let her friend minister to Doña Gertrudis. Neither spoke. Marta, forgetful of herself, thought only of her mother. Ricardo, more egoistical, thought of Maria. The girl's whole soul was wrapped up in the dear being painfully breathing by her side, and without making the slightest error, with the accuracy of a chronometer, she counted her pulse and watched her respiration. Don Maximo and the Señora de Ciudad were whispering in the adjoining room, as though they were making confession. The lady was explaining to the old doctor the character and temperament of each one of her daughters; the conversation was long. In the course of nine hours the sick woman had four severe attacks, leaving her so prostrated that the doctor seriously feared a fatal result. Nevertheless, after the fourth, she remained comparatively comfortable, and passed the day quite easily. The danger, in spite of this, continued.

After the first moments of effusion were over, Maria called her sister aside into a corner of the room.

" Tell me; has mamma made confession? "

" No."

" And why didn't you call the priest?—Didn't you perceive that she was in danger? "

The truth was, Marta had scarcely thought of doing such a thing. Besides, she was afraid of frightening her mother, and thought that this might be bad for her. In the bottom of her heart, likewise, there was a great terror of that tremendous scene, and she wanted to banish it from her mind. Maria chided her severely for her negligence, bringing before her the terrible responsibility which she would have incurred had her mother died. Marta saw that she was right, and hung her head. She sent instantly to summon Doña Gertrudis's confessor, and Maria undertook to prepare her mother. Wonder of wonders! Doña Gertrudis, who during her life had asked an infinite number of times to have her confessor summoned, now felt overwhelmed with surprise and fear when her daughter told her that she must get ready. Possibly the fact was, that when she had asked for it, she harbored the conviction that there was no real danger of death, while now she understood that matters were really serious. At all events, her daughter's words made a great impression upon her, and she raised all the objection in her power against receiving him, urging as an excuse that she felt better; that when there should be danger, she would herself call for him.

Maria opposed this delay, and found herself under the cruel necessity of clearly explaining to the invalid the seriousness of her situation. Doña Gertrudis yielded, but her face betrayed a great discouragement.

When the priest arrived he was left alone with her, all retiring from the apartment. Marta went to weep alone in her room, so as not to sadden her father; he did the same, so as not to frighten his daughters. Maria watched at the door for the signal that the pious act was accomplished. At last the priest left the room, and, with the mask of solemnity which all daily witnesses of death-scenes are obliged to assume, hiding the real indifference logically caused by such familiarity, he said to those who were waiting:

"You can enter; we have finished."

"How is she?" was the question of each one.

"Well!—well!—well!—The poor woman is calm.—I believe that for her to receive the Divine Majesty will be good for her, as well for the body as for the soul."

" That is true.—You are right, Señor Cura," said several ladies.

" I have seen in my own family a very notable case of the power of faith," declared one of them. " My uncle Pepe had a very serious lung trouble, confirmed consumption. He had consulted a multitude of physicians, and had taken more than a cartload of medicine. Well, then it was suggested that unless he were prepared to die, he would not recover. He had the priest called, made confession, received the viaticum, and even wanted to have extreme unction.—But from that very time, I don't know what it was, but it is a fact that he became more comfortable, and began to improve—to improve—to improve, until at last he became what you see him today."

The other women confirmed this opinion. Each one related her experience in support of it, and the priest summed up all the arguments, showing that such miraculous effects were nothing more than was to be expected, granting that the sick person's body received the presence of the Lord of heaven and earth, in whose hands is the safety of all mankind.

At eleven o'clock in the evening they brought the viaticum to Doña Gertrudis with all the ceremony required by such a solemn act. The house of Elorza was filled with strange faces; a throng composed for the most part of working people invaded the stairway, the corridors, and even the invalid's sick-room, with wax tapers in their hands. The priest, with the acolyte before him, and the holy box on his breast, passed by the physician, and entered the sick-room. Don Mariano had gone to hide himself. Maria, with a book of devotions in her hand, read to her mother the prayers which were to be said before communion. Marta stood leaning against the wall, pale and frightened, gazing at the solemn ceremony, as though she saw some terrible vision. One of the women, who made their way into the room, handed her a lighted candle, and she took it without knowing what she did. When the priest brought forth the holy wafer they had to tell her to kneel.

The scene was sad and impressive for anyone: how much more for a daughter! The wax candles lugubriously sputtered in the silence of the sick-room, and cast tremulous yellow reflections on the walls. The voice of the priest, as he raised the Host, was still more lugubrious than the sputtering of the tapers. The invalid, weakened by her illness, had grown terribly pale from emotion; she sat up as well as she could and, supported by Maria, and with her hands folded over her breast, she opened her mouth to receive the body of Jesus Christ. Then the bystanders went out softly, and on the staircase was heard the vibrating tinkle of the sacristan's little bell, announcing that the Lord was departing from the house. Only the intimate friends remained. A group of ladies invaded the sick woman's room to congratulate her, and to ask after her health. Doña Gertrudis said that she was more comfortable; and, taking her daughter Maria's hand, she thanked her for having given her the pleasure of communion. Her recovery was to be hoped for; all the ladies found her very much like herself, and assured her that it would not be long before she was well.

"God can do all things, Doña Gertrudis. When one's accounts are settled with the Lord, there is no fear of any harm befalling. Nothing, this is nothing, señora; you will see how you will soon recover."

"I have offered a mass to the Sacred Christ of Tunis for the day on which our señora shall get well," said Genoveva, Maria's maid.

"Woman, why did you not offer it to the Ecce Homo of Mercy?" asked an old laundress of the house, in some surprise. She had always lighted the lamp before the said Ecce Homo, and kept the chapel clean, so that she came to look upon it as her own property.

"Aye, woman! because the Holy Christ of Tunis is more miraculous."

"A cuckold on *him*," exclaimed the washerwoman quickly, with angry eyes.

A furious altercation arose between the two, until Maria

319

was scandalized, and bade them be still, explaining that the Christ of Tunis and of Grace was one and the same Lord, though every Christian was free to have the most faith in whatever image he pleased.

At last the ladies withdrew, leaving only two,—the widow De Delgado and one of her sisters,—to spend the night with the young ladies. Don Maximo went to rest awhile, promising to return before long. The confessor did not wish to leave the house because he saw no improvement in his penitent, and he threw himself down on the sofa. Ricardo likewise remained.

At two o'clock what Don Maximo feared took place. The attack was renewed, and unfortunately with such violence that the unhappy lady very narrowly escaped passing away in it. Marta, on seeing the danger, recovered the activity which she lost before the lugubrious ceremony of the communion; she prepared all the medicines; she rubbed the sick woman's feet with a flesh-brush; she held her upright a long time, so that she might not choke to death, and acted as Don Maximo had prescribed in the former cases. All those who touched Doña Gertrudis hurt her; only Martita's soft hands had the privilege of moving her from side to side, and placing her in the most comfortable positions without causing her pain. Finally the sick woman came to herself and spoke, but Don Maximo, hastily summoned by the servants, found her pulse so feeble on his arrival that he could not help making a slight gesture of alarm. Marta noticed that gesture, and calling him alone into the passageway, she threw her arms around his neck, sobbing:

"Don Maximo, my dearest, for God's sake, save my mother!—yes, my mother is dying!—yes—she is dying.— I saw your gesture——"

"Don't cry, child," said the old physician, drawing her head to his breast; "as yet there is no reason for alarm.— I will certainly do all in my power, and more, to save her."

"Yes, yes, Don Maximo.—Do it, I beseech you by all

that you most love in this world!—by the memory of your wife, whom you loved so dearly!"

"Don't! try not to cry any more! The thing to do now is to go and give her a spoonful of quinine; then we will put a cataplasm on her stomach."

The good Don Maximo, disguising the presentiment which he felt, succeeded in calming the girl, and he set himself to applying the remedies which his poor science but rich desire suggested.

But he was not able to halt the swift advance of death which in full career was fast approaching the noble lady's couch. At four o'clock in the morning they noticed that she spoke with greater difficulty; her pronunciation halted, and she often stammered. Almost all her words were directed to Maria, asking her numberless times about the events of the preceding night, and insisting on being told, showering boundless praise on her for her bravery, and congratulating herself on having such a good daughter.

"My daughter, beseech God for my safety.—God cannot —deny thee anything."

Maria, perceiving that her mother was dying, replied:

"Mamma, the one important thing is the safety of the soul.—If God wishes to restore you, let it be a miracle to you of his sacred grace——"

"But—am I dying—my daughter?"

"God only can tell.—Do you wish the Señor Cura to come in and give you a short confession?"

"Yes—let him come in—my daughter, let him come in!"

The priest came, and remained a few moments alone with the sick woman. Those who were in the adjoining room kept a sad silence. Don Mariano lying on a sofa, with his cheek resting in one hand, shut his eyes and gave evidence of deep dejection. After the priest had finished, Marta, Maria, Ricardo, and Don Maximo returned. Doña Gertrudis's condition grew continually more critical. There began to be noticeable in her a restlessness of bad augury; she turned her head from one side to the other as though she could not find a resting-place, as though she were already searching for the pillow on which she was to repose eternally. Her vacillating hands picked up and dropped the bedclothes incessantly, while her eyes also restlessly rolled in their orbits, fastening, from time to time, on the ceiling of the room; it seemed as though she found no one on whom to rest them. Soon Martita noticed that her hands were cold, and she mentioned the fact aloud, in a simple manner, without appreciating its unfortunate significance. Don Maximo turned away his head to hide his emotion; the priest let his fall on his breast.

"I feel—very well—now," she said to Maria, raising her daughter's hand to her lips. "As soon as I—I am well—we will go—to Lourdes—together—will we not?—It is very—pretty—is it that one?—very pretty—very pretty.—If you knew—what I see now!—The Virgin—the Virgin coming—surrounded by stars.—Put on my—velvet dress—to receive her.—Come—quick—quick.—Don't you see—I am entering by the door?—Aye! what trials!—Good-day, Señora.—I have a daughter—who much resembles you.—She has a fair complexion—and blue eyes—very beautiful! —very beautiful!"

A slight hoarseness began to choke the sick woman's throat; the last words were rather breathed than spoken! it was a dry, sharp huskiness constantly growing more pronounced. The confessor hearing it made a sign to Maria, and she quickly took a silver image of Christ hanging on the wall, and put it in her mother's hand, saying:

"Mamma, think on the Lord.—Think of what the Divine Savior suffered for us."

"I—am not—dying," said the invalid.

"Yes, mamma—yes—you are dying," replied the young woman with kindled face, full of fear and anguish, fearing that she was not well prepared. "Repent of the sins that you have committed!—You do repent, and ask forgiveness of God for them, don't you?"

"Yes—yes," murmured the invalid.

"Repeat the creed with me!" said the confessor, assum-

ing a more solemn tone: " I believe in God the Father
Almighty—maker of heaven—and earth——"

Doña Gertrudis repeated the priest's words clumsily,
and as though she were not heeding what she did. She
looked at the ceiling with strange persistence, while the
features of her countenance were rapidly changing; a purple circle was drawn around her eyes, and her nostrils became strangely pinched. When the priest was done she
again began to address Maria.

" The truth—is—that I have—no hat—fit to make the
journey—to Lourdes in.—Those that I—have—are—very
old-fashioned.—Do me—the favor—to write to Luisa—
and have her—send me one—in the newest style.—You
also—need a dress.—Attend to it, my daughter—attend to
it."

" Mamma, leave the vanities of the world.—Think on
God.—Consider that you are going to appear very soon in
his presence."

" No—no.—I am not dying."

" Aye, mamma, by the Holy Virgin, I beg you to feel that
you are going to die.—Think on your salvation ! "

" I am thinking about it—yes—I am thinking about it,"
said the invalid mechanically.

The priest began to read from a book the Commendation
of the Soul in Latin. All knelt. Then the dying woman,
raising her head a little, asked:

" Why are you all kneeling ? "

" To recommend you to God, mamma," replied Maria.

And getting up and putting her face near her mother's,
she continued in a whisper:

" Say with me, mamma: ' *My Jesus*——' "

The mother repeated listlessly: " My Jesus."

" *By thy most sacred passion.*"

" By thy most sacred—passion."

" *By the innumerable pains that thou hast suffered.*"

" By the—innumerable—pains."

" *That thou hast suffered,*" repeated Maria.

" That thou hast suffered."

" Pardon thou my offenses."
" Pardon thou—my offenses."
" And save my soul."
" That'll do, that'll do!" said the dying woman, pushing
her daughter away with her trembling hand. "No, I am
not dying.—I am well.—Come here, Martita.—It isn't true
—that I am—dying—is it, daughter?"
" No, mamma," replied the girl, pressing her hands.
" You are not dying, *mamita;* no.—You must get well soon,
and we will go to drive in the carriage as we used—now
the weather is fine."
" Yes, loveliest, yes.—We will go—wait—lift me a little.
—I am uncomfortable in this position."
Marta helped her to sit up; but as she did so her mother's
eyes rested upon her, fixed, motionless, terrible. That look
smote the poor girl to the depths of her heart, and uttering
a frightful, piercing cry, she let her fall back on the pillow.
The Señora de Elorza's head relaxed as though the neck
were dislocated, with open mouth and rigid lips; and still
from the pillow her great glassy eyes continued to follow
her daughter with the same fixed and terrifying gaze.
" Mother of my heart!" cried the girl, instantly throwing her arms around her. " Do not look at me so, for
God's sake! *Mamita mia,* do not look at me so. Aye! do
not look at me so. Aye! how you terrify me!—*Mamita,
mamita!*—Aye! O God, what is it?"
Don Mariano, who, on hearing the cry, had hurried into
the bedchamber with anxious face, and hair standing on
end, tried to draw his daughter from the corpse.
" Come away! my soul's daughter, now you have no
longer a mother!"
" Yes, I have her.—Yes—here she is.—Mamma!
Mamita! You are here, are you not?—Answer me!—
Speak!—Kiss me, for God's sake, *mamita!*—Let go of me,
papa!—Let go of me!—Now she is going to kiss me.—
Wait a moment, for God's sake!—Let go of me, papa dar-
ling!—Let her kiss me!"
The girl had embraced the dead body of her mother with

extraordinary force, and covered it with eager, loud kisses. Don Mariano, terribly excited, almost beside himself, pulled her away brutally, as though the welfare of all depended upon wrenching her from that position. Maria, kneeling in one corner of the room, had lifted her eyes and her hands to heaven, and was praying for the eternal glory of the departed.

At last they succeeded in dragging Marta away, and took her to another room. Without intending it at all, they caused her great harm. The unhappy girl had not sufficiently mastered her grief; by taking her away they choked the fountain of her tears, and they did not flow again. Pale, completely altered, with eyes fixed on vacancy, she neither listened to what was said to her, nor was willing to take what was given to calm her. She did nothing else but repeat incessantly, in a low, somewhat hoarse voice:

" Mamma—Mamma—Mamma ! "

The priest went to her, and said :

" My daughter, calm yourself, calm yourself. It is a test which God sends you that you may show your resignation. Instead of rebelling against His will, you ought to thank Him for His remembrance of you, showing that He loves you——"

" Don't say foolish things ! " exclaimed the girl, in an angry voice, casting upon him a look of scorn. " Is that a proof of God's love, that he has taken away my mother?— Then that's a fine kind of love !—a fine kind of love—a fine kind of love ! "

Marta kept repeating the expression over and over again for some time, in a tone of irritation. When she had calmed down a little the priest said once more,

" My daughter, you should take example of your sister. She feels her misfortune as much as you, but she is giving proof of Christian resignation and fortitude.—She does not rebel, she acknowledges the working of the Almighty hand, and with her prayers is contributing to the greater happiness and glory of her who is no more."

Marta saw that the priest was right; she repented of her
anger and hung her head, murmuring,

"Oh, my sister is a saint!"

"You also can be one, my daughter. The road to perfection is open to all who wish to follow it."

The girl received the counsels of the priest and of the
others who were with him, but did not answer a word.
She continued in the same way, not moving a finger, her
face pale and distorted, and her eyes fixed. Her indifference began to cause them anxiety, and they told her father.
The instant Don Mariano entered the room, she felt a
shock, and suddenly jumping up she threw herself into his
arms sobbing bitterly. She was saved.

The friends of the family, by dint of strong pressure,
made Don Mariano and Martita go and rest for a few
minutes, while the proper arrangements were made for
laying out the body and for the funeral. Maria remained
praying in her mother's room. The pale rays of the dawn
found her still on her knees, with her face turned to heaven.
The wax tapers which she herself had taken care to place
around the deathbed were burning funereally, their crude.
yellow beams struggling with the languid light pouring into
the room. No one dared to call her from her devout meditations; those who penetrated into the dressing-room and
saw her in that attitude, whispered a few words of surprise,
and retired silently with emotion and admiration.

Finally, all the outside people went away, and Maria shut
herself in her room to take the rest which she so much
needed, after the cruel series of changes and the great
labors that she had undergone during the last few hours.
At noon the father and his two daughters met in the dining-
room, to begin the melancholy meal which all who have
experienced a family affliction will recall with horror; a
meal in which tears mingle with the food, and sobs fill the
long intervals of silence. At this first meal scarcely anyone
spoke; no one ventured to lift his eyes lest they should
meet those of the others, and only furtive, grief-stricken
glances were cast at the place left vacant by the being who

had just fled from this world forever. The courses were eaten mechanically, without appetite, and handkerchiefs were lifted to the eyes oftener than napkins to the lips; the rattle of the dishes cruelly wounded their ears, and the rare words exchanged fell from their lips tremulously and without animation. The spirit protested dumbly against the brutal necessity imposed upon it by the body, obliging it, by such a wretched act, to give over the expression of its bitter grief and break the current of its melancholy thoughts.

They arose from the table in the same silence. Maria shut herself in her room again. Don Mariano, accompanied by Martita, likewise went to his. They sat down together on a sofa, with their arms closely clasped about each other for the larger part of the afternoon; the caresses which they bestowed upon each other gradually changed their desperate sorrow into a most tender feeling, melting into tears. They took turns in consoling each other; the girl declared that her mother in heaven would be on the watch for them all, and promised to be always good and prudent, and never to cause her father sorrow; the father pressed her to his heart, and blessed her mother for having given him such good and beautiful daughters. When a servant came to tell them of the call of some ladies, they felt an unspeakable annoyance, a painful impression, as though they had been wakened from some melancholy sweet sorrow to plunge into despair again.

Don Mariano suspected the motive of the call. They wanted to distract their attention, so that they might not notice the noise made by the men in carrying the body from the house. And, in fact, a group of ladies and a few gentlemen endeavored, by repeated entreaties, to persuade them to go to more retired apartments; but their efforts, as far as Don Mariano was concerned, were in vain; he strenuously urged his friends, in a tone which gave no chance for reply, to leave him alone as they had done, but to take Martita with them.

Alone with his grief the Señor de Elorza felt more keenly

his loss and more deeply his misfortune. In youth there is scarcely any loss that is not reparable; the passions, the feelings are more intense, but at the same time more transitory. One lives for the future, and through the darkest and most furious storms there never fails to shine some bright spot, promising consolation. But at the age which our *caballero* had reached hope is no more; the future exists not. Every misfortune undergone is a new pain, coming to join those that are past, and waiting for those that are to come: the affections which perish, like the hair that falls, find no substitute.

Don Mariano, with eyes closed and head sadly bent upon his breast, let his thoughts fly back over all the events of his long life, and in all of them, whether fortunate or unlucky, he saw the image of his wife, the inseparable companion of his manhood. He saw her awakening in his youthful heart a passion at once tender and ardent; beautiful and pure as an angel, with delicate oval face and blue eyes, looking at him with love. He remembered perfectly the few times when he had had lovers' quarrels with her, and the little reason that there had been for almost all of them. Gertrudis had such a peaceable disposition and such a gentle nature. It always ended in making her weep. He saw her on the day of his marriage, in her black satin (she was still in mourning for her father, the Marqués de Revollar) with which the fairness of her complexion and the gold of her hair made a dazzling contrast. A distinguished gentleman of Madrid, present at the wedding, taking him into a corner of the drawing-room, said to him: " Elorza, you are marrying one of the most beautiful women of Spain. I tell you so, and I have seen many in my life." The same day he started on a journey through foreign lands. He remembered, as though it were but yesterday, the intoxicating, ineffable impression, perhaps the sweetest and most blissful of his life, that he felt when he suddenly found himself alone with his beloved, as the coachman whipped up his horses, and they heard the farewells of the relations and friends, who sped them from the door of the palace of Revollar. How the poor little girl blushed when she realized that they were alone, and she in her lover's power! But he was polite and generous. He merely asked for one hand, and raised it timidly to his lips. All the enchanting details of that journey were imprinted on the Señor de Elorza's memory.

Then he remembered the strange sensation of pleasure and surprise which he felt at the birth of his first child, and the deliciously cruel impression which his wife made upon him, by keeping him rigorously away from her during those moments of anguish. But, aye!.in a short time poor Gertrudis became an invalid, and never recovered perfect health. In spite of this, his love for her had never grown cool; he took the greatest care of her, endeavoring, by all the means in his power, to alleviate her sufferings. She appreciated his sacrifices, seeing in him a Providence who always soothed her by his caresses. Even after many years had gone by, and when no one at all took any notice of the good lady's tribulations, still Don Mariano was the one who pitied her most, though he made believe to look upon her attacks with disdain, and she comprehended it perfectly, and she still reserved for him in her heart the same privileged place as in her youth. The harmony of generous, warm sentiments in both, the affection which they had lavished upon their daughters, the deep esteem which they mutually felt, and the ever vivid recollection of their passionate loves, had been so woven into life that neither of them understood it without being side by side. It was the intimate, perfect, and absolute union ordained by God, such as men rarely heed.

A melancholy, ominous noise, heard through the walls of his room, caused him to raise his head, and fix his eyes on space. Yes, there could be no doubt; they were carrying her away, carrying her away. Don Mariano flung himself, face down, on the sofa, and hid his face in the cushions to choke his sobs.

"My wife! wife of my heart!—They are carrying you away—carrying you away forever!—Aye! how terrible!"

And the good *caballero's* tears soaked through the texture of the damask, and his athletic form shook convulsively because of his sobs. Then he felt a great curiosity, that terrible curiosity that exerts a fascination at such moments, and leaves an indelible mark on the memory of him who has satisfied it. He waited attentively and soon heard the heavy shuffling of feet, and after a little the funereal, heart-rending song of the clergy almost under the balconies. Then he got up quickly, and cautiously lifted one of the curtains. And he saw the coffin, the black, gilded coffin, borne like a boat above the throng. The sky was cloudy and gray, leaving the great plaza of Nieva in shadow. The surging multitude extended to the farthest corners, moving with a slow and measured tread. And the boat, preceded by a great silver cross between two lighted candles, was borne away, carrying from him for evermore his treasure.

He let the curtain drop and once more flung himself on the sofa, muttering incoherent words. He knew not how long he remained thus. The light was fading, leaving the room in shadow, and everything was silent.—Everything except his thoughts, which spoke to him ceaselessly, and the sobs which broke from his breast.

And thus he remained a long time, a long time. At last he perceived that the door of his room was softly opening; he turned his head and saw his daughter Maria. She came and sat silently beside him. But he, as though having a presentiment of a new sorrow, asked her no question, said nothing. He merely took her hand and closed his eyes again.

"Papa," said the young woman after a long period of silence, "we have suffered a fearful misfortune, one of those misfortunes which cause even the most skeptical to turn their eyes to heaven in search of consolation. God alone possesses the key to them; He knows their reason, and is able to turn them into a result advantageous for us. This misfortune has confirmed me in a resolution which I made some time since, to consecrate myself to God forever. —I know by a thousand signs that He calls me, and I

should be truly ungrateful if I did not obey His call.—I
am useless in the world.—All its amusements weary me;
thus, then, I make no sacrifice in confining myself in a
convent.—Besides, there I can better pray for you and be
more useful to you than here.—The idea of matrimony,
which you have desired for me, is repugnant to my heart,
where fortunately there has sprung up another and purer
love which is immortal.—This resolution ought not to surprise you.—I believe that you ought not to feel it.—At this
solemn moment in which afflictions weigh down upon you,
perhaps it may be a consolation to you to know that you
are going to have a daughter safeguarded from all deceit,
from all disloyalty, who is living happily in the service of
God and praying for you."

Maria had spoken with frequent pauses, as though she
expected her father to interrupt her. But she ended, and
still there passed a long period of silence without his opening his lips. At last the young woman asked him, timidly,

" Have you nothing to say to me, papa? "

" Nothing," he replied, without looking at her.

" But do you give me your consent to do as I said? "

" Yes."

" Oh, I knew you would!—You are so good—and sufficiently religious.—You are not like other fathers who are
blinded, and would rather their daughters were exposed to
the dangers of the world than be forever servants of the
Lord, in the safe precincts of a holy house.—Thanks, papa,
thanks.—I was afraid—it is true, I was afraid that you
would not approve my resolution.—But God has touched
your heart.—Now I will leave you.—Marta is waiting for
me.—*Adios,* papa!—Let me kiss you.—*Adios!* "

And the door opened and shut again softly. The Señor
de Elorza remained motionless in the same position in which
his daughter left him, sitting with his hands clasped and his
head bent on his breast.

The room remained in darkness. The noises outside
slowly died away. An immense, keen, cruel grief palpi-

tated in that lonely room, and a pair of fixed, stupefied, tearless eyes reflected the few rays of light that still wandered lost in the atmosphere.

How long did he remain so?

Perhaps the little birds that came at dawn to perch on the bars of the balconies might reply. But the pallor of his cheeks, the livid circles around his eyes, and the deep wrinkles in his brow, doubtless told more exactly.

CHAPTER XV

LET US REJOICE, BELOVED!

IN the small but pretty church of the nuns of San Bernardo, in Nieva, there was great bustling. The sacristan, aided by three acolytes, the two serving-women of the convent, and a woman from the city, celebrated for her skill in dressing the saints, were stirring up a more than ordinary noise in brushing the ornaments of the altars with fox tails and feather dusters. They had no hesitation in standing upon them, and even climbing upon the saints themselves, whenever it was required by the need of dusting some carved work or placing a taper in the proper place. The Mother Abbess from the choir, with her forehead pressed against the grating, shouted her orders like a general-in-chief, in a sharp, piping voice.

"A candlestick there! Yonder a wreath of flowers! Lift up that lamp a little more! Place the crown on that Virgin straight." -

In the interior of the convent likewise reigned considerable excitement. A group of nuns was watching at the door of a cell, as one of their companions was giving the last touches to the poor bed which she was making. She had just put up above the pillow the crucifix demanded by the rules. A great silver waiter stood on the table, which was pine, likewise according to the rules. When the nun

332

had made the bed ready, she came out of the cell, addressing a word or two to the others as she passed. Then she returned with a bundle of clothes in her hand, and all hastened to relieve her of them, unfolding them, pulling them, and giving them a hundred turns. It was the complete dress of a novice,—the white flannel tunic, the linen hood, the shoes, the rosary, the bronze crucifix, and other things. The nuns looked eagerly at each one of the articles, as though it were something that they had never seen before, uttering in low voices many different opinions.

"Aye! it seems to me that this rosary has very coarse beads."—"No, sister, take yours and you will see that they are alike."—"I am going to see, just for my own satisfaction.—It's true; they are alike.—What a goose!"— "The flannel is too harsh."—"It is because it wasn't well washed."—"This hood is beautifully ironed!"—"Jesus *mio!* what stitches!—that is not sewing, it is basting!— Who made this tunic?"—"The Sister Isabel."—"Then it's splendid!"—"Don't say so, sister, perhaps you wouldn't have done it so well!"—"I? do it worse?—Come —come—never in my life did I make such a botch!"— "How many have you ever done, sister?"—"Never did I, never!" repeated the nun, in angry voice. "I could sew better when I was seven years old."

At this moment the Mother Superior appeared in the passageway; the nun who had chided her companion stepped aside from the group, and said to her,—

"Mother, Sister Luísa has just boasted that she sews better than Sister Isabel, and she lost her temper because I told her that she ought not to do it."

"Is it true, daughter?" demanded the Mother Superior, in a severe tone.

Sister Luísa hung her head.

The Mother Superior meditated a moment or two; then she said:

"Daughter, you know well that here no one ought to boast of doing anything better than anyone else.—You ought to believe yourself the least of all, for perhaps you are.—For some time you have been very far from humble, and it is necessary for us to begin to correct this fault.— First thing, go and ask pardon of Sister Isabel for your fault, and then shut yourself in your cell and pray a rosary to the Virgin.—Afterwards when I am in the reception-room with the novice, you must present yourself there and kneel, so that the people may see that you are in disgrace."

Sister Luísa bent her head still lower. and hurried away. A smile of triumph hovered over the lips of the nun.

At the same time, the servants of the Elorza mansion were coming and going, hither and thither, with various objects in their hands. Pedro, the old coachman, was polishing the state carriage, while two stable-boys were grooming the horses. Martin, the cook, was preparing a splendid collation. The maid-servants were running up and down stairs, from the principal floor to Maria's apartments, which were full of people, though it was not yet ten o'clock in the morning. The fifteen or twenty ladies who could scarcely find room to turn around, were all talking at once, as is natural, turning that silent elegant retreat into an insufferable hen-roost. Standing in the middle of it was Señor de Elorza's eldest daughter, half-dressed, and around her were several ladies, some of them on their knees, adorning her and adjusting her as though she were a wooden virgin.

Great emotion reigned everywhere. They had already put on her a costly garment of white satin, decorated in front, from the neck to the bottom of the skirt, with a fringe of orange flowers. One lady was just putting on her feet a pair of diminutive and most elegant boots of the same cloth, while another was hurriedly sewing on a number of flowers, which had fallen off. Others were arranging a garland of orange blossoms upon the top of her head. This proceeding caused a great commotion. Amparito de Ciudad claimed that the garland was too large, and did not show enough of her friend's beautiful hair; the rest believed that there was no need of making it smaller. After a lively discussion, it was decided to adopt a middle course by taking a number of flowers, though very few, from the wreath. Frequent exclamations were heard from those who took no share in the preparations.

"Aye! what an expense it takes, *Dios mio!*"

"Can it be her true vocation!—A girl so young and so lively!"

"There is nothing else talked about in town.—Everybody is excited over this fortunate event!"

"Fortunate for her, my dear! I don't know as I shall have strength enough to see the ceremony."

"But I am going to see it, though it should cost me a fit of sickness."

Some were already beginning to shed tears, putting their handkerchiefs to their eyes; others were whispering about the preparations for the festival, and the circumstances which had led the young woman to take the veil. Much was said about a letter which she had written to the Marqués de Peñalta, bidding him farewell, and exculpating herself. Some pitied Ricardo, while others said in an undertone, that he would have no trouble in finding somebody to marry him. "After all, if God called her to Him by this path, had she any reason to turn from Him, because a young lad was in love with her? If she had left him for another, that would be different! but as it was for God, he had no right to complain." This was the same argument that shone in the Señorita de Elorza's letter, written and sent to Ricardo a fortnight before the day of which we are speaking. Thus it ran:

"MY DEAR RICARDO,

"Though it is now some time since the course of our love was interrupted, tacitly, and by virtue of providential circumstances, rather than by my desire, I feel it my duty to explain to thee something about the resolution which I have made, and which, of course, is known to you. I cannot forget, and indeed I ought not to forget, that you have been my betrothed, with the approbation of my parents, and the sincere affection of my heart.

"Before renouncing the world forever, I must tell you that I have absolutely no reason to complain of your behavior to me. You have ever been good, true, and affectionate, and have estimated me higher than I deserve. It is indeed true, that if I were to remain in the world I would not give you in exchange for any other man, and I should count myself very happy in calling you my husband, if I did not count myself much more so in being the bride of Jesus Christ. The preference which I make cannot offend or trouble a man who is as good and pious as you are. Henceforth no earthly love exists between us; there remains only a pure and most sweet friendship, uniting us in the Sacred Heart of Jesus. I shall not forget you in my poor prayers. Forget me, as far as possible. You are good, you are noble, handsome, and rich. Seek for a woman who will deserve you more than I deserve you, and marry, and be happy. I shall pray without ceasing for you.

"*Adios,*

"MARIA."

While the most of the ladies added innumerable glosses to this document, those who were robing the new bride-elect of Jesus were about finishing their task and giving the last touches to her dress, with the same complacency that an artist shows in laying the last shades on his picture, stepping back and coming near a thousand times to realize the effect produced. Here a pin; the throat a little more open to show the beautiful alabaster neck; a few ringlets on her brow carelessly escaping from among the orange flowers; a button that needed fastening. Maria aided her maids of honor with quick motions. All admired her serenity. And, in fact, the young bride could not have shown a face more joyous at such moments. Nevertheless there was a certain agitation noticeable in her joy. Her movements were too quick and eager, as though she were trying to hide the slight trembling of her hands and the tremor that ran over her whole body. Was it a tremor of delight?

Oh, yes, Maria felt an intense delight.

The brilliant rose bloom of her cheeks told the same story; the unnatural glitter of her eyes likewise proclaimed it. Her lips were dry, and her nostrils pink and more dilated than usual. Her white brow was marked by a long, slight furrow, telling of the quick desire, the restless, sensual eagerness hidden in her heart. It was the cheerful eagerness of the epicure, who finds himself face to face with his favorite food after a long fast. Over her excited brilliant face passed a throng of warm flushes, in a vague, intricate confusion of dismay, dread, and voluptuous desires.

She was going to be the bride of Jesus Christ and shut herself forever between four walls, passing her whole life in a mysterious union, whose sweet delight she had not as yet enjoyed in full. A great curiosity overwhelmed her, stirred her unspeakably. The choir of the Convent of San Bernardo, where the half-light pouring in through the lofty windows slept in mystic calm upon the gray oaken chairs, had always fascinated her. How many times she had trembled when she saw a silent white figure cross the floor and sit down there in the body of the church. It was a sweet voluptuous trembling, which made her eagerly long to enter that fantastic retreat. The nuns, with their tall white figures, seemed to her like supernatural beings,—angels come down to earth for a while, who would soon mount up to heaven again.

She was particularly attracted by one who was young and beautiful; when she saw her enter the choir, she could not take her eyes from her. The stern, classic beauty of that sister, and her clear, steady gaze made an impression upon her which she could not explain. In her breast sprang up a certain extravagant attraction toward her, and a quick, eager desire to be her friend, or rather her disciple; to kneel before her and say: "Teach me, guide me." Oh, if she would permit me to give her a kiss, even though it were the

337

briefest!" One evening a tremendous temptation assailed her to ask her for it. The church was empty; she looked back and saw that the beautiful nun had made her way into the choir and was kneeling near the grating. And, without further consideration as to what she was doing, she went to her and said in trembling voice: "Señora, give me your hand, that I may kiss it." The nun made a graceful sign that it could not be, but rising, she offered her the crucifix of her rosary, with a smile so sweet and assuring, that Maria, when she kissed it, felt deeply moved.

Always when she entered the church of the convent she felt the same rapture, a species of voluptuous somnolence penetrating her whole being like a caress. From that choir came languorous, sweet murmurs, calling her, inviting her to leave the pleasures of the world for others more sweet and mysterious, which she had already begun to enjoy without full knowledge of them. Jesus had granted her already rich enjoyments in her prayers, but He would not abandon himself completely,—certainly would not lose consciousness of self in the arms of the bride; would not give His all to her with the infinite, immortal love which she eagerly desired, except within that silent poetic retreat where no sound could disturb them.

At last the day had come for her to satisfy her desire; within an hour she would be within that mysterious choir which had caused her so many dreams, and would cross with floating tunic the warm sunlight falling through the lofty windows. She felt impatient for the moment to arrive. She was nervous, restless, but smiling. Never had she been so self-satisfied. Her friends were not weary of exalting her virtue and heroism; the town regarded her with surprise, and around her she heard only praise and words of admiration. Maria really found herself upon a pedestal. And like everyone who is under the public gaze, our heroine succeeded in hiding the emotions of her soul, and showed a serene and joyous face. It was her day; it was the day of the great battle, and she smoothed her brow and composed the expression of her face, like a general when the hour of the attack has come.

Nevertheless, from time to time she gazed with anxiety at one of the corners of her boudoir. In that corner sat her sister, with her face in her hands, sobbing. At last, not being able to control herself longer, she suddenly left her maids of honor and went to Marta, and bending down her face so that it touched her, she said:

"Do not weep, dear, do not weep more;—there is no misfortune here to make you so sorrowful. On the other hand, think of the great favor which God has shown in calling me to be his bride.—You ought to rejoice, my little pigeon; come, don't weep any more, darling.—Consider that you are taking away my strength."

And as she said that, she kissed her pretty little sister's smooth, rosy cheek. The girl replied amid her sobs,

"Aye! Maria, I lose you forever!"

"No, *monina*, no—you will often see me—and you will speak with me—"

"What does that amount to?—I am going to lose you, my sister."

And Marta could not help saying this "I lose you; I lose you forever"—she could not because it was the only thought that filled her heart at that instant, her heart that never was untrue; she was accustomed to speak freely her beliefs and opinions. Marta accepted without resistance the idea that her sister was doing well to enter the convent, but she was absolute mistress of her heart; there no one held sway but herself, and her heart told her that she had no longer any sister, that all Maria's love, all her tenderness was about to evaporate like a divine essence in the depths of a mysterious, vague something, totally incomprehensible to her.

Just as Maria's toilet was almost completed, a young man came rushing into the room with the violence of a gust of wind. It was that youth with the banged hair, who gradually had made himself indispensable in all festivals, solemnities, ceremonies, and merry-makings of the town.

339

"Mariíta! the secretary of the señor bishop sends me to tell you that his eminence is ready, and is at this moment starting for the church."

"Very well, I shall be right out."

"I have attended to the organ-loft. I notified Don Serapio and the organist.—*Preciosa, Mariíta preciosa.*—Do notice the blue hangings which I put on the picture of the Virgin—"

"Thanks, Ernesto, many thanks; I am deeply grateful to you."

At a sign from Maria all the ladies arose, and hastened behind her down the stairs, but for all that there was no cessation of their impertinent chatter. The young woman went straight to her father's room, and remained shut in it for some time. No one knew what passed within. Those who were waiting at the door heard the sound of sobs, confused sentences spoken in angry tones, the movement of chairs. The ladies, waiting in the anteroom, whispered to those who came in, " She is taking farewell, farewell of her father.—Don Mariano will not attend the ceremony."

Shortly afterward, Maria reappeared, smiling and serene as before, saying, " Come, ladies, let us go ! "

With the same serenity she passed through the great room of the mansion without giving a glance at the furniture, and descended the broad, stone stairway without showing the slightest trepidation, as she walked along in her dainty white satin shoes.

And yet what recollections she left behind her! How many hours of light and joy! The prattle of her childish lips, sweet as the trilling of a bird; her father's somewhat gruff but, for that very reason, all the sweeter singing, as he rocked her to sleep in his arms; the dreams, the fresh laughter of her girlhood; the lovely sun of April mornings, filling her room with light; the constant caresses of her mother, the warmth of home; in short, that warmth which all the treasures of earth cannot buy; all this remained behind her, imprinted on the walls, ingrained in the furniture. And she left it all without a tear!

MARTA AND MARIA

At the door stood waiting a magnificent barouche, drawn by four white horses. Pedro had shown his taste by decorating them with great blue plumes, and by donning a livery of the same color. On that day everything must be blue, the color of purity and virginity. Even the sky, for greater glory, had clad itself in blue, and shone clear and beautiful. Maria climbed into the carriage with the Señora de Ciudad, her godmother, and the others took leave of her for the nonce, and hastened to the church.

Extraordinary agitation reigned in the town. The taking of the veil by the Señorita de Elorza, though expected for some time, nevertheless did not fail to make a profound impression. A young lady so rich, so beautiful, so flattered by all that the world considered gay and desirable! Interminable comments were made during these days, as people met in the shops. "But didn't they say that she was to be married to the *marquesito?*"—"No! not at all! there's no such thing. The *marquesito* was greatly disappointed; the girl, after the strange experience of being arrested, and her mother's death, returned with more zest than ever to her pious occupations; it is decidedly her vocation: there is no fickleness about her."

Some looked upon it in one way, some in another; but as a general thing, Maria's conduct aroused lively sympathy, and over many, especially among the people, it exerted a certain fascination like everything extraordinary, and up to a certain point, marvelous. She had the reputation of being a saint: the quenching of all the splendor of her beauty, wealth, and talent in the solitudes of the cloister was the unparalleled complement of her fame, the crowning stroke in the process of her popular canonization. All those rough women, who pitilessly elbowed each other in order to see her pass toward the church, would have felt themselves defrauded, if she had wedded prosaically, and had they seen her arm in arm with her husband, preceded by a nurse-maid with a tender infant in arms.

The plaza was full of spectators. When the young lady

341

entered the carriage, and Pedro, cracking his tongue and his whip, started up his horses, there was a great tumult among the throng, which reached Maria's ears like a chorus of flatteries. The people separated precipitately, making way for her to pass. In presence of that magnificence, which only some old woman had ever seen before, the peaceful inhabitants found themselves overwhelmed with respect, and equally excited by a great curiosity. The carriage rolled away, at first slowly, breaking the close ranks of the spectators; the horses pranced impatiently, shaking their blue plumes as though they were anxious to carry the bride to the arms of the mystic Bridegroom. It was a royal procession; and, in truth, Maria, from her elegant appearance, splendidly adorned, with her deep blue eyes shining with emotion, and her cheeks of milk and roses, was worthy of being a queen. She was a figure of remarkable beauty, and offered many points of resemblance to the fair Virgin of Murillo, that we see in the Museum at Madrid. The women of the town could not restrain their enthusiasm, and they burst out in a thousand flattering adjectives.

"Look at her! look at her! What a splendid creature,—a woman after my very heart!"

"I should like to devour her with kisses!"

"And what a rich dress she wears!"

"They say that it came expressly from Paris. She did not want to dress in *tisú;* the chasubles which it will make into will be given away separately, and the gown will remain for the Virgin of Amor Hermoso."

"Oh, I never saw such a lovely creature!—She looks like an angel."

The carriage followed its majestic course, and the young woman smiled sweetly on the multitude. From two or three houses a deluge of flowers was showered upon her, and their variegated petals for a moment enameled the white cloth of her dress; a few remained entangled in her hair. The people applauded.

"Woman, this girl's vocation teaches us a lesson."

"How fortunate she is!—Who would be in her place?"

" It can't be said that she was obliged to.—I know that her father was furious when he heard about it, and tried every way to dissuade her."

" Come now, she is wedded to Jesus Christ, and her family doesn't like it," declared a youth, who was listening to this conversation.

The women turned around ready to crush the scoffer, but he made off, laughing.

And the carriage continued on its way under the radiant sun, which made the panes of the balconied windows glitter, and reflected on the white houses of the town with transports of delight. The sky opened up its purest depths, smiling upon all the wishes for happiness, all the joyful aspirations of mortals, even upon those of the beautiful maiden who, of her own free will, was going to lose it from sight and shut herself forever in the shadows of the cloister. The carriage passed by the feudal palace of the Peñaltas, the ancient walls of which, spotted here and there with moss, cast upon the street a mantle of gloom, making still more vivid the blazing light of the sun.

What was Ricardo doing during this time?

Maria did not ask this; she passed by without casting even a furtive look at the Gothic windows; on her lips still hovered the serene, condescending smile. The shadow nevertheless caused in her a slight tremor of chill.

At the church door all her girl friends, including Martita, were waiting for her. The temple was overflowing with people; they made way for her to pass. At the high altar the bishop of ——, who had come purposely to give her the veil, stood ready to receive her. He knelt and prayed for a few moments. The confused murmur of the congregation ceased; an intense silence reigned.

The prelate began to speak in a clear and solemn voice:

" I know, beloved daughter, that you have formed the resolution to shut yourself forever in this holy house, to the end that you may be all your life long the servant of the Lord.—I know, likewise, that your will is steadfast, and that you have been enabled to resist not only the vain seductions of the world, but also those proper pleasures which the goodness of God allows us to enjoy.—But life, my daughter, can be in the midst of mortification and penance more broad than in the tumult of pleasures; and while our spirit remains imprisoned in the flesh we are the target of severe and constant temptations."

The venerable bishop spoke with extraordinary deliberation, making long pauses at the end of his sentences, which lent great dignity to his discourse. His voice was sweet and clear, and rang through the silent nave of the church like sweet music. He went on to trace with terrible accuracy the details of the religious life, spreading out before the young woman's eyes all the apparatus of mortification which it involved; the pleasures of the world entirely forgotten, the senses crucified, earthly affections, even the purest, crushed; and this, not for a day, not for a month, not for a year only, but for all days, all months, all years, until the hour of death always eagerly seeking for pain as others seek for pleasure. But after he had painted the gloomy picture of the mortification, he went on to express eloquently the pure, lively pleasures to be found in it. " To trust one's self to the arms of God, as a child goes to its mother, that He may do with us as He pleases. To find God in the depths of bitterness and grief, to unite one's self to Him.—To possess Him—and to be the beloved child in whom His infinite grandeur can take delight.—To live eternally united to Him.—To be his bride!—Is not that a sufficient recompense for the petty sorrows that we may experience in a life so brief?"

Then began the profession of faith. The bishop asked, reading his questions from a book, if Maria were ready to leave the life of the world and intercourse with its creatures, to consecrate herself exclusively to the service of God. She replied that she had heard the voice of the Lord and hastened at the call. The prelate asked once more if she had meditated well on her resolution, if she had made it from some mundane consideration, wounded by some ephemeral disillusion. Maria replied that she came of her own free will to give herself up to the Beloved of her soul and rest in Him; all the armies of the earth could not make her retrace her steps, for the Lord had made her steadfast and immovable as Mount Zion.

Over the heads of the faithful appeared a great silver waiter, the same which a few hours before was in one of the convent cells, and on it the habit of the novice of San Bernardo. The prelate blessed it.

Then were heard the sharp, nasal tones of the organ, and the procession took up the line of march: Maria in front, and at her side her godmother and Marta; next came the bishop and behind him the clergy. Some of the people followed and some stayed in the church. Near the door was the entrance to the convent, through which they passed, penetrating into a large, gloomy cloister, illuminated at intervals by a bright sunbeam coming through the swell of the arches. At the end of one of the galleries was an open door, and guarding it, silent, motionless, were seen the white figures of two nuns with wax tapers in their hands. The bride-elect again knelt, and instantly rising she convulsively pressed her sister to her heart. It was the last embrace. When she wished to extricate herself, Martita's arms were so tightly clasped about her neck that it required the intervention of several ladies to accomplish it. She also kissed all her girl friends, who wept bitterly, while she, giving an example of sublime serenity, joyous and smiling, entered the house of the Lord escorted by the two nuns.

The doors closed. Though it was the month of August, Marta and her friends felt a sudden chill in the cloister, and hastened to take refuge in the church, where Don Serapio, accompanied by the organ, was annihilating Stradella's beautiful prayer.

All waited some time with impatient curiosity. No one paid any attention to the cracked voice of the proprietor. of the canning factory; the eyes of the congregation were fixed, glued to the choir of the Bernardos, gazing through the bars at the little door in the rear.

At last she appeared. She came, escorted still by the

two nuns. The garb of novice made her look a little older. Yet she was beautiful; very beautiful; for she really was beautiful, that saintly and extraordinary creature. The people devoured her with their eyes, and repeated in a whisper, " She comes smiling, she comes smiling."

Ah, yes, the new bride of Jesus Christ was smiling, in her expectation of the sweet reward for her sacrifice. But the venerable man who, at that same instant, was walking alone through one of the state apartments of the Elorza mansion—he did not smile! And the young man who, at the same time, was sitting with folded arms, and head sunken forward on his breast, face to face with a woman's portrait, was he perhaps smiling?—No, no! neither did he smile.

The prelate came to the grating and said to the novice, " Thou shalt not call thyself Maria Magdalena, but, Maria Juana de Jesús."

The novice prostrated herself before the abbess, and respectfully kissed the crucifix of her rosary. Then she embraced, one after another, her new companions. While this scene was enacting, many of the ladies in the congregation shed tears. The bishop said the solemn mass, and finally all the sisterhood, including Maria, took the Communion. The organ shrilled, whistled, and snorted with more energy than ever, spurred, perhaps, by competition. It seemed as though Don Serapio and the organ had entered into a tremendous contest, a duel to the death, and the violent consequences fell upon the ears of the faithful.

But the organ mocked the manufacturer in most audacious fashion. When he reached the highest point of ecstasy, emitting from his throat some complicated *floritura*, or *fermata*, a horrisonant bellowing broke in upon him pitilessly, leaving him lost and inundated for a long time. Don Serapio struck out again with a tender note, sure of the effect.—*Zas!* the organ, like a bloodthirsty beast fell upon it, and tore it in pieces. Thus it wantoned for a long time, until, tired of amusing itself and intoxicated with triumph, it suddenly broke in with all its voices at once,

346

clamoring in the silence of the church with a monstrous insufferable shriek. The manufacturer remained choked in that diabolical roar, and ceased to appear.

Silence reigned for a few moments, but it was disturbed by a peculiarly melancholy tinkling. It was the curtain of the choir being drawn. Nothing more was seen. They began to put out the lights, and the people withdrew in all haste.

Maria's intimate friends went to the reception-room to give her their felicitations.

The reception-room was a square, and rather gloomy apartment, cut in two by a double iron grating. The novice appeared, accompanied by the Mother Superior.—Still smiling, perhaps?—Yes, smiling.

" What examples you have given us of courage and goodness, Maria," said one to her.

The young woman shrugged her shoulders, with a gesture of throwing from her the glory which was heaped upon her.

" Don't fail to pray for us! "

" Yes, I will pray for you, dear. We "—she added with a little emphasis—" we are obliged to pray for those who remain in the world."

" If you knew how all the servants wept a moment since."

" Poor people!—I love them all so much! "

" Here is Marta, who wants to say good-by."

" Come nearer, Marta.—Are you becoming reconciled yet? "

" What remedy have I, Maria? " replied the girl, struggling to repress her sobs.

" No, sister; you must resign yourself gladly, and be thankful to the Lord for the favors which he has heaped upon me.—You will always be good, will you not?—Console papa.—Don't forget those prayers which I gave you, nor fail to read the books of which I told you.—Come to hear mass every day.—Try to be always earnest and humble."

Ah, no! Martita would not try, would not try. As she was born good and humble there is no need of striving for it. In this regard the bride of the Lord may be at rest.

The small room where the two nuns stood near the grating seemed like a prison cell by its ugliness and gloom. Their tunics stood out like two white spots against the black lattice.

The friends took turns in speaking, or all spoke at once to Maria, with a strange mixture of admiration, of pity, of curiosity, and of affection. They asked a thousand impertinent questions and made many ridiculous requests about prayers, medals, and other things. A few young fellows who had belonged to the old *tertulias* at the Elorza mansion, had slipped in with the crowd, and were gazing with wide-open eyes of wonder at the new nun, but dared not speak to her. She showed herself serene and lovely, and called them by name with a certain reassuring condescension, giving them messages for their families. The boldest was the ceremonious youth of the banged hair, who stepped up, and reaching the grating, very much stifled, called the novice by her new name, saying,

"Sister Juana, I want to ask you a favor; please give me as a remembrance a few orange blossoms from the crown which you wear—"

"If the mother is willing"—murmured Maria, turning her face to the Mother Superior.

She bowed assent, and the gift of orange flowers was liberally and gracefully granted.

At that instant the Sister Luísa, the nun who was to be punished for her vanity, came in and fell upon her knees, but not the slightest trace of a blush passed over her face. The habit of performing such deeds deprived them of all worth.

The conversation wandered off upon festivals, *novenas* to come, the journey of the vicar who was called to be canon of the cathedral, his successor, and other subjects. Insensibly all were lowering the tone of their voices until there was only a monotonous and melancholy whispering.

It seemed like a visit of condolence rather than of con-
gratulation. They continued to extol Maria's courage and
virtue. "Aye, *Dios mio!* to think that she is a prisoner
forever and living a life of so much labor—"

The Mother Superior looking at the novice, with a sort
of half smile not very encouraging, exclaimed, "Poor little
one! poor little one!" But she, turning around with one of
those graceful gestures so characteristic, replied, "Rich little
one, rich little one, say I, Mother!"

Gradually the young men had been getting near the girls,
and without respect to the holiness of the place, or heeding
the stern crucifixes fastened to the walls, they began to
whisper more or less roguish remarks.

"When are you going to follow her example, Fulanita?
The truth is, that if all of you did the same, what would
become of us? But you would be sure to look lovely in the
habit! See here, Amparito! If you should become a nun,
I should wish to be vicar!"

"Now I wish you would be a little more serious,
Suárez."

"How long should I have to be a priest to become vicar?—
The worst thing is the grating.—Can't the vicar get behind
the grating?"

"Be silent, man alive! it is a sin to say such things in this
place!"

Rosarito and her lover had taken possession of a corner,
only from time to time making some insignificant remark
roused into the category of the sublime by the inflection of
the voice and the trembling of the lips. Only the old women,
and a few young girls who had not succeeded in finding
mates, still continued talking with the nuns. At last the
Mother Superior arose from her chair, and Maria followed
her example.

A man, a venerable man, crossed the plaza of Nieva with
rapid strides; he followed the winding streets, he reached the
Convent of San Bernardo, he entered the court, mounted the

stairway, pushed open the door of the reception-room, forced his way through the people, and laid heavy hands on the grating. He intended to say something solemn, something tremendous. It could be seen by the wrathful expression of his face, by the pallor of his cheeks, by the disorder of his white locks.

But he let his head fall, and only murmured,
" My daughter! my daughter!"
And a flood of tears burst from his eyes.

CHAPTER XVI

THE MARQUIS OF PENALTA'S DREAM

THE transfer of the young artillery lieutenant, Ricardo de Peñalta, had not yet arrived. He had applied for it a fortnight before the Señorita de Elorza took the veil. A month had already passed since the great ceremony—and nothing! The influential personages whom our friend had in Madrid, devoted to his interests, this time took little pains to fulfil his desires.

But why was our hero so anxious to leave Nieva? Be it said in honor of the truth, that when Ricardo asked for the transfer he was exceedingly desirous of turning his back forever upon those places where he had been so happy, and where he was going to be so wretched; but now, after the lapse of a month, the violence of his sorrow had somewhat subsided, and he was beginning to get accustomed to his misfortune. Still he continued to be greatly downcast; the whole town noticed it.

From the day when his betrothed had made him that horrible proposition, which he could not remember without being hot with anger, he understood that he should never be the master of Maria's heart. A secret and implacable voice kept ceaselessly whispering this to him. Thus the letter in which she announced her determination to enter the convent

350

caused him no great surprise; for some time a rumor of
this had been current in society. Yet, in spite of his best
efforts, he could not help feeling a quick, keen pang and a
melancholy that prostrated him completely. The more or
less well-founded belief that the beloved woman does not
return one's affection, is by no means the same thing as to
see it confirmed by a material, tangible fact. Not any longer
did he retain the right to lose his temper and relieve his
wrath by calling her perfidious and treacherous, as happens
in the majority of cases. As the sincere Christian that he
was, it became him to look with patience, even with pleasure
(the letter said so distinctly!), upon that pious substitution
of holy, sublime affections for those of earth, noble though
they were. Maria was blameworthy in no respect,—absolutely in no respect; her conduct was worthy of all praise,
and he saw how the whole city spontaneously and warmly
rendered her their tribute. Possibly in this thought the
young marquis found the only possible consolation; for the
certain thing was, that the beautiful girl had not left him
for any other man, but to follow the hard road that leads
to heaven, for which, doubtless, it must require the doing
of great violence to self.

And in this violence our marquis took a little pride by
thinking with delight, and at the same time with pain, on the
strength which the new bride of Jesus must have employed
to tear up the roots of such a solid and long-established
affection. But amid the beautiful foliage of these more or
less consoling thoughts, a sad and cruel doubt often raised
its odious head. Though Ricardo employed all expedients
to get rid of such an idea, he could not help thinking very
frequently that Maria had never professed for him a sincere
and vehement love, like his for her; that she had been his
betrothed through a compromise, through the influence of
the peculiar circumstances in which both had found themselves in Nieva; that perhaps she had deceived herself in
thinking that she loved him, since if she had really loved
him, the idea of taking part in ridiculous conspiracies would
never have entered into her head, still less that of proposing

to him odious acts of treason; that Maria was a girl of much talent and great imagination, admirably fitted to shine in the world, or to undertake some religious or secular enterprise, of no matter how lofty a character, but incapable, perhaps from the very same reason, of delicacy of sentiments, of constancy, of the modest and humble abnegation which ought to characterize good wives and mothers. Finally Ricardo came to the conclusion that his mistress had more head than heart, or else he did not know what he was talking about.

And gradually under the influence of these doubts, which went almost so far as to be certainties, there sprang up in his mind a strong aversion to the amorous memories, which were a drawback to him. When he thought of the Maria of former times, so joyous, so lovely, so buoyant, his heart would melt within him, and the tears would flow; when his thought went back to the day on which, hidden behind the curtains, he saw her pass by his house unmoved and smiling, without so much as casting a glance at his windows, his heart was filled with a bitterness not free from rancor. And when he saw her in his imagination in the garb of a San Bernardo nun, entirely oblivious of the sweet scenes which had been the enchantment of his life, despising them, perhaps, and looking upon them with horror, as though they had been crimes, our young friend—may God forgive him the sin—began to look with hatred upon the bride of Jesus Christ. These doubts which constantly assaulted him were a genuine cautery for his passion, painful and cruel, like all cauteries, but very salutary in its effect.

He did not for an instant cease to frequent the Elorza mansion as before. There he found two human beings whom he pitied and who pitied him. Moreover, it was a habit of his to spend a few hours each day between those four walls, and not only a habit, but a debt of gratitude for the affection lavished upon him, and not only a debt, but also—and why should we not say so?—also a pleasure, a great pleasure, since he could not fail to find it so in being with such an accomplished gentleman as Don Mariano, who had showed that he loved him like a son, and with such a good and beautiful girl as Marta, whom he loved like a sister. Grief had still further limited the circle of his affections.

In proportion as the recollection of Maria became less pleasant to him, the sweeter did he find the love of that family, and he clung to it as to the last plank in the shipwreck of his hopes. If he let this plank escape him, he would be left alone. Alone! alone! This word brought back to him that terrible night spent in the train, when he returned to Nieva after his mother's death. Cruel fate sounded it in his ears when he least expected it. Finally, while he stayed in Nieva, it did not ring with such a mournful and disconsolate accent, because all that he saw and touched in his own house spoke to him of his mother's tenderness; and all that he found in the Elorza mansion recalled Maria's love; but how would it be in the future?—What would the desert fields of Castilla say to him, across which the swift locomotive would carry him? What would the indifferent multitude in the streets of Madrid say to him?—Therefore Ricardo feared more than he desired the transfer which he had asked for with so much eagerness.

Every day when he reached the Elorzas', Martita asked him, " Has it come yet, Ricardo? "

Sometimes he replied between jest and earnest,—

" Perhaps you are anxious for me to go away, Martita? "

" Oh no," would be the young girl's reply, with an inflection of voice that spoke volumes.

But Ricardo did not have the power of reading it. These love-wrecked men, these men wounded by disenchantment, cannot read other life poems than their own.

Marta, after the death of her mother, in whose illness Ricardo had so much aided and consoled her, once more treated him with the same confidence and affection as of old. For some time she had been rather cool toward him. Don Mariano's younger daughter had passed through a terrible crisis, and no one in the house had a suspicion of it. While it lasted she was rather more brusque in her behavior, more restless, more serious and reserved; but at last her calm spirit and her healthy and well-balanced nature came out victorious. Doña Gertrudis's death, which was a more serious and genuine calamity than anything else, had no small effect in calming the disturbances and commotions of her heart. She was once more the same Marta, tranquil, serene, and affectionate as before, always anxious to free obstacles from the path of others, though her own were blocked by an unsurmountable wall. Fortunate are they who in life meet with these blessed beings who find their own happiness in that of others, and who offer the flowers and content themselves with the thorns.

Ricardo spent long hours at the Elorzas'. Whole afternoons, especially, he devoted to Don Mariano and his daughter, going to walk with them when the weather was fair, and staying in the house when it rained. Sometimes, too, he came in the morning, and then Don Mariano would invite him to stay to dinner. While Ricardo refused and the *caballero* insisted, Marta did not open her lips, but her anxiety was betrayed in her face, and her eager desire to keep him shone in her supplicating eyes. When, finally, he accepted, the girl's joy was evident, and her solicitude was shown in the way that she took charge of everything, going to and from the kitchen any number of times, preparing the dishes which she knew were most to the young marquis's taste, and keeping the servants alert; the *beefsteak à la inglesa* (for Ricardo had learned in Madrid to eat it rather rare), the cold fish, the boiled rice, the slice of lemon (Ricardo put lemon on almost all his food), the English mustard, the olives, and other things. But where Marta used her five senses was with the coffee. Ricardo was a perfect Arab, a Sybarite in regard to coffee. Thus it was that the girl bestowed a more lively and vigilant care upon the preparation of this liquid than a chemist on the analysis of some precious metal. While she came and went, making all the preparations, the young fellow did not cease to rally her in the same affectionate tone as of old; and this, too, though Marta, if still a little short for her age, was now a real woman, and not among the worst favored, either, as we have already had occasion to remark. She had grown slightly, nevertheless.

"Come, *caponcita,* when did you stop growing?" said Ricardo, detaining her by one of her braids of hair, as she was passing in front of him.

The girl smiled, shrugged her shoulders, and continued on her way.

From the day on which he had been vexed with her, Martita had never asked him about the transfer, but whenever he entered the house, all gave him a keen, anxious look, as though trying to read some tidings in his face. As it did not come, the girl recovered her tranquillity and resumed her work, which she rarely failed to have in her hands. Ricardo likewise said nothing about going away. Either he did not remember his petition, or affected not to remember it, or wished not to remember it. Perhaps it was a little of all. The Marquis de Peñalta had passed from disconsolateness to melancholy, and from this he was gradually letting himself drift on toward a happier frame of mind. The house where Marta sewed began to inspire jocund ideas of sweet ease and happiness.

One morning, Ricardo, as though it was the most natural thing in the world, as though the tidings did not tear anyone's heart, as though it were some mere trifle of little consequence at issue, came into the Elorzas', and said,

"Yesterday evening at last my transfer to Valencia came!"

Blind! blind! dost thou not see that girl's pallor? Dost thou not notice the painful trembling that runs over her body? Look out! she is going to fall! Run, run to her assistance!

Nothing, the young marquis perceived nothing! He, too, was a little pale. The indifferent tone in which he made the announcement was pure comedy, for I know on good authority that he walked up and down his room the night before, till he was tired out, and that the rays of the morning found him still unable to close his eyes.

Don Mariano made a gesture of disappointment, exclaiming,

"There, my son, there!—I feel that we are going to lose you!—However, if it is your pleasure——"

Ricardo preserved a gloomy silence. Gladly would he have exclaimed, "How can it be my pleasure? My pleasure would be to ask for a discharge at this very moment, and stay here forever and live calmly near you! Near you, the people whom I love most in this world!" But he had the weakness to hold his tongue, and such weaknesses as these generally cost very dear in life.

"And when do you expect to go?" pursued the *caballero*.

"Tomorrow. I must stop in Madrid a few days to attend to some business. I shall reach Valencia the tenth of next month."

"Are you going to some regiment?"

"To the First Cavalry."

"Ah!"

And there was silence. Sadness ruled them all, choking conversation, which usually was very animated, even though it touched upon the details of domestic affairs. Don Mariano renewed it in a sad and distracted tone.

"Have you ever been in Valencia?"

"Yes, sir; I spent a month there a few years ago."

"It is very pretty, isn't it?"

"Yes; very pretty."

"Many oranges, eh?"

"A great many."

"I think it is a very gay city."

"No, not gay; it seemed to me very melancholy."

"Then, my dear fellow, I should think——"

But they relapsed into silence. Their hearts were oppressed, and the indifferent tone of the words was not sufficient to hide it. Marta had not once spoken during all the time, and, as she sat in a low chair next the window, paid close attention to her crochet work. Ricardo was lounging on the sofa near Don Mariano. A thousand melancholy

thoughts sifted through the minds of all three, and that
cheerful room, bright in the pure, brilliant morning light,
was nevertheless filled with sadness and silence. When the
Señor de Elorza spoke to Ricardo again, his emotion shone
through his slightly hoarse and tremulous voice.

"And what arrangements have you made about your
house?—Are you going to dismiss the servants?"

"All except Pepe, the gardener, and César, the inside
man."

"Have you packed yet?"

"No; I shall have time this afternoon and tomorrow
morning."

"And your calls?"

"Really, Don Mariano, the only people with whom I am
intimate are you here.—Three or four other calls, and I am
done.—I shall send cards to the rest.—What I am most sorry
about is to leave the improvements in my garden unfinished,
and the two pavilions in the corners just begun—"

"Don't be troubled about that, I will attend to it.—I will
attend to it.—I will attend to it—"

He could say no more. Emotion choked him. Those
pavilions had been Maria's idea before the engagement was
broken, and this recollection brought in its train many others,
all painful, in which his wife, his daughter, and Ricardo were
mingled, bringing before his eyes the terrible misfortunes
which he had recently suffered. He hastily arose and left
the room.

Ricardo, likewise moved and overwhelmed by great dejection, remained with bent head, and silent. Marta kept on
busily with her task, as though she felt no interest in what
was going on. She did not once lift her head during the
conversation, nor even when her father left the room.
Ricardo looked at her fixedly a long time. The girl's im-
passive attitude began to mortify him. He had presump-
tuously imagined that it would affect Martita very deeply
to hear the announcement of his departure, for she had
always given evidence of being fond of him. He had blind
confidence in the goodness of her heart and the strength

of her affections; but when he saw her so serene, moving the ivory needle between her slender rosy fingers, without asking him anything about it, without urging him to postpone his journey for a few days, without speaking a word, he felt a new and painful disenchantment. And he allowed himself, by the weight of his gloomy thoughts, to be drawn away into a desperate, pessimistic philosophy.

"Then, sir," he said to himself tearfully, "you must accept the world and humanity as they are.—This girl whom I believed to be so tender-hearted.—What is to be done about it?—In woman exists only one true affection.—Can it possibly be that this child is in love with someone?"

Ricardo had no reason to be indignant at such a thought. But it is certain that he was indignant, and not a little. He tried to drive it away as an absurdity, and succeeded only in convincing himself that, not only it would not be an absurdity, but would not even be strange. But as he was downcast, indignation very soon gave way to sadness; deep, painful sadness.

"Aren't you sorry that I am going away?" he asked, with a sort of melancholy smile creeping over his face.

"Not if it is your pleasure to go"—replied the girl, not lifting her head.

Confound the pleasure! Ricardo had no longer any desire to go away; he was furious with himself for having asked to be sent. Gladly would he give everything to exchange.—But he did not say a word of what he thought.

His sadness and depression kept increasing. He felt a cruel desire to weep. He dared not say a word to Marta, lest she should notice his emotion. Besides, what reason had he to speak to her?—Such an unfeeling child!

He found himself in one of those moments of dejection in which everything appears clad in black, and he took a certain bitter delight in it; a moment in which one (if the expression be permissible) wallows voluptuously in sadness, endeavoring to add to it by unhappy recollections and expectations. He dropped his head on the pillow of the sofa, and shut his eyes, as though he were meditating. Our hero had been meditating deeply, deeply, for many hours. His nerves had been on the strain for a long time, and he began to feel the attack of a languor akin to faintness. He lifted his head a little, to prove to himself that he still had the power of motion, and he looked once more at Martita, who was still in the same position; but very soon he let it fall again. It seemed to him as if he were seized against his will, and kept lying there, without the possibility of moving a finger. He still had his eyes open, but they were as heavy as if the lids had been made of lead. At last he closed them, and fell asleep. That is, we cannot say that he slept, or only napped. It is certain, however, that the Marqués de Peñalta, thus stretched out, with eyes closed, seemed to be asleep, and his face looked so pale, there were such dark rings under his eyes, and his whole appearance was so lifeless that it inspired alarm.

In the space of a few moments one can dream of many and very different things. All have experienced this phenomenon. Ricardo had not as yet entirely lost the idea of reality, when he found himself in a room like the one in which he really was. However, there was this difference, that in the new one the window had very thick iron gratings, like lattices, and one of the walls was likewise grated, through which there could be seen in the background, gilded altars, images of saints, lamps hung from the ceiling; in fact, a real church. Looking attentively from the sofa, he perceived that a great throng was pouring into the church, causing a low, but disagreeable noise, until they filled it entirely, and there was no more room. Then he began to hear the tones of an organ playing the waltzes of the Queen of Scotland, which made him suspect that the organist was Fray Saturnino, the *capellane* of San Felipe. Then, rising above the heads of the people, he saw the gilded points of a miter. The organ ceased, and he heard the nasal voice of a preacher delivering a long sermon, although he could not understand a word of what he said. When the sermon was over, he heard a sweet song which made him tremble with delight; it was Maria's sweet voice, singing with more sweetness than ever, the aria from *Traviata:* "*Gran Dio morir si giovane.*" When this was finished, prolonged applause rang through the church. Then all the people crowded up to the great altar, leaving the spaces near the grating free. Something was going on there, for he clearly heard some voices saying,

"Now he gives her the benediction—now—now."

And at the same instant Don Maximo appeared in the door of the room, and said,

"What are you doing, lying down here? Didn't you know that Maria is being married?"

"Whom is she marrying?"

"Jesus Christ! Come and see the ceremony!"

He desired to arise, but could not. Then the physician said,

"Well, since you cannot move, I will go into the church, to see if I can persuade the people to stand aside a little so that you may see from here."

And in fact, he soon perceived that the congregation was making a sufficiently wide passage from the grating, so that he could see afar away, over the steps of the great altar, Maria's proud figure in bridal array. At her side stood another little human figure holding her by the hand. The bishop was giving them his blessing. It was no more Jesus Christ than it was a pumpkin! The person whom Maria was marrying was neither more nor less than Manolito Lopez, that most impertinent and uncongenial of urchins! He was like one who saw a vision! Could it be possible that a girl so beautiful and wise would unite herself to this cub and leave him, who in every respect was a man, abandoned to despair? The truth is, he had reason for serious and painful reflections. But just as he was getting deeper and deeper involved in them, behold the same Maria enters the room in the garb of a San Bernardo nun, and coming directly to him said, sweetly smiling,

"Art thou sad because I marry?"

"Why should I not be?"

"Fool," says the young woman, coming still closer,

MARTA AND MARIA

"though I am wedded to Jesus Christ, yet I love thee the same as before."

Then Ricardo began to sigh and groan.

"No, Maria, you do not love me; you love Manolito Lopez."

"Come, Ricardo *mio,* don't talk nonsense. How could I love this urchin?"

"Have you not just married him?"

"You must be dreaming; don't say any more absurd things.—Wake up, man—wake up—or wait a little, I am going to wake you. But see in what a sweet way!"

And in fact, the beautiful nun came even closer still, and took his face between her dainty hands with an affectionate gesture. Then she brought her own close to his slowly, and gave him a warm and prolonged kiss on the brow.

Oh! wonderful change! Ricardo noticed with amazement that just as she gave him the caress, Maria's face had suddenly changed into Marta's. Yes; it was her bright black eyes; her fresh rosy cheeks; her dark hair falling in ringlets around her brow. But her face seemed so sad and mournful that he could not do less than cry,

"Marta! Marta! what ails thee?"

And the very cry that he made awoke him.

Marta still sat in the low chair beside the window, apparently absorbed in her work. And nevertheless, the young man, though awake, was sure that he had cried out. All that had passed was a dream; but neither the cry nor the warm, moist lips which he felt imprinted on his brow were imaginary; though he were killed, he could not be convinced of it.

What was it? What had passed?

He remained some moments looking at Martita, while he slowly collected his ideas. At last he decided to speak to her. The girl lifted her face which was flushed and disturbed.

"Did I not just cry out?"

Martita grew still more flushed and disturbed, and scarcely could she answer in trembling voice,

"No—I heard nothing."

361

Ricardo looked at her steadily and with surprise. Why was that girl blushing so?

" I was asleep, but I would take my oath that I cried out— and I would also take my oath—such a strange thing!— that you gave me a kiss."

Marta's color, when she heard these words, suddenly changed from rosy to pale, betraying a profound consternation. Her tremulous hands could not hold her crochet work, and dropped it in her lap. At the same time her eyes rested on Ricardo with such an expression of fear, of tenderness, of supplication, of dismay, that he felt a strong shock, like that caused by an electric discharge.

It was the same look—the same that he had just seen in his dream.

He felt himself inundated by a great light, a divine light. At that supreme moment he saw everything, he comprehended all. The mist that blinded his eyes faded away, and he saw himself face to face with the scene in the garden, when Marta seemed so offended because he kissed her hands —and he saw and comprehended. The strange dismay following that scene he likewise saw and comprehended. Then he went back in imagination to the beach on the island. The sun pouring floods of light over the sand; the blue and white waves girdling a peninsula where two young people had been long sitting; the sob which broke the silence of the tunnel; then a girl falling into the water, and a young man plunging in after her and saving her. " Thanks, Señor Marqués, it is not so bad down below there." This also he saw, he comprehended. Then a sudden and extraordinary estrangement: a pair of eyes that did not look at him, two lips that did not speak to him, a pair of hands that did not touch him.

Ah yes; he saw all; he understood all.

He sprang up hastily from the sofa, and bringing his face close to Marta's, said to her in sweet, affectionate tones, but with innocent petulance,

" Don't deny it, Martita; you just gave me a kiss! "

The girl raised her hands to her face, and broke into a

passion of tears. A thousand emotions of fear, of penitence, of affection, of doubt, of joy, of anxiety, instantly
crossed the heart of the young marquis who bent his knee
before her, exclaiming in accents of emotion,

" Marta, for God's sake, forgive my stupidity.—I am a
fool!—I just dreamed such sad things, and they suddenly
all ended so well!—I could not resign myself to let happiness
escape so—an absurd idea came into my head, inspired by
the very idea of seeing it realized.—But no—no! I cannot
be happy on earth.—I was born to be unfortunate.—Luckily
I shall die early, like my father—and like my mother.—
Forgive me that momentary folly, and don't weep.—Do you
want to know what I was dreaming?—I am going to tell
you, because perhaps it will be the last time that you will
see me—I dreamed—I dreamed, Marta, that you loved
me."

The girl opened her hands a little, and ejaculated with a
certain wrathful, but adorable intonation these words, which
were immediately cut short by sobs,

" You dreamed the truth, *ingrato!* "

The Marqués de Peñalta, beside himself, entirely carried
away by his emotions, his heart ready to burst, pressed her'
in his arms without being able to speak a word. At last,
very softly, very softly, with the sublime incoherence of the
heart, like a murmur of celestial harmony, he whispered
into the ears of his companion the hymn of love. *Dios mio!*
how sweet sounded that hymn in Marta's ears! I do not
intend to repeat it: no; the pen cannot reproduce that mysterious language which comes directly from the heart,
scarcely touching the lips,—accents escaping from heaven
and hastening to take refuge in the breast of virgins,—for
the earth does not understand them, notes perhaps lost from
the song with which the angels celebrate their immortal
bliss.

Marta listened. Tremulous, confused, she hid her head in
her lover's breast, shedding a flood of tears. Ricardo pressed
her closer and closer to his heart without wearying of repeating the same phrase,—the most beautiful phrase that God

ever suggested to man. Once the girl raised her head to ask in low and tremulous voice,

"You will not go now, will you?"

Little desire had Ricardo at that moment to go away! Not for all that was precious in earth and in heaven would he go away. His spirit did not dare to pass by even the window-panes, fearful lest it should lose the bliss in which it was bathed. Nevertheless, he had sufficient self-control to tear himself away a moment and rush to the door, crying,

"Don Mariano! Don Mariano!"

The Señor de Elorza, alarmed, nervous as he had been for some time, came in haste, fearing some new misfortune. Ricardo's face, wherein shone the deep emotion which overmastered him, was not calculated to calm any one. What was the matter? Why did they call him?

"Don Mariano," said the young man, and his voice stuck in his throat—"I have the honor of asking the hand of your daughter Marta."

That was a thunderstroke; but what on earth! Had he gone crazy?—What did it mean, sir? We shall see, we shall see! Nothing; Don Mariano could say nothing, could do nothing, could think of nothing, for before he could say, do, or think of anything, his daughter's arms were around his neck, and she was weeping as though her heart would break.—What was left for the noble *caballero?* To weep likewise. Why, this was exactly what he did, pressing his beloved child with one arm, and squeezing with his other hand the Marqués of Peñalta's.

"You will not abandon me, will you, my children?" entreated the venerable man, lifting his noble, manly face bathed in tears.

Ricardo pressed his hand more warmly. Marta clung to his neck more fondly.

There were a few moments of silence, during which all the angels of heaven swept through the room, which was bathed in the morning sun, and gazed with radiant eyes of joy upon that interesting group. But now Martita lifted her face a little from her father's breast, and, smiling through her tears, asked her lover coyly: "Will you dine with us to-day, Ricardo?"

"Yes, *preciosa mia*," replied the young marquis, falling on his knees, and kissing the girl's hands again and again; "I will today, and tomorrow, and every day forever!"

Marta hid her face again on the paternal breast! Her heart was so full of joy! The three shed tears in silence; but what sweet tears!

O eternal God, who dwellest in the hearts of the good! are they perhaps less pleasing to Thee than the mystic colloquies of the Convent of San Bernardo?

THE END

www.ingramcontent.com/pod-product-compliance
Lightning Source LLC
Chambersburg PA
CBHW031057030726
47496CB00002BA/268